Knight of Rome Part II

By

Malcolm Davies

Chapter 1

The blades whirled and locked with a clang. Both of the combatants felt a quiver race through their arms to the shoulder joint. They strained for advantage and then swiftly broke apart, the edges of their weapons scraping out a vibration to set teeth on edge. They stood looking into each other's eyes, seeking an advantage, searching for some clue to signal the next onslaught. It came without warning and simultaneously. For long minutes they attacked furiously, defended desperately, came together and moved apart in a dance dictated by the length of steel in their right hands.

The early morning sun rose over one wall of the courtyard in which they fought sending their shadows wavering to the same frantic rhythm. The heat of the day increased. Sweat beaded on their foreheads and ran down to drip off their noses, their tunics began to cling to them. At last, the tall, heavy-shouldered man stepped back and grounded the point of his sword. The woman grinned.

"So, you give up?"

"It's no shame for a warrior to surrender to beauty," he said.

She rolled her eyes and tutted as if to dismiss the clumsy compliment.

Otto Longius, son of Badurad of the Suevi, Imperial Prefect and Knight of Rome, spent half an hour every day he was at home teaching his wife, Lollia Alba, how to handle the legions' weapon of choice, the short sword. There had been a gap in her training during her pregnancy and the weeks of her recovery after giving birth. At first, Otto had instructed Lollia in the basic moves; step, thrust, recover and parry. Lollia was naturally strong, nearly six-feet tall and the daughter of a Gallic warrior, now an army veteran and also a citizen and a knight. She had inherited her father's fierce spirit and as she became confident in handling the sword, her skill and strength developed until she had become formidable.

They propped up the dull-edged practice weapons behind a terracotta pot of basil in the corner of the courtyard and strolled off, arm in arm, to their bathhouse. Swordplay was a scandalous occupation for a well-brought up young Roman matron so it was kept a strict secret by the entire household as was Otto and Lollia's habit of bathing together, scarcely less acceptable. They lay relaxing in the hot water, legs entwined. They had no need to speak. Eventually they emerged and helped each other scrape the dead skin, sweat and fragrant oil from their backs with the blunt-bladed ivory strigil designed for the purpose. Her body was firm and supple with only a faint spider's web of silver lines over her hips which had been left by the stretching of her skin when carrying her unborn baby. His skin was palest white where it was not exposed to the weather.

Dressed and at the veranda table, Lollia's maid, Didia, brought their son, Lucius Albus Longius, named in honour of Otto's best friend and his father-in-law, to sit with them. He was a sturdy blue-eyed child, rosy and healthy but then he had been born and lived his life so far in his parents' villa outside the walls of nearby Luca, free of the stink and dirt of the city. At two and a half, he was developing a will of his own. He escaped Didia at every opportunity to explore, to her constant terror. Now he loudly demanded to sit on his father's knee and be fed with pieces of bread dipped in honey. Tullia, the scar-faced cook, her little son Pollux, her assistant, Plotina, and Libius the male general help and decorator made up the total of the domestics.

Libius had gone out early. Illness in adulthood had left him deaf. He was a skilled painter of flowers and wildlife. With practice on Otto and Lollia's walls, his perspectives had improved beyond measure. He was now regularly commissioned by the discerning families of Luca who managed to suppress the Roman aversion to any physical impairment while he was painting his gardens full of blooms and birds or glades with deer and other wild animals on their dining room walls and ceilings. All the servants were former slaves freed by Otto and returned his generosity with unquestioning loyalty.

At the far end of the table sat former legionary decanus, Evocati Felix, who had first come to Otto and his friend Lucius as their soldier-servant. He had re-joined the legion with an oath given under the eagle in spite of his game leg, smashed by a German axe. He had gone on to be decorated with a gold chain and a medal for his courage and enterprise. Now he slurped bread soaked in milk out of a bowl. He did not have enough teeth left to be able to tackle a crust. The majority of adults were missing teeth. If you had a bad one pulled, a false replacement was possible if you did not object to it being pushed through the bloody hole in your gum into the jaw socket. Few availed themselves of this service.

The six cavalrymen who formed Otto's military escort slept in a small barracks block built near the stables and were fed separately by Tullia and Plotina.

This was Otto's household on that early April morning in the nineteenth year of the reign of Emperor Augustus to whom Otto gave his unstinting service, receiving status and moderate wealth in return.

The clunk of military boots crossing the tiled veranda and a discreet cough from the bottom of the steps told Otto one of his men was standing by waiting for the orders of the day. Otto was an Imperial Prefect reporting directly to the Emperor. He oversaw the efficiency of the city garrisons of Spedia, Pisae and Luca. He and his men undertook to assist the city magistrates with the security of travellers on the roads. Unless he was on a mission for Augustus, he was free to define his own duties but he was conscientious and scrupulously honest. He and his men rode their patrols in good weather and bad on most days. Few bandits were foolhardy enough to ply their trade on the triangle of highways between the three cities under the guardianship of Prefect Otto Longius.

In half an hour he was fully armoured and inspected the men and their mounts. The cavalrymen were immaculate, their mail, helmets and weapons free of any spot of rust and gleaming. The horses were glossy; manes and tails combed and flowing free, hooves oiled and glistening. He stood down two of them; there was no point in tiring all the horses everyday as long as they were exercised enough to keep fit.. Today was a routine patrol. He had no information of anything amiss in the district but it did no harm to be seen and let everyone know they were there. "Boots on the ground," Augustus had once said to him, quoting his old friend General Agrippa. In this case it would be hooves but the principle was the same.

"The Pisae road," he said and climbed onto the back of Djinn, his black charger.

Otto felt the immense power of the stallion through his thighs and buttocks as the horse shook his head and took his first dancing steps. Djinn was always restive when they started out. He needed to use those great muscles and get his blood pumping. He fretted at the bit and skittered sideways a little. Otto did not correct him. It was Djinn's expression of eagerness and he would calm down after five minutes or so. The sun rose higher. The day was hot but not as oppressively as it would be in high summer. Buds had burst into full blossom on the fruit trees they passed, the grass was a vibrant green and the blue sky full of birds. It was a day to feel blessed simply to be alive, young and riding a good horse; Otto smiled broadly at the sheer delight he felt. They walked, trotted and cantered in sequence along the well-paved road between fields, orchards and woods.

There was plenty of traffic: carts loaded with goods and produce for the markets, heavy ox-wagons hauling jars of oil and wine as tall as a man, travellers on foot or riding mules, some alone, some in family groups. All who could, moved off the carriageway when they saw the soldiers. The heaviest wagons simply stopped and their driver bowed his head.

The patrol gave a wide berth to the grim fortress occupied by the Second Lucan legion. Otto had been one of its officers until forced to resign: a sacrifice to favouritism and political manoeuvring. He still felt bitter even though the Emperor had revived his career. They bridged a small river and on towards the River Arno crossing at Pisae.

The centurion commanding the garrison had resented Otto at first. He was a competent, experienced soldier and did not want to be answerable to this ridiculously young upstart, even though he came with a reputation for courage in battle. However, Otto proved to be neither overbearing nor lacking in understanding of military matters. They had become friends over the past few years, particularly after Otto had arranged for the legionaries to be re-equipped with the latest kit. Garrison troops were always the last in line to be given new amour and weapons. They ate a lunch of soldiers' bread, cheese and smoked sausage together, washed down with watered wine. The centurion dipped his bread in garum, the fermented fish sauce beloved of

Romans. Otto hated it. They discussed business. Otto gave his suggestions, leaving it to the local commander to adopt them or not as he saw fit. The horses had been unsaddled and their backs dried before they were lightly fed and watered. After an hour and a half of rest, they were ready for the return trip.

The sun was two hours past its zenith and the heat of the day had increased. The crickets in the grass now chirped their chorus to a largely empty road. They had crossed both bridges when they noticed a solitary man walking towards them. He stopped and looked around then darted off the highway into a clump of oleanders. Otto swept his right arm out. His men moved level with him on either side and at a second gesture, they urged their horses into pursuit. Djinn was not going to let anyone be in front of him. He bunched up his massive back legs and leapt forward, instantly into a dead gallop. They burst through the thicket in a ragged line as their quarry, head thrown back, arms and legs pumping, raced into an orchard of plum trees. The horsemen were forced to slow as they wove between tree trunks and ducked under branches. The fugitive changed direction, doubling like a hare with the hounds on his trail but eventually he could run no more and slumped, panting, a lance point hovering over the base of his throat.

Otto looked down at him. He was a wispy-haired man in his late twenties, thin and gangling.

"Explain yourself," Otto ordered.

"I am a journeyman mosaic-layer on my way to Pisae for a job. I have a letter."

"Tip out your pack."

A collection of small trowels, chisels and two pairs of pincers fell out. He held up a folded piece of parchment. Otto took it and read it. As their captive had said, he was engaged to repair a floor in a noble house of Pisae.

"You're an escaped slave and you've stolen these tools and this letter." Otto accused.

"No I'm not," he squeaked indignantly. He pulled up the sleeves of his tunic to show his arms then tugged at the neck to reveal his upper chest. "No brands on me. I'm a free man and a citizen."

"Well then citizen, why did you run?"

"Because I knew you were going to hunt me down," he replied.

"No we weren't," Otto told him, a hint of exasperation in his tone.

"But you did didn't you?"

"Only because you ran, otherwise we would have let you go in peace."

"Well, that's what you would say now, isn't it?" the journeyman replied, nodding his head to confirm the truth of his statement.

Otto threw back his head and laughed.

"Pick up your kit and I'll give you a ride back to the road."

Hauled up onto the crupper behind Otto, he clung on while they cantered the half mile back to where he had taken off when he had first seen the patrol. Otto let him down. He turned his back and marched off with aggrieved dignity.

"Aren't you going to thank Prefect Longius for the lift?" one of the cavalrymen called out.

"Least he could do under the circumstances," the man shouted back without stopping.

They were still shaking their heads and chuckling about it when they all arrived back home and were grooming their mounts and cleaning kit and saddlery. Felix was not amused.

"Should've kicked his arse, cheeky sod," he grumbled.

Otto was still thinking about the incident when he and Lollia lay down in their room. Each time she nearly dozed off, the bed shook under her husband's suppressed laughter. Eventually she sat bolt upright up and punched his arm hard.

"Will you stop giggling like a little child and get to sleep?" she complained.

"Sorry but it's so funny…"

"Not if you weren't there it isn't," she pointed out.

Shortly afterwards, they slept.

In the morning, Otto rode out on his tall gelding accompanied by the two troopers he had rested the day before. Djinn was outraged at being left behind and ran along the paddock fence snorting and kicking out in his jealousy. The patrol was to be shorter; a circuit of the walls of Luca to demonstrate to the citizens and anyone going in or out that the Imperial gaze was upon them. The garrison commander, one-eyed Centurion "Cyclops" Massus and his men carried out the same procedure on the city streets.

The horses trotted in a rough circle anti-clockwise about a mile away from the walls. There was no paved road to follow; they rode down cart tracks or across meadowlands, sending beetles and grasshoppers into the air trying to avoid the heavy hooves. Opportunist birds spotted the activity and fluttered behind them pouncing on any unfortunate insect which was too clumsy or slow to get back into the cover of the grass. The day was cooler than yesterday with a light breeze blowing off the hills making the branches of the trees in the orchards quiver causing flurries of petals, pink and white, to tumble to the ground beneath them. Slaves and free labourers toiled in the fields, cattle and mules grazed, roosters crowed, pigs rooted; occasional farm carts passed them. When their route intersected a paved highway, they saw plenty of people travelling about their business.

Otto had never got over his first impression of this land when he and his friend Tribune "Boxer" Longius had viewed it spread below them from a high mountain pass. They had been coming to Boxer's home on leave from the Second Lucan Legion. Otto could barely speak Latin in those days. He had spent his entire life in his native German forests and with the army on the Rhine. He had never imagined anywhere could be so rich in people and livestock and crops as the valley of the River Auserculus. Boxer's family had eventually accepted him and his grandmother Aelia had taught Otto how to read and write. Now he owned hundreds of acres of this paradise himself, thanks to his own courage and the favour of the Emperor. He sometimes wondered why he in particular had been singled out by the gods to be so fortunate. There was no answer; it was sufficient to offer them his humble thanks and try to be worthy.

Late in the morning, two thirds of their way around the city, they struck the river which flowed from the mountains to the sea close by Luca. A stretch of it further downstream formed one of the boundaries of Otto's estate. They kept the river to their right and followed its course for a while. There were few boats on the water but men were fishing off rickety jetties thrust out from the banks. In between them, one man stood alone, taking small objects out of a basket at his feet and tossing them one by one as far as he could out into the middle of the stream. As they drew level, they could see he was drowning unwanted puppies. This was not an unusual sight nor one which would normally have moved Otto and his men but the last puppy wriggled in the man's hand and nipped his thumb.

"You little bastard," he growled and shook it.

"If you don't want it, I'll take it," Otto called out on impulse.

The little creature's brothers and sisters had whimpered and accepted their fate but this one had shown courage. It was the quality Otto valued beyond any other in friend or foe, man or beast.

The owner stepped forward and held up the squirming bundle of brown fur.

"What'll you give me for him?" he asked, with a sly grin.

Otto frowned. "But you were throwing them all into the water," he replied.

"Ah yes, because I don't want any of 'em but you do. So if you want him, I'll need paying."

"Very well," Otto said coldly. "Give the pup to me." When it was placed in his hands, he gestured to the nearest trooper. "Let this man have a suitable reward."

The cavalryman knew Otto well enough to understand what was required. With a friendly smile on his face he brought his horse up closer then reversed his lance and cracked the man across the side of the head with the ash wood butt.

"Ow!" his victim cried out, clutching at his swelling ear, "Ow! What did you do that for?"

"To teach you not to bandy words with us and especially with Prefect Otto Longius. Now piss off before we sacrifice you to Dis too."

At home, Otto put the pup down on the veranda just as Lucius Albus appeared out of the house chased by Didia. He was escaping as fast as his short legs would carry him. The boy saw the pup and stood stock still. The pup saw the boy, lifted his head and froze. Then they ran together. Lucius went down on his knees, the pup rolled over to have his belly rubbed and that was it. Boy and dog were united as if by some magnetic attraction. That night Lucius howled the place down until his dog was allowed to sleep in the room he shared with Didia. Sulkily she went to the kitchen and asked for an old basket for the puppy to sleep in.

"Look at the face on you!" Tullia said. "What's up?"

"The new dog has to be in with me and Lucius Albus every night. The damn thing'll just widdle all over the floor."

"Well, here's an old dishcloth to mop it up with your ladyship," Tullia said and lobbed one at her.

Didia left with her nose in the air.

On the fifteenth of the month, the estate steward came over and spread his books and accounts on a table at which Lollia was seated. He took his place opposite her and nervously licked his lips, glancing over from time to time at Otto who reclined by the window paying minimal attention. Otto's size and ferocious reputation had intimidated the young man when he first began to run the affairs of the estate. Lollia terrified him equally with her lightning grasp of figures and ability to spot the slightest error. She ran her finger down columns of figures with one hand, slamming beads across the wires of her abacus with the other. If she stopped to make a note on her wax tablet, he winced.

Unless she had been born into a noble house, the wife of a knight was not at the highest pinnacle of Roman society, constantly under public scrutiny. This allowed her a certain leeway to conduct her own business, although no woman had any part in public life. Many ran complex and profitable commercial concerns through the proxy of a trusted freeman or woman while their husbands were engaged on official duties. Otto had been away on a mission for the Emperor once already in their short marriage. It made good sense for Lollia to have a complete understanding of their financial situation and the management of the estate. In any case, she was a better accountant than her husband. Satisfied, she clicked the lid of her wax tablet shut with a flourish and smiled as she thanked the steward for his punctilious care. He bowed and left; feeling yet again as if he had got away with something although he was completely honest and hard-working.

The month wore on in the same even tenure in which it had begun and which had been the pattern of Otto's life since he had completed his mission for Augustus in Britain over two years ago. Since his return, he had been at peace apart from the occasional skirmish with robbers on the highways. He had visited or been visited by his in-laws or the Longius family, he had ridden over his lands, hunted and inspected barracks, kit and legionaries in Luca, Spedia and Pisae. It was a full and enviable existence and Otto knew it. He also knew that sooner or later the order would come from Rome calling him away to undertake some service for his Emperor but in the meanwhile, his time at home was to be relished.

One late afternoon, a party of travellers approached. There was a white-bearded, older man in the lead followed by a younger pair, all mounted on riding mules and leading a string of eight pack mules. They came to a halt in the front courtyard of the villa and waited politely to be invited to dismount. Felix limped out and saluted the old man.

"Greetings sir," he replied, still on mule-back. "I seek the house of the Equestrian Prefect named Otto, formerly of the Second Lucan Legion I am told."

"Well, you've found it, stranger. Do you have business with him?"

"No business but I am charged with a message from an old friend of his."

"Dismount and wait here, I'll ask him to come out. What is your name?"

"It is Reuben but he does not know me," he told Felix and climbed stiffly from the saddle.

In a few moments, Otto strode out dressed in a tunic and soft boots but with a sword at his side and his pugio dagger sheathed in the small of his back. Felix had left the villa by a side door to alert the cavalrymen, just in case. Otto examined his visitors as he approached. They wore long robes and round caps. Their beards were full and the side locks of their hair hung down to mingle with them. The younger men had curved swords scabbarded on their belts and two round shields hung on their mules' saddle horns. Otto stopped in front of Reuben who put his right hand on his heart and bowed.

"You are the officer called Otto who served on the Rhine, sir?"

"I am."

"Then I have a letter for you from your old friend Prince Aldermar."

"You mean Prefect of Auxiliary Horse Aldermar?"

"He is no longer with the army of Rome and has taken up his royal duties amongst his own people."

"Has he now? I didn't know; the message?"

Reuben handed over a leather tube sealed with wax at the opening end. Otto took it.

"You will sit in the atrium with me and take some refreshment while I read it? Your men…."

"They are my sons, sir."

"Then they are welcome to join us."

"They will stay here with the animals, if you will kindly lead on."

Seated on stone benches at the marble table beside the tinkling fountain over the pool with its mosaics of nymphs and fishes, Otto called for wine, water and bread. To his surprise, his uninvited guest produced a finely chased silver cup out of the folds of his robes and smiled up at him while Otto filled it. Reuben tore off a corner of the flat loaf and nibbled at it while Otto broke the seal and took out a scroll of parchment. He unrolled it and began to read the words which burst the pleasant bubble in which he had been living. The surprising source of the letter had already intrigued him but the contents threw him into confusion. It was difficult to make sense of it.

"To my friend Otto of the Suevi, now Otto Longius, Greetings.

When I first saw you in our Legate's headquarters, barefoot, dressed in a second-hand tunic and spitting hatred at that poor slave who tried to abuse you, I would never have dreamed that you would rise so high but you have and I applaud you: an Imperial Prefect no less! Not a senator yet? You must try harder my young former comrade. But Knight and Roman gentleman as you now are, you began as Otto son of Badurad of the Suevi and none of us can completely hack away our roots.

So I write to you to tell you that one of my men has heard a rumour that the widow of Badurad and her daughter are alive and were in the country around the River Lippe in early March of this year.

If you wish to come to me, I will tell you more.

Salutations, Prince Aldermar.

Otto paled and stiffened. He took a gulp of wine and had to read the scroll again, before he could take in the meaning of the words. Then they exploded in upon him. He grinned broadly and slapped his hand down on the table so hard that Reuben started.

"Welcome news, sir?" he asked.

"A miracle, a gift from the Gods!" Otto shouted.

Reuben looked slightly pained but said nothing.

Otto rolled up the letter and put it back in the scroll case. Reuben noticed that his hands were trembling. His innate good manners prevented him from asking what news the soldier had just received. Otto recalled his own duties as a host.

"Sir," he said, "it is too late to set out on the road tonight. Perhaps you would accept what hospitality I can offer? There is a clean dry barn where you and your sons could sleep securely and we shall feed and water your mules…."

"A Roman officer calls me, "sir"! This is a day of miracles for both of us."

"Age should be respected," Otto smiled. "Let me offer you dinner."

Reuben shook his head. "Our religion places strict dietary laws on us. If you could point out a spot where we could build a fire to cook our own food…"

"I'll have a charcoal burner brought out to you."

"Then I shall retire to see to my party if you will permit?" Reuben asked and rose with a second graceful bow before walking over to his sons and explaining the arrangements to them.

Chapter 2

Otto sat alone for a moment trying to disentangle his thoughts. Then he did something that no Roman of status would ever have done. He had spent his earliest years in a society where women were by right strong and independent, property-owners, counsellors and even warriors. He had been astonished that their Roman sisters were excluded from having their say in all but the most trivial decisions. He thought of Lollia as his partner and her blood on her father's side cried out that she should be treated as his equal. He called her to him and showed her the letter.

He stared at her as she read, trying to see if the expression on her face would give him a clue to guide him. Lollia finished and looked into his eyes.

"Can you trust this Aldermar?"

Otto nodded. "He's the prefect who trained me how to handle a cavalry alia. He is a Roman citizen of German descent, a knight and a decorated officer. We have gone into battle together."

"Then you have no choice. You must go and find out more, perhaps find your family."

"So it seems to me," he agreed.

"But before you make any arrangements, take advice from Vitius Longius and Centurion Massus…" Otto opened his mouth to protest but Lollia raised a hand to silence him. "… Vitius is astute and he's the father of your best friend. Massus is a distinguished veteran and also close to you, you met me through him, remember? It won't do any harm for us to consult older, more experienced heads and they'll both have our best interests at heart."

That night they made love. Afterwards neither slept. Lollia could sense his wakeful tension and it troubled her. She moved closer and laid one of her arms across his chest.

"What is it?" she asked.

Long suppressed guilt and doubt poured out of Otto in a flood of words. The witch's prophecy which had set him on his life's path, the death of his father under a hail of Roman javelins, the cloud of acrid smoke over his village when he marched away with his new liege companion Lucius Longius and the deep sorrow of never having known his mother's fate.

"Perhaps she will want nothing to do with me. Perhaps she will think I'm a coward and a traitor to my father's memory…".

"Hush, hush," Lollia soothed him. "You are never less than honourable and never could be. You acted according to the will of your gods that the wise woman interpreted for you. If you had done wrong, would they have rewarded you as they have? No, your mother will love her son, a mother can do no other. Now sleep."

He did, but lightly and was awoken just after dawn by the distant sounds of Reuben getting ready to set out. He pulled on a tunic, went to his strong box and took out three gold coins. He dunked his head in the water butt, wiped the droplets off his face and ran his fingers through his close-cropped hair. The mules were saddled and the men about to leave when he arrived.

"I have come to wish you a safe journey and to thank you," he said.

"I am grateful to you in turn for a night's shelter, sir," Reuben replied.

Otto held out the three gold coins.

"Your reward, one for you and the others for your sons."

"I regularly trade with Aldermar and this time part of our bargain was that I would bear his message to you. I have been paid."

"Not by me and the news you gave me is a gift of the gods…" again a quick spasm of distaste passed across Reuben's face "…please accept my thanks. It is a long way from the Rhine to Luca and you have faithfully carried out your mission; many would not have done so and that deserves recognition."

Reuben took the coins

"He who sows righteousness receives a true recompense," Reuben said. "The words of the wisest man who ever lived, Solomon, an ancient king of my people," he explained.

"The Greeks would argue with you about his wisdom," Otto laughed.

"The Greeks argue with everyone, including themselves," Reuben replied, climbed into the saddle and, with a wave and a bow, rode out at the head of his small caravan.

The next day, Otto sat in the private study of Vitius Longius' villa in Luca with Centurion Massus. Wine and bread had been served and then the door firmly closed. Vitius had ordered Pinerus, his major domo, to wait in the corridor, well back from the door and ensure none of his household eavesdropped. The letter was read by both of Otto's chosen advisors. His host composed his features into an inscrutable mask of Roman dignity and said nothing once he had finished and passed it over to the centurion. As he read, he momentarily raised his eyebrows. When he reached the end, he gave a short whistle.

"Bet that knocked you sideways," he said and passed the scroll back to Otto.

"The question is," Otto began, "What to do about it."

There was a pause. Vitius and Massus looked each other then Vitius spoke.

"Clearly you wish to find out if there is any truth in this message. Where is the River Lippe?"

"Over the Rhine."

"In Germany? You would have to go into hostile territory?"

"Of course."

"Could someone go on your behalf, an envoy perhaps?"

"No, it'll have to be me. I don't know anyone who might act for me, let alone be trusted with the task," Otto said, with a shake of his head.

"You can't just go swanning off in any case. You are an Imperial officer. You'll have to ask the Emperor to be excused duties and to leave the Empire," Massus told him.

"He won't refuse me; it's my mother and sister after all," Otto responded with conviction.

"Sure of that, are you?" Massus queried.

Before he could answer, Vitius broke in.

"And what is the purpose of this proposed expedition?"

"As I've said, to see if they're alive."

Vitius leaned back in his chair and steepled his fingers, collecting his thoughts, then he spoke slowly giving a solemn weight to his words.

"It seems to me, Otto that there are four possible results of undertaking this dangerous journey. You cannot find them. You find their graves. You find that they are alive, well and happy. You find them living in difficult circumstances, sick or impoverished. In the latter cases, what will you do next? If you discover they require your help and support how will you give it?"

"I had not thought that far ahead," Otto told him ruefully.

"Well, you'll have time to ponder it," Massus said. "Write your letter to the Emperor and I'll send it off with the next courier."

The meeting broke up. Otto spent half an hour talking with Aelia, now whitehaired and unable to walk without the aid of a stick. Poppaea, the daughter of the house had married a young man who was eminently "suitable" in the eyes of her mother, Sabina Pulchra. She was visiting her in her new home across the city. The old lady talked about her grandson, Lucius to whom Otto had been oath-tied, not so long ago. She clearly missed him.

"I am old Otto. I find I want my loved ones closer these days. Tell your friend the Emperor to send our boy home to us."

Otto smiled and said his farewells.

"I am sorry but I must go. I have some urgent business."

"The young generally do," Aelia sighed.

Massus marched briskly to the barracks and went into his private quarters. He bolted the door and took out a small strongbox which he unlocked, removing from it a short hexagonal baton of hard wood. He then carefully wrapped a narrow strip of parchment around it making sure the edges of the spiral he had formed did not overlap. He dipped a steel pen in black ink and began to write along the length of the rod, turning it to the next of its six faces and carrying on once he had reached the end of the first one. He wrote, "*You will shortly learn a friend who eats figs wishes to cross the water. His eyes and ears could record a story to be told when he returns. From the Hand of Cyclops.*" He blew on the ink to ensure it was dry then uncoiled the parchment. Stretched out flat, it appeared to be nothing more than a random series of letters, but if the person to whom it was to be sent had an identical baton to wrap it round, the message would make sense once more. It was hidden in the cap of a scroll case, sealed and on its way to Rome within the hour.

Over the years, several people had speculated why Decimus Massus, an experienced centurion awarded a silver spear after saving his legion in Africa, was content with garrison duty in a backwater like Luca. Massus had his own reasons for accepting the posting which he had once explained to Otto and Vitius Longius but he had never mentioned his role as a covert agent of the Emperor. He was ideally placed for passing or receiving intelligence along the Tyrrhenian seacoast, based far enough out of Rome to avoid scrutiny by the Emperor's political enemies but close enough to the capital for speedy communication.

Otto took hours over the composition of his letter to Augustus. The initial draft was flowery but then he remembered how his elaborate speech when he first met the Emperor had been greeted with derision. Next he tried flattery, then entreaty but neither rang true. Finally he wrote frankly and simply, which was the best thing he could have done.

"To Emperor Augustus, Father of the People, Greetings.

Sir, I have received information that my mother and sister may be living in the River Lippe country in Germany. I earnestly request leave of absence and permission to cross the Rhine to search for them.

Salutations from your loyal officer, Prefect Otto Longius".

By the time it arrived on the desk of the Emperor's secretary, the coded message sent by Massus had already been received.

Otto did not have to wait long for a reply.

"To the Equestrian, Imperial Prefect Otto Longius, Greetings.

I am instructed to inform you that your duties are too important for you to be allowed to absent yourself from them. You will remain serving in your present capacity until or unless you receive orders to the contrary.

Menities"

Otto was stunned at the brusqueness of the unexpected refusal. He stalked around for a week full of resentment, growling at everyone except Lollia and Lucius Albus but even with them he was remote and withdrawn. Massus had a quiet word with him.

"There's more to being a good soldier than waving a sword around in battle. There is accepting an order you disagree with and cheerfully getting on with it. Just because he won't let you have your own way this time don't forget you owe our Emperor your rank and your status as an Equestrian. He's already given you plenty, eh?"

Otto scowled and made no reply but he knew that he had behaved badly. He shared a flask of the best wine with the centurion by way of admitting he had been in the wrong. He began to smile again, although he inwardly grieved for his missed opportunity. He was unaware of discussions in the Emperor's modest house on the Palatine Hill.

"Aldermar is one of my confidential correspondents. Why did he write to Prefect Longius directly?" Augustus asked.

"Perhaps he regarded this rumour as a purely domestic matter too trivial for your attention, sir," Menities replied.

"Not his business to decide that sort of thing."

"It will be of advantage to have the insights of a proven officer on the situation on the far side of the Rhine. There are of course risks…"

"Name one" Augustus demanded..

"He might possibly re-join his tribal kin and take sides against us," Menities suggested.

"Nonsense. I'd back him to be true to the end. Old-fashioned fidelity. I like that. We need a scheme to get him in and out. Can't simply ride up in his uniform and say, "Morning, ma," can he? Rest of 'em will chop him to bits," Augustus chuckled.

The major hazard was that Otto would be taken prisoner by hostile tribesmen. That could result only in a long drawn-out and painful death for him but worse for Rome, a major propaganda coup for the enemy. Menities and Augustus took a week to finalize their plan. The Emperor sent for Praetorian Tribune Cassius Plancus. By the time the tribune presented himself in front of his Emperor, Menities had already despatched confidential orders to Massus and Aldermar.

"That smell coming off you?" Augustus demanded.

"Yes, sir," the handsome, exquisitely dressed and groomed young officer replied.

He wore the plain white tunic and toga of a praetorian in Rome. His hair was curled and gleamed with oil. His white calfskin boots were laced with gold cords ending in tassels.

"What is it?"

"Patchouli, sir. I can have some sent over to you if you wish."

"Insolence! Go around like brothel keepers the lot of you. Gold bootlaces, Gods above and below! Now listen tribune, you are always pestering me to send you on active service and your mother is adamant she will publicly commit suicide if I do. Everyone's mother's causing me difficulties at the moment but I digress. A compromise for you. Take thirty or so cavalry to Luca the day after tomorrow, there you will receive further orders. Report to Prefect Otto Longius. You met him a few years ago. Tall, burly chap. Kills barbarian kings. Tell no-one your destination. No-one. Campaign kit and supplies only. No mirrors and jars of disgusting scent, let alone your barber and pastry cook. You be will out of Rome for some while but within the boundaries of the Empire. That's the compromise. Dismissed."

"Oh, thank you, sir," Cassius Plancus beamed.

"Thank me on your return, tribune," Augustus told him with a sardonic smile.

The Emperor was in an unusually good mood for the next few days. Menities was bold enough to remark on it.

"You appear to be in very good form, sir."

"Thinking about Tribune Plancus roughing it in some mud hut. That'll cool his campaigning ardour."

"I think Prince Aldermar lives quite well," Menities reproached.

"Where's his Greek statuary? Egyptian bed with silk hangings? Eats lark tongue pie and honeyed dormouse does he? Poor young Plancus!" he said and laughed aloud.

"Poor young Plancus" rode out at the head of his thirty-two-strong cavalry turma accompanied by fifteen mules carrying tents, kit and supplies handled by five civilian drivers and camp servants. Among them was a tall, strongly built young man, blue-eyed and blond haired. He was one of the Emperor's bodyguards, a member of his Germani Custodes, each of whom had sworn their oath to the person of Augustus. He had disguised himself as a civilian and slipped in among the muleteers as ordered without the knowledge of Plancus.

The party travelled at a brisk pace north along the well-paved Via Aurelia. The praetorians were feared by the general population and resented by the regular army. By day traffic scattered in front to them and at night, they were avoided by other travellers in the waystations where they slept. They made good time in generally fair weather and without incident.

Massus was expecting them. He had received a letter with the palace seal and on opening it, found a strip of parchment had been concealed inside. He wrapped the strip around his baton and read,

"*VI end in case of discovery. From The Left Hand of the Sphinx.*"

The sixth line of the letter ended with the words "in case of discovery" and "The Left Hand of the Sphinx" was Menities' code name, or one of them. Augustus had once used the symbol of a sphinx as his personal seal. Satisfied that it was genuine, he read the message, beginning to smile as the detail emerged. However, he had not been informed of the whole scheme, only the first part. He was to pass it on to Otto and Plancus verbally and leave the rest to Aldermar. He took charge of a second letter to Otto but left the seals unbroken.

Some days later, early in the afternoon, Massus met the praetorian cavalry on the road two miles out of Luca. He had posted one of his men in advance to warn him of their approach. He saluted the tribune.

"Centurion Decimus Massus, sir. I am to escort you to the estate of the Imperial Prefect Otto Longius and give you both your further orders."

"Lead on, centurion," Plancus said in reply but did not condescend to introduce himself.

The household had seen and heard the horsemen coming so Lollia stood in the yard at the foot of the front steps of her home with

Didia holding Lucius Albus' hand behind her to her right and Felix to her left, all ready to offer a formal welcome. Massus dismounted and walked over to her. He bowed and she returned his greeting.

"Domina Lollia, may I present the noble Praetorian Tribune Cassius Plancus?"

Plancus slid down off his horse in a practised, flowing motion, came forward to take Lollia's hand, bending over it. He looked up into her eyes.

"It is my honour to make the acquaintance of the wife of my old friend and fellow officer," he said in his cultured accent and with his most charming smile.

As she was the taller by three or four inches and it was a hot day, a reek of horse, stale sweat and some faded perfume she could not identify rose into her nostrils from his hair and body, ruining the effect for which he had been aiming.

"You are most welcome, sir," she said and took back her hand which he had still been holding. She gestured to Felix. "This is Evocati Felix, our major domo and my husband's former military companion."

Felix had dressed himself in a soldierly way with his gold chain of honour around his neck and a sword at his side. He bowed and received the most cursory of acknowledgements from the tribune.

"Your husband, domina?" asked Massus.

"He is out with his men on the Spedia road. I expect him in an hour or so. I take it you will need somewhere to bivouac. Evocati Felix can show you a pasture on our land at the river's edge, if he will be so kind. Perhaps you would care to use our bathhouse, tribune, while we wait for Prefect Longius. Didia, show the gentleman the bathhouse and come straight back. I'll take Lucius Albus for now."

Lollia turned away with a gracious smile and left them to their arrangements.

When Cassius Plancus had bathed, his aide de camp, the decurion who normally commanded the cavalry turma, was waiting for him. He saluted.

"Camp set out for your inspection sir," he said with a salute.

The tribune waved his hand vaguely in reply, "Lead on."

They walked through the gently sloping garden, threaded a coppice of young hazels and out into a water meadow. Four large tents had been pitched in a square. Two smaller ones for the tribune and the decurion were set up a little distance away. The civilians would be making do under a shared canvas awning. The horses and mules were picketed to long ropes stretched between poles knocked into the turf. Stones had been collected from the river and laid out to make fire pits. The troopers had knocked two short stakes into the sand at the river's edge and fastened a narrow plank on top of them to make a crude bench. This was the latrine. The men would squat over the plank and open their bowels straight into the stream where the current would carry their waste away. There was even a sponge on a stick for wiping and for once, plenty of water to rinse it before the next man used it.

Plancus suppressed a shudder at the rudimentary sanitary facilities and commended his second in command on the layout.

He made his way back up to the villa thinking about Lollia. He was as appreciative of her beauty as of her faultless good manners and modest demeanour. She was clearly not of pure Latin stock with those blazing blue eyes and her size. He had seen only Northern slave women who had been so tall and, well, large, but she was all in perfect proportion,

"Impressive, that's the word for her," he mused, "lovely and powerful; the Goddess Juno incarnate."

As he came back into the garden surrounding the villa, he saw Otto had arrived and was sitting with that centurion (Massus was it?) at an outside table. He walked up to them and held out his right hand. Otto stood up to take it. He towered over the tribune.

"Gods, I'll swear you've grown since last we met! How are you old thing? You look well, if enormous," Plancus said with a broad smile. "Your lovely wife kindly offered me the use of your bathhouse. I expect she found me a bit whiffy but was too polite to say so. My chaps are comfortably sorted out in one of your fields; so that's all jolly good isn't it?"

Cassius Plancus and Otto were not close friends. They had met once when Otto had been in Rome and had spent only a day or so in each other's company but Plancus treated everyone on or near his social class as an intimate friend of long standing.

"Perhaps you would care to sit and take some wine, tribune?" Otto asked, a little put out at the effusive greeting Plancus had given him.

"Tribune? Oh, it's going to be all stiff and military is it? Then thank you Prefect, sir." he laughed and sat down beside Massus. "Shift up a bit centurion, there's a good fellow."

Massus grudgingly moved a little way along the stone bench. "Prefect Longius I have a letter for you from the Emperor. Do you wish to read it before we begin?" He handed it over and Otto opened the proffered scroll case. Plancus turned and looked directly at Massus.

"What on earth did you do to lose an eye? How ghastly for you!"

"He lost it to an arrow the day he saved the army and was awarded a silver spear," Otto said without looking up from his letter.

"I say, well done,!" Plancus told him and offered to clink wine cups.

The centurion could not help smiling, even if he was beginning to wonder if the effete Tribune Cassius Plancus was the right man to escort Otto on an arduous journey to the northern edge of the Empire. Otto finished reading what the Emperor had written.

"To *my Equestrian Imperial Prefect Otto Longius, Greetings.*

Your recent letter recalled former Prefect of Auxiliary Cavalry Prince Aldermar to mind. Loyal friend for many years. His people still enlist in my service. Need to let him know he is not forgotten. Tribune Cassius Plancus is to escort you on a diplomatic mission to his capital.

Give Aldermar my warmest sentiments of undying friendship and all that. Menities has sent detailed orders to the garrison commander in Luca, he will liaise with you both. Pay the strictest attention to what he says, Nothing in writing. Salutations

By the hand of Augustus Imp.

Post Scriptum. Aldermar may have further news of your mother and sister. Fortuna with you, my Otto."

"The Emperor says you have detailed orders for us, Centurion Massus." Otto said.

"I have sir, but they are to be communicated to you verbally. The paperwork I need to consult is locked away in my quarters…"

"Then that's where we shall go. I'll quickly wash and change. Perhaps you wouldn't object riding over in the mule cart, Tribune Plancus?" The tribune nodded his assent. "Good; it isn't far and we can relax in the back while Felix drives us."

Lollia stood by with a towel while her naked husband leaned over a bowl splashing his face, neck and armpits with hot water out of a bronze ewer in their bedroom.

"You're getting it all over the floor," she scolded. "Here, give me the flannel, I'll wash your back. Tullia wants to know if she and Plotina are supposed to feed all those soldiers."

"No. I'll send some wine down to them this evening. She will need to cook for the tribune and his decurion though; they'll be eating with us this evening."

"And Decimus Massus?"

"Yes, we'd better invite him as well."

She finished rinsing him and handed over the towel.

"So, what's going on? Why has a small army invaded us without a declaration of war?"

"Don't know precisely. Augustus is sending me to Aldermar but there's more to it, I think."

"Well, it's part of what you wanted at least. Your feet smell appalling. Wash them too."

Dressed in a clean blue tunic and soft boots but with his treasured pugio in its sheath belted at his back, Otto sat in the cart with Massus and Plancus. The tribune manged to drape himself elegantly with one arm dangling negligently over the side as they swayed and jolted into the city.

"This is the way to travel," Plancus drawled. "Bags of time to look at the view and no saddle rubbing your backside raw, eh?"

Once through the city gates, Felix turned right for the barracks, hitched the mule cart and they walked inside behind him.

"Wotcher Felix, old mate," a legionary called but stiffened to attention and fell silent when he saw the officers.

They went into Massus' rooms.

"Evocati Felix, with Prefect Longius' permission, please stand outside three paces from the door and let no-one come any closer. My lads are a lot of nosey bastards," the centurion called out in an unnecessarily loud voice, just to let them all know he meant business.

Once inside he seated his visitors and took the papers he had received from Rome out of his strongbox.

"Right gentlemen," he said taking a chair, "we are all soldiers in a private office in barracks and here we can speak frankly and openly to one another…."

"On our own, the centurion and I are on informal terms," Otto interrupted for the tribune's benefit.

"Very well, Cassius it shall be," he agreed.

"Thank you," Massus said with a nod of approval. "The Emperor orders you to present his compliments to Prince Aldermar in his city in Lower Germany. Your designated route passes through Lugdunum and towards Noviodunum via Agendincum. You will cross the River Sequana well upstream of the island of the Parisi. Aldermar's guides will find you when you are near Noviodunum. I have a detailed map for you and permits to draw supplies at any army outpost or legion camp on your way. You are to be frank about the nature of your mission to anyone who enquires, consistent with your own security. In other words, if some dodgy sod starts sniffing around, do 'im without making too much fuss. The rest of the orders are for you, Otto. You are to ride through all inhabited areas in full uniform wearing your gold torque and arm-rings. Will that charger of yours allow anyone else on his back?" Otto shook his head. "Thought not; in which case you are to bring along your grey gelding as a spare mount. Is he up to it?"

"Yes, he's fit enough."

"Well then, that's it. You leave first light tomorrow."

"Seems odd," Cassius commented. "Secret orders, nothing in writing and yet we are to let any stranger know our business. Don't quite add up, old thing."

Massus shrugged. "Not for us to question orders."

"I wouldn't lose money betting you know a lot more than you are prepared to tell us."

"Now, Cassius, you know as well as I do what curiosity did to the cat. I'm saying nothing."

"Fair enough, then," said Otto. "Will you dine with us this evening?"

"Thank you and thank Lollia. A dinner prepared by the hands of Tullia and Plotina is not to be refused. I'll ride over when I've finished here."

Otto's troopers carried two amphorae of wine down to the praetorian lines as he had mentioned to Lollia. The dinner was excellent. The centre piece was a kid seethed in milk and dressed with rosemary and basil. The bread was straight out of the oven, still warm and carrying the slightest scent of yeast. There were side dishes of river fish, sausage and fresh vegetables, cheese, fruit and nuts. Tullia and Plotina had tried to ensure that their kitchen and their mistress' table would not be found wanting by the two officers newly arrived from Rome. Cassius Plancus regaled them with the gossip of the day circulating in the capital. Most of it went over Otto and Lollia's heads; they did not know any of the people concerned. Massus largely ignored the talk; he was too busy doing justice to the best dinner he had eaten for a long time. Felix was the first to rise from his place at the table. He wanted to put Otto's armour and weapons into the best possible order before he left in the morning.

"Bit eccentric to dine with the servants, most entertaining," Cassius remarked when he had limped out of the room.

"Felix stood beside me in an ambush and a siege. I've been glad enough to eat the soldier's bread he baked for me. Why should he not have a place at my table, when he chooses?"

"No reason whatsoever," Plancus replied, unruffled by the implied rebuke. "Just that it's not something one sees every day."

The dinner party broke up shortly afterwards. After effusive thanks from the tribune, he and his decurion returned to their lines. Otto walked Massus over to his horse.

"This Cassius Plancus, are you sure he's up to it if things turn rough on the way?" the centurion asked.

Otto laughed briefly and slapped his friend on the back, unintentionally making him stagger.

"You have more in common with him than you think. He also was rewarded with a silver spear and promotion to the praetorians after saving his legion's eagle and rallying them. It was out east somewhere. Don't be fooled by his manner. I've seen the scar across his belly he brought home with him."

Massus sighed. "I'll never get my head round some of these aristocratic officers; off-duty dressed in silk, perfumed like dancing girls but hard as nails. Listen, I'll keep the best eye I can on your household while you're away but I can't promise not to have to use your troopers."

"I know you will, goes without saying. Gods with you, friend Decimus."

They shook hands, the centurion mounted up and disappeared out of view in the deepening night.

Chapter 3

Lollia and Otto went through the long ceremony of a loving couple saying farewell in the dark privacy of their bedroom. She did not know precisely where her husband was going or when he would return, if ever, but she made no complaint. They got up by lamplight so he could make his final preparations. Felix had loaded a pair of mules with his campaign trunk, tent, ground sheet and camp bed. He had added two spare lances and an oval cavalry shield wrapped in greased leather to protect it against rain and damp. He brought Djinn around to the front of the house just as the praetorian cavalry formed up.

The sun had fully risen but the dew was still thick on the grass. Lollia stood on the bottom step of the veranda her face a mask of Roman fortitude. She held Lucius Albus by the hand. Otto's people were ranged on either side of her. He kissed Lollia on both cheeks, ruffled the hair of Lucius and Tullia's Pollux then put on his helmet. He swung up into the saddle. Djinn had an instinctive sense of occasion. He reared up a little and took two curvetting strides on his back legs, pawing the air with his front hooves before settling back to earth. Otto patted his neck. He raised his right hand in something between a wave goodbye and a blessing. Everyone except Lollia bowed and he was no longer part of their domestic world, a soldier on service now.

They formed column with Cassius Plancus and Otto at the head of the first group of twelve horsemen. The mules and Otto's gelding, led on a halter (which he did not like), took the centre, followed by the remaining twenty troopers under the command of the decurion. A turma of praetorian cavalry with two additional officers was a formidable fighting unit but a small one. They were vulnerable to ambush and would have to employ some lightly armed local scouts once they were beyond Lugdunum. For the moment, they were in Italia and it was not until they were deep into Cisalpine Gaul that they would be in real peril. They trotted back onto the Via Aurelia with the growing heat of the sun on their left, up into the foothills, heading north along the paved highway.

Sundown comes early in the mountain valleys. They had climbed for most of the afternoon and when their shadows were long, they found a place to camp overnight. They discovered a semi-circular bay with protective high cliffs and a spring at the base where stone had been cut away from a rockface to break up for surfacing the road. Cassius set out his dispositions, keeping the men and animals several yards back from the sheer faces in case of falling debris. They did not unpack their tents as the night was dry but prepared to roll up in their cloaks. Fires were lit and rations were cooking when a voice hailed them out of the darkness beyond the circle of firelight. Instantly, the troopers were on their feet, weapons in their hands, without an order having been issued. Plancus called them into defensive ranks with the mules and horses behind them.

"Come slowly forward where we can see you," the tribune shouted into the night.

A middle-aged civilian in a plain tunic and travelling cloak appeared. He had his arms raised to show he was not carrying a weapon. He stopped abruptly on seeing that he was facing a shield wall with glittering spear points emerging from it. Unblinking eyes stared fiercely over the top.

"Sirs," he said, his voice shaking with nerves. "Sirs, I mean no harm."

"State your business," Plancus barked.

"I am a carpenter returning home to Spedia with my family. We have been visiting my father-in-law's farm. We are benighted, I beg the favour of your protection until the morning."

"How many are you?"

"Five sir, six with me, I mean…" his fear was making him confused.

"Do you have a wagon?"

"A cart, sir, a covered cart."

"Bring it up."

He vanished and reappeared leading a pair of aged horses harnessed to a two wheeled cart with a canvas hood over it.

"Get your people off,"

The carpenter hesitated.

"My children certainly but my wife and her sister...."

"Tell them all to climb down and stand by your vehicle."

Three young children and two women emerged, all looking terrified. Plancus gestured to a couple of his soldiers who each seized a burning stick out of a fire and peered inside by their flickering light.

"All clear sir," one of them reported.

Plancus sheathed his sword and smiled. He stepped over to the family,

"Have no fear for the safety of your people, especially your womenfolk. Bring your vehicle up to the fires. Rest in security tonight. My men will guard over you and you shall come to no harm."

"Blessings on you noble sir," one of the women babbled took his hand and kissed it.

"Compose yourself my good woman, you are safe now,"

Half an hour later, one of the little girls was showing a trooper how to make a cat's cradle out of string while his tentmates laughed at his clumsiness. A young boy was sitting by a fire chewing bacon with a soldier's helmet balanced on the back of his head, so big on him it looked like a bucket.

As he rolled up in his cloak and went to sleep, Otto wished that Massus could have seen how quickly languid Cassius Plancus had transformed into a decisive field officer. Centurion Cyclops would not have believed his one eye.

In the morning after the grateful carpenter and his charges had left them, Otto rode up alongside Cassius.

"That was decent of you, offering comfort to that family," he remarked.

"No choice, old thing. We are the army. We exist to protect Rome which boils down to its citizens, don't you think? Even dreary plebs."

They came down out of the mountains into Cisalpine Gaul which had been spared the worst of Julius Caesar's ethnic cleansing. These were cities and townships whose people had traded with Rome for over a century. In them, smiths forged weapons for the legions and where all the red-glazed table and cookware used in Rome and its provinces was fired. The inhabitants benefitted by the commerce and by the roads, bridges and aqua-ducts the Romans built as they spread their tentacles of control and what they chose to call progress, whether the natives wanted it or not.

They rode thirty miles a day for six days then took a day's rest. At this rate, they could be expected to arrive in under thirty days; provided there were no delays, provided no horse went lame and provided none of the men fell sick or was injured. Whenever possible they stayed overnight in waystations or legion outposts. They rarely pitched their tents nor did they eat into the rations the mules carried other than at the noon halt.

At first Otto had been enthusiastic about retracing his previous journeys. He had happy memories of travelling these highways with Lucius Longius but that had been some years ago. Everywhere he saw new roads, new buildings, more people: although he could not say why, it saddened him a little. He soon lost interest. What had begun as almost an adventure became a monotonous slog towards their far-off goal. Day followed day in the same routine through sunshine and late spring rain. Nothing of note occurred until they were two days north of Lugdunum.

Under lowering clouds they saw a column of around one hundred men marching eight abreast towards them. They were not fully armed but wore various pieces of army kit, swords at the hip. A very young tribune rode in front of them and as the praetorians approached he shouted an order and turned his horse off the highway. The column halted but did not move aside. The cavalry began to slow and stopped facing them..

"I order you to make way!" the tribune shouted at his men.

"Piss off sonny," someone called out.

He went red in the face with humiliation and rode up to Otto, saluting him. "So sorry sir, they have all received their discharge and they seem to have forgotten how to behave like soldiers."

"So they are civilians now?"

"Yes, sir."

Otto walked Djinn past him and right up to the first rank.

"If you are no longer soldiers who obey an officer, who leads you?" he asked loudly.

A tall man pushed to the front. He was weather-beaten and lean, hardened both physically and mentally by twenty years of the legionary life. He grinned up at Otto showing brown, jagged teeth. He eased his sword in its scabbard by way of an unspoken threat then let his hand drop from the hilt. He folded his arms and straddled his legs wide.

"I lead them," he said. "I am…"

He never finished his words. Otto nudged Djinn with his knee. The horse made a quarter tun to his left freeing Otto to draw his long cavalry sword above his head and send it slashing down on the man who had defied him. His victim was so shocked that this unknown officer had drawn a blade on him that he was welded to the spot. His mouth fell open in a look of stupid disbelief just as he was struck between the base of his neck and shoulder. An arc of bright arterial blood sprayed ten feet into the air; he staggered and fell dead.

Otto straightened Djinn so that he was directly facing the rest of them.

"Clear the road for the Emperor's Praetorian Cavalry!" he roared, his voice ringing out like a brass trumpet.

They began to shuffle out of the way, two came forward to drag the body clear.

"Leave him," Otto barked.

They fell back. The turma and its pack mules stamped the body raw as they cantered over it.

They spent that night at a fortified supply depot. The troopers had previously kept themselves aloof from Otto; he was not one of their own but they now gave him quick smiles of approval as he passed among them. He had demanded a clear road in their name, so they had adopted him.

Cassius raised a wine cup to Otto over the small fire that lay between them in the depot yard.

"Bit harsh on that chap today, don't you think?" he asked.

The alternating light and shadow of the flames danced across Otto's face as he answered.

"Cavalry at a standstill is vulnerable to close quarter infantry attack. We were outnumbered and most of them had swords, a few javelins. I stunned them into obedience to avoid a general conflict. It's pity that a man who had served Rome for so many years should die on the road like a slaughtered mule."

"Oh quite, appalling really awful."

During the next day's stage, the country around them began to change abruptly. Farmsteads and small towns had become less frequent and those few that they saw were heavily stockaded behind defensive ditches. The tree cover grew thicker, the road narrower and less well maintained. They put the livestock in the centre of their camp and slept fully armed in a ring around them during the hours of darkness.

"We need some local scouts," Otto said.

Cassius consulted the map. "There should be a legion outpost ten miles east of here. There's a river marked as well, no name though. They might know a couple of locals who can help us out."

Following Caesar's maxim never to split your forces in hostile territory, the entire turma veered off eastward on a half-overgrown path through the trees. The legion fortress was nearer fifteen miles away than ten nor did it house a full complement of troops. The wall surrounding it was leaning in parts and the ditch overgrown with weeds. No-one challenged them until they were at the gate when a legionary with no helmet on poked his head out of the watch tower and shouted down at them.

"Lost?"

Otto and Plancus looked at each other in amazement.

"Praetorian Tribune Plancus and Imperial Prefect Longius seek admittance. Open up."

The soldier's eyes went wide and he vanished without a word. After a few moments, the double gates were heaved apart by four legionaries, none of whom were in full uniform. The cavalry filed in and at an order from the decurion, the men dismounted and stood at their horses' heads looking around them. Slovenly soldiers leaned against buildings or squatted in groups over boardgames, passing around pitchers of drink. Some sorry cows were penned at one corner of the parade ground. Chickens squawked and bustled away when one of the skinny dogs skulked too close. A few native carts and horses were grouped on the far side. Drab women with naked children clutching their skirts stopped working at their wash tubs or cooking pots and peered over at them.

"Who commands here?" Plancus asked one of the soldiers who had opened the gates.

"Prefect Velius," he said with a smirk and a badly restrained chuckle.

"And that amuses you soldier? Or perhaps you find me comical?"

The legionary realized he had made a bad mistake and came to attention, staring straight in front of him, his face expressionless.

"Where might Prefect Velius be found at this time of day?" Plancus asked.

"In his quarters, sir," the unhappy man replied pointing at a low building with a turf roof.

"Very good, thank you. Now, you obviously found me diverting judging by the look on your face when you first addressed me. It's only fair that you now entertain me. Run out of the gate and down the track until it gets dark then turn around and run back. I will really enjoy that, how I'll laugh to myself while you're gone. Of course, if you are back here before dawn tomorrow, I shall know that you have cheated and you will be flogged. Off you go old boy, that's the ticket."

The legionary turned on his heel and jogged out of the camp. The three officers rode over to the prefect's quarters. Otto and Plancus dismounted, the decurion held their horses' reins. There was no sentry posted outside the commander's door. Otto knocked but there was no response. He knocked again, harder, making the door shake on its rusting hinges.

"What?" an irritated voice shouted from inside, followed by a brief burst of coughing.

Plancus nodded at Otto and they stepped in. The shaft of daylight that entered with them lanced across the unswept floor of a dirty room. Opposite them, a man sat on the edge of the bed with his bare feet on the dusty planks. He had not shaved for several days, his dark hair was greasy and tangled. He wore a rumpled tunic and no loincloth. His flaccid penis poked out from below the overhang of his belly. He rearranged his testicles, pulled his tunic down and stood up.

"Who are you?" he demanded.

"Tribune of Praetorian Cavalry Cassius Plancus and Imperial Prefect Otto Longius; may we assume that you are Prefect Velius,?"

The unkempt officer walked over to the table and sat on a bench, reaching for an earthenware pitcher. He poured a yellowish fluid into a mug and drank it back in one gulp. He looked over his shoulder at the bed.

"Get out," he snapped.

A surly woman crawled out of the heap of blankets, picked up her shift from the floor and padded out.

"No wine. Want some ale? Looks like piss, tastes like piss and makes you piss," he offered.

"What has happened here?" Otto asked.

"What d'you mean?" Velius asked with a truculent air.

"No sentries, men dirty and not in uniform, farm carts leaning against your walls which are half-falling down; do you want me to go on?"

The prefect slapped his hand down on the table.

"You come in here all full of military virtue and judge me? What the fuck do you know?"

"I know that something had gone wrong here, Prefect Velius, could you explain?" Plancus asked mildly, trying to calm him.

Velius sighed and poured himself another drink. "Very well. I came here five years ago with six hundred good men. We built our camp and patrolled the area. There's a river half a mile away but the ground in between is nothing but swamp. Pools of black water, stinking mud and reeds and clouds of stinging insects. By the end of the first year, I had lost fifty men to disease. They sweated themselves to death in their bunks. A supply convoy came through after twelve months. I sent a message back with the quartermaster in charge. Next year, he returned. No answer and never will be. Men began to desert. We caught them and executed them. So many, it sickened us and we no longer had the will to punish them. More men died of fever, killed themselves or faded away in simple despair. Five long years; no orders, no replacements, abandoned, forgotten other than for enough supplies to keep us alive, though there's plenty left over these days. So do not rush to condemn me, my highly polished gentlemen. Do you know how many men I have left? Three hundred and twenty-one at the last muster, though the Gods only know when that was; probably less of 'em by now."

"Can you not put some spirit, some soldierly pride back into this camp?" Otto asked.

"Five years," Velius stated bleakly. "Five years," and fell silent staring down at the scarred table. "Anyway, what do you want?"

"Scouts, if you have any to spare," Plancus told him.

"A couple of the natives who hang around here might want a job, feel free to ask."

"Thank you we shall enquire. And something else; when I get back to Rome I will raise your plight with the authorities."

"I suppose I should thank you but I know it won't do any good. It's too late. Things here have gone too far. If they suddenly notice this command now, I will be disgraced and cashiered, my remaining men decimated. Not much of a prospect is it?"

Neither Otto nor Plancus wanted to argue the point. They left him to his ale pot and went on foot over to a small group of locals squatting around a smouldering fire. None admitted to speaking Latin.

Otto tried in his German dialect and one of them understood. Otto explained he was looking for two or three men to act as guides and scouts. They would be paid and fed but must provide their own horses.

"Where do you go?" the man asked.

"We need to find a place to cross the Sequana," Otto told him.

"Three days to river then must find a way over," he responded and named an extortionate fee.

Otto squatted on his heels and haggled for the traditional minimum of twenty minutes before agreement was reached. They now had two guides who would scout ahead for them and show them where the river was fordable. Their new companions left the compound and came back within quarter of an hour astride light horses. Each man carried a lance and a round wicker shield. A third native had passed out through the gate with them but he did not return. They mounted up and gladly left that forlorn outpost, trotting back the way they had come. Ahead, a soldier was running steadily in the same direction. Plancus urged his horse on and caught up with him.

"Halt," he called as he drew level.

Sweat coursed down the panting legionary's red face and he stumbled to attention.

"I have spoken with your prefect. Your situation is as about as bad as it can be, man. Say to Velius that Praetorian Tribune Cassius Plancus advises him to march out of that fortress, burn it behind him and make his way to the nearest legion outpost that has a full set of officers. He can use my name when he tells them his story, Cassius Plancus, remember that. Here," he flipped the weary man a silver coin "go back and pray for better fortune."

The cavalrymen were all in a sombre mood that night. The usual banter around the hearths once they had fed and groomed their mounts was missing. Their two scouts made their own fire and sat over it muttering casting furtive glances at the horses and the mule train. Otto and Plancus took a stroll around the picket lines.

"If ever I saw something to chill the blood and suck the life out of a man it was that outpost," Otto remarked.

"I wouldn't be at all surprised to find out that friend Velius had offended an influential man in Rome or someone on the general staff, no other explanation," Cassius suggested.

"What is being done to those men is wrong."

"'Course it is but it happens, old thing. But I think we have more pressing problems than the plight of Velius, don't you?"

"So you noticed that third man who left through the gates with our two…"

"Oh really, Otto! Now we're deep into this ghastly wilderness do you imagine you are the only one with your wits about you?"

"Who was he and where did he go?" Otto asked, ignoring the criticism.

"In answer to your double question I have to say I don't know. But I don't like it."

"We have lost a day so we must press on to the river. Let's be vigilant but do nothing to make those two think we are suspicious." Both of them turned to look over at the two natives, huddled, heads together, talking low. "They are definitely plotting, time for us to make some plans of our own."

"Difficult if we don't know what they're up to," commented Cassius.

"Are you telling me that a nobleman raised in the scheming, back-stabbing cesspit of Roman politics can't turn the tables on them?" Otto laughed. "Time to make use of your education in the school of dirty tricks, Cassius...old thing!"

Mid-morning on the third day, they crested a ridge and saw the river a quarter of a mile away below them. The sun was bright, the water sparkled reflecting the blue sky. Blackbirds sang and the thorn bushes had exploded into clouds of white blossom. It was an idyllic scene. They rode down to the river's edge and looked across. It was about fifty yards wide at this point with firm turf banks which were swept clear of undergrowth and most trees by the annual floods after the snow and ice thawed upstream. They studied it for a long five minutes before Otto came to a decision

"We swim the horses across here," he said. "We'll build a couple of rafts to carry the weapons and armour and the supplies."

"Let's make a start then," Cassius responded by way of agreement and turned in his saddle to look back at the forest edge as if checking for likely timber.

"No, sirs, no." one of the scouts interrupted urgently, forgetting that he had implied that he spoke no Latin. "River dangerous here, deep holes, drag horses under, mud, currents, very bad for you, very bad. All drown. Half day upstream ferry take you over tomorrow easy sirs, easy."

"Secure these men," Cassius ordered. Instantly they were surrounded by grim-faced troopers. Unwavering lance points were aimed at their chests. Other cavalrymen dismounted and dragged them off their horses. Cords were produced and their wrists tied behind their backs.

"Decurion, get a work party of twenty of the chaps stripped of their armour. The rest, form a screen at the edge of the trees. Let's get on with these rafts."

It took them three hours to lash-up all of the rafts they needed. Saplings and sheaves of brushwood were cut and roped together give them enough flotation. They poled them across with a combination of yelled encouragement and filthy oaths, spinning two hundred yards downstream before they reached the far side But reach it they did, with some of the kit dripping wet but their food supplies complete and dry. All Roman soldiers were taught to swim if they did not know how when they enlisted, so men, horses and mules made it safely over the river. The prisoners were carried across with the armour.

By two hours after midday, fires had been lit and men were drying themselves and their mounts ready to move off. It was time to deal with the scouts.

Plancus took charge. "You lied to us and you tried to lure us to the ferry you spoke of, why?"

"We did not lie there is big mistake sirs," said one of them.

"Crucify them both on the nearest tree," he ordered the troopers and began to walk away.

"No, no", the other scout screamed. "I tell you. There are men waiting for you on this bank where the ferry lands."

"How many?"

"Maybe twenty, not much more than that."

Plancus laughed. "Now you are the one who is lying. Twenty men aren't enough to defeat this cavalry."

"But ferry only room for six horses. Kill six Romans, have weapons, horses, is good plunder."

Plancus sighed and gestured to one of his troopers who drew his pugio and cut the man's throat. Then he dispatched the scout that been had questioned first.

"Tie their bodies together and throw them in the river. Bring their mounts along with us; they'll do as packhorses if nothing else."

Otto and Plancus moved out of hearing of the men.

"What now?" Otto asked.

"I don't think we have a choice. We know a small, hostile force is half a day away upstream. How many miles do you think?"

Otto shrugged, "Twelve, fifteen?"

"We've lost time already but we can't ignore them. We could get out of the immediate vicinity as quickly as possible, double marches, but when we don't turn up tomorrow they might come back downstream. If they do, they'll cut our trail in a day and then what?"

"Horses stolen and throats cut in the night."

"Exactly.

"These are your men, Cassius, I'll support your decision."

Plancus called the unit over to him. "About fifteen miles from here is a ferry. The two pieces of carrion we have just disposed of were trying to get us to use it. When the first six of our comrades had crossed over to this bank, they were to be ambushed and slaughtered while the rest of us could do nothing but watch. I won't sleep well while these insolent savages remain unpunished. We push on as fast as we can upriver until dark. Cold camp tonight, chaps, no fires. At dawn we move out and when we find them we'll show them how stupid they were to even think about attacking Praetorians, what do you say?"

They cheered briefly and saddled up.

At seven in the evening, it was too dark to continue but they had ridden hard and covered just short of twelve miles. The night sky was cloudless. The stars were bright but only a sickle of moonlight shone down onto the forest glade where they were encamped. Horses and mules stamped and snorted steamy breath out of their nostrils amongst the sleeping men huddled in their long cloaks. At the first light of dawn they rose like the dead come back to life, silvered with dew as curls of white mist rolled across the leaf mould under the trees. They proceeded slowly and as quietly as nearly forty men and their animals could, turning slightly inland. Every half an hour, the nimblest of the civilian muleteers climbed a tree and spied out the land ahead. Three hours after dawn, he practically flung himself down out of the fir tree he had been perched in.

"Ahead, sirs, less than half a mile, it's them. I'm sure," he gabbled breathless in his excitement.

"Calm yourself, my fine fellow," Plancus told him. "What exactly did you see, every last detail mind."

"A ferry on the other bank beside a hut and a cable stretched across the river. On our side there's bushes with a track through them where the people who come off the boat must make their way inland. Behind that, horses…"

"How many?"

"Can't be sure sir, more than twelve anyway.

"How far is this thicket back from the river and what's the ground behind it like?"

"Maybe sixty, seventy paces and then it's clear for a long way apart from a few trees."

"You have done well."

Plancus called his decurion to him and gave his orders. The turma was to ride inland for around twenty minutes then cut round in an arc to come up behind the thicket and flush the ambush party out into the open.

"Mule train to stay where we are," he said.

"What about us?" one of the civilians bleated. "We'll be unprotected! How will we defend ourselves?"

"If I were you I should take a spare lance off one of the packsaddles and point it while shouting fiercely. That should do the trick. Look at it another way, if we don't come back, you are better off by fifteen mules loaded with military supplies. Your lucky day, eh?"

They walked their horses for a few hundred yards then began to increase the pace as they swung into an arc, closing on their prey. Shields up and lances at the ready, held upright in a position to strike downwards overarm. The group of tethered horses came into view, poor things for the most part, a dozen, fourteen and then a man bearded and long-haired, left at the rear to guard them. He had been looking the other way, towards the river and when he turned his head and saw what was coming down on him and his comrades, it was too late. The praetorians urged their horses into a canter. He managed one warning shout before a lance tore out his throat and then they were riding through broom and alder, green shoots of bracken uncurling among the thin trunks of the saplings. The main body of the ambush party was lying in wait at the front of their screen of cover, nearest the river. When they heard the warhorses crashing towards them and felt the ground shake under their hooves, they instinctively ran out onto the riverbank. If they had held their positions, some of them may have survived. There were twenty-two in all, variously armed with axes and spears, some with shields, others with helmets and mail shirts. They stared in horror as the cavalry emerged into the open. Some broke and ran up or downstream. The troopers on each end of the line pulled out and around them to prevent their escape and drive them into the milling crowd being edged towards the water. The praetorians raced in, cast a lance and spun away, never getting close enough to come within range of an axe. Some spears were thrown at the horsemen. They were caught on shields apart from one which grazed a horse's rump.

In less than five minutes, the men who had planned to destroy at least six of the Romans were all on the ground, dead or dying. The cavalrymen dismounted, picked their victims up by shoulders and feet and tossed them into the Sequana, even those still agonisingly alive and screaming for the mercy of a swift stab to the heart. A rider was sent to bring up the mule train. Otto insisted that the best of their enemies' horses were hitched along with the mules and they moved off along the track, north and west without a backward glance.

Chapter 4

"What's he like, this Prince Aldermar?" Cassius asked.

"Noble," replied Otto.

Cassius sighed. "Look Otto, when this journey isn't dangerous, it's boring. Have you heard of the art of conversation? It lightens the weariness of the day and fosters friendship between men of goodwill. You really should try it some time. "

"Aldermar is noble of appearance, noble of bearing, noble of mind and of noble birth," he responded.

"So then, taken overall, would you say he was noble?"

At that moment they came to the highest point of the ridge they had been climbing all morning. Below them was a wide panorama of rolling green like frozen waves. Green so dark it was almost black, blue tinged, in some places fresh and vibrant in the sunshine, but onwards and onwards that ocean rolled unbroken to the far horizon.

"We have to find our way through that?" Cassius demanded.

"No, we'll skirt around the south western edge and find the road to Noviodunum. That vastness you see below us is the Ardennus Forest. It's the home of savage Aurochs that will rip a man's guts out with their horns, long-tusked wild boar the size of ponies, bears and wolves. Strange clans live all their lives in its heart and never come out. They are at one with the spirits of nature and find all their needs are met but they have no love for the rest of humanity. There are other men in its depths. The worst of men; men who have killed their fathers, raped their kinswomen, stabbed unarmed comrades in the back. When there is nowhere left to flee, they go into the Ardennus. They do not come out again."

After a few minutes, Cassius said, "The other thing you should know about conversation is that it should be cheerful…"

Otto threw back his head and laughed aloud. But as he did so, the thought of home suddenly broke in on him. With a pang, he remembered happy faces around the table, Felix's wry comments but above all, Lollia with her full lips spread in a wide smile and her eyes sparkling. A great longing to be with them almost overwhelmed him but he pushed the feeling away. If the Gods loved him, they would give him other such times to be enjoyed; for now, his duty was all that mattered.

The smoke of Noviodunum was a grey smudge over the endless trees a few miles ahead of the cavalcade when two riders came out on to the unpaved road in front of them. They were mounted on tall, heavy horses with long fringes of hair around their fetlocks almost covering their hooves. Both men wore mail shirts and helmets of a Roman pattern. They carried lances and oval shields like the praetorians. Both lifted their hands high to show their peaceful intent. Plancus stopped the column and they approached.

"Hail Romans, Prince Aldermar greets you. We are to lead you to him."

"Is he near?" Plancus asked hopefully, tormented by the throbbing of his bruised buttocks, punished by day after day in the saddle.

"Yes, only three days,"

Otto laughed at the disappointed expression on the tribune's face. They followed their new guides off the road.

Very early on the third morning, they came to the edge of a broad open valley. At the head of it, two wide streams, some would say small rivers, ran either side of a hill on which Aldermar's people had built their fortified city. Caesar himself had invited them to cross the Rhine into Gallic lands and settle there more than a generation before. They had copied the architecture of their neighbours and built an oppidium; a township in a defensible position protected by a ditch and a wall which served as their stronghold in times of danger. Aldermar's forebears had no need to excavate on three sides of their city. What appeared as two separate water courses was really one which forked on the far side and flowed around the base of their hill. They had dug a deep trench across the front from stream to stream and let the waters flow into it like a moat. It reminded Otto of "Boxer's Canal", the earthwork his friend Lucius Longius had designed to protect the Second Lucan's permanent camp on the Rhine.

The oppidium was large enough to accommodate fifteen thousand people and their livestock in an emergency. It boasted wells, granaries, workshops, orchards and gardens as well as the wooden houses of the inhabitants. On the summit of the hill, a high timber gable supporting a newly thatched roof, golden in the sunlight, marked Aldermar's royal hall.

There were hamlets on the surrounding forested slopes where some of his people herded pigs, kept bees, made charcoal and cut timber. Horses and cattle grazed on the meadow lands below, separated from the cornfields by thorn hedges. Even the praetorians found it impressive, as used as they were to the temples and theatres of Rome.

A thin tendril of white smoke rose into the clear air a few hundred yards downhill. They were directed towards it. A small fire had been lit against the dawn chill and beside it stood Aldermar attended by three of his warriors. Plancus took his first look at him and saw exactly what Otto had meant when describing him. In the prime of his manhood, he was as tall as Otto with tawny hair flowing over his armoured shoulders and the back of his long blue cloak that reached down to his booted heels. His beard was neatly trimmed and his blue eyes bright with intelligence. He smiled in welcome.

"A truly noble looking barbarian," Plancus thought, but there he was wrong; Aldermar was much more.

The man he was scrutinizing had been a highly trained and decorated Roman officer. He was a member of the Equestrian Order as were his father and grandfather before him. He had been educated in Rome for several years in his boyhood; spoke, read and wrote fluent Latin and passable Greek. And, although Cassius Plancus would never know it, he was a valued confidential correspondent of the Emperor.

"Get down off that poor nag staggering under your weight and let him rest, Otto, and introduce me to your fellow officer. Let your men dismount, tribune," he called.

"Prince Aldermar, may I present the Noble Praetorian Tribune Cassius Plancus," Otto said.

"You are welcome here, tribune. Plancus? The Divine Julius had a legate called Plancus in his Army of Gaul did he not?"

"A great uncle," Cassius replied, pleased at the recognition of his family name.

Aldermar turned to Otto. "How glad I am to see you here, my young friend. We have some history together you and I," he looked over at Cassius. "Ask him about the first time we ever spoke together when you have the leisure. You will not believe it, nor will you believe how far Otto Longius, son of Badurad of the Suevi, has come since that day. The Kingkiller, as my men named him. Sit with me," he gestured to a ring of rough log benches around the fire.

"Prince Aldermar," Otto began, "thank you for your welcome. We do not come to you as beggars but have a gift of horses. They are not of the best, we collected them on our way to you…

"Along with the heads of their owners," Aldermar interrupted with a brief laugh.

"... Our Emperor Augustus instructs me to confirm his friendship and highest regard for the loyal service of you and your men..."

"I am sure he does but that's not why you're here." He gestured for his men to move away out of hearing then produced two parchment scrolls from under his cloak. "Your further orders. One each. I suggest you read them before we go on."

They broke the seals both read, looking at each other in surprise when they had finished.

"Are you aware of the contents of these letters, Prince?" Cassius asked.

"Oh yes, intimately. You Otto, are to cross the Rhine and travel up the valley of the Lippe on that personal business of which you informed the Emperor. On the way you will speak to as many people as possible to get a sense of what is going on and the mood of the people. Something's afoot and Augustus needs intelligence. You will provide it. Tribune Plancus, you are to be my guest along with your men until such times as Otto returns or we know for a fact he never will. You will stay with me in my hall and your men will be comfortably accommodated in the city. Perhaps they can train with my cavalry and we can gain insights from each other. You might enjoy your time with us although I regret I cannot offer you "Patchouli Oil" something the Emperor writes to tell me you may miss."

Cassius went red in the face, spluttered and then guffawed until his eyes watered. "Apologies sir, the Emperor does not approve of the latest fashion."

"He never did. I was sometimes admitted to his company when I lived in Rome. He was always on the austere side. We went to one of his dinners for the honour of it, not the quality of the food. Speaking of which Otto, your friend the tribune will be feasting in my hall but you will not. You will need conditioning before you can pass as a young warrior of the Suevi in your ancestral lands…"

"Conditioning?" Otto protested. "I exercise, I ride many miles daily…"

"Exactly. You ride, you do not walk, you do not run and when you've exercised you eat a good dinner with soft bread, olive oil and wine. You are carrying too much bulk to pass for a man who is often hungry. You must live like a simple warrior for a while before you go over. Espionage is a deadly business, Otto; there are no second chances. The Emperor has placed you in my care and I am about to demonstrate it."

He beckoned one of his companions over and sent him across to the mule train. He came back with the tall German muleteer.

"Tribune Plancus, will you please order your decurion to lead all your people and their animals down into the valley now. One of my warriors will show them the way," Aldermar requested.

Once they were out of sight, he spoke to the mule driver.

"You have words for me?" he asked.

"I am to say I have come from the left hand of the Sphinx, lord."

"And you speak good Latin?"

"Not as well as you, lord."

Aldermar nodded. "Then take off your clothes. Otto undress as well and give this man your armour, boots, sword, everything. You need not exchange loincloths," he added with a grin and lobbed over a leather satchel. It fell at Otto's feet. When he was undressed he opened it and took out a plain tunic, a buckskin cloak, a pair of soft leather shoes, flint, steel, a bone-handled knife, a horn cup, a rope, and a length of cord. He put on his new clothes and looked at the other man now wearing his armour and trappings.

"Listen," said Aldermar, "we do not know how many unfriendly eyes have seen a tall, fair-haired Imperial Prefect riding north. Now he is about to ride into my city with me. It is unlikely that anyone will remark that a civilian has left the party. Just as we are sending you out as a spy, Otto, others watch us. We must give them nothing to report to their masters." Aldermar gestured to the muleteer in Otto's uniform. "Tribune Plancus, you will now call this man "Otto" and treat him in exactly the same way as you are accustomed to treat our friend. This is vital; you are an essential part of the deception. Show any of your Roman hauteur towards this, shall we say, temporary, prefect and it will certainly be noticed, understand?"

He nodded his agreement.

"Good, and now Otto it's time for you to begin." He whistled and two scouts mounted on small horses, scarcely more than ponies, materialized out of the undergrowth. One of them grinned at Otto.

"Do you remember me, lord?" he asked.

"Oh yes," Otto replied warmly. You are the "Ghost" who took our message into the legion fortress when it was besieged."

"That was me. You rewarded me with a silver arm ring in front of the whole army."

"You earned the recognition."

"Now, lord, you will come with us. My real name is Grimwald and this man is my cousin Hrolf."

"Greetings to you both and I would be happy to accompany you but I have no horse…."

"That is the point Otto. Spend some days roaming the forest on foot with Grimwald and Hrolf. They'll bring you back when you're ready. Go now," Aldermar told him.

The two scouts turned their horses uphill into the thicker trees. Otto picked up his satchel and went after them.

They kept ahead of him, just in sight for the whole of the day. At last they stopped and lit a fire. Otto collapsed beside them. Hrolf broke off a corner of the coarse flat bread they carried and tossed it over to him. They had smoked meat and sausage as well but they did not offer to share.

"Prince Aldermar says we can give you food to stop you dying of hunger, no more than that. You must find your own, lord," he said.

Otto was too tired to argue the point and he was sure that it would do no good. His legs ached, his feet were sore and his belly rumbled hungrily but he managed to sleep. In the morning, he was alone. His bag with its few, meagre possessions was gone. They ashes of last night's fire were cold; they had not lit another when they rose. Otto felt panic, then took a deep breath and began to think clearly. He cast about the edges of the small glade in which they had slept until he found some fern fronds that had been bent over. The soil under them was damp so they had been pushed down after the dew had fallen during the night. He walked carefully ahead scanning the ground and was suddenly a boy again, his father beside him patiently pointing out each snapped twig or torn leaf as he taught his son the story the forest tells of who or what has passed by. Otto smiled to himself. He had been born and raised to this. Two mounted men were easier to trail than a deer.

He came up on them near midday, beside a gushing, rocky stream with dark pools where the force of the water had swept sand away from under the mossy banks.

"You must try to feed yourself, lord," Grimwald told him.

"Give me back my belongings and call me "Otto". A lord is not on foot while others ride nor is he weak with hunger."

He took off his shoes and slipped into the tumbling, icy water and crouched, moving upstream and studying the shadows near the banks Sure enough, he saw the flickers of a fishtail as it beat slowly to maintain its position against the force of the current. So cautiously, so gently he put his hands under the surface and slid them either side of the trout's body. Then he scooped, gripped convulsively and flicked it out onto the bank. It flopped and writhed but he was on it and had snapped its vertebra before it could wriggle back to the safety of its natural element. It weighed only about a half pound but it was a meal. He went back in and caught another, giving up when he lost a third. Hrolf and Grimwald had watched his efforts impassively and without comment.

He cooked one fish over a small fire and ate it whole, head, fins and bones. He split the other one open and hung it on a twig. He ripped up some damp grass and fed his fire with it. Smoke rose up and enveloped his second trout. It would not be a complete preserving process without salt and time but it would now last him until supper.

That night he talked to Hrolf and Grimwald but they kept smiling to each other as he spoke.

"You talk like a Roman who had learned our language and speaks it well but you have lost your true Suevi voice," they told him.

Otto noted what they said and spent at least two hours each day in conversation with them when they were together. Some days, they vanished and he was left to get by completely alone as he followed their trail. Late spring is a bad time of year to survive by foraging. There are no nuts or berries, no mushrooms, no wild fruits. There were fresh salads to be had but they loosened his bowels and gave him gripes. He found a drift of cones under a tree and spent hours picking out their pine nuts but the rewards were scanty for the effort required to gather a few mouthfuls. He ate them one by one, chewing slowly to give himself the illusion of a full belly. He pounded Evening Primrose roots and roasted them on a flat stone with wild garlic. He picked and ate Ground Alder leaves. He ripped dried, decayed looking bracket fungi from tree trunks and cooked them slowly over his fire after soaking them in water in his horn cup.

The sole benefit of this time of year was that there were many new-born or hatched animals and birds to be had, if they could be caught. One day he heard the distinctive clap of a wood pigeon's wings as it took off. He found its nest and climbed as near as he could to it then threw his rope over the slender branch on which it was built, tearing it down. The untidy mass of twigs and grass fell to the ground with three young birds in it. They were, almost fully fledged but not yet able to fly. He ate well that day.

Day after day he walked and ran for hours behind Grimwald and Hroth's horses. He was weakening and exhausted but forced himself to go on, if not cheerfully, then without complaint. Sometimes one of them would be gone for a day and that night they always had new bread and sausage so they must not be far from other people but the mazy ways they took him through the forest meant Otto had no idea of where he was.

Wandering on his own, he came to a tangle of brambles with a narrow path through it. In spite of the thorns, he crawled through and discovered a small pool hidden in the middle. The tracks around the edges showed that it was used by deer and wild pigs. He cut a hazel rod and thrust one end into the ground, bending the other until he had an arc of springy, new wood. He held it place with some of his cord attached to a peg he had carved. Then he made a loop with the remaining cord and spread it carefully, tying it to the hazel. He slept close by, alone at night for once. The cold and his insistent hunger pangs woke him early and he found his luck was in. A young forty-pound roebuck had become tangled in his snare and strangled himself trying to break free.

He dragged it out, slashed opened its paunch and reached deep into the guts.

The two scouts found him tearing at a dripping hunk of liver with his teeth. It felt like a blood-transfusion to Otto. He could feel energy coursing through him as he ate the sweetish, soft flesh. He skinned the buck, lit a fire and cooked the heart and a steak, eating them greedily as soon as they were cooked. He jointed the rest and wrapped it tightly in its own skin to protect it against the blowflies. That afternoon, when they had moved on another ten miles, Otto made a rack and hung thin strips of his venison over it above a smoky fire which he tended deep into the night. In the morning, he had ten pounds of dried, smoked meat; enough to last him a week. He offered Grimwald and Hrolf the remaining haunch in return for a loaf of bread.

Grimwald shook his head. "Prince Aldermar said we must not feed you all the time."

"But you aren't giving me anything, we're exchanging meat for bread. If I came across a settlement they would do the same."

They could not deny the truth of what he had said. With food for a fortnight now, Otto really did feel like a lord.

He had been in the wilds for sixteen days, he had walked or run two hundred miles. He had lost twenty pounds in weight, his beard and hair were long and tangled, his face thin but he felt strong and as if he could endure in the forest forever.

The next day, they met Aldermar. He stood beaming, again beside a small fire, this time with a pot steaming over it. "Now I see a hardened young warrior of the Suevi. Where has that Roman officer gone? Otto you look as if you have never crossed the Rhine; exactly what is needed. Sit down on that log," Aldermar said.

One of his men came up with a razor in his hand. "To shave your head, lord," he explained took the pot off the fire and dipped the razor into the hot water it contained. He rasped the razor over the sides and back of Otto's head, leaving his topknot untouched. It had been nearly two moths since Otto had last visited a barber and his remaining hair was long enough to look something like the traditional "Suevian Knot".

Aldermar examined it and nodded approval. "It will grow longer and the shaved skin will darken in a day or so. Now, how do you feel? Don't tell me hungry and weary, I know that."

Otto thought for a moment. "I feel as if I've walked in the forest with my father again and remembered all he taught me. My thanks to Grimwald and Hrolf."

"I've brought writing materials. I would like you to write to your family and tell them where you are and that you are safe. I will have to read it before it is sealed, I'm sorry," Aldermar told him.

Otto understood precisely what was required. There was every possibility that his message home would be intercepted and examined by unfriendly eyes. As well as giving comfort to Lollia, it must support his cover story. When he had finished, he passed the parchment to Aldermar who scanned it and sealed it into a scroll tube without comment but a wry smile at the last line.

To my wife Lollia Greetings.

I am safely arrived at the city of Prince Aldermar to carry the Emperor's good wishes and respect to him. My journey was not without its perils but all our party completed it without harm. Tribune Cassius Plancus sends his compliments. I hope all is well with you, Lucius Albus and our people. I look forward to returning to you,

Fortuna permitting. The Prince has shown me the most unusual hospitality for which I shall always be grateful to him.

Salutations, Otto

"How is my replacement managing?" Otto asked.

"Very well. He really enjoys being an Imperial Prefect. You might have to fight him to get your rank and armour back when you return. As for Cassius Plancus! He is the darling of the women of the city, even though he can barely greet them in our language. For the first week he fought hard not to show his contempt for our barbarian homes and rough manners, now he hunts and feasts and boasts as well as one of my own warriors. He has to have an interpreter of course but that doesn't seem to slow him down much. Well, let's get you kitted out. You're going to be a warrior with a couple of horses to trade. Your two good friends will see you to the boat."

Grimwald and Hrolth led Otto around the city and then uphill to the north and west. They stopped on a high point so he could get his bearings. Hrolf pointed with his lance.

"North is the river. We follow it downstream for two days until we come to the jetty," he explained.

Otto was riding again. Wearing a crudely mended mail shirt over a tunic and breeches with boots on his feet, he was mounted on a sturdy grey horse. He had a Roman infantry helmet on his head; it was battered and pocked with badly hammered-out dents but serviceable. He carried two lances and an oval shield. His pugio was once more belted around his waist and the tiny, white marble finger given to him by a grateful sculptor in Rome on his first visit hung on its gold chain around his neck. He had a few silver coins in a leather purse. His trading stock was made up of another three horses, one carrying a sack of provisions.

They rode alongside the Rhine. It was slower moving and wider here. Marsh lands spread out from either side. Herons stood stiffly in pools watching for small fish or careless frogs. Reeds whispered and waved to the faintest breeze. Bulrushes grew out of the shallows. Clouds of gnats and dragonflies whined and hovered in the fetid air. The wooden jetty thrust a long way out in the river. Around it were clustered some ramshackle huts, canoes upside down on the mud and fish traps. Moored against it was a wide flat-bottomed barge. It had a ramp at each end which could be let down to allow livestock on and off. Otto negotiated a fee in silver for himself and his horses and said his farewells to Grimwald and Hrolf.

"I have no gifts for you to thank you but I won't forget you when I return."

"If," Hrolf muttered under his breath. Grimwald heard and glared at him.

The boat swung into the current and was soon in mid-stream. Otto went to the stern where the pilot was pushing his long sweep against the flood. The six rowers took occasional short strokes with their oars as the far shore glided towards them over the water.

"Your crew are having an easy time of it," he said to the pilot.

The man looked at him and spat over the side. "Yes, for now. They are just giving us steerage way, the river's doing all the work. When we get into the Lippe you'll see them bend their backs."

"Is it strong flowing?"

"No, it's sluggish. It wanders all over the land in loops and bends, Ten miles in a straight line would be twenty on the Lippe but they'll be opposing the current you see, real work."

The Rhine became discoloured with washed-down silt as they neared its juncture with the Lippe. The boat turned slowly in a wide curve to keep it in the middle of the new watercourse as they passed mudflats on either bank. The rowers took the strain and heaved their ponderous craft upstream, shipping oars one side then the other according to the pilot's shouted instructions as he negotiated underwater hazards. For two hours they battled until they rounded a final bend and a saw another jetty a little way ahead. Waiting at the far end were a group of men, each standing beside a tall basket of live eels they had caught and another holding the halter of an ox. The boat thumped into the jetty and was briskly moored. The ramp banged down on the planking and Ottos was ashore with his horses.

Chapter 5

A broad track led away from the river, across the boggy ground at its margins and inland to dryer soil underneath the first of the trees. The river valley was a wide swathe of flat territory stretching for scores of miles to the east and north. There were no ranges of hills, only infrequent rock outcrops which seemed more dramatic because of their rarity. Oak and ash grew huge in the rich soil which fed thousands of people in small villages and farmsteads.

Otto was surprised to feel a thrill of excitement as he breathed the air of his homeland for the first time in many years. He laughed at himself and shook his head. Half a mile from the Lippe, under the fresh green canopy of the trees, the track forked. One way led due north, the other to the east. Otto took the eastern path. He was charged with listening to as many people as he could which suited him. The more farms and holdings he visited, the more he would learn and he could use the opportunity to ask about his mother and sister. He clicked his horse on and tugged the lead rope of his stock animals.

He was never without a place to spend the night. The laws of hospitality were strictly observed. If he stayed at a poor man's farm, he chopped firewood, drew water to fill troughs or once, helped look for a lost cow to return the kindness he had received. In a wealthy chieftain's village, he paid with his stories. He told of his voyage to

Britain and the land of the Belgic tribesmen who had conquered a broad area from the channel to the Irish Sea. A newcomer with an interesting tale to tell was welcome everywhere. Offers were made for his horses but he always found a reason to turn them down. He wandered and meandered, changing direction and doubling back on himself like the Lippe but always edging slowly north, always listening always asking after the widow and daughter of Badurad without success. One night sitting around a notable warrior's fire, a man stood up and raised his ale cup in a toast.

"To he who is coming!" he shouted. Everyone drank and thumped on the tables.

"Who is coming?" Otto asked

His question raised the immediate suspicion of the men on either side of him.

"How do you not know?"

Otto did not reply directly but diverted their attention with the story of how he had lived in Britain after surviving a storm at sea. He left early on the following morning but they had given him a thread at which to pull.

He approached the subject of "he who is coming" with caution whenever he could and gradually learned more. He also took careful note of those who were present among the company drinking with the chiefs. There were tribesmen he judged to be from far off in the east and the north, not the natural allies of the local clans. All seemed to be on friendly terms and more than once he saw the strangers engaged in confidential talks with their host or an elder.

According to the rumour circulating, a miraculous child had been born. He would grow up to be a great warrior who would annihilate a Roman army and free Germany of the invaders for ever. He did not come across anyone who cast doubt on the story which was rapidly gaining the status of a prophecy sure to come about. People were certain that in twenty years or so, the Romans would suffer a humiliating defeat at the hands of the promised one. Faith in the reality of the tale was drawing together clans and tribes that had been at each other's throats since time beyond remembrance. It was the catalyst for co-operation among all the tribes of Upper Germany, if not their unification. Otto had a lot to think about as he roamed the land searching for his mother and sister.

On the twentieth day of June, Otto came to a shallow brook running into the Lippe. On a whim, he decided to follow its course upstream. He had ridden for less than two hours when he reined in beside a group of women doing their laundry on the bank of a shady pool under a spreading ash tree. One of them looked over, stared hard then walked towards him. The world stood still. Otto recognised her.

"What God has brought you back to me, my son?" she asked, reached up and took his hand.

All the days, weeks, months of travelling had come to this, a chance meeting. If it had been raining, she would not have chosen this day to do her washing. If he had not decided to follow up the stream he would have passed her by. If he had been two hours later she would have been finished and gone home. But if the time is right, everything comes easily. This day, this hour, this place had been right.

Odila had hardly changed since the last time Otto had seen her. She was still the strong, free-striding woman his mother had always been. But Otto was altered beyond recognition by anyone except her. As Odila later said, "I saw my husband sitting on a horse looking at me but when I realised he was not a ghost, he could only have been my son, the living image of his father."

Otto dismounted and took her in his arms. He breathed in the scent of her and stroked her hair.

"Oh mother, Oh mother," was all he managed to say again and again.

A young woman waded out of the pool and strode towards them. She was golden blonde, blue-eyed and moved with natural grace.

"Mother?" she said enquiringly

Odila unwound Otto's arms from around her. "Saxa, this is your brother Otto," she announced

Saxa's eyes grew wide and she drew a sharp inward breath.

"This is real? This is truly happening?" she demanded.

A complicit glance passed between mother and daughter. Odila nodded.

"Fetch the washing, Saxa; we'll finish it another day. We must go, straight away."

"To your home?" Otto asked,

"Yes," Odila told him, "after we have we have made an important visit."

With the basket of wet washing slung precariously over the back of one of the horses, they walked together up the stream bank then turned off onto a narrow path through a dense thicket of rowan and alder. They emerged into a bright glade dominated by a curious structure in the centre. The hollow stump of a lightning-blasted, ancient oak reared twenty feet into the air behind a dome of woven branches and thatch to which it was connected. The oak was miraculously still alive and had sent its green shoots to tangle into the roof of the dome. A thin tendril of smoke rose up the natural chimney of the stump.

Otto tethered his string of horses by the low entrance, a tunnel through which they made their way bent double. They had just entered when a deep, melodious female voice called out, "Welcome Otto son of Badurad, welcome Odila and Saxa."

The gloom was relieved by a few oil lamps and the glowing embers in the fire circle. A woman sat cross-legged on a pile of skins and furs covering a huge log. She was in the mature prime of her life, full breasted and serenely confident. Dressed in her kilt of wildcat skins, festooned with necklaces of beads and bones, she smiled down at her visitors and gestured for them to sit on the low stools at her feet.

"The last time you came to see me Otto, it was your father who brought you. You were more fascinated at the sight of what is between my legs than my words" she said and laughed at his embarrassment. "Oh, you were only a boy then, no harm and no offence. Now Odila brings her son to me as I knew she would and he has become a man. I know you have followed your fate as the Gods willed. I have glimpsed you in the smoke and the ink pool." She reached out her right hand. "Give me the object you value the most," she commanded.

Otto immediately took the gold chain holding the marble finger from around his neck and passed it to her. She turned it over examining it closely.

"Delicate workmanship, look how perfect the tiny nail is. I am glad your heart is uncorrupted by the world's love of possessions, Otto. You gave without hesitation. Here take it back." He lifted it from her open palm and replaced it around his neck. "Gold will soon be all around you, Otto Kingkiller, remember, not all men can resist its glamour."

"I have nothing for you lady, other than silver money. Will you take it?"

"I want for nothing. By coming here today you have confirmed me in my faith in the rightness of things that are and are yet to be but can be seen. That is a great gift. Go now, all of you. Otto and Saxa take my blessing." She leaned forward and placed a hand on their heads, muttering under her breath. Then she sat back and smiled a farewell.

Sitting in his mother's hut, Otto listened to her story of the aftermath of the Roman raid. Odila knew from the wise woman that her son had been fated to come the oath-companion of a Roman and that that was the path the Gods had decreed for him but Otto knew nothing of what had happened to her and his sister.

"We women saw the smoke from the hillside where we were harvesting chestnuts. There was little left when we returned to the ashes of our winter homes. We buried the dead all together but we had almost nothing to put in with them for the next world. We did what we could. Our grain pits had not been disturbed so I sent a boy to find my brother Baugulf and he came back with wagons and warriors to fetch us to his village. We were welcomed. I like to think we would have been equally welcomed if we had been empty handed but three wagonloads of corn helped, I'm sure. The girls grew up and found husbands, some of the younger women remarried…"

"But you did not?" Otto interrupted.

Odila lifted her chin and squared her wide shoulders.

"I am the wife of Badurad of the Suevi. Is there another equal to him to be my husband? I don't think so. Now tell me of you. The wise woman has seen that you are a great battle chieftain among the Romans and I have heard other rumours. Are they true?"

Otto talked for over an hour. He told them of his visit to Rome and his meeting with the Emperor. They knew of Augustus; they had seen his portrait on a coin. They could not conceive of a city housing a million people, nor what sum "a million" represented. Saxa, sat open-mouthed as this strange man who was her brother was speaking, Neither she nor Odila could grasp the idea of living in the same place in a house made of stone all year round. Odila was delighted that he had a wife and a son.

"What's her name?" Saxa asked.

"Lollia Alba."

Saxa tried to pronounce the name then giggled at the strange sound of it.

"What does she look like?"

"She is very tall for a Roman woman, nearly as tall as me. Her eyes are blue and her hair dark, almost black.

"What does she wear?"

"Clothes, ladies' dresses," Otto replied, a little puzzled.

"What sort of dresses? Are they different colours?"

Before he could answer, Odila asked her own question.

"And my grandson?"

"He is called Lucius after my best friend, the man to whom I was hand-fasted and Albus for Lollia's father who was a great warrior among the Gauls and later served Rome. Lucius Albus is tall for his age, he will soon be three years old and loves to be in the open air playing with his dog."

Otto stayed the night under his mother's roof. In the morning, he took an axe from the side of the hut and strode over to the woodpile where he spent the best part of the morning chopping and splitting firewood for her. Saxa sat on a log bombarding him with questions. Most of them he could not answer. Some of the replies he gave confused or annoyed her. How could a fire heat the floor of a house and not burn it to the ground? How could a Roman woman tolerate having no place in council or battle? When he was done, he stripped and plunged into the stream to wash. He took a clean tunic from his pack. Odila rushed off with the dirty one, scrubbed it and laid it over a furze bush to dry in the sun.

"How much wood do you think I use Otto? You've built me a wall of split logs!" she scolded but was touched that he had thought of her needs.

They ate a noon meal of bread, eggs and cold pork. After they had finished, Odila's face clouded over. She took his hands in hers and looked deep into Otto's eyes.

"The Gods have given me more than I could have hoped for by letting me see my dear Otto after so many years but now you must go, carrying a mother's blessing with you."

Otto looked startled. "I've only just arrived!"

"Our time together has to be short," she sighed. "These are difficult days for my brother and it is dangerous for you to stay. Also, stories are told of the son of Badurad who killed King Helmund for the Romans. Sooner or later, you will be discovered and taken. They will avenge Helmund on your body very slowly my son, then kill you."

"Tell me about my Uncle Baugulf," Otto asked.

"His horse tripped and he broke his left arm when he fell. It never healed properly. It's withered and he has no strength in that hand. He cannot lift a cup to his lips with it let alone hold a shield in battle. His son, your cousin Gerlach is a fine young warrior but he is only twenty and has little experience. Others see Baugulf's weakness and want to replace him…"

"Arnulf and his two sons, Eberulf and Bermar, foul animals!" Saxa spat.

"Have they laid hands on you?" Otto asked, his voice harsher than any raven.

"They would not dare!" Saxa told him, her eyes flashing. "They leer and whisper foul suggestions when there's no-one to overhear their filth, that's all."

"But Baugulf is a noble chief, will none of the other warriors stand with his son to protect his honour and family?"

Odila shrugged. "They see that my brother is weak and Arnulf is strong. They see he has one young son while Arnulf has two and older.

They do not want to risk being on the losing side. Gerlach can't defeat three warriors on his own."

"Then I shall drink ale with my uncle this evening."

Odila looked at him and saw the wintery glare of his eyes that she remembered so well from her husband. She knew there was no point in speaking further but in any case, it was not her place to interfere in the matter of a warrior's honour.

Otto's mail shirt was rusted and travel-stained so it was hung it on a branch pushed through the arms while he and Saxa scrubbed it brighter with a stiff brush and river sand. Felix would have winced at the sight but it was at least not completely red with rust when they had finished and he put it back on. He put an edge on his lance blades and slipped his arm rings over his muscular forearms. Otto waited until the sun was almost gone and strode into the grove where Baugulf drank with his men

Under the cover of the leafy branches, forty men sat on rough benches around a central fire. Boys came and went filling cups and horns from leather jugs.

He had left his shield and lances at the edge of the ring of trees with everyone's weapons. When men had drunk too much, tempers became short and it was better to keep the inevitable violence to an acceptable level. Otto kept his pugio in its sheath at his back. If pushed, he would claim it was an eating knife.

He marched up to the highest bench under a deer hide canopy. Sitting at its centre was a broad, strongly built man with marks of pain on his face. A youth bearing a strong resemblance to him sat on his right. Otto bowed.

"Greetings Lord Baugulf, I am the son of Odila and claim kinship with you."

All eyes turned to him. Of course, they all knew by now of his arrival but this was a formal introduction.

"Greetings nephew, you are most welcome," Baugulf replied.

Nearly everyone smiled but Otto noticed a group of three men at the right of his uncle and cousin who scowled. The one on the end was a burly warrior in his mid-forties; shrewd, powerful, Beside him sat a pair of much younger men who looked at Otto with clear hostility. All of them shared the family trait of flaming red har.

"Ah," Otto thought to himself, "I know who you are so let's begin."

He walked over in front of the man he correctly took to be Arnulf and bowed.

"I wish to sit in a place of honour to drink with my kinsman but I shall not ask you to move, sir, as you are an old man and I respect the aged." The sound of muffled laughter rose in the background. Arnulf went red with annoyance.

Otto pointed to the younger man sitting next to him. "You, shift! I want to sit where you're resting your arse."

"Do you know who I am?" he shouted at Otto who stood smiling broadly.

"Yes. You're the boy who's in my place."

"Boy? Boy?" he roared. "I am Eberulf."

Otto hesitated for a moment as if thinking, "No, never heard of you. Eberulf? That's a wild boar isn't it? Oink, oink; move it or I'll drag you out by your piggy snout."

"Have a care, young man," Arnulf warned. "He is my son and his brother is beside him. There are three of us and only one of you."

"I don't think I'm alone. I believe my cousin Gerlach will stand by me…"

"That I will," came a clear voice from the other table.

"But this is no time to speak threats and talk of sides as if there was to be a battle," Otto said in a friendly voice. "I claim my right to a blood kinsman's place. Your son is keeping me out of it: that is a matter between him and me. Either I can throw him out of his seat in front of everyone or he can do as he's told and give it up."

"Neither," yelled Eberulf, flinging off the restraining hand his father had placed on his forearm. "I'll not stand for this."

"It will have to be as you wish then," said Otto with a flinty gleam in his eyes, belying the smile on his face.

They walked from under the trees and stood waiting while torches were lit and set into the ground in a ring around the pair of them. The combat circle was thirty feet across. The flickering glow of the yellow flames was augmented by the rising moon. There was enough light to kill by. Eberulf took up his shield and a long-handled axe. He thumped the rim with the flat of the axe and snarled over at Otto.

"You come here to mock me and insult me. Well, the crows will be laughing at your jibes when they pick out your eyes. I'll have your arm rings and your mail and you will have a grave on the midden with all the other shit."

Otto nodded pleasantly. "You want my mail? Gerlach help me." His cousin stood forward and together they hauled it over his head and flung it to the floor. Otto took off his tunic as well and dropped it down at his feet with his arm rings.. "Here, Eberulf, it's all yours. And here's my shield and my lances, have them as well, with my best wishes. All you have to do is pick them up. But do you want to? Do you want to die because you are a stupid village boy who lets his pride overcome what little sense his father gave him?"

Bare-chested, Otto drew the pugio from behind his back, took two long steps towards the middle of the circle and beckoned his opponent to come to him.

Eberulf stopped, a worm of unease gnawing at the back of his mind. "You're going to fight me with just a dagger?" he asked.

Otto glanced down at it. "Why not? Or does the sight of a bare blade make you piss yourself?"

He was gambling but he felt the odds were on his side. Angry men do not make good decisions; his enemy was spluttering with rage. Eberulf was fierce and strong but his technique and reactions had not been honed in years of warfare. Otto was sure that he would run forward, barge with his shield then swing his axe obliquely over it to strike Otto down. The trick was not to be where the axe fell.

Sure enough, Eberulf roared and hurtled towards him, eyes glaring and spittle flying from his lips. At the moment when their shields should have slammed together with the force of two heavy men behind them, if both men had been fully armed, Otto took a step to his left and pirouetted completely around on the spot. For a perilous fraction of a second his back was to Eberulf and then he was standing sideways on to him on his shield side. He thrust the broad dagger into the spot below the ear where the jaw meets the neck. It sank in half its depth. Otto twisted his wrist and withdrew the blade. Eberulf toppled to the ground like a felled tree, dead. A stunned silence followed the swift end of the combat. It was broken by Otto.

"Well that was easy enough," he chuckled.

Arnulf went over to the stacked weapons He picked up his sword and shield and motioned for Bermar to do the same.

"Now there is blood between us. I will be revenged," he told Otto. No shouted insults, no rage; cold fury perhaps, with a calculating mind behind it.

"I see you are an experienced warrior, Arnulf, will you give me time to prepare myself to kill you?"

He nodded. Otto shrugged into his tunic and mail shirt then took up his shield and a lance.

"Gerlach are you with me?" he shouted but his cousin was already at his side. "Concentrate on Bermar, keep him away from me as long as you can," Otto instructed.

There is little to choose between a lance and a sword at close quarters. The lance point has the longer reach but the wooden shaft can hacked in two by a swift cut. All the swordsman has to do is be on guard, defend and wait for the moment of over-extension when he can bring his blade down and chop his enemy's weapon in half.

Arnulf shuffled half a pace towards the killer of his son, crouching to cover his body from nose to ankles with his shield. Otto took the longest step he could with his left leg, leaned back then bent his body forward over the tremendous leverage his long limbs gave him, hurling his lance at full force. He had been the champion of the Second Lucan Legion for many years, outdistancing everyone in throwing the heavy Roman infantry pilum. The light German cavalry spear he had cast was a dark blur, humming through the air as it flew at Arnulf. It hit him with such power that it penetrated his shield, his left arm holding it across his body and his chest, bursting his heart. He fell over backwards, dead without a sound.

Otto looked around to see where Bermar was and saw that he and Gerlach were well matched. It occurred to him that it would be better for all his kin if his cousin could defeat Bermar without his intervention. Gerlach was neither highly skilled nor particularly fast but he was competent and determined. Above all he was relishing the fight. He had waited a long time to be let loose on Bermar or his brother. The fight did not last long. Gerlach changed from a high to a low attack, broke Bermar's shin and stabbed him through the throat as he lay writhing in the dirt.

Otto turned to the stunned men of Baugulf's clan.

"It should not have taken me to begin this. You have witnessed how well your lord's son Gerlach fights. If you had been his father's true oath men and stood with him, these vermin would have been just as dead as you see them now. Go down on your knees and beg forgiveness of Lord Baugulf and the noble Gerlach."

Otto picked up his remaining lance and walked away, whistling. He stopped by the water's edge and washed his pugio blade clean of clotted blood, dried it on his tunic hem and returned to his mother's home. She had lit a fire outside the entrance and thrown pine knots onto the blaze to give a sweet smell and bright flames. She looked up at him with an anxious face but put her fears aside when she saw her son untouched, unconcerned and smiling. He had been gone less than half an hour. He sat down beside her and accepted the horn cup of mead Saxa offered him.

"Did you meet your Uncle Baugulf?" Odila asked when she saw that he was obviously not about to begin a conversation.

"I did and he welcomed me as a kinsman."

"Did you see Gerlach too?"

"Yes, a fine young man worthy of his father and of you, his aunt."

"Was foul Arnulf there with his dogs of sons?" Saxa asked bitterly.

"Indeed they were, then they left."

"What do you mean they left?"

"Well, to tell the truth, they became dead."

Odila's hand flew to her mouth. "No more riddles and half-answers, Otto. Tell us everything. "

"I killed Arnulf and Eberulf. Gerlach killed Bermar."

Chapter 6

Before he could continue, Saxa pointed out the wavering flames of a torch coming towards them. It was held by Baugulf; Gerlach was walking with him carrying two swords and a small bundle. They both sat by the fire and took the mead Odila offered them.

"Cousin," Gerlach began, "here are the swords and ornaments of the men we fought tonight. What do you want us to do with them?"

"All that was Bermar's is now yours, Gerlach, by right of conquest. I claim no part of it.," Otto told him.

"And all Arnulf's property now belongs to you, nephew, according to our laws, and Eberulf's as well," Baugulf advised.

Otto opened the bundle and took out a very fine arm ring of twisted silver decorated with gold wire. He handed it to Gerlach.

"Please accept this gift in memory of the night we stood shield to shield in the face of our family's enemies."

Gerlach's eyes shone. "I am proud to have fought beside you."

Otto selected two more then re-tied the bundle. "As for the rest of Arnulf and Bermar's property uncle, I make you a gift of all they had, provided you free their slaves."

"Arnulf was counted a wealthy man among us, are you sure?" Baugulf enquired.

Otto looked askance. "Since when do the Suevi lust after riches? In any case, it is little enough to recompense you for the protection you have offered my mother and my sister over these many years."

"There is no question of "recompense". Odila and Saxa have the right to call on me."

"I know uncle, I know, but you acted with honour and I want to show you I'm grateful."

"There is more gratitude on my side, I think. Tonight you have destroyed my enemies…"

"With Gerlach's help. Don't forget your son."

"…I do not. When your arrival allowed him to act he played his part like a man. No, I do not forget, nor do my warriors, Bermar was no mean opponent. However, your presence here is already widely known. By tomorrow sunset, the news will have travelled twenty miles in every direction. By the end of the week, the whole valley of the Lippe will be speaking of it. You are hated and feared equally among the Suevi. Not only are you blamed for the death of Helmund but when you were at the Roman fortress, many warriors crossed the river swearing to return with your head. None came back. Everything is changing among us. Men pass through my lands who would have been hunted down in previous times. Now, they are greeted as friends for the time when he who is coming unites all the tribes to destroy Rome. Where will you be then, Otto? There will be no safety for you in Roman lands," he paused and sighed. "That is all in the future but for the moment, I am afraid seekers after vengeance or reputation will come here after your blood. We must prepare and be ready to fight...."

Otto laughed gently. "Uncle, do you think I want to bring the world down on you? I am moved that you say you would fight for me but it won't be necessary. Tomorrow my mother and sister will be gone. I'm taking them over the Rhine to my home where I can care for them..."

"Oh no," Odila told him, "that will never do. I am a free woman of the Suevi; these are my lands and my people. Here I shall remain but Saxa is to go with you. The wise woman told me that when you returned, it would be a happy interlude and then I must say goodbye to both my children."

"No, mother," Saxa shrieked, "I'm staying with you..."

"Now listen girl," her mother told her taking both her hands. "Why do you think the wise woman blessed you and Otto? It was because you must leave, together. That is the will of the Gods and if you refuse to accept it, your life will be cursed. Be honest with your mother, are you not already half in love with the idea of seeing far-off places and new things?"

Saxa could not deny what Odila had said. She dropped her gaze and shrugged.

Otto began to protest but saw his own unshakeable resolve reflected in Odila's eyes. He turned to his uncle.

"If men seek me out, you can tell them I am crossing the Lippe and going west to the coast.."

"Is that true?" Baugulf asked.

"If you say, "Otto son of Badurad told me he was going west to the coast," then you will not have lied."

Gerlach stood up and put his hand on the arm ring Otto had given him.

"I swear on this token of the blood bond between us I shall freely give your mother, my Aunt Odila, all the protection and support in my power. Let the Gods hear my words."

With this most sacred of oaths, the two men left. Otto sat with his mother, neither speaking but content to share a few brief minutes in the firelight. She smiled at him, her eyes bright.

"Your father would be proud of you, my son," she told him and went to her bed.

As the stars faded and the faintest light of dawn revealed the outline of the trees against the sky, Saxa and Otto mounted up. He had pressed most of his money on his reluctant mother and given her the two spare horses which she gladly accepted. Brother and sister rode away. Odila watched them out of sight, her eyes almost blinded by the tears she was too proud to shed.

For six days they followed the Lippe downstream as fast and straight as they could go without attracting undue attention by their haste, making for the jetty and the Rhine crossing.

In a tavern in Luca, three men leaned forward speaking softly to avoid being overheard. It was not a respectable inn but they were not respectable men. They were like any other citizens at first glance but on a closer examination, there was something shifty about each of them. Together, they looked like they were up to no good, which they were.

"And I'm telling you that big German bastard who's supposed to be an officer isn't there," the bald, unshaven one said.

"What about his cavalry. They're billeted at his villa," his broken-nosed companion pointed out.

"Yeah, and probably taking turns on that snotty tart of a wife of his while he's away but they go out for hours, all day some days…." the first speaker responded.

"What about the others?" the last, jug-eared, man asked.

"What others, a broken-down old soldier with a gammy leg and a handful of slaves? Slaves don't fight back, why would they? No lads, we just have to keep an eye out until those troopers are off the premises then go in. It'll be stuffed with loot, that place…."

The hottest morning of the year so far. The sun so bright it hurt the eyes to look at any part of the sky. Insects churring and chirruping in the meadows and the garden. The magistrate of Pisae had demanded that all of Otto's six troopers patrol the roads near his city. Travellers were being accosted and robbed by a new band of brigands who had just come into the area. Tullia and Plotina were in the kitchen peeling vegetables and chatting, mostly chatting. Felix was in his room polishing Otto's spare armour as he did every morning. Libius was in the dining room repainting part of one wall. Lollia was in her own room. Lucius Albus and Pollux were in the garden with the puppy, much bigger now with enormous paws. He would be a monster when he was fully grown. Didia was supposed to be keeping an eye on Lucius but had nipped inside to have a word with Tullia.

The men burst in. They had spent the early morning drinking to get their courage up, which was a mistake. They were not drunk but a little slow, a little lacking in judgement. They kicked open the kitchen door which crashed against the wall with so much force, it sent a tremor through the entire villa. They saw two women at a table with a pile of vegetables and a younger woman standing open-mouthed by the inner door.

Tullia, Plotina and Didia saw and smelled three scruffy men reeking of wine pushing in through the back of the house. They all stood motionless like a frieze of temple statues; then bedlam erupted.

The men roared threateningly, expecting the women to scream and run. Didia scuttled away, after snatching up a kitchen knife. But Plotina and Tullia jumped to their feet and began to pelt the intruders with vegetables, pots, pans, dishes, anything they could lay their hands on.

"Slaves don't fight back…" but they were not slaves; they were freed women prepared to defend themselves and their home. The trio of thieves stopped where they were for a few seconds protecting themselves from the hail of kitchenware but as the ammunition began to run out, they pushed forward into the central corridor which stretched the length of the house, widening into the atrium at the front.

The cooks had delayed them and made enough noise to alert Felix. He was hardened in conflict and knew better than to act without preparation. He took a shield off the wall and picked up a sword, hefting it in his hand before stepping out of his room. Lollia had rushed to her door and saw the men bursting out of the kitchen. She turned and ran, pulling her skirt up around her waist to avoid tripping.

The bald one sprinted in her wake, aroused by the sight of her scissoring thighs and near naked buttocks as she shot down the corridor and out of her home. In the instant they passed, Felix had taken up his stance, covered by his shield with his sword held horizontal in the ready position. The two remaining thieves skidded to a halt on the tiled floor and looked at him. Old cripple he may be but he was blocking their progress and there was no way around him.

Didia had rushed into the room where Libius was working. She wrenched the paintbrush out of his hand and thrust the handle of the kitchen knife at him, pulling on his arm shouting "Come on! Come on!", even though she knew he could not hear her. He did not have to. The urgency with which she was dragging him and the look of terror in her eyes told him all he needed to know. He strode out in front of her.

He saw the backs of two men, both armed with long knives and beyond them, the steady eyes of Felix staring over the top of his shield.

Libius had never raised his hand to any living being in his entire life but he knew a crucial moment had come. He took a firmer grip on the kitchen knife and stepped forward, lunging it into the back of the man with the big ears so it would sink deep into his flesh. At least, that was his intention but the blade bounced off a rib. His victim howled with shock and pain. Libius struck again and this time found his mark. The man twisted, groping with one hand for the knife embedded near his spine and sank to his knees. His companion turned to look at him. Felix saw his chance, shuffled forward and sank his sword into his belly, ripping it diagonally to do the maximum damage. Blood flooded the mosaic floor as he screamed and fell, spilling his intestines.

Lollia had run out of the front door and hard left into a walled courtyard. Her pursuer stopped at the entrance and licked his lips.

"Stupid cow," he thought, "there's no way out for you over those walls, my lady."

She dashed to a corner and reached behind a large plant pot, bringing her hand back with a sword in her fist. It was one of the practice weapons, its edges and point ground down and rounded off to minimize the possibility of accidental injury but it was still a twenty-inch length of steel weighing a couple of pounds. He took a better grip on his long cudgel and advanced with a sneer. Lollia's first thrust took him under the breastbone. It did not penetrate but punched the soft end of his sternum into the vagus nerve. Suddenly he was unable to breath or feel his legs. A second thrust to the base of his throat smashed his hyoid bone and windpipe cartilage. He slowly choked to death at her feet. Lollia did nor look away until he was still.

He was still fighting for his last few breaths when Felix came into the courtyard, doing his best to run but hindered by his permanently bent leg. The dying man convulsed and went still. Lollia followed Felix back into the villa. It stunk of blood and excrement. The man Libius had stabbed was scrabbling on his knees and elbows towards the kitchen mewing like a kitten. Plotina squelched through the mess and took the sword from Felix without a word. Holding it double-handed, she chopped down on the back of the crawling robber's neck. They all heard the bones crack. She handed the weapon to Tullia who stared down at the disembowelled intruder. He was still alive, grey-faced, staring in horror at his own guts which had fallen to the floor through the rent in his tunic. She spat on him then put the point of the sword against his throat and slowly pushed it in and twisted. He thrashed, screaming and went silent.

Lollia was horrified by the brutality and opened her mouth to rebuke the pair of them but Tullia raised an open hand to silence her.

"This was nothing compared to what they would have done to us if Felix and Libius, and you madam, hadn't stopped them.

Plotina nodded her defiant agreement.

"I think we had better send for Massus," Lollia said.

"I'll go," Felix told her.

Massus and his men took the bodies away and crucified them outside the city gate. They nailed a placard to a post beside them. On it was written, *"These men tried to rob a household under the protection of the city garrison of Luca. Other wrongdoers be warned."*

The centurion had been puzzled by the dead man in the courtyard. Black, purple bruises at his throat and chest showed where he had been struck but there were no open wounds, no blood. He looked at Felix quizzically but Felix innocently returned his gaze and said that he had also killed this one. Massus asked no questions.

Lollia was grateful. If it had become known that Lollia Alba, daughter of Julius Albus, the wife of the Imperial Prefect, practised with a sword and had taken the life of a robber, the scandal would have run through the city in minutes but her notoriety would have been lifelong.

The thieves had left a small but decent horse harnessed to a two-wheeled cart under the trees at the edge of the grounds. It had been intended as their means of escape. Lollia gave it to Libius as a reward. He could carry his paints and plaster in it when he went into Luca on a decorating job.

In Germany, it was ten days since Otto had left his mother's village and he was having difficulty in relating to Saxa. She was a young woman and, with the exception of Lollia, he had no experience of females of her age. She seemed to talk incessantly, asking questions then flitting to another subject before he had time to answer, remarking on everything they saw, never silent. He did not understand that Saxa was talking so much because she was terrified, beginning to wonder if she had made a huge mistake in leaving the security of her home to ride day after day through a world much bigger than she had imagined with this taciturn stranger who was her brother. Her chatter was a nervous release.

They unselfconsciously bathed naked everyday in a pool or brook so he could not avoid the sight of her body. Saxa was straight limbed and high-breasted, not as solid as their mother although her shoulders were wide. Her feet and hands were calloused as a result of going barefoot and hard work. At night when they slept huddled close to share warmth, the smell of her sweat and womanhood was inescapable. He found their unavoidable physical closeness unpleasant. As they rode through the margins of the swampy lands, he suddenly understood that he had become accustomed to smooth skins, manicures and perfume. He laughed.

"What a Roman you've become; you're almost another Cassius Plancus!" he thought.

"What's funny?" Saxa asked.

"I am, my dearest Saxa," he replied and his hearty laugh made her join in.

They arrived at the jetty late in the afternoon. There was no boat to be seen on the river so they spent a miserable night beside a deliberately smoky fire trying to keep the mosquitoes away. In the morning their faces were black with soot and they still had itching bites all over their arms and necks. Five men labouring under the weight of baskets of eels came up and sat near them. They had emptied their traps at dawn and were crossing the river to go to the nearest market on the far side. They were coated with mud that had been greenish brown when wet but now dried in the warmth of the sun to a grey powder. They spoke among themselves, glancing over at Otto and Saxa from time to time. At last one of them came over and shyly offered a handful of fresh, broad leaves. He mimicked rubbing them on his arms.

"For the bites, the itching…" he said.

Otto tried one. It did seem to relieve the worst of the irritation. He and Saxa used them all and called across their thanks which brought broad smiles from the eel catchers.

The rowers brought the boat alongside, shipped oars and moored. The pilot collected the fares and they boarded. He looked Saxa up and down.

"Not bad," he said to Otto.

"What's that supposed to mean?" he shot back.

"Oh, hold on there, hold on young man. No offense intended. Those horses you took up the river to sell weren't anything special but your slave woman's a real beauty. Well done, you got a bargain; that's all I'm saying."

Otto was about to explain then thought better of it. He was supposed to be a simple trader and it was in his best interests to maintain his cover.

"Sorry," he said. "I'm tired and covered in mosquito bites. Just want to get home."

Saxa staggered as the boat shifted under her feet while it was still tied to the jetty. She clutched the gunwale with both hands to hard that her knuckles went white. When they pushed off into mid-steam, her face paled and beads of sweat broke out on her forehead.

"If you're going to puke do it over the side," the pilot shouted.

Otto supported her and lifted her hair back as she retched and threw up spectacularly. She sank to the deck and stayed there motionless but groaning as they left the Lippe, breasted the flood and made their way over the Rhine. Once they had landed, she crawled up the ramp and sat several yards away from the water while Otto retrieved their horses. She recovered a little as they rode but looked a mess. Her breath smelled of stale vomit, the front of her tunic was stained with part of her stomach contents and her smoke-stained hair clung to her scalp in greasy tangles. Otto stopped at a farmstead and bought bread, eggs and a cake of gritty homemade soap. They made an early camp by a spring tumbling out of a rock cleft with a small pool beneath it. Washed, combed, wearing a clean tunic and with a supper of roasted eggs and fresh bread to fill her empty belly, Saxa was restored.

"I shall never go on a boat again as long as I live," she swore.

Otto told her the story of his voyage to Britain and the great storm which drove his ship to find shelter in the Sea of Vectis.

"It wasn't so bad. I survived,"

"I notice you've never done it again," Saxa pointedly remarked.

As they were climbing the slope on the other side of which lay Aldermar's city, Grimwald and Hrolf materialized out of the trees on either side on the track.

"I see you have survived, lord," Grimwald remarked.

"So I have," Otto replied.

No-one mentioned Saxa, although the two scouts acknowledged her existence with slight nods.

"I am to lead you through the kitchens to Prince Aldermar's private quarters." Hrolf informed them.

Grimwald rode on ahead, no doubt to give the news of their imminent arrival.

Saxa was amazed at the number of cattle, horses and the abundant crops she saw around her as they passed through the valley towards the walled city on the hill.

"Your friend Prince Aldermar must be one of the richest men in the world!" she exclaimed.

Otto was transported back to the time when he had thought the camp of the Second Lucan Legion was Rome itself.

"He is a noble and prosperous man, certainly," he told her.

She nearly broke her neck twisting from side to side in the saddle so as not to miss any of the shops and houses lining the streets.

Aldermar's private room was furnished with a desk and chairs in the Roman style. He stood up smiling and bowed in greeting as Otto came in with Saxa behind him. The only other person present was Cassius Plancus, sporting a curly chestnut beard, tanned and fit. He strode over and embraced Otto.

"You've grown thin my friend and you look tired…" then he stopped abruptly as he noticed Saxa behind him. "And who is this with you?"

"Saxa."

"Of course she is. What is she doing here?"

"She's coming home with me," Otto replied.

Cassius stood back, the smile slipping from his face. "Perhaps she is a new slave for Lollia?"

"Certainly not," Otto snapped.

"Look old thing, hardly for me to comment on a chap's private affairs, but is the wife likely to be happy when her husband brings a beautiful young girl into the nest?"

Otto laughed long and hard, slapped his knee then indicated Saxa with a sweeping gesture. "Praetorian Prefect Cassius Plancus, my I introduce my sister, Saxa of the Suevi?"

Cassius looked at a loss for a fraction of second then recovered his debonair manner, walked up to Saxa, took her hand and kissed it.

She looked over at her brother with raised eyebrows but he smiled his approval. She had not understood a word of what had passed between Otto and Cassius but now Aldermar addressed her in his German dialect, very close to her own.

"Welcome to you, Saxa, sister of Otto. I think we must call you Lady Saxa, since your brother is a great lord among the Romans. Would you like to go with the women to refresh yourself and change your clothes?"

"Thank you prince," she replied, relieved that she would be among people with whom she could communicate for a while.

Aldermar called for his wife, Leikflad. She entered the room dressed in a blue wool gown to the floor, belted with a woven silk cord. Her thick, red hair hung in two plaits to her waist. She was round and apple-cheeked, kindness and simplicity shone out of her. She walked up to Saxa and took her hands.

"I am Leikflad. Oh, dear child, you do look weary! Come on, we'll find you somewhere to wash and change. Then we can have a proper talk, out of hearing of all these men…" she bustled Saxa out.

"Time for you to resume your rank, prefect," Aldermar said and led Otto to a chamber, leaving him at the door.

It contained a bench and table on which Otto's armour and uniform was laid out together with his trunk and spare clothing. A single bed had been placed against the far-side wall. A barrel cut in half steamed with the hot water it contained. There were two men in the room. One was the German bodyguard who had impersonated Otto on his absence, now dressed in a plain tunic. The other was a barber, given the additional duties of bath attendant. Otto stripped and groaned with pleasure as the warm water closed around him. He was scrubbed, rinsed and dried. Then the barber exercised his proper skills and shaved him. Finally, he cut Otto's hair so that it was the same length all over his scalp. With a bow he left, taking his bowls, tools and towels with him.

When they were alone, the bodyguard spoke.

"Welcome back, sir. You look very fit, if I may pass a remark."

"Skinnier, anyway," Otto said and began to dress.

"I am to tell you that there is to be a feast and Prince Aldermar requests that you attend in your dress uniform."

"How did you like being a prefect while I was absent?"

"It was grand for the first few days, everyone saluting and that but I must say it got a bit lonely. Prince Aldermar and Tribune Plancus tried to keep it going but they ran out of things to say. I'll be glad to be back with my mates, to tell the truth."

"Gods willing, you soon will be. In the meantime, thank you for the way you've looked after my equipment. It's immaculate."

"I'm a member of the Emperor's personal guard, sir. I know how to keep a soldier's kit in good order." he said with pride.

"That you do," Otto told him, unlocked a small box on the table and took out two gold coins. "Please accept one of these gold pieces as my thanks and I'm going to ask you to earn the other one on the way home."

"How, sir" he asked with a slight hesitation.

"I've brought my sister, Saxa across the Rhine. She doesn't have a word of Latin. I want you to teach her what you can while we travel. What do you say?"

"With pleasure sir and I'll be respectful. Oh, and if you give me that pugio of yours I'll polish it up. Something seems to have dried and gone black where the hilt joins the blade." He looked at Otto, the picture of innocence, as if he did not know exactly what was staining the weapon and how it had come to be there.

When he was dressed and armed, Otto felt as if everything was a little loose on him. He knew he had lost weight but the physical effort he had endured had re-sculpted his body. His muscles had stretched and hardened and his face was thinner, the features more sharply defined. He would never regain the bulk he had lost but remained lean for the rest of his days. He took another gold piece and a handful of silver out of his strong box, picked up the two arm rings that had belonged to Arnulf and went to find the feasting hall.

He sat at the top table with Aldermar to his right and Leikflad to his left, Saxa beside her. Her hair was plaited with green ribbons and she wore a flowing green gown, borrowed from one of Leikflad's women. Cassius was beside Aldermar. Two long tables on either side were filled with the prince's household warriors.

Roasted pork and fowls, bread and green vegetables, ale and mead were fetched and rapidly consumed. Aldermar's men grew noisier and very soon Leikflad rose from the table with Saxa to retire and leave the men to their drink and bragging. Otto stood up and pressed a gold piece into Saxa's hand. She had never seen such a thing and turned it over, examining it in wonder.

"Lady Leikflad, may I ask a favour of you? Tomorrow, will one of your women go with Saxa to buy some new clothes and necessaries? We have been travelling hard and fast and she has nothing with her."

"Lord Otto, you are not asking a favour of me. I'll happily go shopping with your sister and enjoy myself helping her to pick and choose."

When they had gone, the ale horns were filled again and the men settled down for some serious drinking. Otto asked Aldermar to call Grimwald and Hrolf forward. They came and stood in front of the high table. Otto walked round.

Speaking quietly so only they could hear he gave them both several silver pieces and said, "This is your reward for half-starving me and running me through the forest like a stag with the hounds snapping after him. I told you I would not forget you."

"Thank you, Lord," they mumbled, clearly unimpressed.

Then Otto produced the two arm-rings and held them up so everyone could see.

"These are the spoils I took from a great warrior of the Suevi in fair fight. Grimwald the Ghost and Hrolf, Prince Aldermar asked you to perform a service for me and you did it well, to the honour of your prince and to you. Take them as a well-deserved reward."

They beamed, the hall resounded with cheers and the thunder of fists banging down on tabletops, and to Otto's amusement, Cassius downed yet more ale and joined in.

Chapter 7

In the morning, while Saxa was having the value of a gold piece demonstrated to her in the shops and booths of the city, Otto walked over to say hello to Djinn. The black warhorse was in a paddock of his own. Otto called to him. Djinn pricked his ears up and ambled placidly up to his beloved master, putting his head over the fence and snorting gently. Otto could not believe the change in his horse; where was the fire gone, the energy? Normally he would have trotted across showing off his proud, high-stepping gait. Otto stroked his nose and turned accusingly to Aldermar.

"What have you let them do to him?"

"Nothing, I swear," Aldermar replied. "He's been in this field, well fed and groomed all the time you have been away. He may have covered one or two of my mares…."

"One or two? He's spent. He looks like he's tried to mount your whole herd!"

Aldermar spread his arms wide in a gesture of innocent appeasement. "If he went too far it isn't my fault. Nobody made him; he just sort of kept volunteering…"

Otto gave him a disgusted look but said no more.

Saxa showed him her new gowns and riding boots, her hooded cloak and girdle then handed him a purse full of silver and copper coins.

"What's this?" he asked.

"The money that was left over."

"It's yours Saxa, keep it…"

"But it's so much! How could anyone spend all this money, brother?"

"I expect you'll learn." Otto said with a smile. "Listen, we are not counted among the rich in Rome but we are far from poor. Like Prince Aldermar I have land, although not as much, and people to work it. You will begin to see things differently in the next few months."

After dinner that evening, a sober affair since Plancus and his troopers would be leaving in the morning to escort Otto home, Aldermar took them into his private room. Over a cup or two of mead, he explained that Massus would have further orders for them once they arrived.

"I must offer my grateful thanks for your generous hospitality to me and my men, Prince Aldermar," Cassius said.

"Oh, no need to thank him. He'll be amply rewarded when next year's foals arrive," Otto told him.

Aldermar raised his cup in a mock toast, "To the art of horse breeding."

Otto laughed and joined him as did Cassius who had no idea what was going on between them.

"Are you keeping the beard?" Otto asked the tribune.

He stroked it with both hands. "I am about to start a new fashion among the discerning young gentlemen of Rome," he replied.

"Not for long when Augustus sees it," Aldermar laughed and then changed his tone.

"Otto, I need to speak to you seriously for a moment about Saxa; have you thought about her staying here? Leikflad has taken a great liking to her and would be happy for her to live with us in my household. She could do worse than make a life here; she would soon find a husband among my oath men and you could make provision for her dowry. I swear that she would be honoured among us."

"I don't doubt it but the thought hadn't crossed my mind."

"You know that I was educated in Rome for some years? Part of my studies was the law," Aldermar went on. "Once within the Empire, Saxa has no rights at all, not even of personal liberty. Anyone could take her up and enslave her without penalty..."

"That's ridiculous," Otto interrupted with some heat. "She is the sister of a Roman knight..."

"Lollia Alba has her rights by birth. You have yours as a reward for your services to the Emperor but Saxa? Believe me when I tell you she has none."

"Slavery corrupts this Empire…" Otto began fiercely but Cassius stopped him.

"Oh come off it. Every nation has slaves and free men, Germany included. I bet your father had slaves, even if you have this eccentric aversion to the institution."

"I ask both your pardons but the thought of finding my sister again then having her carried off to some atrocious…well… brothel. It appals me. Aldermar, is there anything I can do?"

"You could adopt her," Cassius suggested.

Aldermar shook his head. "No. A citizen cannot adopt a slave. There is a way around this but you will find it distasteful."

"Tell me," Otto asked.

"When you get to Luca, go before the magistrate and formally free Saxa as if she was your slave. She will then have Latin Rights as a freed woman. If her eventual husband has at least the same status, her children will be citizens."

"How can I call my own flesh and blood my slave? In any case, there is no bill of sale."

"You don't need one," Aldermar told him. "If Tribune Cassius Plancus will witness that you brought her into the Empire from Germany, that will confirm she is your property. Then you can free her."

"Look at it this way, Otto old thing, all women belong to someone; their fathers, their husbands or brothers; you can't have them just flapping about the place, now can you? This way Saxa will be freer than most of 'em." Cassius added.

"Saxa must make her own choice," Otto said.

She was brought in and listened intently while her situation was explained. She raised one eyebrow and gave Otto a withering look when he told her that legally, she was now his slave. She bowed to Aldermar.

"Prince, your lady has been very good to me and your offer of a life in your hall moves me almost to tears with its kindness. I am torn but I want to see my brother's home and family."

"Very well Lady Saxa," Aldermar responded. "However, if Otto permits, you can return to us once you have stayed with him and Lollia Alba for a few months."

"I most certainly "permit" Prince Aldermar. Saxa has only to ask and she will be escorted to you and the gentle Leikflad," Otto told him.

The next day, they set out for Italy and Luca.

Centurion Massus had been short-tempered with his men ever since the attempted robbery at Otto's villa. He found fault with their kit, their drill and their timekeeping. The truth was, he felt guilty and the garrison were suffering for it. He believed that he had let his friend down by not ensuring that at least two of the cavalrymen were always on the premises but the magistrate of Pisae had sent him an urgent request and what could he do but comply? A legionary poked his head around the office door.

"Two veterans to see you, centurion," he said.

"What do they want?" Massus growled.

"How should I know? It's you they want to see."

"Watch your lip, soldier. Send 'em in."

They stood at attention in front of his desk. One was squat, a round, powerful barrel of a man with sloping shoulders and long arms. His comrades in the legion had given him the ironic nickname of Macer, meaning skinny. The other had a bulbous nose over a rubbery mouth and receding chin. He was Bellus; "Handsome".

"We want to sign on as Evocati, centurion," Macer said, speaking for both of them.

"Let's see your discharge papers," Massus demanded holding out his hand.

He read the documents. Both had received honourable discharges from The Second Lucan.

"You served your full time and three months later you want to be recalled to the army? What happened to your bounty?"

They looked embarrassed.

"Well, first we opened a shop," Bellus told him.

"And then we went bust," Macer finished.

"I see," said Massus, not without sympathy. "Now I'll tell you how it is boys. Say you were selling kitchenware…"

"It was leather goods," Bellus corrected.

"…it doesn't matter," the centurion continued, "it always works the same way. All the other shopkeepers who sell kitchenware or leather goods, get together and go to the wholesalers. They tell them to charge you more than the going rate or else they won't put in any more orders. Then when you put your goods up for sale, all the rest of 'em discount their prices. Result,? You're fucked. How much money have you got left?"

"Nine hundred between us."

"How much did you start with?"

"Six thousand four hundred."

Massus whistled. "Well, they roasted you, boys and then they turned you over and browned the other side. Pity you didn't have a word with me first. Now I'm going to add to your misery. I have no provision for increasing my garrison numbers, only for replacements and I want younger men for that. Sorry lads…."

They saluted and made a smart about turn to leave and that was when Massus had his inspiration.

"Did either of you serve with Evocati Felix under Prefect Otto Longius?"

They both grinned.

"I should say!" Macer told him. "We was in that siege with both of them up on the Rhine…"

"Give 'em some more oil Felix!" Bellus chuckled

"Then lads, kindly old Centurion Decimus Massus may be able to let you in on a good thing…."

Lollia Alba received a message asking her to visit Massus in Luca on an urgent matter. She immediately thought of Otto. Had he been wounded, killed? She fought down her panic and forced her face into a mask of Roman fortitude although her heart would not stop its hammering. Half an hour later, Felix drove her through the city gates in the mule cart accompanied by Didia.

There were proprieties to be respected. Lollia could not be seen alone in the company of another man while her husband was away, which was why Didia had been brought along. She most certainly could not enter the barracks under any circumstances, nor could she stay outside on the cart like some farm girl. She could sit, veiled, on the marble bench under the portico of the court building with Didia standing behind her and this Lollia did.

Felix walked across the square and came back fifteen minutes later with Massus and two men she had never seen before. One was built very like an ape and the other was extraordinarily ugly. The centurion saluted her.

"Domina, I am very conscious that through no fault of my own you have recently been left vulnerable to attack by criminals…."

"Thank the Gods that Felix and our man Libius were there to defend the house."

"That was fortunate, lady but I am proposing that you consider employing these men you see before you as guards. Both have received honourable discharges from The Second Lucan Legion and both served under Imperial Prefect Otto Longius in Germany."

"Do you vouch for them, Felix?" Lollia asked.

"I know the pair of them; good, steady soldiers. Subject to your approval, they can be hired for half a legionary's pay plus their equipment and keep."

Lollia looked them over. They were not prepossessing but they were not being taken on to ornament the place.

"As you recommend them to me, Centurion Massus and you know them personally, Felix, I agree but on a probationary basis. When my husband returns he can decide whether to make the arrangement permanent. Is that agreeable to you both?"

It was.

"What are your names?"

She struggled not to giggle when she heard them.

When Otto's party came to the Sequana, they found the water level had dropped a little as the summer wore on. They decided to cross it as before, a combination of swimming and rafts for the arms and equipment and for Saxa.

She took one look at the gigantic floating birds' nests weighed down by kit and weapons and refused to get on one. The boat on the Lippe and Rhine had been bad enough; to sit perched on one of these

She reluctantly slid to the ground. Otto kept hold of her hand and led her forward. A burly man in a plain tunic with a sword belted at his waist came over, saluted and took the horses' bridles.

"Macer, sir; formerly of The Second Lucan, now one of Domina Lollia's guards."

"Thank you Macer," Otto replied in a distracted voice and walked Saxa over to Lollia who stood smiling on the bottom step.

"Welcome husband," she said.

"Lollia, this is my sister Saxa…" he ran out of words.

Lollia was astounded. Otto had made no mention of bringing his family back with him. If this was the sister, where was the mother? Lollia's thoughts raced but she did not let her smile slip, stepped forward and took both of Saxa's hands.

"I am very happy to see you here, Sashta," she told her.

"No lady. I Saxa, Otto is brother to me," Saxa responded in halting Latin.

They looked into each other's eyes which were almost on a level. For once, Lollia was not hunching herself so as not to tower over another woman. Saxa had expected a cold person, haughty and much shorter than she was. They were both relieved and that feeling gave rise to an instant liking.

"I'm sorry, *Saxa*. Now, this is your nephew Lucius Albus…" the little boy made a bow and Lollia proceeded down the line until she arrived at Bellus who greeted her with his unique version of a pleasant smile.

She was given a tour of the villa, gaping open-mouthed at the furniture and the painted walls before being shown into a guest room.

"This is your room," Lollia told her.

Saxa clearly did not understand. Lollia lay down on the bed, got up and then pointed at Saxa who touched a finger to her own chest with an enquiring look on her face. Lollia nodded. Saxa beamed and sat on the edge of the bed bouncing a little; she had never slept on such a soft mattress in her life.

Outside, Felix and Otto had walked the two horses over to the stables and were tending to them.

"So, who are these two new characters? Otto asked.

"We had some trouble while you were away. None of us hurt and nothing stolen but Massus recommended them as guards. Old comrades of ours, the pair of 'em, from up in Germany," Felix replied.

"What sort of trouble?"

"I think you had better hear it from the Domina,"

"Alright," Otto said, with some reluctance.

"It would be better. Anyway, Macer and Bellus are on probation waiting your approval."

"Do you think they'll do?"

Felix nodded. "Sound lads, had some bad luck, lost nearly all their bounty so they're happy enough to have three squares, a roof and flimsy constructions looked suicidal. While the cavalry was milling about getting organized and the first troopers had begun to cross, she stripped off her clothes, clutched her horse's saddle and swam strongly beside it over the river. The men were scandalized; she was the prefect's sister, standing naked and dripping water for all to see! Two of them rushed over and enveloped her in their cloaks. Otto was furious.

"Saxa you go too far! I'm ashamed," he yelled, "Roman ladies don't…."

But she interrupted by shouting back, if anything even angrier. "Roman ladies don't do this and Roman ladies don't do that! What do they do other than sit on their fat backsides waiting for their slaves to feed them and their families? I am not a Roman lady. I do not want to be a Roman lady. All these men here, aren't their mothers made like me? What is the shame? Tell me that."

"Perhaps you should have stayed with Aldermar," he bellowed.

"Perhaps I should, brother. At least I would not be constantly belittled in his hall," she shot back, just as loudly.

The troopers were beginning to enjoy the slanging match and even though they could not understand it, they could see that Saxa was getting the better of the exchange. They gave her a cheer. Saxa understood that they were on her side and smiled in triumph at her brother.

"Silence in the ranks there," Plancus added his voice. "Decurion, take the name of the next man who opens his mouth."

Neither Otto nor Saxa spoke to each other for the next three days but she could not keep up her resentment in the face of all the new sights rolling out before her everyday. Her enthusiasm soon disarmed him and Otto often rode alongside his sister answering her questions and commentating on anything that caught her attention. Paved roads were a source of delight, Agendincum and Lugdunum were wonders. When they crossed over into Italy and she felt the soft southern breezes on her cheek for the first time, Saxa felt as if she had entered a new world. But it was Otto and Lollia's villa that truly astounded her.

She had some undefined idea of her brother's wealth and status but the reality was beyond what she had been capable of imagining. With a smile and a wave from Cassius Plancus, the praetorian cavalry veered off and went straight to the meadow where they had first bivouacked on their arrival from Rome. Otto and Saxa trotted their horses to the front of the house where Lollia, Lucius Albus and the staff were waiting to welcome them. Otto dismounted and reached out a hand to help Saxa but she made no move to get off her horse. He looked up and saw sheer terror on her face. This vast palace in brick and stone with its soaring columns, as she saw it, frightened her. She felt inadequate as if she had no right to be in a place of such splendour.

"Don't be afraid, Saxa; you are at home here. No-one will harm you," Otto said soothingly.

something to spend. They get on alright with the rest of us and don't try to take advantage of the womenfolk."

Didia looked into say Lollia was taking Saxa to bathe.

After ten minutes she reappeared scarlet in the face.

"The domina says you must come to the bathhouse, now, straight away, urgently…"

Equally red-faced, Lollia stood at the entrance. "Otto, Saxa has hair all over…her…her body. I mean, all over. It's most distasteful but we can't ask her if she wants help to remove it. You must find out."

"Won't it hurt, doing what ever you do….?"

"Yes." Lollia replied but said no more.

Otto called Saxa who came out, wrapped in a towel and with a bewildered expression.

"Lollia and Didia want to know if you would like them to get rid of all your hair, under your arms, your legs, all over in fact?" he asked.

Saxa looked at him for a moment and burst into laughter. Then she realised he was not joking.

"Do Lollia and Didia have no hair on them?"

"No."

Saxa looked both of them up and down with amusement edged with scorn.

"I think that is disgusting. Why would a grown woman want to look like a little girl?"

"Saxa thinks it, as you said, "most distasteful", to have the hairless skin of young girls when you are both grown women. She wants to know why you do it."

They looked at each other and shrugged. "Because we do. It's the custom. No decent Roman woman will use the baths with her if she doesn't do something about it," Lollia told him.

"I see. But you said it hurts. Can we sort it out a bit at a time. Say, start with her underarms and work down?"

After negotiations carried out through Otto, Lollia and Didia accepted the compromise, as did Saxa.

"If it is the custom brother, I will not make Lady Lollia and Lady Didia uncomfortable."

"She is not "Lady Lollia" she is just Lollia, your sister and Didia is a servant, but thank you."

That night, when they had recaptured their breath and lay relaxed, legs entwined in their bed, Otto told Lollia what had happened when he had discovered his mother and sister in Germany.

"My mother refused to leave with me so I did all I could to make her future secure. Saxa had to come. The wise woman pronounced it is the Gods' will."

"Did you tell your mother about me?

"I did."

"What did you say?"

"That you are strong and beautiful and you have given me a son.

She pressed closer and then told him every detail of the raid on their home.

"My part in it must never be known. Everyone has sworn to keep the secret. If it came out, I would be the subject of gossip and mockery."

In the morning, Otto lined up the household and thanked them for the part they had played in defence of their home. He gave each of the women twenty silver denarii. Libius he embraced in front of them all and presented him with a gold piece.

"What about Felix," Lollia asked when the others had dispersed about their duties. "Doesn't he merit a reward?"

Otto and Felix chuckled.

"I wouldn't insult him by offering," Otto told her.

"But why…" she began.

Felix intervened. "Domina Lollia, I am a decorated veteran of the legions. My trade is killing. They are only civilians, for them it was something special."

The next morning, Otto and Cassius visited Massus who was not his usual self; a little diffident.

"About that business at your villa, what happened was …."

"What happened was, you had to send the troopers out on patrol. It was your military duty and you did it. If there is any blame, it rests on those scum who tried to take advantage of their absence, not that it got them anything but death and disgrace. There's no more to be said." Otto told him.

Massus blew out a deep breath and grinned. "Glad you see it that way. How are those lads I sent over getting on?"

"According to Felix they're settling in well and everybody's happy, for now.

"Good but you won't be happy, gentlemen, when I pass along your orders. Quite simply, you're off to Rome as soon as any necessary repairs to your men's equipment have been made and your horses rested. The Emperor wishes to see you in person, in full dress uniform and wearing all your decorations. I have to inform him as soon as you arrive so a courier will be going out this afternoon. I reckon you can get away with two days, then its back on the road. Further instructions will be issued when you report to the Praetorian Barracks on your arrival."

"Shit!" Cassius said.

"And my compliments to you, tribune," the centurion replied.

"I meant, shit, back on a bloody horse."

"I'm sure it's hell for you, sir, not like the joy of foot-slogging the width of Africa."

"Sore feet or sore arse, you choose Centurion Massus," Cassius asked him with a grin.

"When you put it like that, I see your point, sir."

As they road back to the villa, Cassius asked what Otto's initial discussion with the centurion had been about.

"Three robbers attacked my home during my absence. Felix cut down two and Libius settled for the third one. Plotina and Tullia finished them off."

"Ferocious household you've got there," Cassius remarked.

"They aren't slaves. They're free people with something to fight for," Otto replied, making his point.

The news did not go down well with Lollia. She wanted her husband home with her for a while but most of all she was worried about Saxa. The girl had no decent clothes, her hair and nails were a mess and she could not make a single sentence out of the few words of Latin she had learned. It was going to be awful. Then Lollia thought again. She would make Saxa her project; she had a practically blank canvas with which to work.

"We're going to have to buy Saxa some dresses and take her to the hairdressers …." she told Otto.

"Spend whatever is necessary, I leave it to you…."

"As usual!"

"But I need Saxa this afternoon, she has to go before the magistrate with the tribune and me."

"Why?"

When he explained her legal position, Lollia was angry. "That can't be right, Saxa is your sister and you are a knight."

"Prince Aldermar told me what to do and I trust him to know what he's talking about. He was educated in Rome…"

"Was he? I never knew that."

The magistrate was a busy man and had other things to do but he was certainly not going to make an Imperial Prefect and a Praetorian Tribune wait in his outer office, even if they agreed to do so, which was unlikely.

He looked up from his desk as they marched in. He sighed quietly. Why did these military types stamp their feet like they did? They weren't on parade or anything. They clanked towards him in gleaming armour, helmets in the crooks of their left arms, between them, a tall, strikingly beautiful young woman.

He heard their depositions which his clerk noted down and prepared a document of manumission. He called the young woman forward; she had been making a minute study of the floor mosaics. After some instructions from Prefect Longius in some barbaric tongue, she smiled, allowed her thumb to be inked and pressed it down on both copies of the papers. An entry was made in a ledger, a fee paid and Saxa the "German slave" became Saxa Longia, freed woman with Latin Rights.

"I wouldn't mind going over the Rhine to bring back another one like her," the magistrate thought as they left.

Lollia declared they must have a celebration feast. It was held early the next evening since Otto and Cassius would be riding for

Rome at dawn. Saxa had the place of honour wearing a crown of flowers. Two flute players trilled in the background and Tullia, with Plotina's help, had excelled herself once more. Otto noted with satisfaction how Saxa surreptitiously copied the way Lollia ate the unaccustomed dishes. It was a great success ending a significant day.

Chapter 8

The streets of Rome were even more packed with jostling humanity than Otto remembered and stank worse. The German "muleteer" slipped away as the others were being paid off and would soon be resuming his role in the Imperial Bodyguard. The mounted troopers made steady progress towards their barracks on the Palatine Hill; the crowd melted away in front of them as soon as they recognised who was monopolizing the middle of the road.

The air was sweeter in the central square of the Praetorian Barracks but no cooler. The officer of the day marched over as the cavalry were stood down in a barrage of shouted orders and salutes thrown back and forth. An orderly led Cassius' charger away to the stables with Djinn, who had recovered from his debauchery while under the care of Aldermar,.

"What's that on your face Cassius?" the officer in charge asked.

"That my friend is a luxurious but well tended beard. You'll see, everyone will be growing one in a few days."

"Right, well then, orders. You are to remain in barracks awaiting a summons to attend the Emperor. One of Augustus' staff flunkies will give you detailed instructions on how you are to present yourselves on the day. I have to inform them of your arrival in Rome. Imperial Prefect Longius, I understand that you have brought all your military decorations, please hand them over to the tesserarius for safekeeping. He will deposit them in our strong room and give you a receipt. You no doubt wish to bathe. Dinner in the officers' mess this evening."

Coming out of the baths, Cassius took Otto by the arm and pulled him aside.

"Look here, old boy, cover for me won't you? It's three hours 'till dinner and I must make a quick appearance at home. If they find out I'm in Rome and don't instantly rush over to see them, I'll never hear the end of it. Thanks, you're a real friend."

Otto lay relaxing on the bed in the quarters assigned to him. It was a relief to think that he had a few days when he would not be riding from dawn to dusk. He slept for a what he thought was a few minutes until a knock on his door roused him and he was shocked to see that was evening and the sun had almost gone.

"Officers assembling in the mess, sir. Have you seen Tribune Plancus?"

"He's around somewhere," Otto replied.

As he was about to walk into the dining room Cassius hurried over. They entered together. He was clean-shaven.

"Your beard?"

"Mother," Cassius snapped and pursed his lips in an angry line.

Otto thought it better to ask no more but his friend looked odd. His nose and forehead were tanned, his cheeks were white where his beard had been shielding his skin from the sun and wind but his throat and neck matched his forehead.

After a good dinner and a few cups of the good mess wine to which minimal water had been added, Cassius mellowed and told his story.

"I toddled over and said hello to the respected parents. Father saw the beard and raised an eyebrow but Mother fell back on her couch and started gasping. Her women rushed over and burned feathers under her nose to bring her round. So she sat up, said the smell of singeing was making her feel sick, took another look at me, pointed and fainted again. More feathers. Then she said I had turned into a German barbarian. She could not bear it. She would never be able to leave home and go out into society again. She asked why I was trying to kill her. I took Father's advice and called for the barber. Damn shame: it was a fine beard."

Otto consoled him with another cup of wine.

The "flunky" was a harassed middle-aged freed man who had spent his life in the service of the state. He met Otto and Cassius in the office he had requested for the purpose.

"I am the Emperor's Master of Protocol. It has fallen to me to arrange your meeting with him, others will be present." He consulted a list. "Prefect Longius, you have been awarded a Military Crown and a Civic crown, which will you chose to wear during the audience?"

"I don't know; the Civic Crown I think."

"Very well. Tribune Plancus, you are the holder of a Silver Spear, I believe.?"

"That's correct," Cassius told him.

The functionary scribbled some notes on a tablet read them back to himself under his breath then nodded approval at what he had written.

"Very well, this is how it will be done. When the double doors of the audience chamber are opened, you will enter side by side preceded by two impressive soldiers. One will carry the tribune's Silver Spear, one a cushion bearing the prefect's Military Crown. They will march up centre of the table, it's a half circle, bow to the Emperor, salute him and move aside. You gentlemen will then take their places. Do not let your crown fall off when you bow, prefect. You will both wear your parade armour, polished to perfection, helmets to be carried. I am told the prefect has other barbaric ornaments won in combat, please display them about your person. I think that is all. I shall oversee the selection of the men to carry your honours."

"You don't think all this is perhaps a little too much?" Cassius asked.

"I am tasked with arranging the most impressive military display possible with just the two of you and a pair of soldiers. It is not for me to question why Emperor Augustus wants things done this way and it is certainly not for you to do so."

"No disrespect to your office was intended, Master of Protocol; we are a little surprised at the degree of formality, that is all," Otto told him.

He nodded his acceptance of the apology and abruptly left.

On the appointed hour and day, they made their way up the Palatine to Augustus' modest home, surrounded on all sides by praetorians carrying shields and long wooden clubs. Two centurions with their own arrays of bronze and silver medals welded to their armour marched in front of Otto and Cassius. They stopped at the entrance and were admitted almost instantly before proceeding along a corridor to the double doors that the Master of Protocol had mentioned. They were flung open; the centurions stepped in followed by Otto and Cassius, exactly as planned.

Augustus sat opposite the doors in the middle of the table, five men were seated on either side of him. They wore the purple striped togas of senators. Among them were previous Consuls, the highest elective office of the state. Their ages varied but they had certain characteristics in common. All were immensely rich and wielded the influence money can buy to win an election for themselves and their allies or bring a riotous mob out on the streets to shout slanders against an enemy. Each had the calculating eyes of a man who fought every day to hold on to his power, his fortune and his life in the merciless arena of Roman politics. Augustus was not only the Emperor but also the Princeps, the first man of Rome. It was as the Princeps he ruled, accommodating the Senate wherever possible. He needed their cooperation to avoid daily, destructive conflict but many noble families had long memories and good reasons to hate him.

The two soldiers bowed and moved to the ends of the table. Otto and Cassius stepped forward and saluted the Emperor. Menities stood behind him, as ever, a wax tablet hanging on a cord at his waist. Augustus smiled serenely. Otto found his handsome face was unchanged since their last meeting but for a few new lines of strain around those fine, expressive eyes.

"Tribune Cassius Plancus, one of these decorated centurions holds your silver spear. Tell us how you earned it," he demanded.

"The aquilifer of my legion was killed and our eagle fell with him. I took it up and fought off some of the enemy trying to take it. Once they could see their eagle again, the men rallied to it, took heart and we won a victory for the Senate and People of Rome and for our Emperor, sir. "

"And you were wounded; badly?"

"I managed to fight on and recovered in a few weeks."

"You delivered Prefect Otto Longius to a friendly tribe on the Rhine. While doing so you turned the tables on a treacherous enemy, came on them by a ruse and punished them. Step forward, tribune."

Cassius marched up to the edge of the table. Augustus stood up and hung a silver medal on a ribbon around his neck.

"In recognition of prompt action. Successful completion of your primary mission. Well done."

Cassius saluted again and returned to his place.

"Prefect Otto Longius," Augustus said, "you have two crowns, Why are you wearing that one?

"Sir, the Civic Crown was given to me by your own hand which is why I chose it. My Military Crown was given to me by my general, the Noble Drusus Germanicus, your late son."

"And that thing round your neck?"

"It is the golden torque of so called "King" Helmund of the Marcomanni. He dared to lay siege to the fortress of the Second Lucan Legion. I defeated him in single combat and claimed the spoils."

"And what do the bracelets you wear on each arm represent, Prefect Longius?" one of the senators asked. He spoke in a mellow, cultured voice which should have sounded pleasant but somehow managed to make Otto very careful in choosing his words.

"Each one is taken off the arm of a German warrior I have killed. It is a custom to demonstrate personal prowess and to honour a brave enemy."

"You are not Roman by birth, prefect, that is apparent to all but yet you have somehow become a Roman officer. Why, I ask myself, would you continue to uphold a German tradition?"

"Sir, I have served on the Rhine border with native auxiliary cavalry and relied on local scouts. They prefer to be led by an officer who shows some respect for their ways and is of proven combat experience. I think you may find that many of the men who fought in Germany, including members of the Patrician Class, now wear arm rings or torques, as tokens of their service."

Augustus remained unmoved but Menities' eyes were darting round the room, judging the reaction of the senators to this exchange.

"Thank you for your explanation, Prefect Longius, I found it instructive," the senator told him with a perfunctory smile.

"Now, two experienced officers …." Augustus began but was interrupted by another senator.

"Very young officers…"

"But old in war," the Emperor shot back, hiding his irritation. "Not generals relying on written reports. Men who fight the enemies of Rome face to face. Sword in hand. Real experience."

The senators cross-examined Cassius about the thwarted ambush on the Sequana. They seemed outraged that anyone would have the effrontery to attack elite Praetorians. He acquitted himself well in his usual, urbane manner. Then Otto was asked to report on his solo expedition into Upper Germany.

"I crossed the Rhine and into the valley of the River Lippe where I travelled for several weeks…."

"I am astonished, prefect. One supposes that these fearsome Germans were so impressed with your bangles that they dared not approach you," the senator who had originally questioned Otto remarked.

Another man, on the far side of Augustus, laughed aloud. The Emperor did not intervene but Menities could see an angry pulse beating on one side of his throat.

"I did not wear them all, sir and I dressed as a civilian to pass myself off as one of them."

"Of course you did, nothing easier, eh?"

"As you say, sir. The basin of the Lippe Valley is flat, marshy country and the river is sluggish, wandering in loops and bends. I followed it upstream for many days, staying overnight in farms or villages. Everywhere I went I was struck by the number of strangers wandering the land. Warriors of the far north and east who have been regarded as enemies for generations were welcome guests. I saw more than one local chieftain engaged in intense discussions with some of them. The people believe a child has been born who will grow up to destroy a great Roman army and end Rome's ambitions in Upper Germany."

There was a moment's silence when he finished followed by a burst of laughter from a small minority.

"And what is he called, this holy, saviour child?" a voice called out.

"I do not know his name" Otto advised. "But there is nothing supernatural about him in the story as it was told to me."

"And what are we to make of this nonsense?" yet another senator asked. "What you will gentlemen. I was asked to report and that is what I have done," Otto said, hoping he was finished but they would not let him go without probing deeper.

"But surely, even if this wild tale is true, what difference could one additional barbarian make to their perceived cause?"

"I beg to remind you that when the Gauls found their one barbarian, Vercingetorix, even the Divine Julius, the greatest commander of our epoch, was hard pressed at the end," Otto reminded them.

"But the victory belonged to Rome!" a triumphant voice shouted.

"Indeed it did, but at an enormous cost which was off-set by the seizure of the wealth of Gaul. There are no oppidia, no manufacturing industries, no seaports or cities in Germany to make conquering it worth such an effort."

"I myself viewed the Ardennus Forest from a high vantage point, sirs," Cassius broke in, supporting Otto. "It was a blood-chilling vista of trees as far as the horizon and beyond on three sides. Twenty armies could not subdue it. To that extent, I am with the prefect."

"So you two feel confident to set Rome's foreign policy do you?" asked the first senator to have spoken. "I tell you now that if Publius Quinctilius Varus was brought back from Syria and given just one army, let alone twenty, he would pacify the whole region in months."

"I give way to your superior knowledge, sir," said Cassius with an exquisitely but deniably insolent bow and a smile.

"Time to move on to other matters. Prefect, Tribune, our thanks. You may leave."

Putting the regalia back in the strong room in the barracks, the centurions were chuckling.

"That old bugger of a senator gave you a rough ride, sir," one of them said to Otto.

"Mind your language soldier," the duty officer reprimanded him.

"Apologies sir, fine body of men in the senate, utmost respect for 'em," he said snapping to attention.

"Goes for me double, sir.," his comrade told the officer. "Pleasure for us to lay down our lives for the likes of them, any old time."

"Oh just sod off, the pair of you."

They saluted. "Sodding off as ordered," one of them said. They did a smart about turn and marched away, arms swinging.

Before Otto and Cassius had walked over to the officers' quarters, a messenger ran up to them.

"The Emperor wishes you to attend him in one hour's time gentlemen."

Divested of their armour, in tunics and soft boots, they knocked on the "palace" doors once more; both of them with sinking hearts. The earlier meeting had been on the edge of acrimonious and no doubt they were to be blamed. They were wrong. Augustus was sitting in his garden under a pergola over which a vine grew, giving him and his single companion some shade from the noon sun. As they drew nearer, Otto saw the upright figure with the Emperor was his first commanding officer, Publius Quadratus. He had some silver in his hair now but was as slender and elegant as ever. He rose with a smile and held out his right hand.

"My dear Otto, How glad I am to see you."

"And I you, sir."

Augustus grimaced at Cassius. "Old comrades. Nothing more boring. "Remember when this and that?" Should remember the rest of us weren't there. Take a seat both of you. Eat?"

He clapped his hands and a servant brought at tray with more olives, cheese and bread. He placed it on the small table around which they sat.

"So Tribune Plancus, Germany suit you?"

"Prince Aldermar was a very generous host."

"All the roast pork a man could want washed down with fermented barley water and not a goose stuffed with pine nuts or a drop of decent wine in sight," he laughed. "Hellish for you. Heard about the beard. Agree with your mother for once. Now then, what did you make of this morning, eh?"

"I thought some of the senators, one in particular, was unnecessarily hostile to Prefect Longius, sir."

"Nothing to do with the prefect. That was his way of attacking me; I elevated our Otto to the Equestrian Order and made him an officer. I was right. Faith in him justified. The senator was using Otto to question my judgement. Unbelievably, not everyone loves their emperor. Daren't publicly oppose me so belittles my protégé, d'you see? They enjoyed the sport but they showed their hand. Publius, give these innocents a lesson in politics."

Publius Quadratus took a sip of the chilled wine in his cup and nodded to the Emperor.

"Rome needs victories, they are what confirms our greatness to the Roman mob and the entire world. To gain victories, one needs armies which must have generals to lead them. That is where the difficulty arises. Generals come from a narrow social class divided into factions, each jostling for power. Get one or more of your party appointed a general and suddenly you have the implied threat of his army to add to your influence. Hence the call for Varus to be transferred to Germany, closer to Rome. Is that a fair summary, sir?" he asked Augustus.

"Wish the rest of 'em could say as much in as few words. Pompey Magnus and the Divine Julius. Evenly matched until the last battle. Pompey lost and the treacherous, womanish Egyptians took his head. But it was no fluke that Caesar was cut down beneath a statue of Pompey. Political statement? I fought his sons for years. One of 'em held Sicilia. Spain was a Pompeian stronghold, which is where you two come in. Imperial goldmine subject to attacks and losses of treasure. What's behind it? Go to Spain, find out and stop it. No-one is to know anything of this. Publius Quadratus will fill you in on the logistics."

"Gentlemen, you are invited to a small dinner party at my house on the Esquiline this evening. I shall send one of my men to fetch you. His first words will be "Lucan on the Rhine", if they are not, kill him. Dress inconspicuously."

Their guide knocked on a door in the high, blank wall surrounding Quadratus' home. A Judas grill opened and a guard checked his identity before they were all admitted into a garden still sweetly scented by flowers in the gathering dusk. As they entered, the doorkeeper asked their guide if they had been followed. When he was told they had not, he stepped into the empty street and whistled. Two men in dark cloaks appeared out of the deeper shadows and made their way over.

"Just a precaution sirs; we like to keep a few eyes on the neighbourhood. Please follow me."

Quadratus was waiting for them in a small dining room. He rose to greet them and dinner was quickly served. The only sign of luxury was the delicate ewer and drinking vessels of gold-etched glass from which they took their wine. Later, Cassius described the house and gardens as of "refined good taste"; in keeping with the character of their host. The conversation was light-hearted while they ate but once they were done and the dishes removed, Quadratus got down to business. He took the cap off a large leather tube and removed a sketch map which he spread on the table.

"You both are to proceed to Tarraconensis; precisely to this location," he put his index finger on an area shaped like the bow of a great ship thrusting out from the massif of the Pyrenaei Mountains. "This plateau stretches twenty miles from the mountains to its endpoint and is four miles across at its widest. There is one passage to the summit on the eastern slope which is relatively gentle and could be improved to allow access by wheeled vehicles; otherwise, bounded by sheer cliffs; split and jagged in places. Its surface is almost level and three hundred feet at its highest. The Emperor's goldmine lies to the west. This means that bullion has to be transported around the base for thirty-eight miles through broken, boulder-strewn country to reach the nearest decent highway to the coast. It could have been designed with ambush and robbery in mind…."

"Is it not possible to build a road from the mine up the western side and then simply cross to an accessible slope?" Otto asked.

"No," Quadratus replied. "There is another feature I have not yet mentioned. A ravine runs the full length, north to south, it as if it had been cut through by some titanic sword. Your mission is to support our engineers in building a western road climbing to the top. In addition they are to bridge the central cleft at a suitable point. The bridge is the key to transporting the Emperor's gold as Otto suggested. Tribune Cassius Plancus, you are to leave Rome with your cohort augmented by another two hundred and fifty men and march to Veii. You will take control of the cohort there and continue your journey to Emporiae on the coast of Tarraconensis. Ostensibly you will be rotating the Veii Praetorian Garrison. By the time it is widely known that you are not, you will be well on your way. Their commanding officer will receive orders to stay where he is until further notice. You will travel light; heavy transport will be awaiting at Emporiae where you will liaise with a party of engineers under their prefect. They will be accompanied by an ala of three hundred auxiliary cavalry. Imperial Prefect Otto Longius will lead this force."

"How many engineers, sir?" Cassius asked.

"Around two hundred with a small number of artillerists. Yours is the overall command, tribune but I most strongly advise you to consult your prefects. This will be written into your orders."

"Around two thousand men for a short length of road and a bridge?"

"No; a strong force to investigate and bring these marauders to justice, and, incidentally, to protect the engineers. Every effort must be made to keep this operation secret. Trust no-one in Rome and no-one in Spain, up to and including the governor. Now, let us enjoy a flask of wine and speak of other things. You will both sleep here tonight; I would be a poor host if I let you run the gauntlet of the streets after dark."

At breakfast, Quadratus was his gracious self until they had eaten, then as he had last night, he became serious.

"Tribune Plancus, here are your orders to assemble your troops and march to Veii. I include sealed orders for the praetorian tribune there, as discussed last night. All other documents are in this tube," he tapped the leather with his index finger. "They give details of your mission together with maps and permissions to draw on civilian supplies for what you may need to the account of the Emperor. You may also demand the complete cooperation of any legions you encounter on your journey. It also contains some other papers which are matters of state, for your information only. They are to be opened strictly in accordance with the instructions also enclosed. I am reluctant to let you leave the safety of this house with it. Who knows what prying eyes might have been bribed to discover our plans?"

He lapsed into silence and absent-mindedly rolled breadcrumbs into pellets while he thought.

"It seems to me," Otto said, "that disclosure ceases to be a problem once Tribune Plancus has picked up the men in Veii. After that, we shall be committed to the mission. What if I took them out of the city discreetly and travelled separately?"

"What would you do with them?"

"Have Centurion Massus in Luca put them under guard in his quarters."

"And you trust him with confidential papers?"

"The Emperor does."

Quadratus gave Otto a swift, penetrating glance, understanding immediately what Otto was implying. He nodded.

"Very well. Two of my men will accompany you while you return to barracks and pick up your horse. They will bring you back here to pick up the documents and then lead you to the city gate."

"As you say, sir. My crowns and parade armour can stay in the praetorians' strong room, probably the safest place in the Empire. I have a receipt from the tesserarius. Tribune Plancus can bring along my helmet, arm rings and torque; I'll need them on campaign. He will be marching up the Via Aurelia so it should be easy for me to join the column when he is close by Luca."

"Excellent, do you agree tribune?" Quadratus asked.

"First class plan, sir, if Imperial Perfect Longius is sure he is ready to take the risk. Perhaps an escort of two or three cavalrymen?"

Quadratus shook his head. "I understand your concern for Otto but only important people need armed protection. Alone, he will be just another undistinguished traveller among many."

Cassius wanted to say, "Undistinguished, him? On his horse?" but kept his thoughts to himself.

The men Quadratus employed were experienced and skilled in observation but in the thronging streets of the capital, who could say that they had not been watched as they took turns to stroll nonchalantly a pace or two in front of the man on the black charger?

Otto wore a horseman's cloak covering the dispatch tube on a loop over his shoulder and his long, cavalry sword. Once clear of the city, he adopted the method of covering the ground which was second nature to man and horse. He mentally divided the hours into quarters. During the first, he rode Djinn at a walk, upped his pace to a trot and then to a canter before dismounting and leading his horse on foot until he judged it was time to remount. It was not the quickest way of proceeding but still ate up the miles and kept his horse fresh. He looked back at the travellers going up and down the Via Aurelia a few times during the first three hours but saw no-one who appeared to be following or taking any particular interest in him. Djinn attracted a few admiring glances but nobody looked twice at his rider.

Traffic grew less as Rome faded into the distance. When the sun was two hours past its zenith, Otto found himself on a long stretch of empty road with a derelict farmhouse close to the verge a little ahead. Two riders were lying in wait for him concealed behind one of the tumbled-down walls. They burst out and faced him only a few yards away. Their ambush had been well planned and executed but it did not take into account the skills of Otto and his warhorse; they had survived a hundred skirmishes and sudden attacks.

Otto twisted his torso, sat back in the saddle and nudged with his left knee. Djinn reared up on his hind legs, spun around, and was into a gallop back towards Rome in three strides. The speed with which the manoeuvre been carried out startled the ambushers and Djinn had gained thirty yards on them before they could kick their mounts into motion but they did, hurtling after the fleeing Otto.

He kept twisting his head around to watch the pursuers, checking his horse's gallop a little to let them gain then giving Djinn his head and surging clear. After a mile, he grinned. They had fallen for it. One of them was ahead of his companion and the distance between them was widening. When he judged the moment had arrived, Otto slowed his horse once more and the first man caught up with him, pulling over to the left to give him an unhindered swing with his sword. Otto heard the swish of the blade and caught the glitter of the three feet of steel slashing towards him and dropped forward over Djinn's neck. The blow passed harmlessly over his head. He sat upright and lashed his own sword across the man's face. Blood, teeth, a flopping jaw and he fell out of the saddle with a scream and then a crack as his skull bounced off the paving stones.

In an instant, Otto and Djinn had reversed their direction and now tore down on the second man who had been shocked at the death of his comrade and was in two minds whether to run or fight. His brief hesitation cost him his life as Otto's sword thrust burst through his chest.

He quickly rifled the bodes for identification but there was none. However, both wore military boots and their swords were standard army issue. They were, or had been, regular cavalrymen. One of them had a heavy gold ring, old and worn with the inscription, "Pom.Mag." still faintly legible on the inside. Otto took it.

Chapter 9

Otto resisted the impulse to get away from the bodies lying on the road as fast as he could. Djinn had regained his wind while Otto had been examining them, so they proceeded at a gentle hand-gallop. He would not look like a horseman fleeing the scene of butchery to anyone who saw him. After twenty minutes, a carriage with outriders forced him off the road. Otto waited patiently, head down, until they had passed him by then continued on his way. The outriders would drag the corpses off the highway and collect their mounts, reporting their find at the gates of Rome or maybe not; they were good horses. By the time anyone came from the city to investigate, the dead men would have been stripped of their boots and clothes, lying naked and unknown in the heat under a humming cloud of flies.

He did not remove his cloak to keep what he was carrying concealed while he ate in the waystation dining rooms and went to his bed early, bolting the door behind him. He took quick breakfasts and left at dawn each day. There was no more trouble but the strain of constantly looking around for pursuit and anticipating a sudden attack told on him. Otto was a mentally exhausted man when Djinn's hooves clattered onto the street of Luca. He asked for Massus at the garrison post but the centurion was out and not likely to be back for at least two hours. Otto unsaddled Djinn and hitched him up outside with a half a pail of tepid water then waited in the guard room with his back to the wall, facing the door. When Massus arrived, he took one look at the prefect's haggard face and shouted to one of his men.

"Bread and wine in my office." He gestured to Otto to follow him, went in and shut the door behind them. Otto took off his cloak and removed the dispatch tube. He laid it on the table.

"Centurion Massus, The Emperor has charged me with carrying his documents. Will you lock them in your strongbox under guard?"

"Of course…"

There was a knock and a soldier came in with a tray of food and drink for them. Otto threw his cloak over the tube to conceal it. Massus noted the importance Otto was placing on secrecy. When the tray had been put down on the table and the soldier had left, Massus heated some wax and dropped a blob on the join between tube and lid.

"Press your thumb into that," he instructed. When Otto had complied and there was a clear wax seal bearing Otto's thumbprint, he took the precious item and locked it away. He did not ask what it contained or to where it was to be delivered. Experience had taught him there were times when it was best not to know.

He watched the tension drain out of his friend's face as they ate and drank their wine in silence.

"People will be interested that two men tried to stop me just outside Rome. They're dead," Otto said.

Massus nodded and smiled slightly. Otto learned quickly. He knew that the centurion was one of the Emperor's confidential correspondents but he had not mentioned the names of the "people" who should be informed. Massus said nothing but they both knew his meaning had been understood.

"Also, I found this on one of them," Otto said and handed over the ring.

Massus' eyes widened when he read the faded lettering inside. Again he said nothing directly but rose and put it into the strongbox.

"Pompey Magnus, "Pom. Mag.": he's long dead. Surely he cannot have any influence on the living?" Otto conjectured.

Massus filled their wine cups. "Sit back and listen to a history lesson from old Cyclops Massus; I sometimes forget how young you are and that you never picked up these things as a lad. Julius Caesar stood for the common people and new ways of governing the state. Pompey was the champion of the rich and the nobility who wanted things to stay as they were. They were fated to clash. Pompey fell but that didn't settle matters, just drove a lot of his support in Rome underground. After Caesar was murdered, Augustus or rather, Octavian Caesar as he was called in those days, took power along with that shit, Marcus Antonius. The Divine Julius was known for the mercy he showed to defeated political opponents, that's why there were enough of them around to stab him to death. Octavian and Antonius were the opposite, ruthless and harsh. A lot of Roman gentlemen were executed, assassinated and their estates confiscated. When Octavian and Antonius fell out things got even worse but now they are much better, entirely due to Augustus. Rome is always full of plotters so, if you are one of his envious rivals, you can invoke the name of Pompey Magnus and claim your cause is justifiable. It isn't, of course. They simply want to replace our Emperor and the Gods help us if they succeed. The end."

Everyone at home was pleased to see Otto but surprised that he was alone. After he had greeted them all, omitting no-one to avoid hurt feelings, he bathed and sat on the veranda talking with Lollia.

"I am under orders. Cassius will be here soon with his praetorians. I have to join them."

"When is soon?

"A week, perhaps less."

"And then?"

"We march. I can't tell you where nor for how long I'll be away; months I expect."

"Then we must make the best of you while you're with us, my love,"

Saxa's reaction was as explosive as unexpected. "You're going to go off and leave me with these people? The swine Didia is ripping every hair out of my body one by one, their food's vile, everything dipped into little bowls of rancid fish sauce, I can't understand what they're saying to me most of the time. It's killing me to live here," she ran out of breath and the stream of high-volume German yelling ceased.

"You wanted to come," Otto reminded her.

"Yes, to be with my brother and his family, not to be alone and friendless..."

"Lollia is a friend to you."

"Oh her," Saxa said dismissively. "She's alright but so useless and spoiled, like all these Roman women. She'd faint if she broke a fingernail."

Otto said no more but woke Saxa early the next morning.

"Come with me, there's something you might like to watch."

She stood in a corner of the enclosed courtyard while Otto and Lollia clashed blades, ducking, dancing backwards, lunging, parrying in a complex whirl of steel, too quick for the eye to follow at times. After ten minutes, he called a halt and offered Saxa his sword. She hefted it in her hand, grinned and ran at Lollia who stepped aside and brought the flat of her blade down on the hilt of Saxa's weapon. It flew out of her hand and clattered to the floor. She flushed and took it up again. This time Lollia parried her wild swing and counter thrust, forcing Saxa to stand perfectly still with Lollia's sword tip gently resting between her breasts.

Otto put the swords back in their place and took one hand of both of the young women. He spoke alternatively in Latin and German.

"Well sister, useless, fainting over a broken fingernail?"

Saxa had the good grace to smile and apologize.

"Would you teach Saxa swordplay while I'm away? It will keep you in practice if nothing else," he asked Lollia.

"Oh, that would be really good but you must explain it has to be kept between us, no-one can ever know."

Saxa was doubtful. "But the servants have already seen you both."

"They have," Otto conceded "but they will never speak of it for two reasons. Firstly, they love Lollia and don't want her to be mocked if it came out. Secondly, Lollia killed a robber armed with a club. They owe her a great debt for that."

Saxa was shocked. Perfumed, well-dressed Lollia with her smooth complexion and finicky table manners killing a man? If it had been anyone other than her brother who had told her, she would never have believed it. It was settled; Lollia would teach Saxa sword craft.

Otto was content. He had raised his sister's opinion of his wife. He had given them a shared secret which would forge a bond between them. And, although he pushed the thought to the back of his mind, an extra blade in defence of his home and people might not come amiss.

It was a morning of swords. He watched Macer and Bellus at their drill. Their performance was exactly as he had imagined. Solid veterans efficiently going through the stock legionary moves. They were competent workmen who had learned their trade well.

"Right lads," he said when they were finished and standing in front of them. "I'd like to make a permanent arrangement with you. Here are my terms. In any military matters you're under Evocati Felix's orders. We'll get a post put up and you'll practice for an hour every day. You can go boozing in Luca one night a week but only if at least four of the cavalry troopers are here. There may be some labouring work about the place from time to time, I expect you to muck in. What do you say?"

They looked at each other and after a moment's hesitation, they both agreed.

"Very good, I'm glad you'll be staying. So, since you're on the strength, full legionary pay for both of you, how's that?" Their beaming faces told him it was very good. "I'll see Felix about getting you some helmets and kit. Centurion Massus will have some spares he can "lose" eh?"

Massus had already wound a strip of parchment around his scytale baton, written a dispatch on it and given the sealed message to a trusted courier.

"Two men attacked the friend who eats figs outside Rome. He killed them. One wore this ring. From the Hand of Cyclops."

Felix approved of the terms Otto had offered Macer and Bellus. "They'll do us proud," he said. "I'm not even going to ask about going on campaign with you, after what happened while you were up north."

"I'm glad you're here, Felix. With you in command and our two soldiers, I'll sleep better at night. See Massus about kitting them up will you?"

He spent long hours with Lollia, listening to her plans and schemes, the gossip of the town and news of the families they knew, savouring every minute. He walked with Saxa along the river, which she loved to watch, if not to voyage on. He played with the boys and threw sticks for the huge puppy.

"That dog needs a name," he told Lucius Albus.

"Got one. He's called "Lion"."

"You can't call hm that. A lion is a kind of cat. No dog wants to be called a cat, now does he?"

"Lions is big and brave."

"Well then, you've chosen a good name, my son."

Djinn, his gelding and two mules were re-shod. Felix waxed his subarmalis and a spare, polished and oiled his mail shirt, greased the spare and wrapped it in canvas. Swords and lances were sharpened. Tullia and Plotina laundered tunics and underwear. Bellus and Macer stretched out his leather tent on a line and waterproofed it with sheep's grease. He was as ready as he could be when the rider from Cassius galloped into the yard.

"Compliments of Tribune Cassius Plancus, sir. The column will be five miles north of you on the Via Aurelia at midday tomorrow if you would care to join us,"

Otto recognised Cassius's way of speaking in the words; all that was missing was "old thing" at the end.

That evening he took twenty gold pieces out of his strongbox and put them in a leather purse. He gave it to Lollia.

"Promise me that if I don't come back you'll give this money to Saxa and have her escorted to Prince Aldermar's people. They wanted her to stay with them...."

Lollia looked down at the purse in her lap, up at her husband and tears welled up at the corner of her eyes. She cuffed them brusquely away; she did not want the mask of her Roman stoicism to be shattered as the possibility that he might be lost on this mission became suddenly real to her.

Saxa came in and demanded to know what was going on. When he explained, her bottom lip trembled and fat tears coursed down her face.

"You mustn't leave us, brother," she said.

"The Emperor has my oath," he told her.

That was enough for her to follow Lollia's example. The whole of her culture and upbringing told her that oaths were sacred. If men and women did not keep their given word what was left other than chaos? Her brother had no choice.

Eventually he managed to get a smile out of the pair of them but that night Lollia made desperate love to him, as if she would never let him go.

The morning dawned under an angry sky, the clouds slashed red in the rising sun. He went into Luca and collected his "item" from Massus.

"Mars and Fortuna with you," he called to Otto's retreating back.

A few spatters of rain fell on Otto as he led his gelding and pack mules out towards his meeting with the column. For all his readings in philosophy, Otto was not a man given to wrestling with the great questions. What the nature of human existence is and what is an individual man's part in it were not things that troubled him. He studied the words of the great thinkers of his age to try to understand the actual world in which he found himself and the best way to live in it. But as he rode alone towards the highway, his mind ranged back over the last few days. He realized he had been truly happy. He held on to the memory as a treasure he could recall at will to try to conjure up that contentment again. Without knowing it, Otto was becoming bound to his home and land.

He came on to the main road and headed north for half an hour until he saw the praetorians spread along the verge taking their noon break. He noticed they were resting in three distinct groups. None of them cast more than a cursory glance his way: just another civilian trotting through the spitting rain. Cassius was sitting at a small folding table under the shelter of an awning stretched out from the back of a two-wheel cart. The remains of his lunch lay on a silver plate. A fat young man stood behind his chair with a napkin draped over one arm.

"Oh there you are, Otto. Jolly good of you to turn up so promptly. How's the family doing?" he called with a nonchalant wave.

Otto dismounted and pointed at the cart.

"What's all that about?"

Cassius pretended that he did not understand for a moment. "Oh the wagon thingy. A few essentials."

"Such as?"

"A bed, the odd comfortable chair, a rug or two, something to eat off and drink out of…"

"And him?" Otto pointed at the waiter.

"Who? Nestor? Also essential; you can't expect a man to cook his own dinner. After the privations I've already been through for Augustus this year, that would be intolerable…"

Otto grinned and shook his head. "Well it's essential that I arm myself. Can I use your wagon and would Nestor kindly help me?"

"Of course, feel free. Nestor, there's a box marked "Otto" somewhere with this gentleman's belongings in it. Be a good chap and assist."

Nestor doubted that Otto merited the status of "gentleman" but when he saw him in his gleaming mail shirt, gold torque, arm rings and a cavalry prefect's helmet, he changed his opinion.

"Put your kit and spare clothes in my wagon, they'll keep dryer," Cassius offered.

Nestor stowed everything, helping him with the heavy tent.

Otto handed Cassius the sealed tube containing their orders. "Can't tell you how happy I am to be relieved of it," he said, jumping onto Djinn's back and heading off to find the transport officer to hand his gelding and mules into his care.

When he cantered back, the troops sat up and took notice. Cassius had them fall in ready to renew their march. From the back of his own horse, he introduced Otto at the top of his voice.

"Imperial Prefect the Equestrian Otto Longius holder of both Military and Civic crowns has joined us. He fought with the praetorian cavalry at the ambush on the Sequana. We are fortunate to have the services of an officer of his reputation. Centurions, lead off, march!"

"To repeat your words to the Emperor's Master of Ceremonies, perhaps a little too much?" Otto remarked.

"What did you want me to say? "New chap arrived boys, be nice to him?" Come on, we've a long way to go."

The legions marched twenty-five miles a day on paved roads in friendly territory. But these men were praetorians, the elite; they would cover thirty miles. Even so, it would be the best part of a month until they reached their destination, following the Tyrrhenian coast then turning east, edging the Ligurian Sea and finally, a short stage southwards into Tarraconensis. They would all be a little leaner and a lot fitter by the time they made Emporiae.

Otto saw that the men were as divided in their march as they had been at rest. Cassius' cohort took the lead, the Veii cohort followed them and the half cohort seconded from the Praetorian Barracks took up the rear with the mule train and vehicles. The gap between each unit was wider than would be expected but only an experienced observer would be able to see it. The next day, the half cohort took the lead and the others had to suffer the dust. Cassius rotated his men every day.

"What's wrong with the men?" Otto asked one evening as they sat at Cassius' camp table enjoying an excellent dinner prepared by the invaluable Nestor.

Cassius sighed. "My chaps are sulky because they don't know where they're going; that's the Emperor's fault for demanding complete secrecy. The Veii lot are unhappy for the same reason and because their tribune has been left behind. The half cohort are bitter because they think they're only here to make up the numbers and will eventually be given all the dirty jobs. Happy days!" He lifted his wine cup in a mock toast.

"Can't you move centuries around so, say, three from Veii join you, two of yours march with the half cohort and so on?"

Cassius shook his head. "Won't do. If I divide 'em up, morale will sink even lower and however I organize it, I'll be accused of favouritism. Please understand, I'm not courting the good opinion of the men but I need them to become an integrated force and shuffling them about won't help. Then I'm going to have to integrate over two hundred engineers and they're always bloody-minded...."

"Plus three hundred cavalry...."

"Oh, you'll sort them out old thing, no worries there," Cassius told him with a smile.

Day followed day and the men became even more sullen as the road passed under their hobnailed boots. On rest days, the units kept apart but their discipline held; there were no quarrels, no catcalling, just a studied dismissal of the existence of the others. Cassius called a meeting of the senior centurions and told them of his concerns.

"Can't order a man to be happy, sir," one of them said which summed up the general attitude.

It was miserable time for all concerned; no singing, no banter around the fires at night, no ribald comments shouted through the dark.

The Greeks had built their trading city of Massillia on the southern coast of Gaul long before Rome had become a great power. They then established an outpost on an island in a river estuary in Spain. It was known in Greek as "Emporon", a place for trading. The Romans took the word and changed it to emporia then took the place, adding townships on either bank of the river. Because there were three locations involved, they gave it the plural name of Emporiae, and now Cassius' men were on their final approach.

Otto rode ahead to find the engineers, always supposing everyone had their timings right and they had arrived. Sure enough, rows of heavy wagons were drawn up in a rectangle outside the town on the northern bank of the river. Men in a mixture of legion uniforms and tunics under leather aprons were busily stripping down and rebuilding jacks, pumps and artillery pieces. It was the characteristic of engineers that most puzzled Otto. They dismantled everything simply to put it back together whenever they had nothing else to do. It was their abiding obsession. Djinn did not like the smell of the oil and grease and he did not care for the look of these oddly shaped masses of timber and iron spread in his path. Nostrils flaring and ears twitching, he took delicate mincing steps to show his displeasure. Otto asked a group of men for their prefect. They ceased work, looked up and gave him an impatient salute. It was obvious they thought he was interfering with some vital task.

"Over there, sir" one said, gesturing to a table spread with papers beside one of the wagons.

A man was bent over it studying a diagram.

Otto rode over and called out, "Greetings, Prefect".

The Prefect of Engineers lifted his head from his work. Otto looked into hazel eyes separated by a badly bent nose. He leapt down off his horse and wrapped his arms around the burly, broad-shouldered man.

"Lucius, Boxer, I never dreamed it would be you!"

Lucius Taurius Longius, "Boxer", Otto's first and best Roman friend, the man to whom he had given his oath, was overwhelmed.

"Otto, Otto, how are you here? Why? They told me praetorians…"

The engineers were treated to the sight of the two officers, slapping each other on the back, pushing each other away, grinning into each other's faces then embracing once more. Eventually they stepped apart, both short of breath but still smiling.

"I was expecting a cavalry prefect but not you," Lucius told his friend. "Come and drink a cup of wine with me and tell me what's happening at home."

An hour of questions and answers barely broke the surface of all they had to say to each other but duty intruded.

"My cavalry?" Otto asked.

"They're camped two miles upstream where they think the grazing is better. At least, that's what I thought the one who believes he can speak Latin was saying."

"I'll go back to the column and tell them you're here and then introduce myself to my men. Cassius…"

"Not Cassius Plancus that we met in Rome? Him? What will he do for spit-roast peacock out here?"

Otto laughed again. "Don't be fooled. There's more to him than you think. He's leading the infantry. He'll be here in three or four hours. So if I'm to get back and then visit my command, I'd better get going."

Dressed for war, arms glittering with silver rings and a king's golden torque around his neck, Otto cantered Djinn into the cavalry camp. He pulled the warhorse to a halt. Djinn, with his sense of the theatrical, showed-off by rearing a little and taking a few steps on his hind legs. Otto patted his neck and he snorted and stood still.

"Greetings, I am your prefect," Otto shouted. "I am Otto Longius, son of Badurad of the Suevi and Knight of Rome."

"You are Otto Kingkiller?" one of the men shouted.

Otto nodded his head. "Some men have called me that. Where are your decurions?"

Two bearded men in mail shirts stepped forward and bowed. "We are all Prince Aldermar's men, lord. Many of us know you. Some fought alongside you when you won that torque you wear."

Otto was pleased but kept his face stern. "I must return to the tribune who leads us and tell him he has the finest cavalry for which a commander could wish. Tonight, I'll pitch my tent among you."

They cheered him as he rode away.

That evening, Cassius invited Otto and Boxer to dine with him. It was a balmy night under a sky blazing with stars. For twenty minutes nothing was said as they attacked the food in front of them. Full, they leaned back and relaxed.

"Thank you, Nestor, that was a fine dinner," Otto told him. Nestor smiled and bowed in acknowledgement of the compliment and cleared the dishes away. Cassius raised one eyebrow.

"You'll give him ideas above his station," he said with a smile but it was still a rebuke.

Otto bit his tongue. He wanted to say that treating Nestor like a human being might discourage him from poisoning Cassius one day but did not want to put the thought into his friend's head; that might not go well for the cook. He changed the subject.

"It's an amazing coincidence that we are all together for….."

Before he had finished, Cassius, who had just taken a mouthful of wine, started to laugh, choked and sprayed it across the table. He spluttered and coughed, cleared his airways, looked at Otto's puzzled face and laughed again until the tears ran down his face. Shaking one hand in apology, he left the table and walked around, guffawing until he had collected himself. With a final chuckle he took his seat once more.

"Apologies, gentlemen. Otto, old thing, you are the most astonishingly naive person I have ever met. For all your poring over your books at night, you seem to have no idea of what goes on around you. You have a complete blank when it comes to politics."

"I don't understand…."

"Exactly!" Cassius said and banged his hand on the table for emphasis. "Let me bring light into your darkness. Augustus sees that substantial amounts of bullion are going missing from one of his Spanish mines. Gold buys votes, public offices, weapons and men to use them. He suspects someone is trying to accumulate enough treasure to fund a move against him. Who can he trust to thwart the plot? Well, his praetorians are sworn to him personally. He knows Otto will be loyal to the gates of the underworld. He publicly rehabilitated your family, Lucius, so your devotion is assured. He sent me up to Prince Aldermar's city so that Aldermar could look me over and give his opinion. It must have been favourable because I command and we have his auxiliaries with us. I'd bet one of his conditions was that Otto would lead them. Add to that, neither of you two have any connections in Rome and are good friends. He saw how I supported Otto at the conference when that senator verbally attacked him and will have concluded that Otto and I are also friendly. Would any of us betray a friend? No. Gentlemen, we are flies in the Emperor's web and what a jolly cunning old spider he is." Cassius raised his refilled wine cup. "I give you Augustus, Father of the People and the best of Emperors."

They drank, Boxer and Cassius smiling at Otto's face on which realization was dawning. The mood soon became darker. Cassius explained his concerns over the divisions between his men.

"I can't see any way to improve matters."

"Do you have the authority to bring in a man capable of resolving this?"

"I am entitled to do, I quote, "any and everything to ensure the success of this mission". What did you have in mind?"

"You appoint an outsider as camp prefect. No-one could accuse him of favouritism, simply because the men are an unknown quantity to him."

"Can you think of anyone suitable?"

Otto nodded. "I can."

Chapter 10

Two olive groves covered a pair of south-facing hillsides to the west of Tarraco. The slopes folded together leaving a steep path between them which ran with water during the winter rains. Sheep grazed among the trees and the air was shrill with cicadas. Lizards basked on baking stones, birds fluttered down after the insects attracted by the sheep dung. The sun had a cloudless sky to himself and punished the land with oppressive heat.

At the foot of the hills stood a modest white house with a red, terracotta tile roof. The door was of solid oak reinforced with iron bands, the windows small to minimise the glare and barred for security. At one side of the door rested a wooden bench. To the rear, high walls enclosed a courtyard with stables. There was a well and a fig tree in the centre. In one corner a heavy-set man, shaven-headed struck at a post embedded in the ground with a rudis, the weighted wooden sword used for training legion recruits. But this man was no beginner. He was in early middle-age, powerful and competent. Every blow made the post quiver. They were delivered expertly with slight foot movements to get the maximum force behind the strike. He sweated freely but did not pant for breath or look as if this violent exercise was causing him any distress.

A woman sat on a cane chair in the shade of the tree fanning herself and rocking a cradle in which a small child slept undisturbed by the tock, tock, tock of his father's weapon-drill. Her inky black hair cascaded almost to the ground and reflected deep blue highlights as the sun caught her rhythmic motion. Two men came out of the house.

"Three German horsemen coming up the road," one of them said.

The sweating swordsman stopped.

"How long?"

"Twenty minutes."

"You know what to do," he told them, went over to the well and poured a bucket of water over his head. He was sitting outside with a mug of heavily watered wine in his hand when the riders pulled up, a jug and a bright sword naked on the bench beside him. His two men had armed themselves with spears, left the courtyard by the back gate and now stood out of sight at the side of the house.

"Greetings First Spear Centurion Titus Attius," Otto called.

"Former; a civilian these days, unlike you in your martial glory. Climb down all of you." He turned and called out "Stand down boys, friends." His men came around the corner. "Take these two lads and the horses into the courtyard and give them something to drink."

As they came forward, Otto recognised the tall, thin one.

"Don't tell me, Second Lucan, first cohort, second century. You were a decanus," he suggested

The veteran beamed. "That's me sir," he replied, delighted to have been remembered.

Otto sat on the bench. He nodded at the two men leading the horses away. "I see you're well prepared to receive visitors," he said.

"We look after ourselves out here. There's no-one to do it for us. I have this house, olive trees and an oil press, livestock, chickens and above all a wife and a son to defend.

"Congratulations, Titus, I also have a son."

"Still in Luca?"

"Nearby."

They lapsed into silence, then Attius spoke again.

"It's good to see you, young Otto and you're welcome to the hospitality of my home but you haven't ridden all the way out here to socialize."

He did not pose his remark as a question but a statement of fact. Otto told his story

"Up at Emporiae, a force of two and a half cohorts of praetorian infantry, two hundred and odd engineers and my three hundred cavalry are preparing to march inland. There are the usual support personnel, priests, medics, cooks and the rest. About two thousand two hundred in all. Our mission is to protect the engineers while they build a bridge and to stop thefts from an imperial goldmine. Praetorian Tribune Cassius Plancus commands, but…"

"Ah, I was waiting for the "But"," Attius said, interrupting Otto's explanation.

"One of the full cohorts is his own, the other is out of Veii and had to leave its tribune behind, the last one is only half strength and engineers are always troublesome…."

"I can see the tribune's problem. A legion has a chain of command to rely on but he has a couple of units vying to be top dog and the poor sods in the half cohort feel like they're going to be left to pick up the shit when the parade has passed by," Attius summarized. "Thank you for letting me know you have a problem."

"To solve it we need to introduce another officer subordinate to the tribune but out-ranking all of his centurions. How do you like the idea of taking a commission as Camp Prefect?" Otto asked.

"On what terms?"

"The duration of the commission will be a year and a day from the date you're sworn in or until given leave to resign. A legion prefect's pay and allowances for the full period whether served or not. I can offer you a signing-on bounty of three thousand denarii which I have in my saddle bags. We leave in ten days."

"Your tribune is prepared to make me this offer without ever having met me? Bit rash isn't he?"

"What I didn't tell you is that Boxer is building the bridge…"

"Young Lucius Longius?"

"The very same. We both spoke up for you…"

"Damn decent of you," Attius said, drily.

"You know what I mean, Titus. So, what do you say?"

"I say come in out of the sun and meet my household."

With that he rose and led Otto into the relative cool of the dim interior. The wife was clearly a local woman, her dark skin an inheritance from her ancestors who had come out of North Africa with Hannibal. She was strongly built, pretty and had luminous eyes. She and Titus spoke in a language Otto did not understand.

They ate a simple midday meal together then Titus pushed his chair back.

"I did not take kindly to being pushed out of my legion by that well-connected fop of a Broad Stripe Tribune; it left me with a sense of unfinished business, so I accept the offer. My family will go to my father-in-law's home in Tarraco city with my valuables and the good furniture. My lads will keep an eye on this place and two of my brothers-in-law will attend to the olive harvest and press the oil. Family, bloody useful when they aren't poking their noses in. You're leaving in ten days, you said?"

"I did," Otto replied with a grin.

"Then I'll be with you in good time. And Otto, thank you; perhaps after this I'll be able to say goodbye to soldiering and truly settle down."

The logistics of collecting supplies for over two thousand men and transporting it all were complex but the Roman Army was disciplined in more than battle. They made lists, counted goods in, gave receipts, passed counterfoils on so that the quartermaster's central ledger could be marked up. Wagons, spelt, fodder, horseshoe nails, oil, grease, saddlers' wax and thread, anything and everything they would need to travel to their destination and establish themselves was all docketed and loaded strictly according to plan..

Titus Attius had arrived two days before they were due to march. He was presented to Cassius, saluted and gave a short speech

"Sir, I am of the Centurionate. As I see it, the function of a camp prefect is fundamentally that of a senior centurion. You and the other officers should not have to be involved in the practicalities of the men's daily routines. You command and it is my task to ensure your soldiers are ready and fit to perform their duties. Do you agree, Tribune Plancus?"

"I do, Titus Attius."

"Then it is my privilege to take the oath as Camp Prefect under you, sir."

He spent his time walking around observing everything but saying nothing. He gave no orders. He made no comment. Cassius was on the verge of asking him what he was playing at but Titus forestalled him at dinner on their final night in Emporiae.

"I've seen all I need to see, sir. Tomorrow I intend to let the men know what I am all about. It will delay us for a couple of hours at most but it will be worth it. Do I have your permission?"

"As we agreed before you officially went onto the strength, such matters are for you to determine. I'm looking forward to seeing what you intend."

It was an invitation for Attius to expand but he said no more.

Men, horses, vehicles and draft animals were lined up for the inspection of their commanding officer before the order to move out was given. That was Titus Attius' chosen moment. He strode up to Cassius who was mounted on his charger, came to attention and saluted.

"With deep regret, Tribune Plancus, I must advise you that your soldiers are not in a fit state to proceed," he said in a booming voice which most of the assembled praetorians heard but none saw the wink he gave the tribune. Attius turned to face the men.

"Time I greeted you properly, boys. I am former First Spear Centurion of the Second Lucan, Titus Attius your Camp Prefect but you may call me "sir" or address me by my rank. Now, stands to reason I'm going to need a camp to be prefect of, but when I look at this fine body of men, do I see you all have a forked stick over your shoulder with a basket to collect the earth you dig up for me? Do I see an entrenching tool? No, I do not. Going to scrabble away at the ground with your bare hands to make me a ditch and rampart were you? Fall out by centuries and get your tools. First Cohort, first century, run! The longer you make the tribune wait, the angrier he will be with me and be sure I'll take it out on you lot. Second century, on your way, shift!" As they raced away to the transport and each hurried back with a standard legion forked pole, a "furca", with the required kit attached, Attius went on. "I know there are a few men among you who are praetorians because daddy arranged it so you could play soldiers in Rome and parade in front of the pretty girls. My sympathies, you didn't bank on this did you?" A low chuckle rose over the parade and a few faces flushed. "I also know that most of you are here because you've proved yourselves to be the finest soldiers and were rewarded by a transfer to the Praetorian Guard. But even the best of us get soft in garrison. Today, we begin to earn our pay again, lads." They were all equipped to his satisfaction but Attius was still not finished with them. "Senior centurion of the half cohort, on me at the double." The man trotted up and saluted. "Congratulations, you are now promoted to Camp Prefect Adjutant. Even I can't be everywhere at once. Get your optio over here." When he arrived he was given a temporary field promotion to centurion. Attius now played his final card. "Adjutant, since your men no longer have a senior centurion, they are to be integrated into the two full cohorts, half in each,. Your centuries will be allocated a number after the present second century but before the second from last. Liaise with the other seniors and all three of you bring me your plan by the end of the day after we have all eaten." He turned to Cassius and saluted once more. "With deepest apologies for their slack attention to detail, sir, I can confirm your men are finally ready for inspection."

He had taken just over one hour to solve the problem that had so troubled Cassius from the first day they had left Rome. Otto and Boxer had been right; Titus was a revelation.

"Masterly, Titus," the tribune told him over dinner.

"Thank you sir, just experience of soldiers. As soon as their senior centurion was removed, the half cohort felt uneasy. The seniors of the other two cohorts are now squabbling to get the best of 'em so they've become valued, not just the leftovers. Everyone's happy, for the moment."

"Quite, jolly well done. Tonight we can see the lights of Emporiae and have a secure line of retreat in case of attack. That will not be the case tomorrow. I propose to construct a full marching camp at the end of every day and dismantle it before we move on the next morning. Boxer, I understand that engineers are excused general construction duties on campaign, that privilege is withdrawn. Tomorrow your men will have to do their share. If you need any of them excused for a valid reason, see the Camp Prefect. Otherwise, they are expected to contribute to the ditch, rampart and palisade. Let me expand on my decision. Firstly, we are not a full legion so we don't have the numbers available to do all the work. Secondly, having to protect your wagons nearly doubles the length of the required perimeter. Your men will complain. Let them, as long as they dig."

Boxer bowed his head across the table to indicate his acceptance of the order. For the first time, Titus Attius looked at Cassius with respect for the man, not simply his rank.

The optio in charge of the four artillery pieces and their crews presented himself to Prefect Lucius Longius as soon as he heard the bad news.

"The tribune's order is for engineers, sir. We're artillerymen so it seems it don't apply to us."

"Not to you, optio, but the rest of your men better find themselves entrenching tools by the end of the day."

"Can't blame a man for trying, sir," he said with a grin.

The oxen that lumbered along the dusty roads hauling the heavy wagons defined the distance the column could travel each day. The marching men and the cavalry could not outstrip them without leaving their supplies and equipment open to attack. Progress was slow, especially since they were travelling uphill towards the faint blue smudge of the Pyrenaei on the horizon, but at least it was uneventful; until the eighth day after they had left the coast.

Their route took them through a semi-open region rich in olive groves and orchards of nut and fruit trees. In the distance, they saw a carriage flanked by four outriders converging on them from a side road. It drove onto the highway at the junction, a hundred and fifty yards ahead. A figure climbed down and walked to the front of his mules. He was portly, wearing a blindingly white toga in spite of the heat. He raised his right hand in a gesture for them to halt. Cassius cantered forward with Otto and Boxer on either side of him.

"I have the honour to be a member of the council of the Procurator appointed to govern this province on behalf of the Emperor. The Procurator is astonished that you have not shown him the courtesy of requesting an audience to explain your presence here..." the stranger declaimed in a rich baritone voice.

"Prefect Longius," Cassius barked.

"Sir," Otto and Boxer responded simultaneously.

A quick expression of irritation crossed the tribune's face.

"Otto, bring up a dozen of your men. They are to seize the bridles of this gentleman's mule carriage and lead it off the road. Do no damage. If anyone resists, deal with them severely."

The soldiers were still coming on, the German horsemen surrounded the vehicle and dragged the mules' heads around so they pulled it back onto the side road. The outriders sensibly raised their hands and followed it. The council member stood alone with a cloud of dust descending on and around him. The leading praetorians were now ten yards away and showed no sign of slowing their pace, let alone stopping. He leapt to the safety of the verge, astonished and furious in equal measure, ignored by the soldiers marching past.

At the midday halt, Cassius called an informal meeting of both prefects, Attius, his adjutant and the two senior centurions.

"Gentlemen we are fortunate to have with us Prefect of Engineers Lucius Taurius Longius and Prefect of Cavalry Otto Longius. Today I had urgent need of cavalry support and called for Prefect Longius. Of course, both officers answered. It occurs to me that this could be dangerous in an emergency. Suppose we were hard-pressed and I sent a runner for "Prefect Longius", who would attend me? Things quickly become confused in battle, if we let them. So with their permission, I propose that Lucius Taurius Longius is called "Prefect Boxer" among us. He was given that affectionate name in his first legion and I believe all the engineers and artillerymen use it among themselves. Will you agree, prefect."

"Certainly, sir, to avoid any future problems."

"Thank you. In all official correspondence my clerk will refer to by your proper name. Our cavalry prefect will be Prefect Otto. Camp Prefect, adjutant, centurions, you will see that this instruction is passed down through the ranks."

It was Boxer who raised the incident with the Procurator's official at dinner. Cassius glared at him.

"My men halt on my command, the order of the Emperor or if we need to deploy in face of an armed challenge; never because some local chief book-keeper wants to know our business."

But it did not end there.

Three days later they were confronted again, this time in an area where the road was bordered by broad pastures. A force of one thousand armed legionaries were formed up in three ranks across their path and the fields on either side. Four mounted officers stood in front of them, one holding a leafy green branch as a sign that they wanted a parley. Cassius responded by wheeling his horse around on the spot and shouting a stream of orders.

"Camp Prefect, triple rank on a front of four hundred. Remainder central reserve, less sixty to the wagons. Prefect Otto, one hundred and twenty troopers on each wing, the rest, join the wagon guard. Boxer, how quickly can you get me some artillery?"

"One scorpion still mounted on its cart to each flank in six minutes, sir"

"Do it."

Orders were bellowed in harsh voices, bugles sounded. Soldiers glided into their positions like machine parts. Eagles swayed on the end of their poles as they found their places in the line where men could rally if necessary. Horses cantered out onto the grass and reformed in two menacing masses of nodding manes and plumes, lance points glittering and winking. Dust swirled and settled. The artillerist frantically wound the torsion springs of the scorpions and then squatted at the ready with their three-foot iron bolts to hand. Suddenly all was silent again except for the sound of the horses champing their bits and their eager snorts as they pawed the earth.

It had been an awesome display. In minutes, a column of men had transformed into a battle line with a reserve force to the rear and cavalry on each flank. Cassius was now the only mounted officer in front of his men.

"Forward, slow march!" he yelled.

Titus Attius stood ahead of the centre of the front rank with his vine staff of office in his right hand and his sword still in its scabbard at his hip.

"Thump your spear against your shield with each pace lads. On me; one and two and one and two…"

The praetorians rolled forward with a rhythmic "Boom" each time the spear shafts hit the shield rims and their leading feet thudded into the hard ground. Thirty inches at a time, boom, boom, boom, they closed the distance between them and the unknown legionaries who confronted them. They no longer seemed to be an assembly of individual men but some great beast, scaled and spiked with iron and steel.

The din frightened the horse the officer holding the green branch was riding. It skittered and bucked making the leaves wave frantically which in turn scared the horse next it. That one reared up on its hind legs and backed into the front rank of legionaries, bowling over four of them. It kicked out as it was pushed away by the men still on their feet, flattening another two. Their long rectangular shields protected them from anything more serious than bruises. The confused knot of struggling men and whinnying horses enraged their leader who turned towards them and screamed out a torrent of threats and abuse. Order was restored by his First Spear Centurion who looked disgusted at the spectacle his men had made of themselves in the face of the praetorians advancing at the slow march.

When the opposing forces were twenty-five yards apart, Cassius considered he had achieved the desired effect.

"Halt!" he bellowed and sat calmly astride his horse. He stared at his opposite number who was purple in the face above his ornate cuirass moulded with abdominal muscles the owner had never possessed in reality. Since it quickly became obvious that Cassius was neither going to say nor do anything, he was forced to ride over. He opened his mouth to speak but the tribune was too quick for him.

"You can see that I lead praetorians, the Emperor's personal troops. I suggest that you remove your men from the road."

"I am the Procurator of the Imperial Province of Tarraconensis...."

"How nice for you. Tell me, do you enjoy the job?"

The Procurator spluttered, spittle foamed at the corners of his mouth as he fought to frame a reply. He took a deep breath.

"I demand to know who you are and what you are doing in my province...."

"Your province? Surely it is the Emperor's."

"You will not go on unopposed until I have some answers."

"Prefect Otto!" he called. Otto galloped in from his position on the right flank, pulling up with a flourish. "Ride over to my clerk and ask him to give you the document marked "Pass" in my valise." Otto saluted and spun away on Djinn who arched his neck and stepped proudly, showing off as he habitually did when all eyes were on him. While they waited, Cassius, smiled pleasantly, admired the view, inspected his nails and smiled once more, fully aware he was driving the Procurator to the verge of a seizure. Otto handed him a folded parchment. Cassius opened it and looked up at the man in front of him whose complexion had gone from purple to livid.

"I am going to read it to you first," he said. *"Let no-one hinder or impede the holder of this pass or his men anywhere in the Empire on pain of my deepest displeasure. On behalf of The Senate and People Of Rome Aug. Imp. Princeps"* Cassius intoned in a sonorous voice. Then he turned to Otto. "I am going to hand this document to the gentleman who is standing in our way. At the slightest hint that he is about to tear it or thrown it down into the dust, kill him for showing contempt towards our Emperor.

The Procurator looked at Otto and suppressed a shudder. There was no suggestion in those ice blue eyes that this German-looking officer would not do as instructed.

He read and returned it. "It seems I must move aside."

"Oh, a bit more than that, I think. Get them at least two hundred yards back off the road to avoid any unnecessary unpleasantness when we march on, there's a good chap," Cassius drawled.

"At least may I know your name?"

"Of course, Tribune Cassius Plancus, delighted to meet you."

A glint of triumph gleamed in the Procurator's eyes; the expression of a man who has unexpectedly turned the tables on an enemy.

"Well, young Cassius Plancus, you would be surprised how many people I know in Rome who will not be happy at the way I have been treated today."

"Was my late great-uncle Proconsul Lucius Munatius Plancus one of the people you know? The one who was The Divine Julius' general? Perhaps it is my father, the senator or his brother, also a senator. Maybe you know my mother's brother whose consulship ended three years ago? We all know people in Rome, Procurator. Good day to you."

They hired two guides at a village. Deep-chested, swarthy young men with powerful, short legs; mountaineers born and bred. Their Latin was basic but Titus Attius rattled away with them in the language Otto had first heard him speaking with his wife in their home.

"Local Iberian dialect," Titus explained. "My grandparents spoke no Latin, my parents used both tongues so I grew up with it. There may be others among the troops who understand it... might be useful to identify them"

There were six in all; two Praetorians, three engineers and an artilleryman.

The road became narrower and more pot-holed every day. Eventually they reached a gap between two jagged boulders. The guides pointed along the track between them.; this was the route they must take. They trudged on their way getting closer to the base of the mountains that now loomed above them casting long morning and afternoon shadows until they came out onto a grassy plain studded with rocks. They had arrived at their destination. The wheel-rutted path they had travelled led on southwards around the base of a sheer escarpment, the faces of which were broken and scarred with deep gullies. The rockface was not of one colour but light and dark in alternate bands which looked as if they had been spread one on top of the other like thick blankets but the layers rose and fell in frozen waves. They could see a few pine trees overhanging the top and some hardy shrubs had found toeholds in crannies where enough rainwater could accumulate to keep them alive. A zig-zag road had been carved up to the summit. Cassius and Otto looked at it in horror.

"We'll never get our wagons up that," the tribune said with finality.

Boxer laughed. "Never as bad as it looks at first, sir. Soon have it sorted out. I'll go up with a few of the more experienced men and study the ground then we'll be able to tell you how long it will take to make it fit for our transport."

"You mean how many months," Cassius said with a brief laugh.

Boxer looked at him reproachfully.

"Days, sir, days; you have the men and equipment, leave it to your engineers."

Boxer stripped to a tunic and boots and jammed a most unofficerly straw hat on his head before toiling up to the summit with half a dozen similarly dressed companions. They stopped at various points, obviously discussing what they saw, gesticulating and pointing and then reached the top and disappeared. Titus stood the men down. Horses were unsaddled and draft animals taken out of harness. Sentries were posted at strategic points and everyone else, man and beast dozed in the heat, flapping at the flies. Two hours later, Boxer was back. He took off his disreputable hat, wiped the sweat off his brow and saluted.

"Good news sir. Although its difficult to see from here, the face is sloping away from us."

"Marvellous," Cassius replied. "That's cheered me up no end. Tell me, what's good about it?"

"All to do with gradients. In fact, we have less to do than I thought. We shall clean up and fill in the existing road and then make two turning places for the oxen by widening the bends. Easy enough; we cut into the rock face and use the spoil to patch and level."

"Apologies for being flippant, Boxer. Your area of expertise is unknown territory to the rest of us. I now ask again but with more confidence this time, how long?"

"Three full days, all being well. Also, there's water up there. A spring comes out of a cleft in the mountainside. It runs away down into the ravine at the moment but we could build a culvert and use it."

"Very well, get us up there as quickly as possible. Otto, tomorrow you and fifty of your cavalry will ride with me all the way round and have a look at this fabled goldmine...."

"May I suggest you take one of my men with you? He's skilled in drawing plans and sketch maps. He could record the outline of the escarpment and estimate heights and distances..." Boxer said.

Cassius thought for a moment. "I can see how that might be useful. Can your man ride?"

"He would be better on a mule, sir."

A mule it is then. Let's hope for his sake we don't get into a fight; can't engage an enemy on muleback, eh? Camp Prefect, assume command in my absence."

Chapter 11

After riding for an hour, the nature of the road changed under the feet of Cassius' reconnaissance party. Deep wheel ruts where heavy transport passed diverged away from the cliffs towards the south and east to be lost from sight between the chaos of rock and stone strewn around the landscape.

"Bullion shipments," Cassius said to no-one in particular.

They followed the wagon tracks around the land-locked peninsula. Towards sundown, they found a trickle of water emerging from under a large rock which was enough to let men and animals drink their fill, then they settled for the night. Three sentries climbed onto high points and the rest clustered together, men and horses, in the light of a feeble fire of thorny branches. In the morning they rode on. Around noon the ground began to rise and fall steeply. The cliff face to their right was less fissured and almost vertical. After a midday break, they crested a rise and saw the mine laid out below them. It was astounding and completely unexpected.

Both Cassius and Otto had thought they would see the entrances of tunnels cut into the rock but there were none. Rectangular constructions of stone and concrete perched high on the mountainsides. Aqueducts, culverts and leats ran into and out of them, some dry, some filled with water trickling down into the natural bowl below them.

Smoke rose from the tall chimney of a building hidden with many others behind a palisade on the hillside opposite them. They saw a large group of men climbing the far-side hill and collecting at the foot of a wooden tower halfway up. Faint whistles blew, a flag rose and fell on the top of the tower. A torrent of white water burst out of one of the structures on the mountain into a sluice which directed it onto the hillside beneath. The water smashed into it, ripping bushes, soil and gravel down in roaring, foaming, brown chaos into an empty reservoir. Within five minutes, the area was stripped to the underlying rock. The flow diminished then ceased.

Otto pointed up at the mysterious structures they had first seen, "They're not forts or buildings, they're tanks."

"Yes but where's the water coming from?" Cassius asked.

The whole chequerboard of pools, some empty, some filled with yellow water, some with clear, reflecting the blue of the sky, covered a mile in either direction with pathways wide enough for three horses abreast running between and around them.

They had been noticed. A rider threaded his way along the causeways and up the slope towards them. He was in civilian clothing, a cheerful, open-faced man.

"Greetings, gentlemen. May I escort you to the mine superintendent's office? He will be delighted to meet you, I'm sure; we so seldom have visitors."

It took them three-quarters of an hour to descend and ride up to the palisade. The gates were open and they trotted into a large yard filled with smoke and dust and there was an incessant low vibration beneath their feet, unsettling the horses.

"It's the trip hammer, it crushes ore, sirs. We don't notice it anymore," their escort explained with a brief laugh.

The mine superintendent was a man built on epic lines. A massive head sat on a thick neck over sloping shoulders. His chest was deep with a generous belly straining his tunic. He shook their hands in a calloused, meaty fist. He nodded a greeting to the engineer and beamed.

"Welcome, welcome," he said in his usual overloud voice; years of working with noisy machinery had damaged his hearing and he had almost to shout simply to hear himself speaking. "I am Sextus Tubero and I have the honour to manage this enterprise on behalf of our Emperor. Do you want the tour? Of course you do! Everyone wants the tour although we receive few guests. I expect you've already been told that. This way, gentlemen, this way…" He practically, pushed them out in his enthusiasm and led them around his kingdom hurling facts at them, most of which passed by Otto and Cassius but which Boxer lapped up. They saw raw, alluvial gold and some ore being smelted, the product smashed down into granules by the waterwheel-driven triphammers and then re-smelted with salt to remove lead, copper and silver. Finally, an iron crucible was lifted from the furnace with tongs and a stream of pure, liquid gold poured out of it into a mould before their eyes.

"There," said Tubero with immense satisfaction. "What do you think of that?"

"Those hammers driven by water-power, I've never seen anything like it," Boxer said in awe.

"Nor will you have young man. A device developed by the genius Virtuvius and just beginning to come into use. We have the most up to date machinery in the world right here!"

"Magnificent, it will change how we do so many things!"

"Indeed. And now our treasury."

They strode across the gritty yard and stopped at a stone building with an iron-reinforced door. Tubero knocked. A hatch opened. They were scrutinized from inside and then the door was swung back by a legionary who saluted. They were inside an iron cage. Two further soldiers regarded them through the bars before unlocking an inner gate. They were now admitted to the single room contained within the thick stone walls. Barred windows were set into the walls, none of them big enough to let even a boy crawl through.

"Our sentries have to have some light and air," Tubero explained. "We don't want them suffocating or going mad in the dark, ha ha!"

He went to the neat stack of shallow wooden chests in the centre of the floor, flung open the lid of the top one. It was filled with neat rows of gold ingots, five inches long and as thick as a man's thumb.

"One pound in weight, forty to the chest and twenty-five chests, one thousand pounds in all, make up a shipment. This is what all the rushing water, fire and smoke and hammering is all about: these little metal rods. Now, let me offer you some refreshment."

They sat in Tubero's office at a table eating bread and olives with a jug of much better wine than could have reasonably been expected.

"How do you refill those tanks up on the mountainside?" Cassius asked.

"Oh they fill themselves; we diverted a river," Tubero told him casually, as if that was all in a day's work.

"And what are all those pools for?"

"Settlement ponds, we call them. When the water is clear in a pond the silt has sunk to the bottom. We pump it dry and carefully remove the earth revealing the gold bearing layer underneath. Gold is heavy you see."

"Must need a lot of slaves…." Otto began'

"No, not at all. This is highly skilled work. A man who really knows his trade can spend ten years on the mine and go home and buy himself a nice little farm if he's careful with his money. There are some slaves of course to do the menial work but we need top-notch, trained citizens here."

At that moment the door opened and a soldier stepped in, removing his helmet as he entered. He saw the two officers, saluted and bowed.

"Centurion Ennius Frugi, sirs," he barked in formal military fashion.

"At ease centurion," Cassius told him and introduced himself and Otto by rank and name.

Frugi bowed again.

"Will you not join us, if the superintendent is agreeable?" the tribune asked.

Tubero nodded and Frugi sat on the bench beside the engineer who moved up for him. Otto and Cassius were trying not to stare. The centurion was the best-looking man either of them had ever seen. His forehead was broad and high under a mass of black curls. His eyes were large and brilliant, wide-set either side of an aquiline nose. His chin was strong and virile and his lips finely chiselled. He had the bodily proportions of a classical Greek statue of a wrestler. If he knew what impression he had made, he showed no sign of it as he reached for the olive bowl.

"You command the garrison here, Centurion Frugi?" Cassius asked.

"I do sir. One hundred and fifty men, almost two full centuries."

"Alone?"

"I have two excellent optios."

"We did have another centurion and a tribune but they were sadly lost," Tubero said.

"How lost?" Otto enquired.

"Robbers on the road to Tarraco. Thanks to the centurion and his men, we are well protected here but our gold is so vulnerable in transit."

"Don't your men escort the gold, Frugi?" asked Cassius.

"That was how it used to be done but after the murder of the tribune and the other centurion together with some of the legionaries, we have changed the system. We now use a haulage contractor who provides his own armed guards. In any case, they are quicker. Our soldiers are all infantry, you see," Tubero replied on his behalf

"Cavalry's next to useless around here," Frugi added. "The ground is so broken up with rocks, there isn't room for them to deploy."

"And is the haulier's wagon ever attacked by thieves?" Otto asked.

"Yes, on occasion. They have lost several men but never an entire load. Two, three chests at most."

"But they add up. The Emperor has sent us here to assist by building a bridge across the ravine that divides the plateau. We are making the far side road usable and when all the works are finished, it will reduce the time your consignments are in transit by two days or more." Cassius informed them.

"There was a native stronghold up there at one time, I believe," Frugi said. "Far be it from me to question your mission, sir, but without a road to the top on this side, I don't see how it will help."

It was at this point the engineer spoke for the first time.

"Unnecessary, centurion; I have noticed a narrow path climbing the cliff but there has clearly been a rockfall at some time which has sheered away the top forty feet or so. However this is not a major problem because all we need is a mule track. A good mule will carry two chests over the bridge to the other side where they can be loaded onto a wheeled vehicle. Half a morning's work with a mule train, sir, your gold under supervision at all time and thirty-five miles cut off your journey."

"That sounds first-rate for us, Centurion Frugi," Tubero said.

The centurion smiled and nodded. Otto thought he had seen that sculpted jaw tighten when the engineer had been speaking. Perhaps it had no significance but a seed of suspicion had been planted by the involuntary facial tic.

"Well, it's been a delight. Thank you so much for the fascinating tour, superintendent; most instructive," Cassius said which was the signal for Otto and the engineer to rise from the table with him.

Frugi saluted and left.

"What is the name of your haulier, superintendent?" Otto asked. "We may need someone reliable for our supplies."

"Pinarius, his warehouse is on the dockside, as you might expect. Can't miss it. It's got "Pinarius and Son" written across the doors."

"What's all this about supply lines, Otto?" Cassius asked that night as they sat by the fire, well on their way back to their base.

"Just an excuse for the question. I think we should take an interest in this Pinarius character. He might be involved in the robberies."

"Agreed. In any case, I shall have to have a word with the quartermaster, tedious man. You're right, we will need to be re-supplied at some point. What about that chap Boxer sent with us, eh? A mule track! Never thought of such a thing did you?"

"No, but one thing serving with our Prefect of Engineers taught me is that they see everything differently."

When they arrived back at their base, there were few men to be seen. Under the gaze of the quartermaster, they were unloading wagons and stacking equipment and supplies.

"What's going on and what have you done with my soldiers?" Cassius demanded.

A decanus saluted. "Up top sir," he said.

"Up top", the plateau seemed bigger than it appeared on the sketch map. It was covered in low scrub and coarse grass through which the tops of rocks, some of them substantial, emerged. Where it butted into the broken mountainsides towering above it, a group of engineers was busily hacking out a ditch. It would be lined with stone to carry the spring water nearer to where their camp was under construction. They walked their horses carefully across. Titus Attius supervised twelve hundred Praetorians, stripped to their tunics who were working with spades, crowbars and improvised wooden levers. The rest stood by, fully armed; Attius was always cautious in ensuring his men had the means of repelling a surprise attack, even three hundred feet above the plain. He threw them a brisk salute.

"Greetings, sirs," he called.

"Report, Camp Prefect Attius," Cassius replied after returning the salute.

"Construction of a stronghold sir. Ground unsuitable for a standard ditch and rampart but we are uncovering a large amount of dressed stones. Must have been a substantial fortress here at one time. We are aiming for a square breastwork with foot-traps around it. Should be six feet high with a fighting step in three days."

"As you think best, where's Prefect Boxer?"

"Over there sir, studying the ravine with his contraptions."

The instruments were the basic Roman surveying tools, the groma, which they had all seen before; an upright rod bearing plumb bobs and a pair of rotating set squares used to set out straight lines but also something new to them. A low table with a sighting groove on the long side, a water reservoir and yet more plumb bobs dangling underneath.

"I give up, Prefect Boxer, what is that?" Cassius called.

Boxer grinned. "It's a chorobates, Tribune Plancus," he said and then fell into silence.

"Alright, what's it do?" Otto asked.

"It measures the level between two points."

"Of course it does, obvious now you mention it. What progress has been made in our absence?" Cassius asked.

"The road is now prepared so we can start to haul everything up tomorrow…"

"So why are men unloading?"

"The ten span ox wagons are too long to go around the bends in the road fully loaded so we need to use the smaller ones. We'll bring up the big wagons empty with a four oxen."

"Can't they just be left there, under guard?" Otto asked.

"They were never intended to go back with us. They were designed to be taken to pieces and the timber used for bridging material. Meanwhile, I've got four men climbing up into the mountains to see if they can find a way to cross this ravine higher up and come back out on the other side.

Otto and Cassius were clearly superfluous so they descended again. Otto rode off to his men who were half a mile away. They had found a meadow with lush grass and a brook at the edge where they were grazing their horses.

Cassius had a long conversation with the irritable quartermaster; he always seemed to be harassed, it went with the job. He reported that they had enough food for six weeks but supply lines should be established as soon as possible.

"Speak to me again after dinner." Cassius told him.

Neither Otto nor Cassius witnessed the arrival of Boxer's men out of the mountains a little before sundown. Two carried long iron spikes, each bent into a ring at one end, the other two had sledgehammers and a bow. They thumped the spikes deep into the stony ground five feet back from the ravine edge and three feet apart. An arrow with a cord tied to it was fired over from the opposite side, it was attached to a rope. They began to pull and steadily drew the cord and the rope over, threaded it through the rings and shot the arrow back. The far-side men dragged it over to them, slid two pulleys on either side and secured it. There were now two parallel ropes stretching the width of the chasm. A three-foot plank was strung under the pulleys with a thinner rope attached to the back and a coil at the front. Boxer sat on the crude seat and began to work himself across, hand over hand.

The rope sagged deep into the gloomy maw beneath him. It creaked under the strain and his narrow perch swung left and right as he changed his hand grip but he carried on determinedly. For the second half, he was dragging his weight uphill as he had passed the lowest point and his slender lifelines now stretched upwards. With burning shoulder joints, he felt a huge surge of relief as his men helped him back onto firm ground. The end of the coil of rope he had carried with him was tied off.

"Well done lads, a good day's work. Let's get back and have something to eat," he told them when he had caught his breath. "One at a time, eh?"

The first crossed but the second man looked down into the depths and baulked.

"Can't I climb back round the way we came, sir?" he pleaded.

Before Otto could answer his comrades rounded on him."No you fucking can't. You're not going to let the engineers down in the face of that lot are you?" he pointed over to where Titus Attius and his praetorians had ceased their toil for the day and were lined up to watch the fun.

"Get on or I'll chuck you in myself," another said.

Whey-faced, he swallowed and straddled the narrow plank. He was partially hauled up the steep side by his comrades across the void hauling on the rope attached to the seat. When he was half dragged onto the lip of the ravine and stood up. The assembled soldiers cheered. Titus did not silence them.

"That was risky," Titus told Boxer at dinner.

"Following your example, Camp Prefect; you never led men where you were afraid to go yourself."

Otto got up, wished them goodnight and went to bivouac with his men as he always did. Cassius watched his retreating back fading into the darkness.

"Centurion at the mine said cavalry were ineffective in this terrain. Not enough open spaces," Cassius mused aloud.

Titus laughed. "Have you ever seen German cavalry in action?" the tribune said that he had not. "No, and neither has that prick, I bet. Our Roman tactic is to position them on each flank and make them ride down on the opposition knee to knee. Germans can do that and a lot more. They're used to fighting in deep forests, along narrow paths. They explode out of the trees howling and they're through a column and gone before the first dead men hit the ground. I've seen them leap out of the saddle, run forward and gut a couple of the enemy horses then remount and go at the rest of 'em with the lance. And I have seen the Equestrian Imperial Prefect Otto Longius in battle…"

"So have I, at the ambush on the Sequana…" Cassius put in.

Titus waved him away. "…That was nothing. See him in the field when hundreds or thousands clash! That's when he comes into his own. Just to know he's there gives men courage; or strikes fear into their hearts. Believe me, he and his men will be effective enough if they're needed."

"The Emperor didn't give us our Germans on a whim. He thinks of everything," Boxer said.

"So you two assert that they are better than Romans?"

"Man for man, on horseback with an axe or a spear, my money's on them every time," Titus told him.

Boxer nodded his agreement.

"Far be it from me to disagree then," Cassius shrugged.

The quartermaster arrived with his inevitable lists, saluted and reminded Cassius that they had arranged to speak after dinner. They talked for a full hour and agreed a procedure. They would buy what they needed in Emporiae as it was the closest large centre. Otto and Boxer were asked if they had any requirements. Otto had none but Boxer wanted more rope and iron rods; engineers always wanted more supplies; they hoarded them like squirrels. In the morning, Otto was ordered to escort the quartermaster and see him safely back once his negotiations were completed.

"And Pinarius at Tarraco?" Otto enquired of Cassius.

"Whoever we approach to buy oil or spelt or whatever will demand outrageous prices so it'll take a few days to come to a compromise. Use that time to have a word with this Pinarius type but don't leave the poor old quartermaster without a couple of men. He always strikes me as a helpless sort of chap, don't you think?"

Otto left with his charge and four troopers. At Emporiae he saw the quartermaster settled and assigned two men to protect him, riding on to Tarraco with the other pair. They descended out of the hills and into the city on a cloudless day. The sea was almost still, brilliant blue with silvery flashes when small waves rose and fell. Keen eyed gulls glided overhead on the lookout for food, celebrating with raucous cries when one of them spotted some offal or a crust. The smell of tar, fish and timber baking in the cruel sun grew stronger as they rode into the dock area. The streets became narrower, winding between high tenements with washing drying on poles sticking out of the upper windows. A wineshop or a brothel advertised the luxury of the establishment on most of the corners. They broke out onto the wide expanse of the waterfront; boats being scraped of barnacles, nets drying in the sun while dexterous fishermen repaired them. Amphorae, crates, barrels in random heaps and everywhere people passing to and fro; some clerks, others seamen, all busy with the commerce of the dockside.

Otto stopped a man pushing a handcart.

"Greetings, friend. Where is Pinarius' warehouse?"

He did not bother to look up but simply said, "Sod off."

This struck Otto as the most absurd response to a polite question. He laughed aloud. The handcart proprietor looked up at the sound. It unsettled him. He trundled off at high speed with Otto's laughter following him. A tall, older man with a wax tablet and a sheaf of dockets in his hands stopped and addressed him.

"Pay no attention to that one, sir. You do right to laugh at him; he is beneath contempt. Did I hear that you are looking for Pinarius?"

"I am."

"Keep the sea on your left and go straight on for half a mile."

"Thank you for your help, sir."

"You are welcome and apologies for that pig who calls himself a citizen of Tarraco."

The high front walls of Pinarius' business premises ran parallel with the dock. The double doors were flung back, one saying "Pinari" and the other "us & Son". A cobbled yard was filled with wagons and carts. Horses stamped in stables along the walls. A cartwright's workshop and a forge hunched under lean-to roofs. A solid, three storey building housed storage areas and an office. Otto asked a worker for Pinarius and he came back with a tiny dark man, brisk of movement with something of the bird about the rapid glance of his bright eyes. He leaned back and looked up at Otto.

"You're a German," he stated, almost an accusation.

"I'm a Roman Citizen, a Knight and an Imperial Prefect."

Pinarius pointed at the troopers. "They're Germans, then," he said.

"They are."

"They look fearsome with the beards and all that plaited yellow hair."

"I command three hundred of them," Otto told him conversationally.

"You must be a tough bastard. What's your name?"

One of the escort spoke a little Latin. He was becoming offended at the way this little man was talking to Otto. "He is Otto Kingkiller," he interrupted gruffly.

"Kingkiller? Why do they call you that?"

"Because I have killed kings."

"Dis and Hecate preserve us all! I'm not a king so you don't have to kill me; I'm Pinarius. Would you care to dismount so you can tell me what you want with me in my office?

It was a high-ceilinged room, cool after the yard outside. To Otto's surprise it was spotlessly clean and neat. One wall was taken up with pigeonholes from which the end of scrolls protruded. Pinarius' desk was clear except for a squared-off stack of correspondence waiting his attention. Two clerks worked at smaller desks in a corner.

"I am Prefect Otto Longius commanding an ala of cavalry to protect the construction work the Emperor requires at his mine. Superintendent Tubero gave me your name, I told him I was looking for a reliable haulier for our supplies. That was not true. I wanted to speak to you about the thefts of the Emperor's gold."

"Thank you for being honest with me, prefect. Do you suspect me?

"I don't know yet. Tell me how the system works."

"Very well, excuse me," he called over to his clerks, "Take a break for a while. I'll call you when I want you." They put down their pens and left. Pinarius smiled at Otto. "They are trustworthy men but when it comes to gold?" He shrugged and left the question hang in the air. He walked over to the pigeonholes and pulled out a scroll which he unrolled and spread out, taking a seat on the same side of the desk as Otto. "This is a record of my transactions with the goldmine. I have carried nineteen cargos for them, see? Monthly, a four-wheeled cart hauled by six mules leaves my yard and returns with the consignment which goes into the garrison fort to be unloaded under military supervision," He pointed at a second group of figures and dates. "Seven robberies have occurred, total amount stolen thirty-two chests...."

"How can you afford to repay this amount?" asked Otto.

Pinarius chuckled. "I can't and I'm not required to. The mine carries the deficit. No-one could contract to indemnify against the possibility of theft on the road. In cases where there have been attacks, I report to the magistrate and make a deposition to him with whatever witnesses he thinks necessary. So far he has accepted that I am innocent of any collusion."

"Who loads your transport?"

"Tubero checks each chest, seals it and the legionaries count it over to me and put it on the cart themselves"

"And your guards?"

"Usually twenty, sometimes more. They're casuals. Tarraco is a seaport as you might have noticed. There's never a shortage of hard men hanging around docks willing to take a risk for ready money. Paid-off sailors waiting for their next ship mostly. I pay them a lot of money and those who come back in one piece think it's worth it. And before you ask me if they could be responsible, they come and go, seldom the same men twice so it's unlikely."

"Surely the soldiers at the mine...."

"Met Centurion Frugi have you?

"Yes."

"The celebrated "Adonis" Frugi; the latest sprig of an old family around here," Pinarius chuckled. "Most of the local women and quite a few of the men around melt if he just casts a smile their way. He has convinced Tubero that the security of the mine depends on him and his men being there, not out on the road. He may have a point, maybe he has other reasons for saying that. Just before my involvement eleven chests were stolen in two raids. One robbery cost the life of a junior tribune, the other a centurion and eight legionaries between them.. That's when they asked me to handle the freight. By contracting it out to me, they hope the mine can keep working on the basis of an acceptable level of loss. Also, anyone who gets killed defending the bullion is of little account to the official mind. Not that I make any money out of the arrangement."

"Master Pinarius, you are a man of commerce, why carry on if there is no profit in it?"

"Prestige, Prefect Longius, prestige; all the ships' captains and merchants know the house of Pinarius is trusted to carry gold for our Emperor. This gives them confidence in my enterprise so they do business with me. I suppose you would say I do profit but not directly."

"Is there anything else you could tell me?"

"The raids have all been within two day's journey of the mine. I'm told that as soon as they've got through the third morning unharmed, my wharf rats give a cheer."

"Thank you for your frank replies and for your time sir," Otto said, rising to his feet. He turned at the door. "Oh, and of course I don't suspect you."

Pinarius nodded and smiled but secretly gave a sigh of relief.

As he rode out through a narrow lane, a prostitute shouted down from her first-floor balcony.

"Oi, General; I'll do all three of you and only charge for two. You can go first if you're fussy. How's that for an offer?"

Otto reached into his purse and tossed her a silver coin. "Better offer, take the afternoon off now you've been paid."

He liked the people of Tarraco. They seemed frank and confident.

Chapter 12

On the face of it, Saxa looked bored most of the time. This was not quite the full story. She enjoyed her discrete fencing lessons with Lollia, she liked to ride out with her around the estate, always accompanied by one of the off-duty cavalrymen on Felix's insistence, but otherwise she felt her life to be without purpose. She visited Sabina and Aelia Longius with Lollia, sometimes they went to see Poppaea Longius who was full of her new husband and house. Occasionally Lollia's mother, Clodia came to visit for a few days. Every social gathering was the same. The women sat and nibbled snacks, drank fruit juice or heavily watered wine and chatted. Saxa's Latin had improved to the level where she could speak and understand easily in a one-to-one conversation but she struggled to follow what was being said in a group when people did not finish sentences or broke in on each other. Mostly she remained silent, smiled when spoken to directly, framing a simple reply.

Sabina did not have a high opinion of her. "That girl sends a shudder through me every time she looks at me. She has those pale, cold eyes like her brother. She's as much a monster as he is."

"Otto is a fine man to whom we owe much," Aelia reproved her.

Sabina shrugged. "He's still a monster though. It's just that he's our monster now."

Saxa had been physically active for most of her life. She had planted and harvested crops, made fires, ground corn and performed the thousand different tasks Suevi women did to keep themselves and their families fed and sheltered. But that was over, there was no contribution she was allowed to make to her brother's household. It had been made clear to her that she was not welcome in the kitchen. Tullia was queen of that realm and there was no room in it for the master's sister. With nothing better to do, Saxa spent her days nibbling with half-understood chatter in her ears or shopping for nothing she really needed in the market. It was not enough.

Libius had a lean-to workshop behind the laundry. It had a tiled roof and a short chimney from which strange smelling steam sometimes billowed into the yard. One morning she opened the door and poked her head in. Libius saw the light move across the wall in front of him, turned, nodded a greeting and shyly indicated a high stool. She sat and watched. He had two pots on his small stove and he was vigorously stirring first one then the other. Satisfied, he poured both into a larger pot and took a stiff brush, beating the contents into a froth. When his wrist ached, he left the brush where it was and flexed his fingers. Saxa stood up and took over. Libius looked unhappy but she smiled and nodded to reassure him.

Eventually he gently held her hand so that she stopped whisking and he covered the pot with an oiled parchment lid. She pointed and gestured making grimaces to try to indicate she wanted to know what he was doing. He looked at her blankly for a moment or two then understood. He took a jar off the shelf and tipped a little brown powder on his bench, then he uncovered the pot and dipped a paint brush into it. He mixed the powder with his concoction and drew the outline of a bird on the wall. Saxa smiled broadly and nodded to show she understood that this was how he made his paints. Their friendship blossomed over Libius' mixture of soapy water and beeswax.

Saxa began to spend time with Libius everyday. She progressed from helping to make the medium to grinding the minerals he used for different colours and, finally, mixing paint. Tullia and Plotina did not approve, which was obvious from their pursed lips when they spoke of the pair of them. Plotina scowled and banged about the kitchen irritably. Didia took it on herself to tell tales to Lollia.

"You must not spend too much time with Libius," Lollia advised her sister in law. "It isn't suitable."

"Why?"

"Well, social rank. He is a freed slave ..."

"So am I."

"Yes but it isn't the same."

"Isn't it? Otto took us both to the magistrate and he gave each of us a paper. How is it not the same?"

Lollia could not say but she was sure it wasn't. She went to Sabina and Aelia to ask their advice about the growing closeness between Saxa and Libius.

"It's grotesque!" Sabina told her. "The sister of an Equestrian and Imperial Prefect consorting with a deaf freed man! Our families will be laughing-stocks. Don't forget Lollia, your husband adopted our name when he was given citizenship so it reflects on us. All this comes of his eccentric idea of freeing everyone in sight. I always knew it would end badly. There is only one thing to do; whip this man from your door and forbid Saxa to see him again."

"If you whip a freed man you might end up in front of the magistrate and I doubt if Saxa will accept being forbidden," Aelia told them.

"But it is wrong!" Sabina said.

"Is it?" Aelia responded. "I don't know about that but it is perfectly understandable. Both of them are outsiders, both of them have problems in communicating; what more natural than that there should be some sympathy between them?"

"All I say is that Otto would not allow it if he was here." Sabina told them with finality.

The camp had changed during Otto's visit to Emporiae and Tarraco. There was now a rectangular breastwork redoubt seven feet high with a shallow ditch around it. It had been constructed with the stone blocks they had retrieved, reinforced with the trunks of the few pine trees that had grown on the plateau. Their timber had also been made into gates in opposing walls. It was big enough to contain all the men and their stores but not the livestock.

The mules and oxen were down below guarded by Otto's cavalrymen who roved the area looking for fresh grazing each day. So many streams and rivulets flowed out of the mountains, that there was still plenty of herbage so late in the summer and no shortage of water for the beasts. If the animals were happy the men were not.

"We are warriors not cattle drovers," one of them complained to his decurion who reported his comment to Otto.

Otto gathered all of them together. "Among the men Prince Aldermar sent me are many who are accustomed to serving alongside Romans. They know that they do not wage war as we do in our own lands or over the Rhine. Here we must wait scores of days for one hour of glory but when that hour comes, it is truly glorious and something you will boast about for the rest of your lives. Be patient, you will have your chance; it often comes when you least expect it."

A number of mature cavalrymen, some with the first hints of grey in their hair and beards, nodded their agreement. Otto secretly shared their discontent. He felt that he and his cavalry were being marginalized but he had to admit he could not see a central role for them in this mission.

There was now a narrow channel carrying spring water into the redoubt where it collected into a shallow pool. A pair of the praetorians who had served in Syria had made a shadouf to lift it into wooden troughs. They set an upright pole with a swivelling cross beam at the top into the ground. On one end of the beam was a bucket, on the other a counterweight. They dipped the bucket into the pool and emptied it in a trough, the counterweight greatly reducing the labour required to heave three gallons of water at a time into the air. The overspill ran out across the ground and found its eventual way over the edge.

Titus Attius had consulted with Boxer and had a latrine constructed one hundred yards downwind of the bridge works. It was a long, suitably perforated cantilevered bench, that leaned two and a half feet over the edge of the outer cliff. Boxer had refused outright to have it over "his" ravine.

"If anyone's constipated, look through the hole before you sit down, that'll loosen your bowels a treat, my boys. Oh, and the man who drops an arse-wiping sponge climbs down and fetches it."

"There's no roof and walls, Camp Prefect," someone moaned.

"Shy are we? There's no cover because it isn't cold and wet. When it is, I might consider closing it in, dismissed."

Seasoned campaigners like Titus Attius knew that positioning latrines as far as possible away from the sleeping tents and cook fires reduced enteric problems among the troops but no-one knew why. It was the accepted wisdom that bad smells caused disease.

Boxer's frail ropeway to the other side of the chasm had been replaced with a stout pair of sheer-legs, secured with guy ropes and carrying thick cables on each side. A cradle on pulleys large enough for two men now scuttled back and forth. A scaffold hung low over the nearest edge to support the engineers who spent all day cutting into the rock with picks, hammers and cold chisels. The effort was so great that they could work two-hour shifts only. Then, covered in dust plastered to them by their own sweat, arm muscles trembling, they gave way to fresh men.

Where Boxer proposed to build his bridge, the gap was eighty-nine feet wide.

"Not ninety, old thing?" Cassius had asked when he was told.

"No," Boxer replied without the slightest acknowledgment the tribune might have been joking. "It has been measured precisely using knotted strings. I intend to widen it to one hundred feet and create a twelve feet wide step four feet down…"

"Wait a minute, you're going to make it even wider?"

"We have to have a level base and a vertical wall each side for the foundations."

"You sure? Seems an awful lot of work to me."

"It is a lot of work but if its done properly, the bridge won't fall down, which is rather the point."

So the men on the hanging scaffolds patiently cut one horizontal and two vertical lines into the living rock every day. When they had gone in deep enough, others used twist drills and wedges to break away the section from above and let it crash down into the void. They were chewing their way through at a rate of between nine inches and one foot a day.

Because he spent the night with his cavalrymen and Boxer was constantly busy during the day, Otto had little time to talk with his old friend, which they both regretted but the officers always ate together. One casual remark of Otto's over dinner the day he came back from his sortie with the quartermaster turned out to be highly significant. He was reporting his conversation with Pinarius when he mentioned Centurion Frugi.

"What, Adonis Frugi," Titus interrupted.

"Yes."

"Met him, have you?"

"Yes, he's the centurion in charge of security at the mine."

"Is he now?" Titus mused. "Last time I heard of him he was breaking hearts in Tarraco; optio in the garrison, he was then. The city girls must have wept buckets when he was transferred. His people go back a long way around here."

"Do you know the family?" Otto asked.

"Not personally but it's general knowledge that the grandfather was one of Pompey's officers. Took his discharge and married a local girl from a mountain village. He had a good farm. His son took it over and they were doing very well then the Civil War broke out. They lost the lot. Adonis's mother was also a local. Some sort of native princess as far as the story goes. Odd lot in the mountains; Iberians and Arverni from the Gallic side all mixed up…."

"Did you say Arverni?" Boxer asked.

"Yes."

"The leader of the Great Revolt that nearly cost us Gaul was an Arverni."

"Oh come off it old boy! He was defeated at Alesia over forty years ago. Are we going to involve the Gauls in the Emperor's conspiracy theory?" Cassius snorted.

Both Boxer and Titus looked at the other two questioningly.

"Prefect Otto, Tribune Plancus, you have not been completely frank with me nor with Prefect Boxer it seems," Titus said coldly. "Why are we here if we don't have your full trust?"

"That's not the case...." Cassius began.

"Then what is?" Boxer broke in.

Otto and Cassius looked at each other. Otto shrugged. Cassius nodded and began to speak.

"The Emperor believes that the gold stolen from this mine may be intended to finance a coup against him by certain disaffected men of influence in Rome. The Civil War was not so long ago and every old wound hasn't skinned over. He believes Pompey's name could be used as rallying cry. That's all. We were ordered to tell no-one."

"Not even the officers serving with you?" Titus demanded coldly.

"No, not even you, unless it became necessary."

"And now it is necessary?" Boxer enquired.

"I believe it is," Otto replied.

"So how much missing bullion are we taking about?" Titus asked.

"Twelve hundred and eighty pounds in less than two years, plus the lives of a tribune, a centurion and I don't know how many legionaries and hired guards," Otto told him.

"Let me get this right. Augustus imagines there is a dangerous group scheming to bring him down. Centurion Adonis Frugi's grandfather fought for Pompey and his mother and grandmother may or may not have been Arverni, so he must be one of the conspirators…All a bit tenuous," Boxer said.

"Never mind Arverni, there are plenty of Iberian tribes who have no love for the Imperial Family. This was Pompey's province, his and his sons, for a long time," Titus added. "Is that everything?"

"Yes," Cassius, nodded to emphasis the truth of his assertion.

"Not quite," Otto intervened. "I left Rome ahead of the column. I was carrying confidential documents. Two men stopped me within a few hours ride of the city. I took a ring off the body of one of them. It had "Pom. Mag." inscribed inside."

Titus whistled and a keen glance passed between him and Boxer. Cassius reddened with annoyance.

"You never told me this," Cassius snapped. "Where is this ring now?"

Otto hesitated, choosing his words with care. "In the hands of a friendly agent."

"Who?" Cassius demanded.

"An agent who is friendly…"

Cassius sighed. "Fair enough." He looked over at Boxer and Titus. "That's definitely all there is. You know everything, including information that was news to me a few moments ago. Thing is, gentlemen, can we go on from this point with confidence in each other?" They agreed that they could.. "I think we should give Otto's information some thought and reconvene tomorrow to address the issues it raises.

The next day Cassius opened the meeting.

"Something Camp prefect Attius said during our first discussion stuck in my mind. If I may quote your words, "This was Pompey's province, his and his sons for along time," is that correct?" Titus confirmed it was. "In which case." Cassius went on, "it is reasonable to presume that a large number of the local Roman population had ties to Pompey. This means that Centurion Frugi's background is commonplace in this area. We do not have anything specific to tie him to the robberies and I suggest we do or say nothing which could damage a brother soldier's reputation…." Both Otto and Boxer grinned at each other at the thought of the fastidious, aristocratic Cassius Plancus with his silver tableware, rugs and cook thinking he was a "brother" to anyone, officer or man. "I have said something humorous, gentlemen?"

The Camp Prefect did not answer directly but asked what course of action the tribune suggested.

"Well, that's it really, I hadn't got beyond my initial reaction."

"I have an idea… "Otto began.

"Oh good, I thought you and your pal were just sitting there smirking and giggling like a couple of schoolgirls. Let's hear it then." Titus told him in a severe tone, instantly taking Otto back through the years to when this man ruled his every waking hour.

Unconsciously, Otto sat more upright and composed his face. "I propose that Tribune Plancus sends a confidential message to the mine superintendent asking when his next consignment will be leaving. We then intercept it and provide an escort of a hundred of my men to see it safely into Tarraco. They don't really need to ride all the way since the thefts have all occurred nearby but it's good exercise for the horses and some relief for the men. From now on we do this every time."

"Why so many?" Cassius asked.

"These bandits have already overcome a small legion force and killed two officers so there must be a lot of them. Pinarius' information leads me to believe that these are hit and run raids; after the first couple of times, it was a question of two or three chests going missing. They must want to get away fast. Fifty troopers in front of the gold cart and fifty behind with a good distance between them should be an effective deterrent. If an attempt is made my men will have a good chance of running them down, whoever they are."

"You're talking about a third of our available cavalry, Otto," Titus pointed out.

"I am but they aren't doing much else of any real use, are they?" Otto countered.

Tubero was delighted and kept the arrangement to himself as requested. So it was that the next shipment of the Emperor's gold was protected not only by Pinarius' hired guards but by one hundred German cavalrymen led by one of Otto's decurions who were happy to be doing something different. They returned deflated because no-one had attacked them so there had been no chance of a good, hard fight.

One week after the return of the escort, two of the engineers jumped into the cradle to haul themselves over to the other side to knock in some marking pegs for Boxer. When they were halfway across, the far side sheer-legs collapsed to the ground. The cradle dropped nearly fifteen feet, was arrested in its fall by the heavy cables and bounced upwards before dropping back again. One man was flung out to pinwheel screaming to his death. The other hung on with one hand for two minutes then his strength gave out. He shouted something that the desperate men on the cliff edge trying to devise some way to rescue their comrade did not catch. He plunged down in silence. Two heartbeats later, they heard the thud of his impact rise from the depths.

Boxer stood on the edge looking down, his hands on his hips and his face ashen There was not a man in the camp who was not unaccustomed to sudden death but this had come out nowhere and the long agony of the engineer hanging on for his life made it more shocking. The original ropeway had never been dismantled. Boxer straddled the plank seat and dragged himself across followed one by one by half a dozen of his men.

The guy ropes attached to the top of the sheer-legs and secured to stakes hammered into the ground had been cut. Without the anchor they provided, the poles had simply toppled over when the weight of the two dead man had been at the mid-point of the ravine. They had not been completely severed, just deep enough so they would come apart at maximum stress but would appear untouched from a distance. Boxer stayed where he was issuing orders for the reconstruction. The three poles of each sheer-leg were raised up and re-fixed with double supports, which was unnecessary but seemed the right thing to do. Only when all his men had crossed back did he come over himself.

On his instructions two fifty-yard ropes were spliced together and wound onto a windlass. He had a beam with a pulley wheel bolted to one end thrust out from the cliff. The beam was secured, the pulley greased and the spliced rope led through. Boxer personally tied a foot loop to the end. That was when Otto intervened.

He had ridden up to speak to the quartermaster about horseshoes. He had missed the catastrophe but watched the aftermath in silence, as had everyone else, respecting Boxer's need to deal with things in his own way. But when it became obvious that he was going down to retrieve the bodies, Otto stepped forward and put a restraining hand on his arm.

"I'll do this," he said.

Boxer shook his head. "They were my men. It's my responsibility."

"I should say something," Cassius told Titus, taking a half pace forward.

"Perhaps not, sir." The Camp prefect replied.

"Boxer, it's the responsibility of those bastards who cut the ropes, not yours. I'll do this," Otto said again.

"Why?"

"Because without you directing up here there could be another tragedy. As long as you're in charge, I'll be fine."

Boxer shook his head. "No, I can't let you."

"Let me?" Otto laughed. "It's been a long time since you could stop me! Let me do this for you, my friend, while you stay in control to keep me safe."

He took off his armour and slipped one foot through the loop then clambered down onto the narrow step cut into the rockface.

Otto took a firm grip higher up the rope and stepped into the void. Immediately he began to spin and swing but Boxer shouted to the windlass men who let him fall rapidly, for a few feet which steadied his descent. They then proceeded more slowly.

Otto looked up. The wide stripe of blue sky above him narrowed. The air grew colder as he went down; there was never a full day's sunlight playing on the walls in these depths. He seemed to be gradually melting into twilight. He brushed against a few outcrops and had to kick himself clear but for the most part the cliff was smooth and almost vertical. Before he realised, he was at the bottom. His feet hit a boulder and slid from under him. He found his footing, stood upright and tugged sharply on the rope twice. It ceased to snake down from the slit of light above. He looked around in the gloom. It was a lifeless place, not even lichen managed to find enough to live on. Fallen stones and small heaps of sand and earth lined the bases of the walls but the centre twenty feet was a smooth path of sand and gravel. Otto thought it was probably washed clean by winter rains running off the mountains. Far ahead of him shone a splinter of light where the ravine mouth opened.

The body of the man who had fallen first was at one side. He was broken and bloody after smashing into the wall as he plummeted to his death. Otto made a running noose with the rope and hitched it under his armpits. He tugged twice. The corpse was dragged a little way over the ground then rose up, arms spread wide as if in blessing, and vanished upwards. The second man who had struggled so hard for life and shouted a last message none of his comrades had heard lay on his back in the centre. He seemed uninjured, as if he was sleeping but when Otto tried to move him, it was obvious that his spine and ribs had been shattered. He was slack, flopping like a half-filled sack of corn. A thud behind him made Otto start, his heart suddenly pounding. It was the sound of the rope end falling to the floor. He struggled with the flaccid weight but at last saw the dead man hoisted out of sight. It seemed a lifetime until the rope was wound down again and he was able to put his foot in the loop and give the signal for them to haul him up. At the top, they hooked the rope and dragged him in and over to the stone lip before pulling him to safety by his arms.

The bodies were already being carried over to the priest for ritual purification. A small coin was placed in each mouth; their fares for the ferryman who would row them over the underworld River Styx to their eternal rest. Wood was stacked and drenched in oil for the cremations. The smoke drifted away on the breeze as their comrades stood saying their farewells. When the funeral pyres collapsed into white embers with rubies of heat in the centre, everyone left except the priest who would hold vigil and collect their cold ashes.

Titus Attius had stood to attention and saluted when the fires were lit then marched away. He had urgent business. He went over to the forge.

"I want five hundred caltrops," he told the smith.

Without a word, the blacksmith began. He took two short strips of iron and welded them together into a cross. Then he bent alternate ends up and down before filing each one to a point. However they were thrown onto the ground, two points would always be upright to pierce the foot and cripple anyone who stood on one.

"Four hundred and ninety-nine to go," the blacksmith muttered under his breath with a sigh.

Titus paraded his praetorians,

"I am posting two centuries on the far side to guard Prefect Boxer's ropeways day and night in rotation. First cohort, centuries three and four, fall out preparatory to volunteering. What is this I see, some reluctance? Lads, lads, have more faith in our engineers and your Camp Prefect. To show you it's as safe as eating your breakfast, my adjutant and I will go over first and shame you all."

The adjutant swallowed and paled a little before marching over to the cradle and clambering in behind Titus. They pulled on the fixed rope and slid smoothly towards the other side. Once out of hearing of the men, Titus said "I've never clenched my arse so tight in all my years of soldiering. This is fucking awful!" The adjutant burst into loud, surprised laughter. When the soldiers waiting their turns heard him, they shuffled their feet and looked sheepish. It couldn't be that bad if the officers were making jokes while they dangled over a couple of few hundred feet of nothing.

As soon as a few of the men were over, they began to jeer at their comrades still waiting to cross who responded with obscene gestures. Titus let it go; he knew it was a valuable way of releasing tension. His entire force assembled, he shouted for order and the praetorians fell in.

"Counting from the right, every third man, one pace forward and come to attention on my command. Go!" The boots thudded as one. "The rest of you, stack your arms. Gather up all the rocks you can find and build a crescent shaped defensive wall around these here crane jobs," He pointed at the sheer-legs with his vine-staff. "High as you like but thick enough so it can't be pushed over easily. Off you go then, we haven't got all day. I'll have some tools ferried over to you."

Back across, Titus walked briskly up to Otto and Cassius who were standing at a respectable distance from the dying pyres. Boxer was saying something to his men who drifted off towards their own lines. He came over to the group of officers and saluted Cassius.

"I've stood my men down for the rest of day and sanctioned a double wine ration this evening, sir, if that's in order."

"Of course, the only thing to do; awful business, quite ghastly." He looked around at the others. "Well, it seems to me that the enemy, whoever they might be, have declared themselves. This has to be in retaliation for our escorting the Emperor's gold to Tarraco. We've needled them. Perhaps they might soon show more of their hand. Camp Prefect, we must move to a war footing."

"Agreed sir. I'm organizing a defensive line on the other side. The men are building a bit of a wall and the smith is making caltrops as we speak. It's likely that we're being watched, so I'll have them distributed after dark. It's more a declaration of intent on our part than anything else. I don't anticipate a mass attack up here."

"Very well, Camp Prefect. Now, Prefect Otto, I consider it is no longer wise to leave our livestock down on the plains. What do you say?"

"There's insufficient grazing up here sir. I suggest they are driven down in the morning and back in the afternoon. Overnight, we can corral them behind the redoubt and divert the water which is just running away at the moment."

"How long is that going to take, everyday?"

"It's the oxen that are the slowest, sir," Boxer intervened. "However, we don't really need them anymore now our gear is all unloaded. Those cables were really heavy but mules can manage the rest of our transport…."

"See to it then. What are we going to do with the redundant beasts?"

"Sell 'em to the peasants. If they've got no money they'll barter for food and oil. Drive them to the nearest market and get what we can for them," Titus suggested.

"Otto, your cavalry can take charge of that. Send one of the men who speaks the local dialect with them," Cassius ordered.

"Keep a few of animals back though. Saturnalia is coming along and the boys will want their roast beef," added Titus.

Otto shuddered at the thought of yet another feast of misrule.

By nightfall, the livestock was gathered at the far end of the plateau and the cavalrymen had pitched their tents nearby.

Otto stayed on after dinner, drinking with his fellow officers. More wine that usual was consumed after the horror of the day. Siting at the fireside warmed by the flames and the alcohol in their bloodstreams, both he and Boxer felt any slight restraint that had grown between them melt away. The doors of memory burst open and they took turns, breaking in on each other and laughing, to recall the old times up on the Rhine. Titus was content to sit quietly with a half-smile on his lips and listen; it brought the past back to him as well.

Cassius was bored rigid after an hour. He remembered what Augustus had said, "Old comrades. Nothing more boring. "Remember when this and that?" Should remember the rest of us weren't there."

Chapter 13

The next day the engineers began to chip away at the cliff face again and the familiar background noise like a flock of persistent woodpeckers filled the air. Titus was unhappy about the length of time it took to move his guards across the chasm.

"Can't you build another of the rope thingies?" he asked.

Boxer shook his head. "No, it's a matter of time and materials. I'm afraid you'll have to make the best of it, Camp Prefect."

"I've had a good idea," Otto told them.

They waited but he said nothing more.

"So, what 's the idea then?" Titus asked at last.

"It's nothing but genius!" Otto said.

"Gods above and below, Prefect Otto, out with it?" Cassius demanded impatiently.

"Why don't you build a bridge so the men could just march over?"

He slapped his thighs and went off into howls of laughter while they stared at him with sour looks on their faces. Every time he pulled himself together, the sight of their frosty expressions set him off again.

Eventually Otto straightened up. He coughed and wiped the tears from his eyes.

"Sorry, I don't often make a joke," he said.

"And now we know why," Cassius told him.

The soldiers who had overheard this exchange thought it was the funniest thing they had heard since they had arrived "up the arse of nowhere" as they put it. Otto's joke went round the camp and became a catchphrase trotted out when ever anything went wrong. A fire would not light? "Ask Boxer to build a bridge over it," someone cut his hand sharpening a sword, "Should've asked Boxer to build a bridge over it." It was childish but silly humour keeps up morale better than any inspirational speech.

Boxer knew that a quicker traverse would be to everyone's benefit. He examined the existing structures, decided the double-guyed sheer-legs would stand the additional strain and made some improvements. He enlarged the cradle so that it was big enough to carry three men. He then changed the single supporting cable into a continuous loop running over pulleys and added a second cradle. As the soldiers pulled across in one, the empty cradle was dragged the other way and passed them in the middle. Men climbed into the empty one on the other side and began to haul their way across, automatically dragging the first back to its starting off point. It was heavier work but there were now three men to pull on the ropes, not just two. The time required to move the guards over and back was more than halved. Not exactly what Titus had asked for but he appreciated both the effort and the result.

One third of the cavalry escorted a second bullion shipment, again without problems. There were no more incidents in the camp and all seemed to be well. Titus was grateful that he had experienced troops under his command. Because nothing was happening, did not mean there was no danger. Old sweats know this, raw troops do not and inevitably get careless, sometimes with catastrophic results.

Boxer finished the foundation step and now had to cut a corresponding one on the other side. The hanging scaffold was taken over and reassembled. He squatted on the step lining up his groma and chorobates. Shouting instructions over to his men to mark the opposing face. It was an ill-tempered process. Once he had established his lines and levels, they had the simple task of using chalk, initially, to lay out where the stone had to be cut away.

Boxer spent hours yelling, getting more and more red in the face. "Left a bit. Left. No, my left you idiot. Down. Not that far! Up now, down from that…." Eventually he was satisfied and they cut the marking grooves horizontally and vertically over the chalk lines.

Once more the picks and chisels gnawed into the rock all day long.

Boxer went into his tent and worked at his drawing table for two days then presented his work after dinner. He had drawn detailed diagrams of twelve lengths of subtly curved timber and written the dimensions beside each of them.

"I need to order these from the shipyard in Tarraco. This will be our bridge, gentlemen, suitably supported with a wooden framework reinforced with iron and based on masonry foundations. We are making progress."

"Why are they curved?" Otto enquired.

"Ah, well, we can't support the centre of the span other than by cantilevers. If it was flat it would sag but by using curves we avoid that. When something heavy crosses it, they are forced down and try to straighten out but they can't. Instead, they push back against the supports and lock them even tighter. Makes everything much stronger…"

"You aren't short of skilled men, why don't you make them yourself?" Titus asked.

"Shipwrights are expert at cutting curves; you never see a straight line in a boat. Also, they will have the seasoned oak we need in stock."

"If this is what you need, you shall certainly have it," Cassius told him. "How do you intend to transport them from the coast?"

"I thought I would have a word with Pinarius. He must be happy with us after Otto's help with his gold consignments."

"Agreed. He must be used to working for the Imperial Navy. I'll write you a note of credit. I'm sure Augustus will be delighted to pay up in due course."

That night, lightning flickered over the high peaks but they heard no rumble of thunder. In the morning, Boxer rode out in bright sunshine with six troopers. By noon, the rain was tumbling out of the threatening sky in blinding sheets. There was a continuous deluge for twenty-four hours. Then it eased to a cold drizzle, soaking through tents and cloaks, dripping down the backs of necks and turning their water channel into a raging miniature river. The rain kept up for five days without a break. When the sun re-appeared, the intense heat had gone out of it. They strung wet clothes and blankets on lines to dry between the steaming tents and looked to their weapons and armour for signs of rust. The change in the weather announced the arrival of autumn. The days of sweating under cloudless skies were over. They worked, drilled and marched through chill showers, frost in the mornings if the night had been clear and increasing snow on the mountain tops.

The first man woke in the middle of the night and stumbled over cursing comrades who shared his eight-man tent. He scrambled though the flap, letting in cold air to another chorus of complaints and made for the latrines. His lower belly felt as if it was being raked from the inside with spikes and even after he had voided his bowels, the sharp pains still racked him. By breakfast, ten others were afflicted. By noon, a quarter of the command was either vomiting or experiencing agonising bouts of diarrhoea. The latrines could not cope; rows of groaning men sat passing liquid faeces to stain the cliffs below while their comrades clutched their bellies and at last, could no longer resist and were forced to squat where they stood. The whole area became a rain-sodden mess of shit and vomit churned up by the boots of the sufferers. By the next morning, after a night of cold, wet hell, half the men were down. They began to die in the early afternoon. The sick had no fever, no rash or other pains to suggest a contagious disease. The doctor and his orderlies were mystified. They could recognise the symptoms of cholera and dysentry but neither quite fitted. They examined the provisions. The bacon was untainted and there was no sign of fermentation or ergot in the spelt.

Titus had seen commands decimated by disease, so had Cassius during his time in Syria.

"Can it be the water?" Cassius queried then shook his head, answering his own question. "No, it flows out of a natural spring."

Both of them had experienced the results of poisoned wells but in this camp they enjoyed a continuous fresh supply from the living rock. Titus shrugged.

"Let's look anyway."

With Otto, they trudged the length of their channel back towards the mountainside out of which their water emerged. A stream of water as thick as a man's arm jetted out of the base of a narrow entrance in the rock, so low no-one could enter without crawling. They stood in perplexed silence as raindrops beaded on their helmet rims and eyebrows. There was nothing to indicate anything was wrong.

"We had no trouble until the weather broke… Something in the rain?" Cassius mused aloud.

Otto leaned forward, peered at the back of the small cavern then recoiled, gagging.

Titus looked at him in puzzlement then pushed his own face in. A taint lingered on the air inside. He drew in a breath and recognised it: that stench of rotting meat and putrescence, familiar to every soldier.

"There's something dead in there," he said. "Very dead."

"Then we'll have to remove it. Will you wait here, Titus, while I fetch some fit men to sort this out? If I can find any," Cassius asked.

"Of course," Titus replied. "They'll need some tools to widen this cave.

Cassius hurried off with Otto but when they were halfway back, the tribune suddenly paled, came to a dead stop and doubled up clutching his belly. He vomited and staggered. Otto did not hesitate. He picked Cassius up in his arms, in spite of his protests and trotted towards the distant tents. His breath came hard after a few hundred yards but he had enough left to shout.

"On me! On me! The tribune has fallen!" Heads turned and a small group of men ran out to help. He handed the groaning Cassius to them. "Get him into his tent and have Nestor look after him." He ran on and shouted for engineers. "Get over to the spring now, picks and shovels. Move it! …and bring a couple of dry torches."

They applied flint and steel to the resin-soaked end of a torch under the shelter of a spread cloak. It flared and the wiriest of the men squirmed into the grotto. Yellow flame illuminated the walls, the torch dimmed and nearly went out but its feeble light had shown enough. He backed out, turned his head away and retched.

"Something big hanging up in the back. Its stinks."

"Can you drag it out, soldier?" Titus demanded.

"No sir, not on my own. bent double. It'll take two of us; might have to open up the entrance and all."

"That will take hours," Otto remarked.

Titus took control.

"You lads, break the edge of the channel and dam it. We don't want anymore filthy water pouring into our supply. Prefect Otto, will you head back and send more men up. Order everyone to stop drinking out of the troughs and collect as much rainwater as they can, they are to use whatever they can find, pans, kettles, anything at all…"

Otto was already on his way, at a sprint this time. He carried out the Camp Prefect's orders but did more. He had the ends of the wooden troughs knocked out so that their contents spilled onto the ground and told the men to throw away any water they had. Finally, he instructed that the shadouf should work constantly to empty the reservoir, in spite of the falling drizzle. The flow of water in the channels was now a trickle and within half an hour it had ceased.

Some of the engineers had dug out the lower side of the channel and blocked it with the rubble. Others had tried to hack at the entrance but given it up as a bad job and somehow squeezed the two smallest men in with torches and scarves tied over their faces. They dragged out the rotting carcasses of two wild boar, their shredded entrails dangling, green and foul.

"They was hung up on a branch jammed across the back, sir. Their guts was right down in the water. Bloody disgusting I calls it, sir," one of them reported.

They scrubbed the walls they could reach and burned a pan of sulphur which filled the enclosed space with noxious, yellow fumes. The channel was brushed out with a stiff brush, a new collecting pond was dug out and stone-lined. They shovelled the spoil into the old infected one and filled it up. They burned the old wooden troughs and shadouf bucket and made new ones. The ground around the latrines was scraped with shovels; the filthy topsoil and stained grass were pushed over the cliff.

The sick fed on thin barley gruel cooked in rainwater for a couple of days and they began to regain their health, although they were weak for some time. As soon as the clean water arrived, there were no new cases. Nineteen had died. A permanent guard was posted on the water source.

The men were bitterly angry towards an unseen and unknown enemy but nothing could be done. The officers insisted on the strictest discipline; surly and frustrated troops can be unpredictable.

Tribune Cassius Plancus did not have the resilience of most of the men. He thought of himself as a soldier and lacked neither courage nor military skills but he had always served as an officer Not for him the years of relentless physical exertion and spells of poor food and bad water the legionaries endured. He had never acquired the natural resistance of Otto and Titus Attius, let alone the rank and file. He recovered a little but was nothing like his previous self. He was pale, weak and gradually losing weight. Nestor tried to tempt his appetite with the best dishes he could concoct but Cassius pushed his plate away after a few mouthfuls. He was barely keeping himself alive on a diet of gruel with a little wine and honey.

The rain ceased. After two days of brilliant blue skies and heavy overnight frosts, the clouds came back; low, bruised-looking with a yellow sheen, bearing snow which fell steadily. The men were now ranging farther and longer in a daily search for wood for the fires. The smiths hoarded their charcoal like misers and would not let a crumb be used for cooking or warming tents. The forge was always crowded with soldiers getting in the way while they rubbed their hands together to warm them. The German cavalry carried on as normal with a complete disregard to the cold. Until the snow was up to the bellies of their horses, they would not call it winter. The weather settled into a pattern of two or three days of snow alternating with a couple of days of blue skies and biting north winds rushing down off the white mountain tops. Clear nights were a blaze of stars. They heard the distant howling of wolves.

On such a day of pale sunshine, a rider trotted up the hairpin roads and into the camp. He had a message from Boxer.

"To Tribune Cassius Plancus, Greetings.

I have the shaped timber we need but conscious that all raids have occurred close to our camp, I ask for fifty cavalrymen to see me home. By the time this message arrives, I should be less than two full days away with Pinarius' men and wagons.

With Respect, Prefect of Engineers Lucius Taurius Longius (Boxer).

Cassius managed the first brief smile anyone had seen on his lips for days when he read the scroll.

Each length of the bridge supports was twenty-five feet long. Boxer ordered them to be carried up to the camp by hand, twenty men for each piece. He had also brought back poles, sacks of mortar, ships' sails and tubs of pigs' lard and sheep-fat. They slathered the sail cloths with a mixture of both for water-proofing and set them up on the poles as awnings to protect the precious cargo. When everything was arranged to his satisfaction, he reported to Cassius.

The sight of the emaciated tribune shocked him. He turned on Nestor.

"How can you let your good master sink to this condition?" he demanded.

Tears welled up in the slave's eyes.

"It's not my fault sir. Nothing I do seems to help."

Cassius' decline had been gradual. Otto and Titus hardly noticed the difference from day to day but Boxer had been absent for weeks. When he left, the tribune was a healthy and vital young man. Now he looked more like a corpse, his eyes sunken, the bones of his face almost breaking out of the yellow skin.

Otto and Titus told him how their water had been deliberately polluted and the result. Boxer calmed down but was still very worried for Cassius.

"He's dying," he told them.

"He is my commanding officer. He is rational and can give orders. Not for me to say anything to him," Titus growled.

"And you, Otto?"

"He's fading."

"So why haven't you two done anything about it?"

"Like what Boxer? I repeat, he is the commanding officer," Titus said, raising his voice.

"Let's ask the doctor," Otto suggested.

The doctor listened to the concerns of the three senior officers in silence before giving his prognosis.

"The tribune's illness has caused a critical imbalance of his bodily humours. Blood and yellow bile have been overwhelmed by phlegm and the proportion of black bile has naturally increased due to the season of the year. He needs to be warmed and fed a diet rich in blood with heating elements; spices and herbs, not available to us here. If he remains with us, he will certainly die."

"And have you told him this?" Boxer demanded.

"Certainly. He told me that his commission is from the Emperor and he will not resign it."

"How long has the tribune got? Titus asked.

The doctor opened wide his hands and shrugged.

"That is for the Gods to decide. It is my opinion that he will pass from us within two or three months unless he leaves for Rome and the best care available. Then it is possible that he will recover. But, gentlemen, he will be too weak to face a winter sea voyage in a matter of a few weeks."

They thanked him and went over to Titus' quarters.

"A delegation. All three of us making the same point?" Boxer offered.

"Agreed," said Titus. "Make it very formal, shaved, polished boots and brushed cloaks. Half an hour?"

Cassius spent his days reclining in a seat padded with blankets beside a brazier. He remained apathetic when they marched up, stood to attention in front of him, saluted and bowed. Titus cleared his throat.

"Praetorian Tribune Cassius Plancus, sir, we are addressing you in the interests of your command as well as your own. You are gravely ill and cannot survive the winter in camp. As your loyal officers, we urge you to take ship for Rome in our strongest hopes of your return to good health after treatment at home."

"Camp Prefect Titus Attius, you forget that I am placed here on the Emperor's orders. Do you counsel me to abandon my commission?"

"Sir, if you die in camp, the effect on morale will be catastrophic. The men will take it as a sign that the Gods do not favour this mission. That is why I say in the best interests of your soldiers you should leave us."

"And you Boxer, are you against me as well?" Cassius asked.

"Not at all, I want to see you restored to serve our Emperor for many more years. You were carried back from Syria with a grave wound, this is no different," Boxer told him.

"I cannot disappoint the Emperor." Cassius replied but it seemed a glimmer of doubt had arisen in his mind.

It was Otto who came up with the decisive argument.

"Just think what your lady mother is going to say to Augustus if you die on active service; she'll tear into him without mercy, Emperor or no. I'm sure he'd give you another medal for saving him from her."

Cassius tried to laugh. They knew they had persuaded him.

There was a gold shipment going down to Tarraco in two days. It was arranged that Cassius should go with it in a mule cart. Eight praetorians were assigned to accompany him to the coast and across the sea to Ostia, the nearest port to Rome, by the fastest ship available.

"Let's hope that we shall find a captain willing to make the voyage at this time of year," Cassius said.

"Begging your pardon tribune, sir," said the decanus of his guard, "but don't fret yourself. Me and the lads will make sure one of 'em's willing enough."

The evening before he left, Cassius called a general meeting including the priest, the tesserarius, the two decurions of cavalry and the praetorian centurions as well as Titus, Boxer and Otto. In a quavering voice he read out a letter his clerk had written for him.

"Greetings to all my officers who have served me so well.

My thanks to you. I regret to inform you that I am no longer physically capable of offering you the leadership you deserve. I therefore relinquish my command to Camp Prefect Titus Attius, to be supported by Imperial Prefect Otto Longius and Prefect of Engineers Lucius Taurius Longius.

I shall report your steadfastness to the Emperor when I arrive in Rome."

Praetorian Tribune Cassius Plancus, read out by me to my assembled staff."

He called on the priest to witness the document then passed it to the safe-keeping of the tesserarius before dismissing everyone except Titus.

"I'm taking my reports to date with me but I'm leaving you my clerk so you'll have his help to write them from now on." He handed Titus the leather scroll Otto had smuggled out of Rome. "Here are the Emperor's orders. I advise you to study them carefully. There is one sealed document which is only to be opened in the circumstances noted on its cover. I have not known you for long, Titus, but I am sure you will see my lads are well led."

When he was alone, a tear ran down Cassius's thin face. He brushed it angrily aside, ashamed of his weakness.

Other tears were shed. A sobbing Nestor found Otto and knelt at his feet. He grabbed one of his hands and kissed it. "It was your words that changed my master's mind sir. I thank you with all my soul. If he lives, it will be because of you."

Sitting on an upturned log beside his fire under a sky where the clouds chased the stars away only for them to reappear brighter than ever, Otto thought about Nestor. Did the slave really have a genuine affection for his master? If so, why? How was it possible to love the person who owned you and had the power to treat you however they wished? Did Nestor not know he was property, to be disposed of at Cassius' whim? Of course he did. Why then was he so grateful? Was it simply that Cassius was a good and fair master and, if he died, Nestor feared being sold to some sadistic brute? Otto was still pondering the enigma of the slave's apparent attachment to Cassius when he fell asleep.

During Boxer's absence, they had cut the second foundation step. He used his instruments to check they were both level and was happy with the result. He then vanished into his tent and spent the next week making his technical drawings of all the elements of construction that would be required. He called the master mason in for a conference, then the chief carpenter and finally the blacksmiths.

Otto gave his off-duty men permission to hunt in the mountains provided at least four went together and were back before nightfall. Wood-cutting parties went out. The praetorians were drilled and worked through their weapons' practices. The cavalry herded the livestock, searching for any pasture not covered in snow which still had some grass, even if it was brown and shrivelled. It was a quiet time, unlike in Otto's household in Luca where dissent and fractiousness reigned.

In spite of, or perhaps because of, the general objection to it, Saxa spent more time with Libius. She liked him and she was fascinated by his artistic skills. Painting and decoration were new to her as were some of the images he produced of gods and nymphs. One day Lollia heard strange noises and hoots of laughter coming from Libius' workshop. She opened the door and heard him say, "Cat" then repeated the word while holding up a board with a drawing of one on it. Saxa was trying to say it herself. They were laughing at each other.

"What's this Libius, you can speak?" she asked in amazement.

They both looked at her. The expression on Libius' face turned instantly to concern. Saxa looked over at her sister-in-law.

"Oh, hello Lollia. Of course he can. It's just that because he can't hear himself anymore it comes out funny. He teaches me new words."

"Well, I want to know why he has never said anything until now."

"He was beaten and mocked so much because he didn't sound right when he tried that he gave up."

"But he'll speak with you?"

"Yes, He's my friend."

That was too much for Lollia. "Well he shouldn't be. You've been told again and again. I will not have you consorting with Libius in my house," she shouted.

"Your house?" Saxa spat. "I thought this was my brother's house…"

Libius hated strife, with good reason. He tried to calm the two women by saying "Please don't," but it sounded like "Pliz doon" to Lollia.

"Oh, just shut up!" she yelled and slammed out of the workshop.

This spat lit the touch paper which led to the explosion.

Lollia and Saxa did not speak for three days. On the fourth, Saxa announced she was going into the city with Libius to help hm with a commission to paint an interior. She had no intention of doing so, she simply wanted to provoke Lollia who ignored her. That left Saxa no choice.

She and Libius were shown into the dining room of a wealthy merchant's house where he had contracted to paint a woodland scene on a freshly plastered wall. Libius did not want her there but was not in a position to say so. Saxa did help him set up his bench and trestle and organise his paints but had nothing to do once he began. He worked quickly laying down base colours and then adding detail before the first paint was dry so he was concentrating and did not notice the two sons of the household enter the room. One was eleven, the other thirteen, well-fed, well-dressed and both with an enormous sense of entitlement. Their father was rich, people deferred to him because of his money and they took advantage of the fact.

The boys watched Libius for a while then got bored.

"He's the deaf and dumb one," the younger of the pair informed his brother who knew that already.

The older boy looked on a little longer then chuckled.

"That big, blonde one with him, do you think he sleeps with her?"

They both contemplated Saxa for a moment.

"I expect so." his brother answered.

"But how does he let her know when he wants a bit. Perhaps he draws what's in between her legs and points at it...."

"Yes... and draws a big cock on its way up her...."

Saxa lost all reason. She grabbed each boy by the scruff of his neck and dragged their hair and faces the length of the newly painted walls. They screamed and then spluttered as their mouths filled with a mixture of soap, beeswax and pigment. When she got to the end, she dragged then back the other way.

"You filthy pigs. Disgusting little animals. You should be whipped raw!"

At this point, the merchant ran in. He shouted for his porter to fetch the city patrol and called his major domo.

"Leave my sons alone, mad woman!" he demanded.

Saxa flung them to the floor; smeared yellow, blue and green, they crawled whimpering towards their father.

"These dirty-mouthed brats belong to you? Then you should have shame." she fired at him.

The major-domo scurried in, a large man as portly as his master.

"Lock this harridan in the cellar until the soldiers arrive," the merchant ordered.

He stepped towards Saxa and made to grab her. "Come along now, woman don't be difficult...."

She bunched her fist and delivered a right hook that landed square in the middle of his round, pink face. He clamped both hands to his bleeding nose and tottered backwards into his master, knocking him into the door jamb where he bounced the back of his head off the marble.

The two opposing sides glared at each other across the room. Saxa's eyes shot blue lightning at the merchant, his bleeding major domo and the frightened boys. They stared back at her with more fear than anger. Poor Libius stood quietly, a brush and a paint pot in his hands looking in sorrow at the ruin of his morning's work and in bewilderment at the aftermath of the chaos. Banging doors and stamping boots signalled the arrival of the forces of law and order led by Massus.

"At last," the merchant said. He pointed at Saxa. "I want her jailed and whipped for assaulting my sons and my man. In my own home, mark you, in my own home! What is Luca coming to when insane foreigners can attack citizens in their own homes."

"Yes, you mentioned this is your home more than once, sir," Massus said, drily. He looked over at Saxa. "What do you have to say?" He spoke as if he did not know her and kept his face straight.

Saxa stabbed an accusing finger at the boys.

"These vermin said that if Libius wants to sleep with me he draws my womanhood and his manhood and then I lie down for him…"

Massus bent over the pair of them so his face was inches from theirs. "True?" he asked.

They looked into his remaining eye and felt the full force of his authority. Hardened legionaries had quailed at it, two spoiled lads could not resist.

"Yes…sort of," one of them squeaked.

"We thought she was deaf as well," the other said, as if that was an adequate excuse.

Massus stood up and nodded then turned to Saxa once more.

"Did you hit that man in the face?"

"The fat man, not the rich fat man, the other one, he tried to put his hands on me. I punched him but only once."

"I see," Massus said and asked the merchant. "Anything to add, sir?"

"Never mind provocation," he blustered, "She has no right to assault my boys and my staff in my own home… "

"In your own home," Massus repeated with a sigh. "Very well, I shall have her taken off to jail as you demand. Imperial Prefect Otto Longius, won't be pleased. "The Kingkiller" they call him, personally known to and favoured by the Emperor, you've probably heard of him? Anyway, as I said, he won't be pleased."

"Why?"

"Because this "insane foreigner" is his sister, the Lady Saxa…." he bowed to her "…who your sons have insulted and your servant has assaulted, by trying to place his hands upon her person…"

"Just a minute," the merchant gasped, paling.

"And the painter is Master Libius, a free tradesman of the city, highly regarded for his talent and a client of said Imperial Prefect...."

The merchant may have been pompous and self-satisfied but he was no fool; he would never have made so much money if he could not think on his feet.

"Centurion Massus, I believe that there has been a grave misunderstanding here, caused by the stupidity of my sons." He delivered a swift and stinging clip around the ear to both of them. "If the Lady Saxa and good Master Libius will accept my profound apologies, no more shall be said of this matter...by anyone."

"Certainly not by me, sir," the centurion agreed.

The merchant let out a sigh of relief. "Perhaps Master Libius could repair my wall painting, but maybe come on his own next time?"

"You see, you grasp a situation right off and come up with the best solution. That's why you are where you are today, sir, in your lovely own home."

A dishevelled Saxa arrived back at the villa where Lollia was entertaining the two older Longius ladies and Poppaea. Without invitation, she recited her story, pacing around the dining room, bosom heaving, eyes flashing. Sabina Pulchra and Poppaea listened in gentle disapproval, Lollia in horror. Aelia laughed and clapped, specially when she mimed punching the major domo. Saxa finished and sat down.

"You see dear, this is why Lollia has warned you about being too close to Libius, decent man as he is. She was protecting you. Other people would think the same way as those dirty-minded boys if they knew," the old woman gently explained.

Saxa thought about it for a moment then stood up and put her arms around Lollia's neck.

"I am sorry," she told her.

Lollia and Sabina Pulchra cried a little. Aelia just rolled her eyes and sighed.

Chapter 14

Boxer's men divided into work gangs according to their specialist skills. The smiths forged iron rods of varying diameters and lengths to be used as nails and reinforcements for the timber and stone. The masons selected rocks from the remaining supply strewn around the plateau and chiselled them to size, some with one side angled to act as wedges. The carpenters toiled with saws, adzes and planes, cutting and shaping wood and forming lap or mortice and tenon joints. Boxer went from one group to the other all day long, listening to suggestions, consulting and adapting when necessary.

Otto watched his friend with open admiration. He remembered how he had struggled with the simple arithmetic Aldermar had made him learn so that he could order the correct level of supplies for his cavalry in the field. But here was Boxer translating complex geometry from drawings on parchment into three dimensional blocks and beams and not only that, having a picture in his mind of how they would all fit together to achieve the final result.

"Look at all he can do, he's a wonder," he told Titus who nodded and smiled.

"Not a jealous bone in their bodies," Titus thought. "A lot of men would be envious of a friend's skill far beyond their own, but not Otto. And Boxer is proud of the crowns and medals Otto won. That's what the Emperor must have seen in them. Otto always says that Fate had made him seek out Boxer. Perhaps it's true; the old bond between them is strong as ever, in spite of the years of separation. They just took up where they'd left off."

Late one afternoon when the sun was a low, red disc casting long, orange shadows across the snow, a hunting party of cavalrymen came out of a gulley in the mountainside. Two of them had a pole slung between them with a black bundle lashed to it. They strutted towards the camp and began to call out and whoop as they came near. A tall young warrior led them. He wore his ash blond hair in two long plaits and a heavy moustache like a Gaul but with the rest of his face shaved. One of his cheeks was flapping open from just below his left eye nearly to his jawline. He was grinning. The party halted in front of Otto and unwrapped their bundle. It was a bear pelt. The wounded man reached down into the bloody interior and lifted out the raw heart of the beast.

Titus had walked over at the noise and now stood examining the pelt. "That was a big bugger of a bear," he thought.

The warrior with the torn face held the dripping heart out to Otto. He took it, clamped his teeth over the end, drew his pugio and carved off a piece. He handed it back with a nod of appreciation. The man followed suit then shyly offered it to Titus who did the same as Otto. A crowd of Germans had now gathered around and the heart passed among them, rapidly diminishing in size as each one took a bite.

"What is your name, man?" Otto asked, speaking in the Suevi dialect.

"Sigbold, lord."

"Ask him if he's the one that killed it?" Titus demanded, in Latin.

Sigbold turned to him and replied in adequate Latin. "I did, Camp Prefect Attius. He came at me out of a thicket. I speared him and over he went."

"But not before taking half your face off. Why aren't you bleeding?"

"I kept slapping snow on it. It soon stopped."

"You are a tough young bugger, lad," Titus told him, offering one of his highest compliments.

"Tell the quartermaster he is to give you all the lye and salt you need to preserve your trophy, Sigbold," Otto said. "Get the doctor to sew you face back together; you'll frighten the horses looking like that."

The feeble joke drew a gale of laughter and the happy cavalrymen went off talking among themselves.

That night Otto left Boxer and Titus at dinner. He had earlier searched through his kit and found a heavy silver arm ring with a bear's head as part of the pattern. He walked through the chilly night to his men's camp. They were sitting around a roaring fire, far too wasteful of precious fuel, but Otto understood this was a celebration and let it pass. He walked into the circle of firelight.

"Sigbold, Senior Decurion, come forward." They stood either side of him. He held up the arm ring so everyone could see it glittering with reflected flames. "Sigbold Bearslayer, I honour you." He slipped it over the young man's right hand. The cheering crashed through the camp. Otto signalled for silence. "Decurion, I appoint Sigbold Bearslayer as your deputy. Let him learn him all he needs to know from you, he could not have a better teacher."

Titus was not pleased when Otto returned and told him and Boxer what he had done.

"You don't promote soldiers for spearing bears," he grumbled.

"You do if they're Germans," Boxer informed him. "They don't follow Otto's orders because he's an Imperial Prefect, they couldn't care less about that. No, to them he's Otto Kingkiller, a famous warrior. He's like a chieftain to them so he behaves like one and rewards his men in their own way."

"You seem to know a lot about it."

"I do," Boxer pointed at Otto. "I've spent long enough sharing a billet with him while he banged on and on and on about honour and reputation."

"You should write a book about it."

"If I do, will you buy a copy, Camp Prefect?"

"Bugger off, Prefect of Engineers!"

They clinked their cups of watered vinegary wine and laughed.

In the morning, the decurion approached Otto. "Do you know who Sigbold is, lord?" he asked.

"No."

"Then it was a happy chance. He is Prince Aldermar's nephew."

The masons began to cut narrow parallel grooves lengthwise on the floor of both steps.

"We make matching grooves on the bottom of the first course of masonry. It helps to bind them together when the mortar is applied," Boxer explained to Otto.

When that was done, skilled men worked with twist drills and hammers to cut three vertical holes.

"What's that for?" Otto asked.

"We sink three upright iron rods each side to reinforce the blocks when they go in."

"Won't the rods just wobble about?"

"They're sized to the holes we're drilling and we pour molten lead in as they're being tapped home."

"Why are your masons working with such small hammers? It would be much quicker if they used a heavy sledgehammer?"

"They have to go carefully. They don't want to crack the floor," Boxer told him and suppressed a sigh.

Otto had taken a sudden interest in the building works and asked incessant questions, mostly about unimportant details which were obvious to Boxer and his teams but he did not have the heart to tell his friend to go away and leave everyone alone. So the engineers worked with Otto as their constant audience.

They strengthened the sheer-legs yet again; they now had four sets of guy ropes and double top fastenings. They replaced the pulleys with larger blocks and threaded a heavier cable through them, greased to protect it from the rain and snow. With a mixture of pride and relief, Boxer announced his men had laid the foundation course of stone blocks.

"We need to cover them overnight to stop the frost killing the mortar and if everything goes well, we can begin the next stage the day after tomorrow."

The mortar set well enough to bear the weight of heavy timber and masonry

"The problem now is we have to build up at the same rate on both sides. Everything supports everything else, you see. Our biggest fear is high winds before we've joined both ends of the cross beams in the middle. Still there is always something to worry about. So far so good…"

There was no moon; misty, high cloud obscured the stars. The sentry looked over the chest-high wall around the sheer-legs into the pitch-black night; he could see nothing. His face was almost numb with cold but he could still feel another dewdrop forming on the end of his nose. He thought about wiping it with the back of his hand but what was the point? Better just to let it drip. He could stand down when the sun rose but that was two hours away. He sighed and stamped his feet to bring the circulation back.

A shrill, swiftly-stifled scream split the silence. The sentry knew what it was. Some intruder had brought his foot down on one of the caltrops. He drummed the shaft of his spear against his shield and bellowed "Alarm! Alarm!" The bugler blew the call to arms and suddenly the praetorians were all in their positions, shield to shield straining their eyes for a glimpse of the enemy.

Other cries of agony rose in the darkness which was lit with a shower of sparks as flint scraped against steel. A yellow flame blossomed, another and another as the fire was passed between pitch coated torches. The first one arced into the air to fall in the frozen slush outside the wall, hissing. But more curved their graceful arcs against the black backdrop of the sky and accelerated as they descended, a few among the soldiers. The attackers came closer; often a torch would fall and splutter simultaneously with a groan or cry from the bearer as he ruined one of his feet on a spike and fell to the ground.

Otto had been halfway out of his cot before the bugler had finished his call. He dragged on his boots and belt with his pugio in its sheath and stepped out of his tent. The alarm was sounding in the main camp. Men mustered as quickly as they could, doing up the buckles of their armour and clapping helmets on their heads as they ran. Otto saw the balls of fire rising and falling on the other side and instantly understood the nature of the incursion. He sprinted to the bridgeworks He shouldered praetorians rushing to their muster points out of his way. From his closer vantage point he saw a lucky throw send a torch spinning into a couple of the greased support ropes. Tongues of flame began to crawl upwards towards the pulley block holding the heavy cable.

Otto leaped into the cradle and grabbed the line to pull himself across. He felt a thud and it swung wildly: someone had jumped in behind him.

"Haul, now haul, bust your guts but haul!" he shouted without looking around.

After what seemed an age, they bumped into the far side cliff edge. Otto scrambled out and ran to the sheer leg. He took a firm grip and began to climb the slick pine pole. Another lucky throw set the sailcloth cover of the masons' awning alight. It glowed as the fat melted then suddenly caught with a whoosh of flame. Otto went up, slid back a little, took a firmer grip and forced his way towards his goal.

The praetorians had begun to hurl their heavy spears at the targets presented when one of the attackers stood upright to throw his torch and was momentarily illuminated. One or two throws had gone home but with the blazing awning behind them not interfering with their night vision but lighting up much of the immediate area, their fire became more deadly.

"Mark your man, boys. Don't waste your ammunition. Mark your man!" the centurions chanted.

The spears transfixed arms and legs or sank deep into torsos. The holding pegs snapped on impact, the wooden shafts fell to the ground and their victims were left with two feet of barb headed iron protruding out of their limbs or bodies.

Otto had now reached the top and steadied himself by gripping with his legs and grabbing onto the pulley block with his left hand. He took out his pugio and sliced through the burning guy ropes. They swayed gracefully to the ground. He felt a surge of relief; if the fire had reached the cable and burned it away, its falling mass might have ripped out the supports on the other side at the least, perhaps smashed everything. There could have been days of delay; weeks if the cable could not be replaced without a visit to the shipyards. Then the pole under him, a substantial pine trunk trimmed of its branches, lurched. He dropped his pugio and wrapped both hands around it.

Boxer had often explained the principle that the strength of any machine or structure relied on all its parts reinforcing each other. Otto was about to have a practical demonstration. His considerable bulk was at the top of one of the three poles fixed to each other like a tipi with no cover. He was clinging on to the outside and had just cut the moorings away. The heavy cable was applying force in one direction and Otto in another. Stressed guy ropes snapped and whipped outwards. The whole thing tilted, all still connected. Slowly at first with creaks and groans but unstoppably, poles, ropes cable and pullies collapsed towards the cliff edge.

Otto had been on the upside when his pole landed with a dull thud that shook the ground. It rebounded a little, jerking him over. His legs lost their grip, he was winded and dazed.. He found himself dangling three feet out over the chasm, his arms on top of the timber and his feet kicking nothing but air. The weight of the cable was dragging him and his support downwards. He was sliding very gradually into the dark, seemingly fathomless space beneath him in a waking nightmare. He fought for purchase and for his life but both were slipping away in spite of his efforts. Just as he reached the point of resignation, a strong fist grabbed the back of his tunic. The sloping pole moved up near to level and he was able to edge along it to safety. The single hand gripping him became two and he was dragged unceremoniously over the edge onto firm ground. He lay on his back in the slush.

Otto breathed deeply, aware of the smell of smoke and the clank and clatter of men nearby. Many of the praetorians had seen the danger and dropped on the other end of the pole so that their combined weight stabilized the wreckage. He turned his head to the right and saw Boxer, also full length on the ground.

"Sorry," he said," I've broken all your pulleys and stuff...."

Boxer burst into gales of laughter.

"Why did you do it, madman?"

"I thought if the fire spread all your hard work would have been wrecked."

"Otto, Otto, it's a few ropes and some timber; not worth your life. I'm grateful all the same. You've saved us from having to do a lot of it again."

"But everything has tumbled over….."

"Have it put right and running two hours after sun-up, thanks to you."

"Was it you who jumped into the cradle behind me?" Otto asked after a moment's reflection.

"Yes," Boxer replied

"You do realize you nearly knocked me out of it, don't you?" he accused.

Titus Attius was less appreciative of Otto's action.

"What do you think they'd do to me if I lost an Imperial Prefect down a fucking great hole? Boxer's the engineer. You're not. Leave it up to him next time."

When day dawned, the praetorians looked out on the result of their night's work. Nineteen bodies lay in a semicircle, the closest just ten paces from their defensive wall. Fifteen had spears sticking out of them at odd angles, the others appeared to be untouched.

"Right lads, get out there and chuck 'em into the ravine. Anyone who puts a spike through his foot gets a flogging for being a careless sod and ruining army issue boots."

The early morning shadows were blue. The snow around the bodies was red. A wide, bloody trail led towards a gulley in the mountainside. A dozen of the men climbed gingerly out and prodded their way through the half-covered tussocks of grass. They moved slowly in straight lines then circled each corpse before grabbing it by the heels and lifting and dragging it back to the immediate base of their wall. The dead had all been sturdy, black-bearded men with long hair, clothed in a mixture of wool and fur. Their soft leather footwear stuffed with moss to prevent frostbite had offered them no protection against the cruel spikes. The soldiers discovered that the four who had not been brought down by spears had cut their own throats. All of them had one mangled foot and a diagonal slash from below the left ear towards the base of the neck. Two still had knives in their stiff hands. The soldiers rifled through their clothes looking for valuables but there were none.

The two centurions leaned over and looked at the heap.

"Scruffy bastards," one of them said.

"Do you think the Camp prefect will want to take a look before they're tossed over the edge?"

"Might be as well to hang on for him," the first one replied.

Titus ordered to them dispose of the dead over the far end of the plateau, not into the ravine.

By late morning, the rope-way had been repaired and was shuttling men and materials from one side to the other, the carpenters were back at work to a chorus of taps and clinks sounding out of forges and masons work areas.

Otto sent a party of his Germans to follow the trail into the mountains. They found another dead man who they left for the wolves but nothing else of note. The attackers had split up into smaller groups and moved on and up until they were lost in a broken tree-lined landscape.

Titus Attius listened carefully to Boxer's damage report and steps taken to make repairs. Otto told him what his scouting party had discovered. The Camp Prefect sat for a long while digesting what he had heard, then spoke.

"First a relatively minor act of sabotage, then the poisoning of our water supply which caused several deaths and forced Tribune Plancus to relinquish his command due to ill-health, now an assault. Open aggression, admittedly only in small numbers but an organized attack, nevertheless. What concerns me most is that they killed themselves rather than be taken alive. Presumably so we could not question them. I am sure Boxer can put up a very fine bridge but it's pointless."

"Why do you say that?" asked Boxer who had been stung by Titus's apparent dismissal of his efforts

"As soon as it's finished and we march away, it will be burned down and totally destroyed," Otto told him.

"If that's true why are they hindering us? They could leave us alone. The construction would be completed and we'd be on our way much sooner without interference," Boxer said, pleased with the point he had made.

"Because they don't know we'll be leaving. Think about it. Even with Boxer's engineers gone, there would be over fifteen hundred men left. Fifteen hundred men who have established themselves on a known strongpoint, secured fresh water, improved the road and opened a supply line to Emporiae. It would be reasonable to think that we're going to maintain a permanent garrison in this position," Titus suggested.

He could see that his idea had set wheels spinning in the two officers' minds.

"So why don't they come in force and try to drive us off?" Boxer asked.

Titus looked grim. "It takes time to assemble enough men, particularly in winter. If we do find ourselves facing a hostile army in battle, it will be a rag tag of tribesmen and mountaineers. They don't have the organising skill of Rome. Warriors will have to be persuaded or bribed to come against us."

"You think we are being delayed to give some unknown enemy time to build up his strength?"

"I don't know, it's possible."

Otto broke in. "We are certainly protecting the gold shipments but the Emperor could have provided Adonis Frugi with an ala of cavalry to do that. With all due respect to Boxer, is a bridge in this location worth the expense to save Sextus Tubero a few days shipping time? I don't think so. I believe the whole thing is a ruse to explain the presence of the praetorian cohorts and cavalry in Tarraconensis and nothing more."

Boxer's faced reddened in annoyance. "So I am wasting my time and the skill and labour of all my men like the Camp prefect said. I've been made a fool of," Boxer said with bitterness.

"You are obeying the orders of your Emperor, that's what you're doing," Titus growled then went on in a gentler tone of voice "No-one has set out to make a mug of you. This goes back to high politics in Rome. A soldier has no right to an explanation of his orders; he just has to follow them."

Otto tried to soften the blow to his friend's pride. "I don't think Augustus has set out to demean you but we are only the pieces in the game he plays. He moves us when it's our turn and only he can see the whole of the board."

Boxer half-smiled and nodded in agreement. "It's a bit hard to take, that's all. We've been giving our all..."

"And that's why the Emperor chose you," Titus told him. "He knows you're loyal to a fault, if that's possible."

"When the tribune and I were given our orders by Publius Quadratus he also said that we should investigate the thefts and bring the marauders to justice. The way he phrased it was a bit odd," Otto reminded them.

"Why's that odd?" asked Titus,

"He used the word "investigate". What's that supposed to mean? If he had simply told us to find them and then get rid of them, fair enough but what are we supposed to investigate? In any case, we haven't done anything about that part of our orders have we?"

Titus and Boxer had to admit the truth of Otto's words.

"So, how do we set about it?"

They agreed to think on the matter, get back together and discuss possibilities.

The next day it snowed. It snowed as if one hundred thousand frantic farmers' wives were all plucking their geese at once. Fat, lazy flakes drifted down, then more and more until visibility was only a few feet and even that obscured by the swirl and eddy of the falling snow when a stray breeze caught it. It stuck on eyelashes and had to be blinked away. It melted on necks and sent an icy trickle down spines. Day after day the drifts mounted. The men shovelled themselves out of their tents in the morning and dug paths to the latrines and fire pits, only to see them obliterated by further falls the next day. There was no possibility of looking for grazing and for the first time, serious inroads were made into their fodder supplies which, up until then, had been used sparingly to supplement the animals' diet. They protected their horses with coats crudely made out of spare blankets and sailcloth. The few remaining oxen and the mules had to suffer through it as best they could. All work ceased. Everyone huddled under cover like mice in their holes, peering out and looking for relief, only to be disappointed. After ten days, the wind veered to the north. The skies cleared to a pale blue, the sun shone without warmth and a chilling wind covered the snowfields with a fine layer of crystalline ice. The livestock turned their hindquarters to the wind and stood miserably with heads hanging low. Just when it seemed that the weather could do no more to them, a sou'wester blew in. The sun was hidden once more by the racing clouds. Awnings were torn into the raging air. Boxer's rope works were whipped from side to side, straining their anchors. Stinging rain lashed down. At the storm's height, the tents shook and bulged threatening to split and then, miraculously it seemed, it was all over. They emerged into a calm morning with everything steaming in the watery sun. The snow had vanished, blown to who knew where, or melted away.

The snow had insulated the grass roots from the worst of the cold. They had put out short and vivid shoots which the animals tore into now they could go down to seek out grazing everyday. But it was not enough to sustain them and the fodder held in camp was running dangerously low. The quartermaster spoke to Titus Attius about it.

"Next time the gold is shipped to Tarraco go along with the cavalry. Take couple of empty wagons with you and bring 'em back full.," Titus ordered.

Then Saturnalia was upon them. No possibility of discussing "investigation" or implementing any scheme. Shouts of "Io Saturnalia" rang around the camp. They slaughtered and roasted the oxen. Double wine rations were served. Otto hid himself away in the middle of his German auxiliaries. He loathed the nonsensical behaviour normally sensible men, and women, indulged in during the days of the festival. The cavalrymen were unhappy not to have any boar for their own end of year feast but they consoled themselves with the knowledge that three oxen had been reserved for them.

In Luca, Lollia and her household were having the best Saturnalia they had ever enjoyed in the villa. Otto, who cast gloom over the proceedings, was away so everyone could really get into the spirit. Libius had soaked scraps of cloth in glue and moulded them so that they dried into the faces of birds and animals. He painted them expertly so that, at dinner, Saxa as a lion sat facing Lollia as a parrot and Lucius Albus wore a dog's face. That was an enormous success. Saxa and Lollia took their masks with them to a party at the Longius' home in the city. Their host, Vitius, stood at the side of his major-domo pouring his wine. Sabina Pulchra, dressed as a cook, brought in a covered dish and placed in the centre of the table. When she lifted the lid with a flourish, she revealed a plate of fish-skins and old bones. The room rocked with laughter. Saxa thought Saturnalia was wonderful, unlike her brother to whom it brought back bad memories as well as his contempt for the whole idea.

The Germans had no priests of their own with them but there was one man among them who had the gift, or curse, of being able to hear the Gods when they spoke. They asked Otto for permission to perform the ceremony on the last night of the year when they would be feasting. He granted them their request. They began to dig a pit but ran into the problem Titus Attius had foreseen when first setting out the camp. The soil was too stony to be able to go down far enough. When they hit rock and could go no farther they embanked the sides with soil and stones to build it up until it was over the height of a man's head.

The Roman priest consulted his water clock and told them when it was a few minutes short of midnight. Otto invited Boxer and Titus along with the senior centurions to witness the rite. As near as possible to midnight, the seer stripped naked and clambered into the hole. The Romans stood in a group to one side as the cavalrymen led a spare horse up the sloping side. Its throat was cut with one deft movement. Blood fountained outwards, strong arms supported the dying animal until its knees buckled and it fell, head and neck hanging over the edge. There was a long silence. The Romans were looking at each other beginning to think it was all over when a voice rose up. It seemed to be coming from the earth itself. It chanted in a sing-song, eery, otherworldly.

"Brothers, listen. Brothers, hear me. The God of Battles is coming. As ever, Death walks with him. I feel his stinking corpse-breath blow in my face. The God of Battles approaches."

The voice faded away. In spite of themselves, the officers other than Otto touched their good luck amulets or made the sign against evil with their fingers. The silence flowed around them, uncomfortable, tense. After several more minutes the voice came again.

"Oh man, go deeper than the deepest grave. Go willingly, without holding back. Then rise again to greet victory."

There was a shuffling noise of falling earth and stone as the blood-soaked warrior climbed out. He was ashen, exhausted and staggered as he walked. His comrades held him up and half carried him to the fireside where they gave him a long drink of heated wine.

The dead horse was pushed into the pit which was back-filled and marked with a cairn.

The Romans all looked at each other speculatively but no-one offered any comment as they walked back to the relative warmth of their billets.

Chapter 15

Titus was cynical. "Not much of a prophecy. In my experience the God of Battles is permanently on his way or has just left. Goodnight gentlemen," with which he disappeared inside his tent.

"It was impressive, though," Boxer said. "But I thought your Gods lived in sacred groves, not holes in the ground."

Otto rubbed his hands together in the warmth of the flames, looking over at his friend sitting opposite.

"They don't; the groves are holy places where they speak with men. The sacrifice was the life of a horse. His blood is the symbol of that life and the seer enters the womb of the earth hoping the Gods will come to accept the offering and grant an insight into the future."

"So where do your Gods live?"

Otto shrugged. "The Gods are the world and everything in it. They are all around seeing and hearing us and all life."

"It seems very strange to me," Boxer told him.

"Stranger than a dozen eternal beings living on top of a mountain in Greece?"

Boxer laughed ruefully. "You have me there."

They lapsed into companionable silence and stared into the flames. After a while, Boxer spoke again.

"Do you ever wonder why we are here? What is everything for?"

"I treasure that scroll of the sayings of great philosophers your grandmother Aelia gave me. It made me want to read more but the more I read, the more I came to understand that the greatest minds agree about very little. What happens after we are dead? We'll find out sooner or later. In the meantime, all we can do is be true to ourselves, our friends and our honour."

"As simple as that?"

"Boxer, you can complicate it as much as you like but that's what it boils down to. Zeno, Parmenides, Aristotle, they are united by an understanding that men know next to nothing. We can only try to make sense of everything out of our limited wisdom. For example, Plato….."

Boxer held up a hand to stop him and smiled.

"No more, Otto, I give in. Once you start on that subject you lose me and I get a headache. I often wish that Aelia had never given you that scroll; it's what sets you off and when you get going nothing stops you…"

"Yes but…"

"Goodnight, sleep well my friend," Boxer said and went to his bed.

Otto smiled to himself as he sat, alone now, thinking of the hours he had spent politely listening while Boxer explained stresses and strains, angles of applied force and geometric principles far beyond his ability to comprehend. "Be true to yourself and your friends," he muttered and turned in.

With the new year, work began again. Boxer's men placed three beams on both sides of the ravine, jutting outwards from the foundations by twenty-five feet. They sloped upwards at the same, precise angle.

They were locked in position by stone blocks mortared together and reinforced with iron.

"Now we have to build a pair of A-frames to lower the first cross-pieces into position," Boxer told them.

The next shipment was dispatched from the mine protected by one hundred cavalrymen along with the quartermaster and his empty carts. The day after it left, the remaining auxiliaries moved off, herding the mules down to search for grazing. Otto watched them for a minute as they headed towards the top of the first of the hairpins bends that led down to the plain. It was a routine sight. He wandered over to see what the engineers were up to. Some instinct made him look back. The main mass of men and animals were still at the top of the road: nearly all of them should be out of sight. He heard faint shouts carried on the breeze. Something was wrong.

He grabbed a spare horse by the halter and rode over as fast as he could. He dragged his mount to a standstill in a flurry of mud and grit thrown up by its skidding hooves and leapt off its bare back. When he looked down, his heart turned over in his chest. Below him he saw a long palisade. Each pair of shoulder-height upright posts was flanked by a sharpened stake leaning outward. Hundreds of men crowded behind it blocking the bottom of the road. Further back stood a second fence but with the cruel points facing the other way.

A dozen cavalrymen had taken the lead with the mule herd behind them and the rest of their comrades further back. The leading troopers had seen what awaited them and halted at the top of the narrow, steep road but the mules wanted fresh grass and water; they were pushing forward. The trapped men had turned and were trying to beat them back but were in imminent danger of being barged onto the dangerously steep slope where their horses would lose their footings, slide and tumble until they crashed against the fence. Men dismounted all around Otto and ran to drag mules away to relieve the pressure on their comrades. As some of the animals were yanked and beaten out of the way, others followed but still those at the front of the mob pushed forward.

In the chaos of braying, kicking and biting, swearing men dodged the hooves and teeth as they hauled on halters, tails, ears, Otto added his own strength and voice but it seemed to be too late for the men forced against the edge of the road. Then one of them leaned forward in the saddle and thrust his lance into the chest of the panicked mule in front of him. It reared and fell dead. He struck again at another. His comrades realized what he was attempting and followed his lead. In less than a minute, they were protected by a low wall of dead animals. The rest backed away from the smell of fresh blood. A bellow of disappointed rage rose up from the warriors in the fenced enclosure when they saw that the disaster had been avoided.

With difficulty, some sort of order was restored. Within half an hour the carcases had been dragged away, gutted and jointed for the pot. They had lost eight mules but saved the lives of a dozen good men and horses. It was well worth the price and the bonus of a good dinner was in store for everyone.

Titus Attius stood with both hands resting on the end of his vine staff gazing down. Otto and Boxer stood with him.

"Like a mushroom, just appeared overnight. How many of them d'you reckon?"

"A thousand?" Boxer suggested.

"More," Otto said, "over twelve hundred."

"Huh, "Titus grunted. "Trouble with these native forces is the numbers change all the time. Remember up on the Rhine? Half of the German besiegers buggered off when they had a setback but even more came along when they thought they were getting on top. It'll be the same with this lot. They'll be close on two thousand in a couple of days."

He screwed up his eyes and studied the warriors assembled between their wooden walls. Some wore metal helmets, some mail shirts, some carried shields but few of them were completely armoured. He saw the glittering blades of long spears, axes and, most worrying, scores of hunting bows. Titus turned and looked at the spring flowing out of its cave. Gullies and faults led deep into the mountains either side of it but they were narrow and steep. Experience told him that a mass assault from that quarter was extremely unlikely. No, they were going to have to deal solely with the men on the plain.

"Half an hour, council of war outside my tent. All officers are to attend."

Otto walked back into the cavalry lines.

"Who was the first to lance the mules?" he asked.

They shuffled and looked at each other, considering whether they should close ranks and say they didn't know. Perhaps some punishment awaited whoever had done it; the animals had been army property and these Romans had a rigid set of rules. After a while, Sigbold stepped forward with his chin high, ready to take what might be coming to him. His face was scarred where the bear had torn it, seamed with a red line and a row flax stitches blackened with pinpoints of dried blood almost ready to come out.

"I was the first, Lord."

"Sigbold, you saved the lives of your brother auxiliaries today. It was well done. Camp Prefect Titus Attius writes a report to the Emperor everyday. I will ask him to mention you in it. Augustus himself will know the name of Sigbold Bearslayer."

Sigbold smiled broadly and some of the tension went out of the troopers. They had been badly shaken by the earlier events. To fall from the road and be impaled on the fence was not a fitting death for a Suevi horseman.

The assembled officers were grim.

"Any thoughts, gentlemen," Titus asked.

The senior centurion of the Rome cohort spoke first. "Attack, Camp prefect. We march on them now before they can improve their defences and attract reinforcements."

Titus shook his head. "There is nothing I want more than to get stuck into the bastards but the ground is against us. The slope's too steep so we would have to go down the road. Think, there are two sharp bends so you'd have your shields on the wrong side for at least one of them and they've got bows; probably slings as well. We can only march on a six-man front, too narrow. Sorry centurion, I know it's the praetorian way but not this time."

"Could we roll rocks down on them?" someone else suggested.

"Certainly that would do a lot of damage but after the first few, they'll just retreat out of the way and use what we chuck at them to improve their barrier. Prefect Boxer, what can you offer us in the way of artillery?"

"I have three scorpions and one medium ballista. Not enough to give a curtain of fire. I could do a lot of damage but it would be the same thing. Once we got started, they'd simply move out of range."

Titus nodded.

"Can we find a place to climb down and go at them from the flank?" the adjutant asked.

Again Titus rejected the idea.

"They've been watching us for weeks. If we try that they'll see what we're up to and be waiting. I'm not interested in filtering men in to die a few at a time. On the subject of being spied on, where are your artillery pieces, prefect?"

"Still under canvas on their transport, sir." Boxer replied.

"Keep 'em that way." Titus looked around at everyone. "Well boys, we're in the shit, no use to say otherwise. But we are soldiers of Rome. We climb out and knock big lumps out of the bastards who pushed us in, eh, Prefect Otto?"

Otto's eyes widened in surprise and then he grinned broadly.

"Yes we do, Camp prefect, we wait a little and then slice pieces off them."

"After all these years, is that confession, prefect?"

"No idea what you're referring to, sir," Otto replied, his face a mask of counterfeit innocence.

"Thank you for your suggestions everyone, dismissed," Titus said and walked into his tent to think.

He was satisfied with his council of war. The officers would feel that they had been consulted, even if their ideas had been rejected. The final exchange between Titus and Otto would have piqued their curiosity. Questions would be asked. The story of how as a boy, Otto, not yet part of the legions, had been thrown into a latrine by a drunken bully and then ambushed him and cut off one of his ears would be retold. There had been no witnesses so Otto had got away with maiming a legionary. If found guilty, he would have been executed. It would give the men something to gossip and laugh about and keep their minds off their situation.

Boxer ordered his artillerists to inspect their pieces and do all they could to make sure they were fit for service without removing their covers. "The Camp Prefect believes we are being observed and he's generally right. Let's not show our hand."

He told the engineers they might as well get on with the project while they could. Soon the background noise of mallets and saws and the ringing of anvils struck with heavy hammers resounded around the camp again, lending an air of comforting normality in their extreme situation.

Titus doubled the sentries and ordered twenty men with a bugler to guard the head of the road against incursions. There was nothing else to be done except rack his brains for a way out of this. His worn features showed nothing of his deep concern about their situation. It was as bad as anything he had come across. Effectively, they were under siege but the standard countermeasure of sallying out in force to drive off the besiegers, if only temporarily, was not open to him. The main thing was not to allow himself to be panicked into rash action

At the following morning parade, none of the guards had anything of note to report. The enemy had spent the night by their firesides singing and probably drinking. Their numbers had not altered. A few arrows had been fired up at the sentries but all had fallen short, none getting closer than the second stretch of road. After inspecting the men and issuing the orders of the day, Titus called Otto over.

"We don't have enough fodder and grazing up here for all our livestock so I want your men to slaughter the mules over the next four days. We can easily buy new ones when this is over but we can't replace your warhorses; we need to feed them as well as possible. We're all gong to be eating a lot of mule from now on. I'm also cutting the men's grain ration by one quarter; they won't need it with all the fresh meat they'll be scoffing."

The praetorians accepted reduction in their rations without complaint but the mood in the camp was subdued. Otto had the flesh of every fourth animal cut into thin strips. They were soaked overnight in saltwater then hung over a smoky fire under cover. It was an imperfect way of preservation but better than nothing. One of the troopers came over to Otto with a sly smirk on his face.

"We could double wrap the paunches and guts in the skins and roll 'em down on the enemy camp. Won't do any damage but it'll really piss them off. Be stinking after a couple of days…."

Titus approved the scheme. When ten rough balls of rawhide had been prepared, he ordered all off-duty soldiers to assemble at the top of the road to watch.

They slung them outwards down the near vertical slopes. The bundles flattened as they hit the ground then rebounded into the air, gaining speed with each bounce. None split. They could see the enemy backing away from the fence, unsure what was hurtling towards them. The first one struck the point of a stake and ripped apart. Entrails, faeces and digestive liquids fountained upwards before spurting through the gaps in the fence. Others flew right over it and burst inside the defences. Their enemies' howls of rage and disgust could barely be heard over the storm of sound made by the laughing, jeering Romans.

When they had quieted down a little, Titus' parade-ground voice boomed out.

"There we are lads. We've had to put up with enough of their dirty tricks but now they know we're even worse than them!"

Morale soared.

On the third day of being bombarded with offal, some of the enemy became so furious they lost all good sense. Around fifty of them rushed up the road towards the Roman camp. They brandished spears and axes and clutched long oval shields. At their head raced a young warrior with leather thongs plaited around his hair and beard, an old pattern legion helmet on his head. They were running as hard as they could in their mistaken belief that large boulders were about to be rolled down on them. The defenders had no such intention.

The bugler blew the alarm when they rounded the first of the hairpins. The remnants of the daily crowd of spectators rejoined the guard party until a full century of men watched and waited for the approaching enemy who were now half-way up the second stretch of road. They had slowed noticeably but were still coming on at a good pace.

"Spears," the centurion called.

After the second bend and on the final stretch, fatigue had taken its toll of the attackers. They had misjudged the steepness of the road and began to realise how rash they had been.

The first flight of the weighted Roman spears dropped four warriors. The praetorians did not have to put much effort into throwing them, launching at the correct angle, gravity did the rest. The shock of the hissing blades plunging into the ground at their feet and the shrieks of their stricken comrades stopped the running men in their tracks. Three more were hit. The survivors raised their shields over their heads but the spears punched through them, knocking over two more. They turned as one and sprinted back the way they had come, the adrenalin rush of terror revitalized their aching legs as they ran like athletes for the safety of their camp.

"Cease fire!" the centurion yelled. "Save your ammunition!"

With eighteen missiles thrown, they had killed or disabled nine attackers, a good return for their expenditure of the single use weapons. The dead lay silently where they had fallen; the wounded screamed or begged for help for an hour before the Romans sallied out and gave them a merciful thrust to end their long agony. They recovered the soft iron blades of their spears; one of the armourers would straighten them and new wooden shafts would be pegged in. The bodies were shoved off the road to roll and tumble limply, end over end, gathering speed until they stuck on the loose scree or thudded against the base of the fence. There was no reaction from the enemy.

Construction continued at pace. They had cut the timber for two A-frames and assembled one with its own windlass on each side of the ravine. The engineers employed them in tandem to sway out and attach the first, straight cross-section to the main support pieces. The full length would be made up of three timbers, lap-jointed together with iron reinforcements. They fitted secondary supporting beams under the main ones which were now load-bearing. The masons' hammers clinked again as stone was cut into shaped blocks to anchor the new timber work. The structure began to resemble a bridge. Any man daring enough could have stepped out and walked across. No-one made the attempt.

Titus Attius had been walking about the camp criticising, encouraging and barking orders as usual. He seemed his unaltered, imperturbable self to the men but inwardly he was in turmoil, his mind raging like a trapped wolf. There had to be a way out of this impasse. He was sure that if he sent his praetorians down they would take the day but their losses would be terrible. He understood that men must be sacrificed on the altar of battle to gain victory but it was a case of deciding when that heavy price had to be paid, if there was no alternative. The moment of decision was not far off; they were running out of mules. Titus ordered the grain ration cut to one half of its original amount and called an early meeting with Boxer and Otto.

"It looks like I'm going to have to send the lads in," he said bleakly. "What's the maximum you can do for them, Boxer?"

"Three scorpions firing three bolts a minute for ten minutes is ninety bolts. Supposing all found their targets, which they won't, means I could inflict ninety casualties but since a bolt often takes more than one down, the number could be as many as one hundred and twenty, theoretically. In practice, I could guarantee no more than sixty."

"Not many out of two thousand," Titus said glumly.

"Two thousand! have their numbers grown that much??"

Titus nodded. "Yes; they've been inviting their mates over for mule gut soup. Can you smash up the fence with your ballista?"

"Not the front one. I've already checked the angle, Because it's down below and butts up tight to the cliff by the bottom of the road, I can't make a falling shot. I could systematically destroy the back fence and drop some stones down among them…."

"If that's the best you can give me, that's how it must be. I'm going to send six hundred men down with a second wave standing by at the top. As soon as the first assault group engages, the second marches. That leaves me only around three hundred in reserve."

"How many casualties do you expect?" Otto asked.

"With the numbers the lads are up against on a narrow front, possibly four hundred," Titus told him expressionlessly. "Trouble is, I've got another dog in this fight that I can't use…"

"What do you mean?"

Titus waved vaguely. "Otto's cavalry is somewhere out there. They must be on their way back from Emporiae but the quartermaster's wagons will slow them up. If they could join the attack it would make a big difference."

"Horses won't charge a fence of sharpened stakes…"

"Boxer says he can smash up the back one facing the road they'll be coming in on," Titus remarked.

"To work, it would have to be a co-ordinated three-pronged attack. Artillery, infantry and cavalry supporting each other. But we don't know where Otto's men are, nor are we in communication with them, so that's that," Boxer said with an air of resignation.

"I blame your miserable hole-in-the-ground prophet for this, Otto. God of Battle on his way? Well, he was spot on there.…"

"What about the problem of the men having to shift their shields over?"

"Oh, I'll sort that with a bit of drill tomorrow," Titus said airily.

He paraded his troops in centuries and made them march in column six abreast. They started with their shields carried on their left arms facing him.

"Left turn!" he yelled.

The men responded without falling out of step. He let them proceed for another few paces.

"Left turn," he shouted again.

They followed his command in perfect unison once more. He allowed them to carry on for a few more yards then called a halt.

"Right lads, think of me as the enemy. You started off with your shields towards me but after the second turn they're on the other side to me and you're completely unprotected. That's what it'll be like when we march down that hairpin road. Note I said "when" not "if". For the second stretch you'll be wide-open to anything they fire or chuck at you. But don't worry. Your Camp Prefect has thought about your welfare and the problem is easily solved. On the command, the line of men on the side nearest the enemy will change shields from left to right arms without dropping anything or tripping over their big flat feet. Back to your starting position and we'll try it, shall we?"

Otto sat watching the heavy infantry marching up and down, the rhythmic stamping of their boots punctuated by shouts of, "Left turn! Left turn!" from Titus who occasionally became exasperated. "Who dropped that lance? You, you dozy sod? You're letting yourself down in front of your centurion and all your mates!"

After two hours they could exchange shield arms from right to left and back again on the march without any problem. Titus now added a complication. A second line was to change arms and also lift their shields above head height, slightly tilted backwards, to give added protection against stones, slingshot or arrows.

They broke up to rest after another two hours and began again, this time receiving their orders from their own centurions.

Otto put his interlaced fingers behind his head and leaned back against the breastwork. The stone was pleasantly warm even though the sun was only a pale disc half-hidden by the hazy cloud above. Boxer was using two flags, one red, one white, to direct the operation of lowering one of the massive curved sections made in the shipyards into place. Both A-frames were employed. An engineer stood beside the sweating crew of each windlass relaying Boxer's signals. They wound cable onto the huge drum, letting the timber rise a little, stopped, allowed it to descend, all the while inching towards its final resting place. "It must weigh tons," Otto thought idly then sighed. The shouted orders and stamping boots of the soldiers being drilled rose up again. His thoughts turned to the sombre idea that so many of them were going to perform their new manoeuvre to the best of their ability but die, nevertheless. His mind wandered to the omen chanted out of the blood pit. The seer had been right. Battle and death were upon them. He thought of the second part of the omen as the great beam swayed over the ravine.

The idea hit Otto with the blinding flash of a lightning bolt. He leapt to his feet rubbing his hands together and staring wildly about. Some men working nearby looked at him askance and moved a little farther off. He had to speak to Boxer and Titus, now, right away, but they were both busy. If he didn't say or do something he would burst. He strode rapidly into the centre of the cavalry lines.

"I need a volunteer to…"

"I'll do it!" Sigbold Bearslayer shouted before he could finish.

"You don't know what it is yet," Otto remonstrated but the younger man would hear nothing.

"It will be a chance for glory, lord, that's all I need to know."

Otto took Sigbold to one side and explained his plan. Sigbold's eyes shone and he smiled widely.

"Oh yes, lord, I'm with you all the way. What a bold stroke it will be; bards will sing of it forever."

"Before that we have to persuade Camp Prefect Attius and Prefect Boxer that we can do it. Have you spoken with Titus Attius face to face?"

"No, not yet."

"Right, this is what you do. Stand very straight with your gaze directed just above the top of his head. Don't smile and don't speak unless he speaks to you first."

Sigbold started to laugh.

"It's not a joke...." Otto said sharply.

"You mean I'm not even allowed to look him in the eye?"

"Correct, not until he has spoken."

Sigbold shook his head in disbelief. "What stupid men these Romans are! Yet they are masters of the world."

Otto shrugged, "Strange is perhaps a better word than stupid. Come on, they will have broken off their duties to eat the midday meal, such as it is."

Sigbold stood straight staring at the crest of the Camp Prefect's helmet.

"Sir, I name Sigbold Bearslayer to you." barked Otto.

Titus looked the tall young Suevi up and down. "You're the one who saved his mates' lives when they were trapped on the road aren't you?"

"Yes sir, I am, sir."

"It was well done. I've mentioned you in my dispatch to Emperor Augustus. He likes a man who's quick thinking. Sit down lad and eat with us. Prefect Boxer, this is assistant decurion...."

"I know of him, sir" Boxer said.

Sigbold bowed and Boxer gave him an encouraging smile. Titus removed his helmet as their meagre rations were placed on the table in front of them. "Who fancies some smoked mule and half a barley cake? Speak up don't be shy!" Titus joked.

"I thought bears slept all winter long," Boxer said to open up some conversation.

"Not all of them, sir. They'll often come out if the weather warms up for a few days or they're hungry enough," Sigbold informed him.

"Nice to have a new face at the table Otto, but you haven't brought this young officer along without a damn good reason have you?" Titus asked.

"No sir. I've come up with a scheme in respect of co-ordinating an attack involving the cavalry that went off to Emporiae with the quartermaster. Sigbold Bearslayer has volunteered to participate and I'm sure that between the two of us, we can make a success of the venture.

"You seem keen, Otto, what's it all about?"

Chapter 16

Otto started to explain his plan. He had barely begun when Boxer froze. He stared at his friend, open-mouthed, a lump of well-chewed meat clearly visible inside. When Otto had finished, Boxer closed his mouth and gulped. The meat stuck in his throat, he began to choke and threw back his cup of wine-tinted water. He spluttered and thumped his chest.

"You're mad," he wheezed, eyes watering from coughing.

"But can you do it?" Otto asked.

"Can I lower you, this deranged volunteer and two horses, into the ravine so you can trot off and bring the cavalry in? Certainly not."

Titus nudged Sigbold and said, "Sit back and enjoy this, son," in a voice too low for the others to hear.

"You got me down to recover the bodies of your engineers," Otto accused.

"Yes but that was just you and you weren't wearing any armour," Boxer replied, implying that it was not relevant.

"I watched you swaying that great lump of timber about today. It must be heavier than a horse." Otto went on.

"That's not the point," Boxer snapped.

"So you admit your rig is up to the weight?"

"Technically, but the beam wasn't panicking and kicking like a horse would."

"We can put a bag over its head."

Boxer thought for a moment.

"We don't have a suitable sling-harness."

"The saddler can knock one up this afternoon," Otto responded instantly.

"It might swing against the rockface and injure its legs."

"We'll wrap them with torn-up blankets and canvas."

"It's possible, in theory, but only in theory mind. Supposing the enemy has posted men in the ravine?"

"Oh, come off it, Boxer. In any case Sigbold and I have taken a good, long look. No sign of anyone."

"The entrance could be guarded though," Sigbold interjected.

Otto and Titus nodded their agreement.

"Alright, it could be done but how are you two going to ride your horses through the pitch black down there, eh? Answer me that?" Boxer asked.

There was a triumphant note in his voice. He clearly thought that they would be unable to come up with a response. The cavalrymen looked at him in astonishment at his assumption that they would be mounted.

"But we'll be leading them, sir," Sigbold replied. "Lord Otto has told me the rain has washed a gravel path down the middle. We shall use that."

"It'll be like it was under siege up in Germany all over again. You risk your neck to ride off into the unknown to try to save us and we wait for days dreading to see your head stuck on an enemy spear as a trophy….." Boxer told his friend with unhappy resignation.

Titus Attius spoke for the first time. "As I recollect that time, if it had not been for your skill and ingenuity, Boxer, none of us would have been alive when Otto returned. So, who saved the Second Lucan, you or Otto?"

Boxer's face reddened. "Oh sir, I wasn't saying I'm jealous…."

"Of course not; back then you were furious because your friend put himself in grave danger without you knowing anything about it beforehand. Now, you're thinking of every possible reason to prevent him doing it again but understand, once and for all, you have no say in this beyond what's practical. Every soldier's life belongs to Rome. It can be hazarded only with the approval of his commanding officer. I approve."

Boxer rose to his feet and stood to attention. "Very well, Camp prefect. May I be excused? I need time think about the best possible way of accomplishing this folly. I hope to come back to you all later this afternoon."

Titus chuckled and grinned at Sigbold. "There we are son. I told you they'd put on a good show. Like squabbling brothers. If you could squeeze them in one skin you would create the greatest man the world has ever seen. With Boxer's calculation and Otto's rush to action, he would be unstoppable. Ah well, you and the prefect better look over your kit and your horses. I'll send a man to find you when Boxer comes back."

The shadows were long when a praetorian jogged up to Otto, came to attention and saluted.

"Camp Prefect's compliments, sir, he and Prefect Boxer are wating for you outside his tent."

Boxer had unrolled a drawing of the road and enemy fortification and laid it flat on Titus' table with the edges held down with pebbles. He asked the others to sit but remained on his feet and began to speak clearly and unemotionally.

"Subject to confirmation, this is what I propose. Otto and Sigbold go as soon as it is dark. I need the praetorians to make a diversion with lots of noise at the top of the road, lighting two fires as if they were moving in strength to take up permanent positions there. I plan to lower both our men down at once, sharing a rope. When they have safely descended, the horses follow one at a time. It's essential that the windlass-men work in harmony. My flag signals are effective but they may not see them clearly at night so I shall need some torches and screens. The carry-sling for the horses has already been sewn together; treble canvas and leather and I'm attaching a pair of hundred foot guide ropes to it. Otto and Sigbold can use them to direct their mounts into the centre of the ravine and minimise the pendulum effect. I propose we employ flags to communicate with the cavalry on its arrival. One flag waved by either Otto or Sigbold indicates they are ready about four hundred yards out. We shall respond with one flag to show we acknowledge their presence on the field, followed later by two together to give the order to charge. Sigbold, you are a hunter. Can you use a bow?" He indicated that he could. Boxer nodded then went on. "In the event of poor visibility, we substitute fire arrows for flags. Sigbold to be provided with the necessary materials. That is all. I await your comments, Camp Prefect."

"As thorough as ever, Boxer," Titus told him. "When it comes to the fine detail, there's no man better. I can't see a flaw in your plan but as we all know, plans usually end up getting pissed on by the enemy." He tapped the drawing with his index finger. "We go with this. Is there anything else?"

"Yes sir," Otto said. "May I use the services of your clerk to write something for me?"

The man hurried up with steel pen, inkpot and parchment. He wrote to Otto's dictation and was asked to read to back it. He cleared his throat.

"*This is the military will of Imperial Prefect and Knight of Rome, Otto Longius. My arm rings are to be disposed of by a council of the senior officers of my cavalry. I leave my warhorse Djinn with his saddle and tack to Sigbold Bearslayer who shares this imminent peril with me. I return my pugio to its original owner, Titus Attius, in the hope he will pass it on to his son and tell him of what we have shared. I leave all the money I have in camp, my personal belongings and my grey gelding with his saddle and tack to Lucius Taurius Longius. My civil will is lodged in the temple of Jupiter Best and Greatest in Luca."*

Otto signed, asked the clerk to witness and take the document over to the tesserarius for safe-keeping.

"What about your sword and your mail shirt?" Titus asked.

"If whoever takes me down doesn't plunder my dead body, they'll be buried along with me. Oh, and a horse to ride in the next world. That's why I've left Djinn and my gelding to Sigbold and Boxer. Otherwise my men would cut their throats and lay them in my grave."

"Not a very Roman send-off then," Titus said drily.

Otto laughed. "I want to spend eternity with my ancestors, sir. You may recollect they are all Suevi......"

In the glow of the torches hidden from the mountainside by temporary screens, Boxer was crackling with tension as he stood beside Otto and Sigbold at the lip of the ravine. His eyes darted everywhere searching for anything that had been overlooked. He wrung his hands, took a deep breath and exhaled.

"We are as ready as I can make us. Mars and Fortuna with you," he said and unfurled both his flags.

The windlasses turned, the ropes tightened and the two men rose gently into the air then outwards over the black void. At the last minute when they were preparing themselves to descend, Sigbold had suggested a lamp so that they could see to take the slings off the horses. One was fetched for him in a leather bag with a flint, steel and a small flask of oil. He slung it around his neck by a string, it was just one more encumbrance. Under their cloaks, both men wore their mail shirts hung about with their weapons. Shields and helmets were strapped to their belts and over their shoulders. They had separate foot loops and wrapped one arm around the rope suspending them and the other around their companion. They were so close, they could feel the warmth of each other's breath on their faces.

The engineers standing by watched two figures glittering in the starlight fade and disappear into the mouth of the chasm. The ropes stretched and creaked as they were fed off the windlass drums. Otto and Sigbold lifted their gaze to the wide blaze of stars overhead, narrowing into a slit of light as they descended. It was three hours past the sunset of a clear winter's day. The moon was two nights off the full and would rise in an hour's time. After a short while, they lost any sense of time passing. It seemed as if they had been in this blind silence for ever. They began to revolve, slowly. It was a peculiar sensation as they could not see the cliff walls on either side of them. It was something like lying down drunk in a windowless room. They heard a faint sound; water chuckling and gurgling and then they were at the bottom, ankle deep in an icy stream. The rain and snow of winter draining off the mountains and plateau was running freely out over what had been a faintly damp gravel bed in summer.

They stepped out of their loops and gave two mighty tugs on the rope. After a short pause, it passed upwards out of their hands. Sigbold splashed to one side and felt around for a flattish stone. He fumbled the lamp out of its bag, over-filled it with oil and struck a shower of sparks to light it. The flame flared yellow in the gloom. He moved it to a position between two rocks where its light was almost concealed. They waited.

If proud Djinn could have seen himself he would have died of shame but he was blinded by the bag over his head. His legs were wrapped around with torn blankets, mummy fashion again and again, taken over his back and under his belly to stop the padding from slipping off. The sling took his weight, the ground went from under his feet. He let his head and neck slump and splayed his stiffened legs.

Time hung heavy on Otto and Sigbold but they had learned a soldier's patience. Eventually, the guide ropes splashed down and they caught them in the guttering light. They took a tight hold and braced to ensure Djinn's landing would be in the middle of the stream. The horse snorted and raised his head when he was reunited with the solid earth, even if it lay beneath three inches of cold water. Otto held his head and the lamp while Sigbold unbuckled the leather strap around his chest and hindquarters. He unhitched the sling under his belly. Otto took the bag off and led him a few paces forward. Sigbold heaved twice on the rope and the sling vanished.

Djinn was quiet but Otto could feel him trembling. "There my brave, my handsome friend. All done now, all over…" he told the stallion in a gentle voice, stroking his muzzle and repeating his soft words until he fears were allayed.

Sigbold's mount arrived; a tall, dark grey with a white face like a skull. They repeated the operation of releasing him from the harness and their lifeline was whisked away; they were alone. Sigbold extinguished the lamp flame and they stood in what at first appeared to them as complete darkness. But as their eyes adjusted, they made out a faint glow above and its reflection in the water under their feet. They walked cautiously forward, following the flow of the current. Neither man spoke. Both were forcing down the same crawling fear. Supposing boulders had fallen and blocked the passage as a result of the masons hammering at the living rock face above them; possibly they could climb over and out but what of their mounts? Supposing it was worse and they were trapped as well, how long would it be before help came from above? They trudged on.

Otto saw a faint wedge of light ahead. He blinked his eyes a few times to make sure it was no illusion but it grew in size with every step he took. Sigbold caught sight of it too and his heart lifted. Starlight and the glow of the rising moon began to show them their path as they neared the entrance, details of the cliff walls on either side of them became visible. The temptation was to hurry on but a possibility of new danger now presented itself. Were there guards, and if so, how many? They could deal with a small number between the two of them but if there were more, they might have to resort to the risky manoeuvre of a mad dash on horseback.

They halted fifty yards in and put the bags back over their horse's heads so they would not budge. Then they piled up their weapons, helmets and shields on dry rocks before creeping forwards. Nearer the entrance, Otto moved to the left and Sigbold to the right. Otto peered around the edge and saw nothing but when he looked across, Sigbold was gesturing to him. Otto took everything in with one quick glance.

His first impression was of the smell of smoke and roasted meat. Then he saw two figures. One slept, covered by a shabby cloak, while the other sat hunched over, dozing and staring into the glowing embers of a small fire. Otto and Sigbold nodded to each other and stepped out. As the seated man turned instinctively, sensing the movement, Sigbold was on him. He grabbed his beard and the back of his head and twisted his hands around and over each other. The neck snapped under his strong fingers with a crunch of displaced bones. His victim slumped, dead, supported in Sigbold's strong arms. Otto pinched the sleeper's nostrils and clamped a hand over his mouth. The man awoke to the nightmare of a pair of merciless blue eyes staring into his until his sight and life faded. He thrashed and was still.

They worked quickly. Within minutes, they collected their equipment, Their own horses were led out and unwrapped, the padding thrown onto the fire to steam and smoke to ashes. They ate the remaining half of a mountain hare off the spit where it had been left, and, riding the guards' meagre ponies, leading their mounts, they trotted off down the streambed where it flowed out between the boulders of the open plain. When the moon set, they slept for a while. At sunrise they woke and unsaddled the ponies they had stolen taking off their bridles and setting them free. Up on their warhorses, they moved on again in the growing daylight. By midmorning they were twenty miles to the south and east travelling easily along the highway.

Titus Attius was sitting at breakfast, such as it was, with his adjutant and Boxer when a party of German auxiliaries strode up and stood solemnly in front of them. Their beards and hair had been combed and plaited, their mail and swords gleamed. They wore arm rings and helmets crested with plumes, wolf-tails or boar tusks; this was a formal delegation. One man with his beard threaded through a silver ornament in the shape of a coiled snake stepped forward, bowed and spoke in thickly accented Latin.

"Camp Prefect, Lord Otto is gone with Sigbold Bearslayer to find our brothers. We know this means there is to be a battle but no-one has told us what our part in it will be."

Attius stood up out of respect but had no idea of how to address the spokesman, he knew neither his name nor rank. He made a quick decision to address him with courtesy.

"Sir, this fight is for infantry, foot soldiers. The road is too narrow and the slopes too steep for your horses."

"You will ignore two hundred spears and axes, the best of Prince Aldermar's men?" the German responded with a frown.

"I have told you, there is no place for your cavalry in my plan," Attius told him a little sharply.

"Then you have not made a good plan," the tall warrior said emphatically.

He turned on his heel and stalked off with his fellow delegates muttering disgustedly in their own language. Attius sat down, equally annoyed.

"Who the fuck do these people think they are? Lot of hairy-arsed savages…" he grumbled.

"You do understand they're all gentry?" the adjutant enquired.

"Gentry? What's that supposed to mean? They're bloody Germans."

"They are from wealthy families or renowned warriors who have accumulated a great deal of loot. The horses they ride belong to them and they equip themselves with weapons and armour at their own expense."

"You sure? Bit of an expert, are you?" Attius replied.

"Yes, the adjutant is quite right. They are what we would call "of good family" where they come from," Boxer confirmed.

"Well I never; I thought Aldermar paid for all of it..."

"In a way he does because they are his liegemen. It's complicated...."

"Then leave it for another time. The point remains, this is an infantry fight."

"I have an idea, sir, that might involve them and unruffle their feathers. Can I give it some more thought and come back to you?" Boxer asked.

"Anything to help will be welcome, especially if it mends fences with those touchy Germans," Attius replied.

"Fences is what it's all about," Boxer said, cryptically.

The praetorians drilled in the shield manoeuvre for hour after hour until they could perform it mechanically, without thought,. Titus wanted them as near to perfection as possible for their own protection in the coming conflict but the marching and counter-marching had another purpose. It kept them busy and prevented them from brooding.

The German Auxiliaries sulked. The engineers carried on with the bridge.

They began to cut six slots in the exposed rock above the steps which had now been backfilled with mortared masonry anchoring the massive, angled supports. When the three main, curved timbers were assembled and lowered into place, their weight would be partially borne on the ground on both sides and not entirely by other woodwork. Each end would slide into one of the slots, in theory; if their lengths had been measured to the quarter inch, if every angle had been correctly calculated, if the levels from side to side were precise, if ..... Boxer could not be certain before the last piece of his jigsaw was fitted into the others. Until then, he had to have faith in his skill and the skills of his men and belief, lots of belief.

Once his engineers were occupied, Boxer took two of them to assist him as he set up his groma in different positions and had them walk off with long strides, counting each one until he shouted for them to stop and push a stick into the ground. They gathered, consulted, moved the surveying instrument to other locations and repeated the procedure. He finished off by taking sightings down the road from different points. He made a few notes on his wax tablet and snapped the case shut with an air of satisfaction and ordered his men to put down a marker stone.

Boxer began to tell Attius what he had in mind but the Camp Prefect held up his hand.

"Before you get going, I should tell you what I intend. I am giving Otto and Sigbold today and tomorrow to find our cavalry and two days to bring them in. We attack on the fifth day whether they're here or not. Our food supply is now so low we can't wait any longer. I don't know if this makes any difference to what you were going to tell me, so please carry on."

"None at all as it happens, sir. The major danger our men face is attacking on a narrow front against a spiked fence. I think I may be able to do something about that. I propose to shoot a grapnel attached to a rope onto the enemy defensive line which must be unstable because they can't dig it in deep enough, as we know from our own attempts. If the hooks catch, we can use the auxiliary horse to haul it through a pulley and rip away a part of ..."

"I thought you told me you couldn't hit the front with your artillery," Attius responded.

"...Not with the ballista. It's a heavier piece, the angle of depression and fire.... "

"I'll take your word for it," Attius interrupted again.

"Thank you sir. I must tell you that we have only one chance. I don't have enough suitable rope for two grapnels; it needs enough to reach them with sufficient slack so we can get a least fifty men and horses to drag the debris back out of everyone's way before the enemy can chop through it."

"Are you sure you can do it?"

Boxer shook his head. "No, it is probable but not certain. In any case, I intend to make the attempt when we start to bombard them with scorpion bolts and smash up their back line of defence with the ballista. It will be just one more in-coming missile in the fire-storm. Remember, sir, as far as we know they are unaware that we have any artillery.

Attius leaned back in his seat and closed his eyes, stroking his top lip with one finger. His years of experience had given him the ability to visualise the development of a battle long before the first bugle call sounded. Now his mind soared over the zig zag road and the enemy's camp like an eagle, seeing every manoeuvre as if the troops had already engaged. He sat forward with a snap, his opened eyes gleaming.

"There's more to this than first appears, young Boxer. I smell panic and it won't be our lads shitting themselves. How long will it take you set up on the day?"

"Twenty minutes if we prepare our firing sites beforehand. My men will have to knock a short thick post into the ground, somehow and then attach the pulley but we can do that tomorrow…."

"See to it but make time to come with me to visit our gallant German allies. Full uniform, you can dress up as a soldier if you like."

The auxiliaries had been told to expect Attius mid morning. The early drizzle had died away and it was a grey, cold day as he sat on the sheepskin spread over an up-ended log they had provided for him. Small fires had been lit to his right and left to take the chill off the air. The entire cavalry force of over two hundred sat in serried arcs in front of him, crossed-legged, their cloaks protecting them from the damp earth. An interpreter stood to one side while Boxer and his adjutant, polished to perfection with their helmets carried in the crooks of their left arms stood behind him.

Attius spoke loudly enough for everyone to hear him but measured his speech leaving pauses for his words to be translated into the mother tongue of his listeners.

"Men of the cavalry, your leaders came to speak with me the other day and I told them that you would have no part in the coming battle. Those of you who are experienced in warfare know that everything can change in a moment. Prefect Boxer now has a plan to tear up the enemy's front defences and destroy their rear. This means there is now a vital role for you to play. I need your strength and that of your horses to clear the way for my infantry, this much is certain. If your comrades who went to Tarraco return in good time, they will assault the enemy camp. Between the cavalry and the infantry, they may break them. If they run, I will withdraw my second wave of foot-soldiers and release you to harry and hunt them down. What do you say?"

Attius had expected a cheer but instead the leaders consulted each other and listened to remarks shouted out by lesser warriors from the back. After five minutes, one of their front rank stood up and spoke.

"Lord Otto Kingkiller told us you were a great soldier and a worthy warrior, now we see why. You are not ashamed to admit you made a mistake by not including us; this is the mark of a great leader. You have made us happy and we shall follow your every order to the letter."

He bowed. The Camp Prefect stood up, his jaw set and his mouth clamped shut, and returned the courtesy before spinning on his heel and marching away without saying a further word. Boxer and the adjutant hurried in his wake.

"Have you ever heard such arrogance?" Attius spluttered once they were out of earshot.

"It was face-saving, sir," the adjutant said, trying to pacify his furious superior officer.

"Whose face got saved? It certainly wasn't mine. I've been made to look a complete prick in front of them."

"Are you sure, sir?" Boxer intervened. "I thought I heard them say they agree with Otto that you are a great soldier and a fine warrior."

"I suppose so," Attius grunted, a little mollified. His eyes lighted on a crude balance suspended on a stout pole. One of Boxer's men was bringing a rock over which he put in one pan. The other rose, hovered and then settled a little higher. "Do you want to explain? The Camp Prefect asked.

"Ammunition for the ballista. If the stones we fire are of a similar weight and shape, overall accuracy is improved. Round ones out of riverbeds are the best but we shall have to make do with what we can find," Boxer informed him. "Let me show you how I'm going to deploy the artillery. Oh course, you may want to make a change...."

"Is that an attempt at humour, Prefect?" Attius snapped.

"Oh certainly not, sir. You might have a better idea, that's all…."

The ballista was to pound the left hand side of the rear defences, gradually gnawing its way into the middle of the line. Two of the scorpions would fire into the main mass of the enemy. The third was to be loaded with the grapnel and aimed at the extreme front right of the fence where the praetorians would attack.

"Swivel your bolt throwers from left to right. That will cause maximum terror and avoid a pile of bodies my men might trip over. How long will you keep firing?"

"I'll leave that up to you, sir."

Titus Attius nodded. He inspected the squat post, dug into the unforgiving ground and strengthened with stone wedges hammered in around its base. The greased pulley was already lashed into position. He slapped a hand on top of it to mark his satisfaction then walked to the head of the road and looked down at the opposition.

Their numbers had grown. There were nearly three thousand of them now, waiting for the famine weakened Romans to come down and be killed then plundered. They had outgrown their camp. A line of tents and fire circles was spread outside the back fence for almost its full length. Women stirred cooking pots and children ran about.

Attius grinned, an old wolf smelling blood and showing his fangs. Once mayhem was unleashed, many of the men would be distracted by the screams of their families and leave their posts. Good, the greater the noise and confusion the better for his purposes.

"Don't let me down, Otto," he said under his breath.

He would have been relieved know that Otto and Sigbold had already made contact with the cavalry.

Chapter 17

Otto and Sigbold had covered a lot of ground on their first day. Djinn had needed to stretch his muscles and feel the life coursing through his great heart. He cantered along the road as if he would never tire, never stop. Sigbold's horse kept pace with only a little more effort. They were both superb warhorses, bred to run and carry an armed man all day long and now they were happily doing what they knew best. They rested at midday and went on until sunset, made a fire and settled down waiting for moonrise.

Sigbold looked sadly at the piece of stringy, smoked mule-meat which was to be his dinner.

"Remember that hare, Lord? It tasted good."

"Not as good as your bear's heart; still warm and sweet, the blood…." Otto replied with a sigh.

The land was lit in monochrome, deep-shadowed moonlight when they heaved themselves back into the saddle and proceeded cautiously. Even though they were on a road of sorts, it was not fully paved and poorly maintained. A single pothole could cause disaster for horse and rider. They had walked, picking their careful way for another five miles when a faint odour of woodsmoke came on the breeze. At that moment a voice challenged them out of a narrow cleft between two boulders. They brought their mounts to a halt as a cavalryman on foot stepped out onto their path with a levelled spear. His stern face lit up with a smile of recognition.

"Sigbold, Lord Otto! What are you doing here? Let me lead you to the camp, this way," he said with evident pleasure.

With the sentry in front, they walked on for a hundred yards then turned off around what revealed itself to be the last in a semicircle of high rocks and saw the quartermaster's wagons, horses, mules and sleeping men spread in a peaceful tableau. Two fires burned low giving a warm glow after the frosty night air.

"Wake brothers, wake!" their guide roared. "Lord Otto and Sigbold Bearslayer are with us!"

The men stirred and came to their feet, some drowsily blinking off sleep, others fully alert. Fuel was heaped on the embers which blazed up, the light of their orange flames licking the rocks all around. Otto dismounted, hands reached out to take Djinn's bridle and tend to him. Sigbold stood by his skull-faced horse grinning broadly as other hands slapped his back in welcome.

The two newcomers went over to the nearest fire and warmed their hands, then Otto turned to the troopers gathered around him.

"Is the seer among you? Stand forward if you are."

A slim warrior with sandy hair came shyly out of the throng and stood in front of Otto. He was an older man, perhaps in his late thirties, with nothing remarkable about him at first glance, except for his eyes.

They were large and luminous in the firelight, one greenish brown and the other periwinkle blue.

"This man had the courage to enter the blood pit and listen to the word of the Gods for all of us. He said war was coming. Well, it has arrived. He said a man would have to descend deeper than his own grave. Sigbold Bearslayer and I were lowered into the depths of the ravine with our horses to come to you. I honour our seer."

He took one of the rings off his arm and handed it to the man who slipped it on to the evident pleasure of his comrades.

"What has happened Lord?" someone shouted.

"Food, drink, and afterwards I will tell you everything," Otto called back.

An hour later, belly full of cold mutton and soldier's bread washed down with watered wine, Otto sat in front of the seated auxiliaries in the same way as Attius had less than three days before. He told them about the siege and the enemy's defences. He recited the saga of his escape together with Sigbold.

"Our Camp Prefect has a plan to destroy these insolent vagabonds who have dared to challenge us. His praetorians will march down on them while Prefect Boxer destroys their rear fence with one of his machines. On the signal, we ride into the gaps and cut them into bloody shreds. Are you ready?"

As one, the cavalrymen shouted their assent. Otto raised a hand.

"We must go quickly but not founder our horses. Rest now, we ride at sunrise."

They drifted away to talk to their friends, look to their kit and mounts. The old hands simply rolled up in their cloaks again to snatch a few hours sleep before morning.

"You're abandoning me, aren't you?" the glum quartermaster accused Otto, who shrugged.

"No choice, how many men of your own do you have?"

"Eight."

"Are they armed?"

"Shields and spears."

"Stay here until the fourth day. If no-one has come for you by then we're dead. In which case, I suggest you and your men leave everything and run for the Tarraco garrison in one wagon."

They moved off in a red dawn, the way before them gleaming with heavy frost.

On the plateau, men woke, tightened their belts another notch over their empty, grumbling bellies and doggedly began the day's work.

In Luca, Otto's household also woke early, if not at first light. Today was going to be special. Lollia's father had business in the city so her mother, Clodia Alba, was staying with her. The Longius womenfolk were coming over for a visit and a daring event had been organized. A woman was going to read everyone's palms; that is, everyone who was brave enough to submit themselves to her ministrations.

She was a Greek who called herself a Chaldean to make herself seem more exotic. Her eyes were black-rimmed with kohl, she had painted henna in delicate filigrees on her feet and hands. Her robes were deep blue spangled with shabby gilt stars and moons. Her profession was a precarious one.

After the defeat of Marcus Antonius and the death of Cleopatra, Augustus became convinced that his victory was due to the benign intervention of the Gods of Rome. He proclaimed that only dedication to Roman Gods and Roman virtues would ensure stability and future Roman victories. He outlawed the worship of Isis, the Egyptian deity, along with all necromancy and fortune telling.

It is one thing to pass a law and quite another to get people to obey it. Romans were addicted to trying to see into the future, it was traditional. They paid lip-service to the new ruling in public but still consulted their favourite clairvoyants in private. "As long as no-one complains, where's the harm?" they thought. So what had previously been done openly was now carried on behind closed doors.

The boys, Lucius Albus and Pollux, had been taken out to go fishing by Felix who disapproved of the whole thing. He did not like it because it smacked of women's magic, their witchcraft. He had a horror of spells and curses in which he implicitly believed. The five ladies sat in a rough circle with a bronze brazier nearby to warm the room. Tullia, Plotina and Didia had not been invited to the party but were allowed to stand in an open doorway looking on. The clairvoyant threw some incense onto the charcoal. It crackled with sparks and sent up a cloud of sweet fragrance. She rolled her eyes back into their sockets so only the whites showed and babbled an invocation to the spirits in some made-up language.

She looked at Aelia's palm first then into the old lady's shrewd, amused eyes. She dropped the hand and bowed her head.

"Domina, you have so much wisdom of your own you have no need of mine," she said.

Aelia returned the gesture and smiled a complicit smile. The palmist acknowledged it with gratitude. Aelia knew this was all nonsense but the look that had passed between them had been her promise of silence.

Sabina Pulchra and Clodia Alba were assured of healthy, successful grandchildren which was exactly what they wanted to hear. Poppaea's future was golden. Then she came to Lollia who held out her open left hand to be scrutinized.

"I see another child…" the woman began.

Lollia raised her eyebrows and smiled around at the others as if to say, "She would say that, of course," but her expression changed as she heard the next part of the prophecy.

"…but it is not a child of this country. A far-off child…"

Lollia snatched her hand away.

"What's that supposed to mean? Don't be ridiculous woman!"

The sooty eyes looked up into hers.

"I see what is to be seen Domina, there is no harm coming to you, only joy. But your child is not of Italia. That much is certain."

Lollia was sensitive on the subject of children. She had not conceived again after the birth of Lucius Albus and he was now far from being a baby. Yes, Otto had been away on the Emperor's service for many months but he had been at home for longer and yet she had no other children. Two children represented the accepted minimum and even then the odds were against both of them surviving to adulthood. Her mother had told her that she would never fall pregnant if she rode astride on a horse. "It will shake your womb up too much," she advised, forgetting that riding around the estate with Otto had been one of Lollia's greatest pleasures when they were first married. Sabina Pulchra had told her to buy a black cat and stroke it every night before she went to bed. Lollia tried to relax and smile but everyone could see she was troubled.

Saxa held out her hand, so broad and powerful compared with the others. The palmist took it and studied it for only a few seconds.

"This is the year of your marriage" she told her.

"Gods above and below, not to that painter fellow, Libius!" Sabina Pulchra muttered to herself but too loudly; they all heard. She looked aghast; it had unintentionally slipped out.

Saxa threw back her head and roared with laughter. "Libius is a kind and good man but he belongs to Plotina…"

There was a shriek from the doorway. Plotina flushed from her bosom to the roots of her hair, threw her apron over her face and clattered off down the corridor as fast as she could. Tullia and Didia glanced at each other and giggled.

Saxa looked round and understood that, not only was it not a joke, but the others had been thinking the same thing. She stood up, holding herself as tall and straight as possible, her blue eyes spitting splinters of ice across the room.

"I am Saxa, daughter of Badurad the Battle Counsel, sister of Otto Kingkiller, Knight of Rome. The man I take will be worthy of them as well as me," she informed everyone.

At that moment no-one doubted her.

"He shall be, lady," the palmist said. "So shall he be."

Lollia took her into the corridor and paid her.

"If you go to the kitchen, you will be fed," she said, quite certain that she would also tell her servants' fortunes for a few more copper coins.

On the fourth day, one day before Titus Attius had committed himself to battle, a sentry at the head of the road spotted the flutter of a white flag on top of a boulder the size of a house several hundred yards away across the plain. It was a bright, frosty morning which made it difficult to make out the flapping cloth against the glare of the rising sun but he was sure he had seen it.. He shouted for his optio who watched for a few moments. There it was again. The optio reported to his centurion. Within five minutes the signal had been acknowledged, bugles were blaring, men arming and saddling horses. The artillerymen trundled their four pieces up to the markers, took them off the carts and began to set them up. They stacked ammunition and loaded.

Otto and his hundred riders had arrived late in the afternoon of the previous day. They had only an hour of light good enough for reconnaissance but what they saw confirmed Adonis Frugi's opinion that this was bad country for cavalry. The ground was so broken and randomly strewn with rocks of all sizes, it was impossible to find a clear route for a massed charge. If they could not come in fast, most of the effect would be lost and worse, they would be vulnerable to a counter-attack by spearmen on foot. He was forced to do something which he did not like; divide his command into three. The first wing was concealed two hundred yards back from the position they were about to storm, the second and third further out. He was going to have to deploy his units according to how well and how quickly Boxer could chew up the spiked fence. It was never good to commit men piecemeal but Otto felt that there was no other option.

On the plateau, one mounted man had picked up the greased rope passing through the pulley on the post. He twisted it around his wrist to give him a better grip and waited. His horse stood at the back of a narrow lane formed by two lines of cavalry facing away from him.

Boxer saw he was in place and nodded to his best artillerist who carefully placed the grapnel in the guide, made sure the rope trailing off the end was clear of obstruction and neatly coiled. Then he too waited, tense and poised like the solitary cavalryman.

Titus Attius looked around at the columns of Praetorians, the German auxiliaries seated on horseback and the few artillery pieces loaded and ranged.

"You all know what you're supposed to do," he told the officers gathered around him. "Mars and Fortuna with us all this day. Begin!"

Boxer raised his right arm and bellowed "Scorpions, fire!" as it dropped to his side. Simultaneous bolts leaped from two of the machines. They arced lazily into the air, reached the apex of their flight, and accelerated back to earth among the shocked tribesman below. Even before they landed, the pawls clacked again as the skilled operators wound the tension back into the curved bow fixed to the front

Boxer shouted his second order, "Ballista, fire!" The machine made a different sound, deeper indicating its additional power. The first thirty pound stone followed a similar path to the bolts: a decelerating upward arc, a moment where it seemed to rest motionless high in the sky and then a murderous downward plunge. It fell two feet inside the end of the fence. The captain of the piece made some small adjustments as his men cranked the torsion back into the human hair springs that powered it. He was not much concerned if his shot fell a little short as it would drop among the enemy. What he wanted to avoid was over-shooting, a waste of ammunition. The second missile fell true, sending a swarm of splinters buzzing through the air around its point of impact and flattening the first of the spiked stakes. He was confident he had the range. With constant corrections, he began to destroy the enemy's rear defensive line, chewing steadily along its length.

Boxer let another ten bolts fall among his panicking victims who dodged this way and that, uncertain whether to run back and risk the ballista fire or huddle in the lee of their defence to be picked off by the scorpions, He judged the moment had arrived.

"Grapnel, fire!"

The missile flew on a flat trajectory. It was heavier at the front end than a standard bolt and was towing hundreds of feet of rope. It dipped in flight and began to descend early; too early, Boxer thought. His heart hammered as he watched the black line snaking out behind it. It was going to fall short, he should have tried to use the ballista...but somehow, it scraped over the fence and disappeared.

"Now, now! Ride!" he screamed.

The single horseman leaned forward and dug in his heels. Hs mount galloped between the lines of troopers who grabbed, left and right at the rope he trailed. They followed his headlong rush, each with a firm grip. One hundred horsemen all moving steadily forward. Suddenly they were checked. The grapnel hooks had bitten and all the slack was taken up. They heaved, the pulley vibrated and shrieked under the friction. Its mounting post slewed to one side. Engineers who had no role in the conflict rushed over and added their weight to the tug of war.

The tribesmen who had constructed their wooden breastwork had experienced the same problems as the Romans. The soil was too thin and rocky for deep post holes so they had tried to reinforce it by lashing horizontal poles to connect each section. This was their undoing. A hundred and forty men felt as if their arms were being pulled out of their sockets as they hauled. The line attaching them to the grapnel was like a quivering bar of iron. Boxer was sure it must snap and then there was a rending splitting sound. A sixty foot length of the fence reared up into the air and fell outwards over the slope above it in a sagging tangle of poles, stakes and men who had tried to hold it in place. As it flopped onto the rough scree, Boxer shouted for everyone to let go. They could not hear him over the banging of the artillery, more intense now as the third scorpion had added its fire, the thud of the ballista missiles striking home and the screams rising from below. Boxer did not want the wreckage to be dragged up over the road where it would impede the praetorians so he did the only thing possible. He drew his sword and struck the rope. It parted on his second blow. One end was dragged away, men falling on their backsides and horses staggering as it went slack but the other end cracked like a cart-whip and slashed him across the forehead below his helmet rim. Blood sheeted down and blinded him. He sat down, dizzily. Someone shouted for a medic. One rushed over and looked at the wound. He slapped some salve and a bandage on it and helped Boxer to his feet.

"You'll do for now sir," he said. "Might have to have it sewn up later."

Titus looked down at his enemy. He saw with satisfaction that men were scrabbling back through the rabble to find their families. Crushed, bones broken, harpooned by flying splinters, they screamed and wept while yet more stones and iron bolts hurtled down on them. But there was still a substantial force of more than two thousand armed warriors ready to oppose his men and the artillery must cease to fire when they closed.

"Time for Otto. Give the signal," he ordered as the column of infantry marched forward.

"Don't trip over all this string these artillery lads have left lying about," the leading centurion shouted.

There was a brief burst of laughter quickly lost under the sound of boots stamping in unison. Two flags were waved, acknowledged and the horsemen waiting on the plain readied themselves to join the fight. Otto mounted Djinn and cantered forward with thirty men at his back. To his left, he saw his other two wings emerge from cover. When he was a hundred yards short of the wreckage caused by the ballista, he flung up one hand and slowed his pace. At fifty yards he saw that the wreckage of shattered timbers, half-hanging pointed stakes and hurled rocks was an insurmountable barrier for his horses. It was too broad to leap and the footing was deadly. He dragged Djinn to a complete halt and jumped out of the saddle.

"Shield wall, on me," he called, and began to march towards the chaos ahead. Men joined him on either side. The other wings saw what was happening and galloped up, flinging themselves off their mounts and running forward.

"Two ranks, two ranks, axes second rank! Otto shouted.

The men shoved each other out of the way then settled into position.

Six hundred praetorians moved as one, never faltering in their stride, left right, left right, again and again their hob-nailed boots striking the ground with a single thud. The centurions marched at the head of each group, conspicuous by the transverse crests on their helmets and the vine staffs they carried. They came to the first bend. As they turned onto the next section of road, their shields rippled from left arm to right like a huge python shaking out its scales in the bright morning. The enemy began to fire their bows, which were largely ineffective but their slingshot caused some damage. A well aimed stone could strike a helmet hard enough to dent it and scramble the wearer's brains. One on the shin or ankle brought a man down. A dozen soldiers had fallen when the senior centurion called a halt.

"Prepare javelins!" he shouted.

The shields flickered again as the rank nearest the enemy went down on one knee, the men who had been holding their shields up to protect their comrades' heads lowered them.

"Cast!"

The order was repeated up the line. Seventy-five weighted throwing spears rose in the air and fell on the defenders below. Before they had found their targets, a second volley followed, and a third. The tribesmen still suffering under scorpion bolts and ballista stones saw the sky darken as this new swarm of missiles brought death down on them.

"Close up ranks. March!"

The implacable glittering beast moved on, rippled its scales as it made the second turn and halted again to give one more close range volley. Three hundred spears had done their damage, ripping through shields and armour, hurling men to the ground. But many still stood firm, determined to resist.

They were the disinherited descendants of Pompey's legions who had been bred up to a bitter resentment of the Caesars, mountain tribesman who had come down from their hovels in the high passes to enrich themselves at the expense of Roman lives, there were notorious bandits and thieves among them, vagabonds and outcasts. They had been drawn to this place at this time by word of mouth; some seeking revenge for past injustices, others by promises of easy victory and a share in the wealth of a looted Roman camp. They were farmers and foresters, hunters and thieves but almost none were trained soldiers. And now the elite of the armies that had conquered the known world was bearing down on them. Some looked over their shoulders for a way out, many more licked their lips and took a tighter grip on their weapons.

The praetorians made the last half turn and now faced them, shields locked. They shuffled forward. Men fanned out from the rear ranks widening their front until forty Romans stood shoulder to shoulder with their comrades hanging on to their harnesses from behind to support them as their officers ordered the advance.

At the instant they clashed, there was a great roar from the back of the field of conflict. The defenders at the rear turned at the sound. The blood chilled in their veins and they fell back into their own comrades now engaged with the Praetorians. A line of mail-shirted giants was running at them, shouting and laughing over their shields from between which cruel lances bristled. Behind them a second line yelling and brandishing long-handled axes.

Otto's men rolled forward with battle joy in their hearts. All the escort duties, all the livestock herding, all the privations of the camp were a small price to pay for these few moments. This was where reputations were made. This is where ancestors looked on ready to welcome the brave fallen. This was what they were in this world to do; bring bloody ruin to an enemy. The praetorians were drilled and efficient, robotic as they pushed out with a shield then stamped their right foot down as they stabbed with their short swords. The Germans shouted insults, invited men onto their blades, recited their previous exploits. It was anarchy but just as deadly. They pressed so close to the defenders that both sides could smell each others' breath and feel the spittle and sweat spattering their faces, shoving and parrying blows while the second rank leaned over smashing their axes down on skulls or hooking shields out of the way to leave an uncovered body open to a sword or spear. Then one of the Germans began to sing a famous battle song. They all joined in the raucous chorus, reciting ancient slaughters.

The praetorians heard them over the din of clashing steel and screaming men.

"Are we going to let those hairy German buggers make more noise than us, lads?" the blood-soaked first centurion yelled. "Rome and the Emperor," he shouted, "Rome and the Emperor." His men took up the refrain and chanted it as they carved their way forward.

Their adversaries were being crushed so tightly together between the two forces that they could not wield their weapons in the dense mass. The ground underfoot was slippery with blood and urine and the contents of voided bowels. They were in hell, imprisoned there by singing, laughing men who cut them down like a ripe crop. It was too much, they broke.

From his high vantage point, Attius saw them push through the fence and run for safety.

"Second Praetorian Cohort, stand down. Cavalry on me!" Three of the leaders walked their horses forward and saluted. He pointed at the fleeing enemy below. "There's your prize. Take 'em all."

The auxiliaries trotted down the road. The few wounded soldiers who had been left behind scrambled out of their way. Otto saw them coming down and shouted for his men to disengage run for their own horses. They had stayed together in a loose, milling herd, nervously snorting at the noise and impact of the artillery but they would instinctively join in any mad charge across the plain, riderless or not.

Titus saw the cavalry spread out over the landscape like wine spilled on a table, dividing into separate streams as they twisted and dodged around the boulders hunting down their prey. It was over. The infantry went among the enemy wounded ending their troubles with a quick sword thrust or a boot-heel stamped on the windpipe. One man, high-ranking by the look of his armour, had been hit by a scorpion bolt. It had penetrated his body near the collarbone and the bent-over point protruded out of his back beneath one shoulder blade.

"Oi, who's your leader then?" an optio demanded, stirring him up with the butt of his spear.

The grey faced warrior looked up at him and spat bloody foam at his feet.

"Now I call that rude," the Roman told him, took hold of the bolt though his chest and wobbled one end in a small circle. "Who's in charge?"

"Rei Vasco," the man hissed in reply and died.

"Who's Rei Vasco when he's at home?" asked the centurion standing nearby.

"No idea, should we tell the Camp Prefect what he said?"

Titus Attius wasn't sure either when it was repeated to him.

"There was a tribe round here called the Vascones. Maybe he meant their king," he shrugged.

Otto led his weary horses and men up the road, ignoring the scene of carnage below as they climbed. The sight of Boxer's face black with blood and the stained bandage on his forehead checked him. But his friend was smiling.

"You are safe," Boxer said with evident relief.

Otto did not reply but stepped forward and wrapped him in a tight bearhug then pushed him back to arms length. "How badly are you hurt, brother?" he asked.

Boxer was greatly moved. Otto had never previously called him "Brother".

"What's all this then? You two Greek chorus boys or officers? Make your reports!" Titus Attius shouted over to them, destroying the moment.

Otto's last task was to send half a dozen riders out on spare mounts to bring in the quartermaster and his wagons. He intended to wash and change but collapsed on his cot, filthy as he was, and slept for three hours.

Chapter 18

The battle was over but there was much to do while Otto slept.

The cavalry was miles away, winkling out the few survivors still on their feet and putting them to the spear. A body of twenty or thirty refugees had run northeast, skirting the foot of the mountains and could not be found. The others lay where the horsemen had overtaken them, some on their bellies, some looking up at the sky with sightless eyes, some curled up like sleeping babies, all soon to be torn apart by scavenging animals.

The artillerists went down to the killing ground searching for scorpion bolts that could be re-used. Where they were jammed in the bodies, they hammered them right through and pulled them out from behind the entry point. Sometimes they found two corpses pinned together by a single bolt, which gave them a good laugh.

The praetorians had rounded up one hundred women and children who would be sent to the slave market in Tarraco. They searched among the debris and made a heap of any metal they could find; spear blades, pieces of armour, kettles, cooking pots, anything at all that could be sold to a scrap dealer. A search of the bodies gave up next to nothing in the way of money and jewellery; a carved piece of bone on a string was the best most of the dead had owned. Still, a share of any plunder, no matter how meagre, was better than nothing.

Best of all, they discovered several sacks of grain and a small flock of sheep penned in a nearby gulley. Tonight, they would go to sleep with full bellies for a change.

Titus Attius received the casualty lists. No-one had been killed but there were over fifty wounded. Most of them had superficial cuts which would be cleaned and be stitched. Provided there was no infection, they would all be fit for service within a few days. He felt a sense of relief that his command had come out of the combat so little damaged, then the tesserarius marched up, saluted and asked if he would accompany him to the surgeon. Titus felt his spirits fall as they walked across the camp together.

A centurion lay on the table in the hospital tent. He was stripped to the waist. His normally rich brown skin was yellow; beads of sweat stood out on his face below the black, woolly curls of his hair. Two of his comrades in the centurionate stood at his head. He tried to smile at the Camp Prefect but it turned into a grimace. He hissed through gritted teeth as another wave of pain passed through him. Titus looked enquiringly at the doctor.

"He was struck by a slingshot. His ankle is shattered and his shin bone has torn through the flesh. I can amputate the foot and if all goes well, this man will have many years of life in front of him. Except he won't submit to the operation and called for you," he explained.

"Sir, he has requested your permission for an honourable death," one of the men standing in vigil said. "He has sworn the soldier's oath and will not desert the eagles without his commanding officer's leave."

Titus looked at the grave faces around him. "Tesserarius, has he made his will?" he asked.

"Yes sir, there is a woman in Rome, the mother of his daughter. There is something for them in the cohort bank…"

Legionaries and centurions were neither allowed to marry nor sleep out of camp. Many had partners who were wives in everything but name. It was not an unusual situation and one which senior officers usually chose to ignore. Titus nodded.

"Then I'll bear the cost of his funeral so they won't be deprived of anything. Give me his sword." One of the men passed it over to him. "All of us together, comrades," he said. They and the wounded man wrapped their hands around the hilt and placed the point over his heart. "Farewell, depart in peace. We shall all meet again where the best soldiers go after this life," his Camp Prefect said as a parting blessing.

One quick downward pressure, the blade entered his chest, he convulsed and lay still with the faintest of smiles on his lips.

Stepping outside, Titus saw a dazed praetorian with a lump the size of a duck's egg on the side of his head, another sling casualty. He was sitting on a folding stool trying to drink out of a cup but the water dribbled out of his mouth, to the great amusement of a soldier who stood idly watching.

"You," Titus barked. The man slammed to attention, the humour wiped off his face. "Fetch me a cup of water." He found a cup, dipped it into the bucket of drinking water by the tent opening and proffered it. "No, that won't do, I want fresh water. Run over to the spring, fill it then run back and find me. What are you waiting for?"

Forty minutes later, red-faced and sweating he held out the cup to Titus who looked at it, pretending disappointment.

"Fill it up I said. Look, it's half-empty, some must have slopped out. Better do it again and this time I mean full."

When the third cup was handed to him, Titus took it and poured the contents onto the ground at the exhausted soldier's feet. "This was to remind you that we don't mock our wounded comrades. Now get out of my sight."

Scores of ravens and hooded crows flew out of the mountains and circled with harsh cries, demanding that the men go away and leave them to their gluttony while high overhead, vultures, also impatient to feed, soared in graceful spirals on the updrafts. The Germans began to return in high spirits as the afternoon wore on. The heads many had taken as trophies bounced against their horses' flanks as they rode. Best of all, some had wild boar draped over their saddles. They had panicked a sounder of boar that dashed into a blind gulley to be slaughtered and carried off in triumph. The cavalrymen gorged on roasted pork with the heads of their fallen enemies stuck on poles beside them facing the fire as if they were invited guests. All they lacked was ale but they did the best they could with vinegary wine. Otto celebrated with his men.

When the fires had died down and the camp was quiet, the sentries could hear the snarling and snapping of the wolves down below as they wrenched the corpses apart and fought over the pieces.

Boxer could not understand how his friend could happily sit chewing greasy, barely-cooked meat with the eyes of dead men glaring at him.

"At times, you're such a savage," he told him in the morning.

Otto grinned. "Not as savage as you,"

"How do you make that out?"

"Well, for the first few years of my life I could neither read nor write nor had I ever seen a permanent settlement. Whereas you had tutors and lived among temples and villas in a city. Yet how many did you kill yesterday?"

Boxer frowned, not grasping the point. "None," he answered.

"Oh no? You used your mathematical skills to direct your artillery while it rained death down on your enemies with no more thought than a boy stamping on ants. If you, with all the advantages of your civilized education can do that, how much more savage must your spirit be than mine."

"Ridiculous," Boxer replied, irritated but unable to frame a counter-argument.

The soldiers scraped a shallow pit well away from the base of the road and heaped it with alternate layers of the chopped up timber from the defensive works and their adversaries' remains. It took a good part of the day so it was late in the afternoon when they finally put flint and steel to it. Dense clouds of white smoke boiled up and hung in the sky before drifting eastwards away from the camp. As the heat built up, the resin in the pine wood and what fat there was in the bodies sizzled out giving a crackling brilliance to the flames at the base. In spite of the wind direction, a smell of roasting meat pervaded the camp. It drizzled that evening but the core temperature of the blaze was so intense that it continued to consume everything, flesh, bone and wood, the air shimmering above it. Next morning, it was a grey and white heap giving off puffs of steam where the raindrops fell on it but the interior still burned fiercely under its insulating blanket of ash.

The surgeon lanced the lump on the soldier's head and removed a spoonful of jellied black blood. His patient felt much better as the pressure was relieved and immediately reduced his headache to a dull throbbing. Boxer's forehead was still bleeding and had to be stitched but pulling the flaps of his wound together lifted his eyebrows giving him a permanently surprised expression. In spite of having punished the soldier for mocking a wounded comrade, Titus could not help sniggering every time he looked at him.

Life returned to the normal, tedious military routine for most of the soldiers. Titus did not believe that a second attempt would be made on his position but nevertheless, improved his defences. He ordered an eight foot high redoubt with an internal fire-step big enough to hold one hundred men to be built at the foot of the road. As they toiled with spades and crowbars lifting suitable stones for their walls, the troops complained that he should have told them before the spiked fences were all burnt to cinders. They were beginning to lay the foundations when a man rode up on a pony.

He was very old, as evidenced by the white beard that fell to his waist and accompanied by two young men on foot carrying green branches as a sign that they had no hostile intentions. He halted a few yards from the labouring praetorians and called out to them in his own language. A few shouted "Bugger off!" and made obscene gestures but the optio silenced them and sent for the Camp Prefect.

Titus came down with his adjutant and one of the Iberian speaking engineers.

"What do you want?" he demanded with no preliminary civilities.

"You are the Roman general?" the visitor asked.

"I am in command."

"Very well, I wish to ransom your captives."

Titus shook his head.

"They go to the slave market at Tarraco."

The old man looked levelly at him and held his gaze.

"You keep them here in the open, breathing in the smoke of the corpses of their fallen kin while you feed them slops. In a day or two, they will begin to die. How many will make it to the city do you think? Half of them, less?"

"My soldiers want silver," Titus replied.

"They also want food. I can offer ten sacks of grain, and five sheep or goats for the release of every ten captives."

"You came here to kill us, why should we treat with you?"

"Yes we attacked you. We were deceived by Rei Vasco who did not tell us you had war machines and northern giants to fall on our rear and slaughter us. Yes, our people are your spoils of war….."

"Who is this Rei Vasco?" Titus interrupted.

The old man laughed bitterly. "A great warlord but not as great as he thinks he is. I have no more to say about him. Come now Roman, hungry men cannot eat silver."

"Thirty sacks of grain, ten sheep and ten goats…."

They settled for twenty sacks and ten animals for the pot.

Titus called a general assembly.

"Men, I am letting the natives buy back their women and children in exchange for supplies," he told the massed troops who did not take the news well. The prospect of money to come was more appealing. "But I know you might think that this is robbing you of your loot. So, I propose that we will take the value of the food we receive from the quartermaster's funds and transfer them to your account. It might not be as much as we would have earned in the slave market but we need the grub and this way we get something now. It's a long way to Tarraco, boys and a lot of 'em wouldn't have made it."

"Our thanks to you, sir!" a voice shouted and most of the others joined in with their general approval, seeing the good sense of the new arrangement.

"Find some scraps of sailcloth and make a shelter for the prisoners; they're worth something now," Titus ordered his adjutant.

The first exchange did not take place without problems. A small herd of animals and two carts loaded with grain were driven out of the foothills to the northeast. The same old man, clearly a respected tribal elder, sat on his pony looking on. The soldiers checked the contents of sixty sacks and counted fifteen sheep and the same number of goats, enough to pay for the release of thirty prisoners. They were now held under a ragged canopy tethered in groups by one ankle and a neck halter. The optio and two of his men untied the nearest thirty and shoved them out. But they had unknowingly broken up family units, separating mothers from children, brothers from sisters. A howl went up, anguished screams; many tried to run back into the shelter, some of those still confined tried to break free. In the confusion, some of the soldiers had unsheathed their swords. Then the old man called out. Whatever he said calmed the situation. Still sobbing and looking back over their shoulders, the small procession of freed captives trudged away out of sight.

Shortly after the transaction had been completed, a party of riders led by Centurion Frugi escorted the mine superintendent to the base of the road. Tubero was astonished to see the captives and the ash-heap, still glowing if the breeze stirred it. Cassius Plancus had wanted to avoid regular contact since his orders had demanded the utmost discretion. Titus Attius had continued to keep his men and the legionaries and workers at the mine apart. The only time they spoke was when a cavalry force was detached to guard a bullion shipment. Although the camp and the mine were only a short distance away from each other as the crow flies, the geography of the escarpment and plateau helped to prevent the two groups from mixing freely. So the unexpected arrival of their visitors put the officers on their guard at first. Tubero quickly broke down their reserve.

"Gentlemen, I'm so relieved to see you all in one piece. Normally we can hear faint bugle calls and see the smoke of your fires but two days ago it was unprecedented. The buglers, chanting men and screaming, then the sky ominously full of crows and the next day such dense clouds of smoke. I won't lie to you, I expected to arrive at the site of some disaster but here you are, carrying on as if it was business as usual.

"So it is for soldiers, Master Tubero. Our life is a monotonous one until interrupted by sudden alarms. We thank you for your concern but as you can see, we are progressing. Would you like to inspect the fabled bridge?" Titus asked him.

All three curved spans had been positioned. Men were clambering about like spiders on their flimsy rope webs adding cross bracing and vertical support. Boxer explained the structure in minute detail while Tubero stood by, eyes shining.

"It's magnificent, prefect," he said when the lecture was finished. "It's so much bigger and stronger than I had imagined…"

"Thank you, my engineers will be pleased to learn of your approval. In a few days we'll start cutting the mule-track on your side. You might like to warn your men to keep well back from the foot of the cliff in case of falling debris. So, the days of carting the Emperor's gold all the way around will soon be over…"

"And then I suppose it will be time for you to depart," Frugi suggested.

Before Boxer could reply, Attius broke into the conversation.

"No so, centurion. We shall not be here in these numbers but a cohort supported by an ala of cavalry will stay on. This location is of strategic value and of course, with the bridge there can be a lot more communication with our men and Master Tubero's staff."

Boxer opened his mouth to ask when that had been decided but quickly closed it again leaving the question spoken.

The blood had drained from Adonis Frugi's handsome face. He stepped backwards and regained his colour. "Excuse me, gentlemen, too close to the edge. I don't like heights…"

"What?" Tubero said. "Since when? You're always going off into the mountains."

"Yes but I keep well back from cliffs with a straight drop."

"Very wise, centurion," Titus told him pointing at the engineers suspended over the ravine as they worked. "Just watching them makes my stomach turn over. Can I offer you something to drink? Some food perhaps?"

As he led them over to his tent, Titus muttered "Keep an eye on that Frugi and your mouth shut, there's a good lad," in Boxer's ear.

They had bread, slabs of cold mutton and the last of the decent wine. Cheese was offered but it was well past its prime.

Tubero enthused about "his" bridge and Boxer modestly accepted the fulsome compliments showered down on him. Titus related the story of the battle to drive-off the besiegers but kept the details of Otto and Sigbold's breakout to himself.

"You were right about this being bad country for cavalry, Centurion Frugi. In the end our men had to fight on foot but they acquitted themselves well enough. Once we're permanently established, we shall be riding a lot more patrols around the foothills to the north and east; don't want to be caught out again. Mind you, we're safe from any incursion as long as we hold our captives, don't you think centurion? Of course, this is something of a home posting for me. I was born in the Tarraco area. I grew up speaking the local language. By the way, Master Tubero, have you ever heard of anyone called "Rei

Vasco"? A couple of the wounded mentioned such a man to me when I was questioning them."

The mine superintendent had not heard the name. The hospitality over, the guests left with grateful thanks for the meal.

"Frugi?" Titus demanded.

"He seemed to get very tense when you mentioned regular patrols. When you asked about our mystery man, I swear I saw a tic start up at the side of his left eye. But since when are we garrisoning this place?"

"We aren't. Wherever did you get that idea?"

Forty more of the prisoners went leaving thirty for the next day.

The two men who had served in Syria and built the shadouf to scoop their drinking water into the trough asked for permission to speak to the Camp Prefect. They had shaved and polished their kit which pleased Titus Attius and made him inclined to give them a sympathetic hearing.

"About them natives, sir and the grain," the first soldier said.

"What about it?"

"Well sir, it's like this. As long as we've got their women and children this other mob have to behave themselves but tomorrow when they hand over the supplies we let the last of 'em go…."

"Yes…"

"So what's to stop them poisoning our grain, eh? They've nothing to lose. Their families will be the other side of the mountains by the time the lads eat it."

"Always up to that sort of trick out east sir; poison you as soon as look at you them Syrians," his mate added by way of background information.

"That's well thought of. Tell your centurion you are excused fatigues for two weeks. This is what we'll do…."

The delegation arrived at its due time. The praetorians counted out the sacks and took charge of a mixed flock of sheep and goats but instead of releasing the hopeful women and children, more soldiers than normal came forward and lined up, barring access to them.

"Today they will be fed on the grain you have just given us. Come and fetch them in the morning if they are still alive," the Iberian speaking engineer told the elder.

He grew incandescent with rage. He spat and shook his fist.

"This was not what we agreed. You are cheating, arrogant swine but what else can be expected of a Roman? We did not ask you to come into our lands and trample us."

"And we didn't invite you to try to starve us and kill us so jog on and come back tomorrow."

In the event, none of the captives took any harm by eating the grain and were returned to their homes and families the next day.

When the quartermaster returned he was outraged at what had been done in his absence.

"You have no right to make this sort of informal arrangement without telling me first. And if you had, I would have said no!"

Titus was so astonished at seeing the normally pre-occupied and timid-seeming officer standing in front of him red-faced with anger and practically hopping from foot to foot, that he did not know how to respond.

"I can't see that any harm has been done," he said.

"Exactly, exactly that. You can't see because you don't understand the system. But understand this I cannot pass my funds to the general account of the men. It's not possible."

"Now look," Titus said, getting onto the front foot. "We had supplies in exchange for captives. You would have had to buy-in grain and some meat for rations. We're eating the grub so you hand over the money, what's the difference?"

"Where are the purchase-orders, delivery notes, acceptance dockets, receipts? You can't tell me because there aren't any. I'm going to be accused of fraud. I'll be cashiered and end up in prison."

"Can't you just write some up and backdate everything?"

"Oh yes, first class suggestion. I add forgery to my other crimes."

Titus raised his eyes to the heavens. "Oh Gods, don't tell me I've got the only honest quartermaster in the entire army to add to my troubles!"

Two days later, the quartermaster was back with some papers, a large leather bag of silver coins and the tesserarius.

"Please sign this sir," he demanded handing Titus a document and a pen already dripping ink."

"What is it?"

"An emergency order to purchase essential supplies from local farmers after stocks were depleted as a result of being besieged."

Titus signed, the quartermaster handed the tesserarius the bag of silver and asked him to put his name to a second document.

"What's he signing?" Titus asked.

"Says here it's a receipt for monies obtained by auctioning spoils of war subsequent to the defeat of the besiegers," the tesserarius told him.

"You will notice that the amount is the same in both cases. I have solved your accounting problem, Camp Prefect, no need to thank me," the quartermaster said looking smug, saluted and marched off.

Now that the immediate threat had been neutralized, Otto's men had been patrolling along the foothills to the north and east where the Pyrenaeum Mountains bulged outwards in cliffs, steep defiles or foothills leading up into the massif. These were not the standard "showing the flag" canters along the roads and byways but detailed examinations of the ground, searching for something out of place. They were expert trackers but this terrain was unfamiliar to them and difficult by its nature. In their native forests, they could spot a low branch pushed out of place by a passing deer or hoofprints on a bed of pine needles but here they were looking for sign on a mixture of thin soil, gravel and flat out-thrusts of rock. However, as well as the skills of hunters, they possessed perseverance.

On the fifth day a solitary trooper bent over his saddle examining an area where a flat pan of naked rock was corrugated like the sand of the sea-shore at low tide. He stopped and dismounted, went down on all four and felt gently along the edge of a ridge with his fingers. He rubbed them together; they were smeared with a gritty paste. He crawled forward and went through the procedure again. Remounting, he walked his horse towards the tangled mass of bushes, scree and gullies a few hundred yards ahead then turned for home.

Sitting with his men, Otto listened carefully to the report.

"You're sure?"

"Yes, lord." He took a stick and scratched the bare earth by the fire into ridges to demonstrate. "A flat plate of rock marked in waving lines. Some of the edges have been crushed by iron tyres. They must have been. Nothing else would make them crumble like that. But why would anyone be driving a cart out there? There's nothing, no path, no hut, nothing."

"And you can find this place again?"

"Yes lord, it's about three miles out."

"Thank you, this was well done." Otto smiled. "If only I had my Ghost to set a watch…"

"Your ghost?"

"Prince Aldermar's best spy and scout. They call him the Ghost because he can move through the night as quietly as an owl in flight or disappear whenever he wants to by day."

"Grimwald Ghost is my cousin," a voice called out of the gloom.

"I wish you shared his skill as well as being kin to him," Otto replied.

He woke with a start in the pitch black of his tent. A hand was over his mouth and the faint gleam of a pair of eyes hovered over him.

"Hush, lord, hush. There is nothing to fear. Light your lamp," a voice whispered.

Not sure if he was dreaming or not. Otto fumbled for the lamp. A fizzle of sparks from his flint and a flame glow lit the tent interior.

The Ghost's cousin sat on the floor beside his cot and grinned at him.

"I have something to show you."

A blade glimmered in the feeble oil flame. It was a sword. Otto tensed then saw it that belonged to the Camp Prefect.

"Are you mad?" Otto asked. "He'll have you crucified for this."

His night visitor shook his head. "It will be back with him in a few minutes and he'll never know it was gone."

"But the sentries…"

"Ah yes, the sentries…."

He blew out the lamp, Otto felt a sudden gust of cold air and he was alone once more.

In the morning Titus Attius was behaving as normal; clearly he had heard or seen nothing. Otto called the thief over.

"You might just be as good as my Ghost," he told him.

"We are a family of ghostly men, lord."

"What is your name?

"Lutold."

"Then you are Lutold Shadow and my chosen spy."

Chapter 19

"Let's sum up," Titus Attius told Boxer and Otto. "thirty-two chests of the Emperor's bullion have gone missing. Supposing whoever swiped 'em hasn't spent any of it, that's twelve hundred and eighty pounds of gold. We believe that if the whole lot had come onto the market it could not have stayed a secret. If it was being sold off bit by bit, someone would have blabbed. So we suspect it's hidden around here. Waiting for what before shifting it, a message, a signal? Who from? We think that Centurion Frugi is involved in some way, he's up to his armpits in it in my opinion but I can't prove it. We know this is tangled up in the politics of Rome and that's the bit that gives me the shivers. If there are powerful men behind it all, who are they and what are they after? Right, I've finished, discuss."

"We know there have been no thefts since we arrived. We know there will be much more commercial traffic once the bridge is finished. We know that the attempts to drive us off have failed. We know we are now in a position to increase the number and range of our cavalry patrols," Boxer said.

"Bit obvious that, Boxer," Titus told him.

"Yes, but it is what we know; not what we believe or suspect."

"Fair point. Come on, Otto, you must have sucked up some of the wisdom of the ancients with all that reading you do. Give us the benefit," Titus cajoled.

Otto thought for a moment, furrowed his brow and began to speak, slowly and carefully as if working out the answer to a problem in his mind as he formed his words.

"Accepting as a fact that the treasure has been hidden close by, our presence ensures that it is not possible to add to it. We also increase the possibility of its discovery. The logical conclusion is that it must be moved and quickly before we find it, either to be used for its intended purpose or to be put beyond our reach. We should intensify the search, as Boxer suggested. This might provoke a hasty action by the thieves or lead to us finding their hoard. One of my men may have already come across something of interest. Will you leave it to me to take the required measures?"

"Vey well, do what you think is best. Boxer, I want your bridge and mule track finished as soon as possible. Double shifts, day and night; if you want soldiers to fetch and carry just ask. Let's get on with it then," Titus told them and closed the meeting.

Lutold Shadow left the camp shortly after dusk. He wore breeches and a tunic covered by a drab cloak. He had soft leather shoes on his feet and was unarmed other than for a long knife with a blackened blade. In a satchel over his shoulder he carried bread and dried meat. He would find water easily enough.

The cavalrymen continued to pore over the ground and Boxer worked on his construction.

The major work all but finished. The last task was to saw up the timber salvaged from the heavy wagons kept for the purpose and lay the heavy planks crosswise to make the surface of the bridge. Once nailed into place, they would help to stabilize the three curved spans. The engineers began to look at the mule track. After careful surveying, Boxer decided to widen it to a minimum of six feet, more where the rock face allowed for easy working. The missing forty feet had to be recut but his masons had a sheer face to work into with no loose stone. Once again the camp was noisy with saws, mallets and the clink of hammers striking cold chisels and drills.

The stars had faded but the greenish glow to the east announcing sunrise was an hour away when Lutold Shadow opened Otto's tent-flap and called softly inside. Twenty minutes later, he was standing beside Otto and Boxer in front of the Camp Prefect's table on which a guttering oil lamp burned. Underlit, their faces looked otherworldly in the shifting light, their eyes expressionless dark pits. Lutold's Latin was not fluent enough to make his own report so Otto spoke for him.

"This is my scout Lutold Shadow. He has been watching a location about an hour's march away where one of my men saw faint signs of cartwheels. When the moon rose, four men came down the mountain and seemed to disappear. He climbed up a little way and saw them together in an enclosed space below. One of the men came out of a cave carrying a box but, get this sir, "the beautiful centurion from the mine", was angry. He beat the man and forced him to return it. They argued for a long time then made their way back up the mountainside."

"Right, get yourselves washed, shaved and properly dressed then come back in an hour. I need time to think; we'll have breakfast together. Oh, and Otto, tell your lad well done, very well done," Titus said, dismissing them.

Titus Attius was in high spirits over their shared bread and heated wine in spite of the cold drizzle the rising sun had brought.

"We're going to nick their loot off 'em, simple as that," he said with a sly grin.

"It can't be this easy," Boxer objected.

"Course it can. We found it because for the first time we made the effort. A couple of hundred horsemen rode out to search everyday, something we hadn't done before. If it was there, we were bound to come up with the goods. Stands to reason. Have more faith in the efficiency of the Roman army, Prefect Boxer," he raised his wine cup to Otto, "and our German Auxiliaries."

"You intend to walk in and take it?"

"You've got it."

"What about the guards?"

"Tell him Otto," Titus mumbled through a mouthful of bread.

"When they raided, I think they probably hid a cart out of sight behind some rocks. They grabbed as many boxes as they could in the melee and dumped them on the cart. The driver took the gold around to the hiding place, unloaded it and drove off. Only half a dozen men are in the know, so why draw attention to the cache? Guards are a security risk; their presence attracts attention, they have to be rotated and sooner or later they talk. I don't believe there will be any."

"But what if…" Boxer began.

"There you go again, trying to work out every possibility like you always do," Otto interrupted. "You can't calculate everything, brother. The future is infinitely unsure. Accept that. Who knows what will happen? Death or Glory!" he said, lifted his cup and poured a little wine on the ground as a libation to the Gods.

"Well said, Otto. Now listen, I speak formally as Camp Prefect and Officer Commanding. After the men have eaten I'm calling a general assembly. The order of the day will be for eleven hundred praetorians and two hundred and fifty cavalry to march and spend four hours searching as far out on the plain below as they can cover in the time. We know they won't find anything, so be it. I am hoping that the scale of this diversion will make our enemies think we haven't discovered their hidey-hole. If they're watching everyone else, they'll have no eyes for us. Because, while our lads are busy, sixty men and thirty cavalry led by me and Prefect Otto will recover the Emperor's property. We shall take the scout with us. While we are away, Prefect Boxer will discretely dismantle and burn his ballista. Metal parts are to be handed over to the blacksmiths for re-use. Any questions?"

"My ballista, why, sir?" Boxer asked in a horrified voice.

"Because it's kept under a tarpaulin on the sturdiest middle-sized cart we have. That's where we are going to store what we are about to recover."

"I shall obey, Camp Prefect Attius. I hope all will be well," Boxer said, desolate at having to destroy his beautiful machine.

"Democritus said that the hopes of the wise are always possible," Otto commented.

"If I'm a mathematical bore, you're an even bigger philosophical one. Otto Kingkiller? More like Otto Greek Quoter," Boxer snapped and left the table.

"What's up with him?" Titus asked.

Otto shrugged. "Engineers, sir. To break up that ballista is as hard for him as putting down a favourite hound would be for the rest of us."

The drizzle increased to a heavy downpour that lasted only a few minutes before clearing the sky allowing the sun to turn the rainwater into steam. The three officers watched the infantry manoeuvring into skirmish lines and poking about in the undergrowth at the base of rocks while the cavalry rode away far to the west, fanning out and performing the same action from horseback. When they had gone about a mile, Titus Attius turned smartly on his heel and barked a stream of concise orders. Just as his smaller force was about to move off, Boxer trotted up and handed Otto several hanks of cord.

"To secure the chests for easier carrying," he explained, then "Gods with you," as he clasped his hand.

The Camp Prefect marched at the head of his two files of men, Otto leading his cavalry brought up the rear. Once down the steep road and out onto the plain, they were indistinguishable from the hundreds of others engaged in their futile search. They swung around to their left and stepped out briskly towards their destination. After a couple of miles, Titus Attius called a halt and let the men fall out while he consulted Otto.

"How much farther?"

Otto asked Lutold who said it was a little more than a mile.

"You'd better get off your horse and march with me," Titus told the scout who looked over at Otto. "Never mind him, I'm in charge here," Titus told him sharply.

"Yes, lord."

"Yes, sir or yes, Camp Prefect."

"Yes, lord sir Prefect," Lutold replied.

"Oh just get on with it," Titus told him impatiently not noticing his sly wink to Otto who grinned.

When they were a quarter of a mile away, Lutold informed Titus and pointed at a scrub covered slope that looked no different from the rest of the broken hillside. At two hundred yards, Titus called a halt again.

"Right son. Go and see if there's anyone home,"

Lutold looked at him blankly for a moment then understood. He took of his helmet and sword belt and shouted for one of his comrades who dismounted and hurried over. Between them they hauled Lutold's mail shirt over his head. In his tunic and breeches with his knife pushed into one boot, he took a few steps into the low bushes and vanished. One moment he was sliding into the undergrowth and then he was gone. Not a sound, not a movement of a single twig to betray him.

They waited in the feeble warmth of the sun for quarter of an hour then saw his figure waving at them beside a tall rock up ahead.

"Otto, wait here and be ready to move in fast if required. Men, advance at the double," Titus ordered.

"Take these, sir. Boxer says to tie them around the chests for easy carrying," Otto said, handing over the cords.

He watched the soldiers move briskly across the intervening space until they arrived at the spot where Lutold awaited them. He was standing in a narrow cleft between a tall jagged rock and a shorter, rounded one which leaned into it forming a tunnel. He darted down it and vanished. Titus blinked in surprise. As far as he could see, there was nothing ahead but a blank stone wall. He drew his sword and went in with caution. At ten paces, the boulder to his left curved inward to reveal a second entrance. Passing through, he found himself in a natural amphitheatre ten yards across and almost completely ringed in by rough walls upwards of thirty feet in height. The ground under his feet was coarse sand and gravel. The beaming scout stood in the centre.

"Welcome, sir," he said bowing and spreading his arms wide like an inn-keeper greeting a rich traveller.

There was a cave, formed like the original entrance by a narrow gap between a pair of massive rocks. Titus peered in. Once his eyes had adjusted to the gloom he saw that it was shallow and the roof came very low just a few paces back from the cavemouth. Rawhides covered a mound in the centre of the floor. He stepped in a pulled the top one aside. A neat pile of wooden chests had been stacked on branches to lift them off the damp floor and further protected with the hides thrown over them.

Titus laughed aloud. He could see unbroken mine seals on the nearest. He shouted for his men and they made their way in. He sent two back outside to cut some boughs off a furze bush and return at the double. In a matter of minutes, thirty-two shallow chests each containing forty gold ingots had been wrapped around with cord and slung over the soldiers' shoulders. They made their way out and formed up, their unburdened comrades taking their shields off them.

"Right, you with the furze branches, they are now brooms. Get it? Furze? Broom? Your Camp Prefect makes a good joke but you don't laugh, you miserable lot!. Go back inside, try to prop up those hides in the cave as if there was still something under them then walk out backwards brushing away all our tracks as you go. I do not want the mark of a single hobnail to show we've ever been here."

They marched back to camp with the soldiers carrying the gold hidden between a file of praetorians to their left and the cavalry moving in parallel with them to their right. When they arrived at Boxer's former artillery cart, there was a distinct smell of burning hair in the air All that was left of the ballista was a neat arrangement of metal parts on the ground. Boxer and the artillery crew stood by with reproachful eyes fixed on the Camp Prefect.

Boxer saluted. "Permission to retain the metalwork, sir. Much of it is forged from the finest steel and can be reused if we make a new one."

"Where will you keep it?"

"With the scorpions and their ammunition."

"Permission granted."

"Pick it all up, get it greased and stowed away," Boxer ordered.

Ingots recounted, chests resealed by the priest, recorded by the tesserarius, sheeted down and under a guard of six soldiers to be rotated every four hours, the command party adjourned to their Camp Prefect's tent. The last flagon of his best Falernian wine, took pride of place on the table. Titus raised his cup.

"To the Emperor. I will not add "and the successful conclusion of our mission" because it is not yet over but today has been a good one."

"When are you going to confront Centurion Frugi?" Boxer asked.

Titus chortled like a naughty schoolboy with some mischief in mind. He wagged one index finger at Boxer.

"I'm not. He's about to discover his loot has gone. He'll think it must have been us who took it but he can't be sure, just the same way we have no cast-iron proof he's implicated…"

"Lutold saw him," Otto reminded him.

"The word of a German spy against that of a Roman officer? No, we can't nail him with that."

"So what happens next?" Boxer asked.

"I believe I know," Otto told him. "He's only one of the players in this game. He will have to make whoever gives him his orders aware of his disastrous situation. He can't desert his post because that would give him away. Therefore, he'll have to send a message, an urgent message. All this leads to Rome, as far as we know, and that's where his contact will be."

"A ship?"

Otto nodded. "That would be quickest and the weather for sailing is improving by the day…"

"We patrol constantly. Instruct your cavalry that no-one must get through to Emporiae or Tarraco without being questioned," Titus ordered.

Tense days followed. The German Auxiliaries scoured the area for someone on a fast horse heading for the coast but reported no sightings. They camped overnight at strategic points blocking the roads but without success.

Boxer's men had covered the bridge in planks, oiled to protect the timber against the ravages of rain and snow.

"Bit dangerous, that," Titus remarked. "Someone could slip."

"The wood will draw the oil in over a few days, you won't notice it," Boxer responded.

"There's no handrails, you could fall off the sides" he said.

Before Boxer could comment, his second in command spoke up with a scathing tone in his voice.

"Better keep to the middle, then. Eh, sir?"

The engineering crew were proud of their construction and were not about to accept any criticism of their beautiful bridge, soaring in its graceful curve over the chasm.

The mule track was almost complete. The masons and their conscripted helpers had taken great delight in roaring, "Heads below!" to any of the mineworkers within a hundred yards of the foot of the cliff each time they pushed the debris of their efforts over the edge. If they made someone jump, they cheered and laughed.

Otto reported that a gold consignment was due to leave the mine the next day and asked if he should provide an escort, in view of all that had happened since the last shipment. Titus was about to reply when he suddenly grasped Otto by his arms, leaned in and kissed him on both cheeks. Otto recoiled but could not free himself from the Camp Prefect's painful grip.

"You're a fucking genius, if you only knew it. That's how Frugi is going to send his message; by one of Pinarius' crew."

Pinarius the haulier did not need to pay for any guards to protect the precious freight since Otto's men had ridden beside his wagons but still employed a few for form's sake. As they were not likely to be bashed on the head, their wages were considerably less than in the old days but there were always a few beached sailors who would take on the job.

The heavy wagon rumbled out of the mine complex and jounced along the rough road to the meeting point with their protective cavalry. Sigbold Bearslayer led the troopers, The quartermaster rode along charged with buying mules: draft animals would be needed to haul everything away when they left their camp for the last time. A further addition to the party was Imperial Prefect Otto Longius mounted on Djinn, who had been specially groomed for the occasion.

The tall officer reflected pale sunlight from the facets of his polished armour. Silver rings adorned both arms. His powerful black warhorse tossed his mane and snorted thin plumes of steam into the morning air. Otto had wanted to impress and he had certainly done so. The wharf rats onboard the wagon looked at him in something approaching awe. He urged Djinn into a walk around both sides, staring at each man in turn. Most of them avoided those icy blue eyes or quickly dropped their own gaze. He halted by the tailgate.

"One of you men is carrying a message to Tarraco. I want it. If you hand it over, you will come to no harm. You have my word. If no-one admits he is carrying such a message but one is found on him when my men search you all, I will cut off that man's hands, slash his hamstrings and leave him at the side of the road. You have my word."

After the briefest of pauses, a burly middle-aged man raised one arm. "It's me you want, sir,"

"Climb down" Otto told him and moved off a few paces.

The messenger craned his neck to look up at him and held out a folded parchment. It was wrapped around with thread and sealed with red wax.

"Who gave you this?"

"Adonis Frugi, sir."

"Where were you supposed to deliver it?"

"To the captain of the "Neptune's Swallow" lying in Tarraco harbour sir. She's a fast vessel that one…" his voice faded into silence.

"Have you ever carried letters for Frugi before?"

"No, sir. Anyway, this is my first trip up here. Missed my sailing you see, and…"

"I can ask your comrades if what you say is true."

"Go on, then, they'll back me up."

"Give me the letter." The anxious man put it in Otto's open hand. He tucked it away under his sword belt. "You may not believe me but today has been one of the luckiest days of your life. No doubt you were promised a reward on delivery but all you would have got was a knife in the back. Here," he held out a handful of silver coins, "take these as payment for your co-operation. Say nothing to anyone and ship-out off this coast as soon as you can. If you mention this to a single soul, you will not live many days afterwards. Take heed, this matter concerns men much more powerful than I am."

The shaken sailor climbed back onto the wagon. Otto nodded to Sigbold and rode for the camp.

Titus Attius turned the letter over and over, his meaty fingers handling it as carefully as if it was made of the thinnest glass.

"Definitely written by Frugi?" he asked.

"So the man charged with it told me," Otto replied.

"Who was he delivering it to?"

"The captain of a fast ship."

"That's enough to nail the centurion to his cross."

"Aren't you going to open it? Otto enquired.

Titus looked at him as if he was mad. "I'd rather put both hands in a nest of vipers. Think, I open it and I see a name, perhaps the name of an influential senator. That scrap of knowledge alone would be my death sentence. No, Otto, it has value as a way of forcing some sort of truth out of Frugi, otherwise, it's poison. We hold onto it and wait."

Boxer walked down to the goldmine to inspect his completed mule track and back up to report the works were finished. That same day, the cavalry came back with strings of mules in tow, the quartermaster and a fat man with two bruisers who he said were his assistants driving an empty cart. He had come to give a price for the scrap iron collected after the besiegers had been driven off. He argued about the price for upwards of two hours until the bargain was struck and the money handed over. The soldiers helped load for him and he rattled and clanked down the road and away, publicly grumbling that he had been cheated but privately relishing the prospect of a future profit.

"There are your mules, Camp Prefect," the quartermaster told him, glum as ever. "My accounts will have to be audited. It's going to be interesting telling my superiors that we needed new transport animals because we ate the ones that headquarters gave us in the first place."

"Ate 'em? I don't remember that do you Prefect Boxer? Titus asked.

"No recollection of such an event, Camp Prefect."

"Oh, very droll, most hilarious," the quartermaster complained and stumped off.

The praetorian centurion stood at attention with his helmet in the crook of his left arm. His vine staff was under his right.

"Greetings Superintendent Tubero. My commander, Camp Prefect Titus Attius, advises that our task here is complete. Along with Prefect of Engineers Lucius Taurus Longius and Imperial Prefect of Cavalry, the Knight Otto Longius…"

"Otto? That big German? Is he a member of the Equestrian order?" the surprised Tubero broke in.

"Oh yes, sir. Appointed by the Emperor in person. He's a highly decorated soldier, they call him Otto Kingkiller. But if I may continue? The bridge will be dedicated at noon tomorrow. You and your senior assistants along with Centurion Ennius Frugi and his optio are invited to attend. There will be refreshments after the ceremony. Prefect Longius will await you at the foot of the mule track an hour before noon. He hopes you will enjoy walking it for the first time."

The Germans had been sent out into the mountains for the past few days to search out enough game for a feast. Spring was advancing and although it was the wrong time of the year and the wild beasts were thin after the winter, they managed to provide wild boar, suckling pigs, roebuck and scores of birds. It would not be a grand affair but there would be sufficient to honour the day. The fire pits were at white heat and the laden spits turning slowly shortly after dawn. The praetorians polished their kit until it gleamed, the cavalry groomed their horses, cleaned their teeth and oiled their hooves. The soldiers wanted to make sure these civilians never forgot the day they had seen the praetorians on parade; the Germans were determined not to be outdone.

A cold dawn, the wind blew out of the north bearing the breath of the mountain snows on it but the day was dry, scudding white clouds in a blue sky. By mid-morning the temperature had risen enough to make it fresh but pleasant. Boxer led Tubero and his party up the cliff on the newly cut pathway. Tubero stopped to admire the herringbone grooves chiselled into the stone to help the mules keep their footing. At the top he turned to look out over at the panorama of his mining complex.

"I've never see it from this viewpoint, it looks so much bigger," he remarked.

They walked towards the bridge in the distance. The caltrops had long been recovered but Boxer still trod warily: one may have been overlooked. The cohorts were paraded in an open square on the other side facing the bridge, the smaller ranks of engineers nearest their achievement with the artillerists. The auxiliary cavalry were ranked behind the infantry. The priest had set up his altar in the very front.

As they approached, Tubero saw the completed bridge for the first time.

"No hand rails?" he asked, sounding a little disappointed.

"They were never part of the design," Boxer told him through gritted teeth. "Your men could build masonry pylons at either end then stretch chains across if you feel it's really necessary."

Most of the remaining carts and wagons had been pushed out of the way nearer to the edge of the ravine to make space for the massed troops.

Tubero and his companions bowed to the command party and lined up at the side of them. Titus raised a hand. Bugles sounded and the priest walked to his altar accompanied by a soldier leading a ram and another holding two black roosters from his small flock of sacred poultry by the feet.

The ram, kept back from the sheep and goats exchanged for the captives, was the appropriate sacrifice to Janus, the god of crossings whose blessing was being invoked by the sacred rites. Blood flowed into a bowl, the liver of the dead animal was examined and the priest proclaimed the offering was healthy and acceptable. Next he walked to the centre of the bridge, cut the throats of the birds and flung them down, one each side, to appease any malignant spirits in the depths below. He ended his ceremony by walking across the bridge and back sprinkling blood out of his bowl with a soft brush, all the while chanting prayers and incantations. The bugles sounded again to signal that the religious service was satisfactorily concluded.

"Parade, stand down!" Titus roared.

The ranks broke up and the men moved away to the spits, their mouths filling with saliva as the smell of the roasting meat filled their nostrils. A table had been set up under an awning displaying the plans and diagrams used in the construction as some of their little remaining acceptable wine was offered to the guests. Tubero and his assistants were fascinated by the papers and discussed them with a sound grasp of the technicalities.

"Not very interesting is it, all this?" Titus said to Frugi. "Tell you what, you've never seen a praetorian camp before, I bet. Come with me, bring your optio and I'll show you something special."

Otto, Titus, Adonis Frugi and the optio put down their wine cups and walked off discretely, passing several parked wagons before turning into the space between two of them, out of sight of everyone else.

Chapter 20

Frugi looked around. He could see the sides of two wagons, the edge of the ravine and an empty space of grass opposite it. He tried to keep the sudden alarm he was feeling locked down as he turned to Titus with a brief, forced laugh.

"I see nothing very special here, Camp Prefect Attius."

Titus held up the letter Otto had intercepted. "No, not even this?" He looked over at the optio. "Centurion Ennius Frugi is renowned for his godlike appearance but I tell you his soul is as ugly as his face is handsome. Adonis? Adonis the poisoner, the murderer, the traitor and the deceiver of ignorant tribesmen. Adonis the thief of the Emperor's gold," he waved the letter. "This is the written proof, optio, let him deny it."

The centurion kept his face expressionless with masterly self-control. "I have no idea what you're talking about, Titus Attius. These are ridiculous accusations. Let me see the letter." He reached out one hand.

Titus shook his head. "Oh no. It's going straight to Rome along with you after your arrest."

Frugi gestured towards Otto. "I suppose you'll let that German savage loose on me if I refuse to submit, is that it? Hiding behind a barbarian?"

"Otto Longius is a Knight of Rome, he has been awarded the Civic Crown and The Military Crown for his service to Emperor Augustus. He can be proud of his record unlike you who gave his oath under the eagles then shat on it."

"Service to Augustus?" the centurion snarled, spit flying off his lips as he worked himself into a frenzy, "that criminal who murdered half the nobility of Rome and plundered their estates with his crony Marcus Antonius until they fell out and he hounded Antonius to death. There's theft for you. Augustus adopted son of Caesar, the one they called the Queen of Bithynia for selling his body to the king of that country, the destroyer of Gaul, the tyrant. What honourable man could serve Augustus? Unlike him, Pompey was called "The Great" in his own lifetime."

"And Pompey is long dead," Titus reminded him.

"Yes, and his veterans thrown off their lands by the usurper, their heirs disinherited. Pompey may be gone from us but the memory of what he was and the harm done to those who followed him still lives."

"Are you also Rei Vasco?"

Ennius Frugi took a deep breath and pulled himself up to his full height, raising his chin proudly.

"My grandmother was a noblewoman of the Vascones, my mother the daughter of their king. I inherited after her father's death.

Yes, I am Rei Vasco, to you, King of The Vascones. It was my men you fought."

"And defeated. I take it you will not co-operate?"

Frugi drew his sword.

Titus drew his. "Between us then," he said.

Both men were armed with a Roman short sword and a vine staff. Since they went into battle without shields, centurions soon became expert in using their staffs of office as weapons in combat, as well as a means of disciplining their soldiers.

They eyed each other, the entire world and their whole of their lives concentrated on this one small spot in this moment of time. Frugi struck first. He leapt in with a sword thrust to the base of his opponent's throat and a simultaneous low slash with his vine staff aimed at the hip. Titus blocked and counter-attacked. They both backed away to weigh each other up after this first exchange.

Then they went in again. Blows, cuts, thrusts, launched and parried, weight changing from foot to foot, ducking, swaying, sometimes shuffling in then back and all the time circling over the ground. The crack of vine staffs, clashing swords, the rasping hiss as blades were dragged across each other, panting breath, grunts of effort and pain, boots stamping the thin grass down onto the hard earth.

At first they had seemed evenly matched but Titus was over ten years older than the centurion who had the longer stride and reach. It told. He began to tire. At first Otto thought it was a ruse but he saw how his chest was heaving as he laboured for breath and that he was no longer attacking. His guard was coming down as the muscles of his arms and shoulders weakened with fatigue.

"Oh fuck it, I underestimated him," Titus thought, "because he's a pretty boy...."

The idea inspired and energized him. He let Frugi come in close then parried his sword strike outwards at the cost of taking a painful thump to the ribs from his adversary's staff. Titus bent his knees, leaned forward, snapped them straight and jumped. The rim of his helmet smashed into that Grecian nose, destroying it in a spray of bright blood. The centurion's eyes watered, his nervous system was short-circuited and for a moment he stood helpless. Titus butted him again, right in the middle of his throbbing, ruined face.

He reeled and staggered without realizing where he was going. Involuntarily he let his sword drop to the floor, cradling his nose in his free hand. He stopped and blurrily saw his heels were nearly overhanging the lip of the ravine. He looked over at the misty figure of Titus through his streaming eyes.

"I curse you," he shouted. "I curse your false Emperor. Hail Pompey Magnus!"

Centurion Ennius Frugi, known as Adonis, King of the Vascones, stepped backwards into the void and was gone.

Titus sheathed his sword and leaned forward, his fists on his knees, drawing in deep breaths.

"Stay here," Otto shouted at the optio and hurried away to return a few moments later with a bucket and a jug of water. Everyone was talking, eating and drinking so he had not been noticed.

Titus sat on the upturned bucket and gulped the water. He sighed and wiped his mouth with the back of his hand. He poured out what was left in the jug over his scarf and scrubbed the blood off his face.

"I didn't know you were going to do that. You should have left him to me," Otto scolded.

"Can't have you killing all the kings can we?" Titus said and laughed before looking over at the optio who was equally bewildered and terrified. He was very young for his rank and it was quite likely he had never witnessed a violent death. Thousands of men served their full terms in the legions and never saw action, it was not unusual.

"Now then, what shall we do with you, lad?" Titus mused aloud.

The optio swallowed nervously but did not reply. Otto took over.

"You heard the late centurion admit to theft and treachery and you heard him curse the Emperor, is that correct?" Otto demanded.

He was answered by a nod of agreement.

"You saw that he could have surrendered or rejoined the combat but chose to seek his own death?"

Again a nod.

"I am sorry that you have been drawn into this. It's dangerous for all of us, especially you. Traitors have accomplices and we don't know who they are…."

"Not me, sir. On my oath not me…" the optio said, finding his voice at last.

"Of course not, son. No-one is accusing you…yet," Titus told him.

"The thing is," Otto went on, "that when this sort of thing gets out, there are enquiries and who can say what their conclusions will be and how many innocent men might be blamed for something that was nothing to do with them?" He left his words to sink into the young officer's mind and stew for a long while before continuing. "I have a suggestion for you. Sign a written statement to which you can swear on oath. It will say, you and Centurion Ennius Frugi were invited to the dedication of this new bridge. Centurion Frugi drank some wine. Camp Prefect Titus Attius offered you a tour and Imperial Prefect Otto Longius went with you. Centurion Frugi fell to his death in a ravine. He was not pushed nor was there anyone within five yards of him when he went over the edge. I believe that everything I have said is true and that you witnessed it all. Can you sign such a document?"

"Yes sir, but what about the letter?"

Titus pulled it out of its place under his sword belt. "This? It's nothing, just a bluff to get him to confess." He let it flutter to the ground. "My clerk will draw up your statement for you and when you've signed, the prefect and I will witness it. All done and dusted but if you wish to have a career under the eagles, never repeat anything you heard here today. If you do, we guarantee this will come back and bite you on the arse, very hard. Now come on, my son. You need a couple of cups of wine and a venison steak to put you back on your feet. Leave explaining to the superintendent to me."

Titus rose and walked back to the gathering with his arm around the optio's shoulder. He looked behind and flicked his eyes at the discarded letter. Otto got the message and swiftly shoved it under his mail shirt before tossing Frugi's fallen sword over the edge.

Otto took charge of the optio and steered him to the Camp Prefect's tent where he called for the clerk to take some dictation. Titus found himself a jug of un-watered wine and a cup, filled it and noticed the slight trembling of his hands. He knocked back the drink in one. He felt a relaxing warmth spreading through his body and gave a relieved sigh. He looked around for Tubero.

The mine superintendent was shocked at the news.

"Were you there? Did you see it?" he asked.

Titus took him over to the table outside his tent where they were joined by Boxer who was not as surprised as he might have been to learn of the tragedy.

"The optio is making a formal statement, Master Tubero," Otto told him. "The military authorities are going to require it."

The clerk finished, Titus and Otto read over the parchment and signed it, the young officer added his name and the version of the event it described became the legal truth.

"Poor Adonis Frugi," Tubero said into his cup with a sigh.

"The last time we ate together, he said he had a fear of heights and straight drops," Titus reminded him.

"Perhaps fate was whispering to him but he took no heed," the mine superintendent suggested.

The conversation ended when the quartermaster came over and asked him if Tubero wanted to make an offer on some cables and materials left over from the construction.

"Won't the garrison have a use for them?" Tubero asked.

A quick glance passed between the three officers. Titus cleared his throat.

"In fact, plans have changed and we shall all be leaving in the next few days," which was the Camp Prefect's public announcement that their mission had reached its conclusion.

The celebration went on for the rest of the afternoon but the goldmine party left early with profuse thanks for the hospitality and "their" bridge which would change their whole way of working in the future. Word soon got round the troops that they would shortly be on their way which added to their enjoyment of the day. Tomorrow they would begin the hard work of breaking camp but for the moment, all was good cheer and happy anticipation.

When they were alone, Titus walked across to the nearest fire pit and threw Frugi's unopened letter into its glowing white heart. He watched until wax, thread and parchment were entirely consumed before returning, going into his tent and coming out with the leather scroll-case Publius Quadratus had handed to Otto in Rome and which had come close to costing him his life. He took out a letter.

"This is a final sealed dispatch to be read only when we have done here," Titus announced.

He cracked the wax with his thumbnail, read the contents and passed it along to Boxer. He scanned it and gave it to Otto who whistled when he had finished looking it over.

"To Praetorian Prefect Cassius Plancus Greetings,

If you are reading this then the civil engineering part of your task is completed and you have no legitimate reason to remain on post. On the presumption that you have eradicated the robbers who plague the worthy mine superintendent and are the source of his many complaints, you are free to return to Rome or to your normal duties if located elsewhere. In the case that you have been able to recover a significant proportion of what has been stolen, you are to proceed to the warehouse of Axios Brothers in the dock area of Ostia. There you will receive further instructions. Your route and method of travel are at your discretion but it is of the uttermost importance that no-one outside your command discovers what you bring with you.

Augustus Imp.

"Well that's clear enough. So what's it to be, land or sea?" Titus asked.

"By sea is quicker but we would have to split up," Boxer said.

Otto gave his opinion. "There are two hazards if we take ship, sinking and pirates. If we march there's only one, "land-pirates" if you can call them that."

"None of us have a clue what's going on at sea but we are a strong and capable force by land, slower but surer, I think," Titus gave his verdict.

As Boxer was walking back to his men's lines, he came across the priest and smiled a greeting.

"You really should have put some handrails on that bridge of yours, young man. Standing near the sides made me feel quite giddy," the priest called over to him.

Boxer's smile changed into a scowl. He did not reply.

Titus Attius had a problem. Normally, when a legion had carried out their orders and was stood down, their legate would issue awards to men who had distinguished themselves. Titus had assumed command by default and the soldiers under him were either praetorians or auxiliaries, with the exception of Boxer's artillerymen and engineers who were the only legion regulars. He did not want to appear presumptuous but felt the men who had been outstanding deserved something. He had a word with the best of the smiths who took a belt buckle in the shape of an eagle the Camp Prefect gave him and welded it to a metal disc then built up a rim around it. Titus watched as molten silver was poured in. He then cut a die in the basic form of a bridge. Once the silver had solidified but was still hot and soft, the smith stamped it with the bridge-die. When the medallion was turned out of its mould, it bore an eagle on one side and a bridge on the reverse. With a hole drilled for a leather thong and some filing and polishing it was just what was required. Titus ordered several.

The day before they were due to march was balmy with a southerly wind. The songs of skylarks were heard for the first time that year. Everyone was on parade in response to a call for a general assembly. Titus stood at his table which was laden with gleaming silver medals.

"Men of the Praetorian Guard, I am not of your number but circumstances led me to command you. You have acquitted yourselves exactly as the Emperor's elite should and I commend you. I have had commemorative medals struck which I am pleased to distribute to the notably worthy among you. Stand forward the senior centurions of the first and second cohorts and my adjutant."

They stood to attention in front of him and bowed as he hung a medal over each of their necks. Next, it was the turn of the two veterans of Syria who had built the shadouf and warned him about the final prisoner exchange. The decurions of the German Auxiliary Cavalry and Lutold Shadow were singled out, with Otto to translate. Then the artillerist who had fired the grapnel and Boxer's second in command. There was one medal left on the table.

"Finally, to a man who we nag and worry, we complain to him and tell him his efforts are never enough yet without him we starve.

Stand forward our quartermaster who kept us and our horses fed and fit to fight."

A roar of approval greeted this last award and the blushing quartermaster strode back to his place in the ranks accompanied by the rhythmical thunder of spear shafts drumming against shields.

"At dawn tomorrow we march for home. Prepare yourselves and your equipment. Tumble our breastworks down so they will be of no use to an enemy. We return with our heads high but never forgetting our comrades who left us here when they took their last journey across the Styx. Dismiss!"

In the early morning light, Boxer stood silently contemplating his bridge. Otto came and stood beside him.

"I'm glad you didn't put rails on it," Otto said, "they would have spoiled the look of it. It's like a bird's wing poised to fly men over the chasm. You should be proud."

At reveille the men were turned out in a bitterly cold dawn with spiteful bursts of sleet stinging their faces. They gathered under their standards and moved down the hairpin road for the last time. Once they were assembled, the order of march was established. The praetorians led followed by the transport vehicles with an infantry guard. The cavalry took the rear with both flanking parties and scouts to range well ahead. They stood motionless in their ranks for several minutes while Titus Attius inspected them. He gave a hand signal. A bugle blew, the call was repeated, echoing off the cliffs behind them, the column lurched forward, men marking time with their hobnail boots until the soldier in front of them took his first stride and then they fell into the rhythm that would take them home. The low sun struggled through whipping clouds to dazzle their eyes as they headed eastwards to the coast.

By the end of the day they had covered eighteen miles and the mountains seemed no farther away than when they had looked up behind them at the start. As the terrain did not lend itself to building a standard marching camp, Titus Attius ordered the wagons and carts to be drawn up into a square and the men to bivouac around them with sentries set and cavalry picquets circling all night. On the third day, they moved onto a paved road and made better time, reaching Emporiae on the sixth day. They camped on the grounds they had used when they had arrived all those months ago. They had been descending throughout their march and here, at the coast, spring was much further advanced than in the foothills of the Pyrenaei.

On the Camp Prefect's instructions, the quartermaster, scrutinized by the tesserarius, gave half the praetorians an advance on their pay and twenty four hours liberty. The other half would have the same privilege on the following day. It took well under the allotted time for the inns and brothels of Emporiae to strip them of every brass farthing. They rolled back into camp in groups, arm-in-arm and singing. The next morning's bugles were a torture to throbbing heads. Provided they held a weapon and a shield and could stand upright unaided, their centurions let their appearance pass. The other party were ready to hit the town by sunset and off they went, after spending most of the day mocking their nauseated and hung-over comrades.

In spite of being warned not to by the tesserarius, the quartermaster asked Otto if his cavalrymen would like to have the same opportunity. Otto looked at him coldly.

"They would not," he said.

"What, they wouldn't like to spend an hour or so with a willing woman?"

Otto pulled himself up to his full height and looked down on the quartermaster with scorn. "They keep themselves pure for their wives. If any man paid to go with another woman he would be shunned by his comrades and could never go home." He stalked away.

"Told you not to ask him," the tesserarius said smugly. "Odd lot these Germans, easily offended."

Boxer and Otto lay on marble slabs in the city bathhouse while two powerful masseurs pummelled their muscles and stretched their joints. They had luxuriated in the heat room, washed and now sighed and groaned as the probing fingers discovered and smoothed out knots beneath their skins. In a few minutes the barber would arrive to shave their faces and cut their hair

"The simple things in life are often the best," Boxer said.

Otto smiled to himself. Only a Roman would think that this was a "simple" activity involving as it did the construction of a tiled building with a sophisticated heating system, a constant supply of hot water and the services of experts in massage and hair-dressing. As a boy, he and his people had bathed daily in a river or stream, sometimes breaking the winter ice before they could get in. That was simple.

They had both replaced their tunics and loin cloths, worn thin with use and hand washing. The final luxury was dressing in their new clothes, as yet unworn.

Boxer studied his friend. "You look taller," he remarked.

Otto shook his head. "No, but I'm thinner. I never put back the weight I lost up in Germany the last time. But you look better. That wound on your forehead is just a pink line now. Your eyebrows are back where they should be but the scar makes you look permanently worried."

Refreshed, cleaner than they had been for months, the column turned north with the sea on their right where it would remain until they were home. They stayed overnight at official waystations wherever possible. Dire warnings about careless talk were repeated to the troops at every stop but they were unnecessary. Civilians avoided the praetorians and were openly fearful of the Germans. Men of other units were not inclined to mix with the Emperor's elite guard, motivated by a jealousy they would not admit, even to themselves.

Boxer and Otto asked if their contingents were supposed to march all the way to Ostia.

"The orders are straightforward. We head for Ostia if we have the bullion, I take that to mean all of us," Titus Attius confirmed.

One night when they were alone Boxer wanted to hear the full story of the end of Adonis Frugi.

"You know it. He fell to his death. You saw me witness the optio's statement," Otto told him, a little coolly.

"I did," Boxer replied, "but there's more, isn't there?"

Otto sighed and nodded his head. "When Titus confronted him he admitted he was behind all our troubles. He was a misguided dupe, I think. He shouted a lot about Pompey and politics but he was being used. Anyway, he and Titus fought. He fought well, did Frugi, I'll give hm that. At one point I thought he was going to win and was ready to jump in but Titus smashed his nose and it was all over. He decided to end his life rather than be taken, so he sought his death in the depths of that chasm. No reason to talk any more about it, eh?"

"Talk about what?" Boxer said with a grin.

Eastwards around the end of the pocket in which the Ligurian Sea lies between Italia and Hispania until it meets the Tyrrhenian, then south, eating up the Via Aurelia at over twenty miles a day. When they were on a line with Luca, Titus asked Otto if he would like a pass to leave the column and visit his family.

"Did you go to see your wife and child when we were close to Tarraco, Camp Prefect?"

"Well, no I didn't."

"Do you imagine I would put my duty second any more than you would, sir?"

"Gods above and below, sorry for mentioning it! It'll be a long time before I offer to do you a favour again."

Three days away from Rome, Boxer suggested that they send a rider ahead to announce their imminent arrival. Titus and Otto burst into gales of laughter. Boxer looked at them both with a confused expression forcing them to guffaw even louder. Eventually, they controlled themselves.

Otto patted his friend on the shoulder. "The Emperor would have been told the day we first set foot in Italia. Have no fears, we won't be dropping in like unexpected guests."

When the permanent, dirty brown smoke cloud over Rome came into view, the first centurion of one of the praetorian cohorts suggested that they left the highway and made towards Ostia without entering the city.

"With this number of men and horses and all our baggage, once we get in we'll be log-jammed by the crowds. Can't kick all of 'em out of the way."

Ostia, the entry port for the corn of Egypt that kept all Rome fed, a vast sweep of wharves, jetties, inner and outer pools. Massive grain ships were moored beside craft out of the Levant, Greece, North Africa, all bringing their goods to stuff the ever hungry belly of the capital city of the Empire. There were a few naval craft among them, guarded by marines and standing ready to defend the sea approaches. Men of all colours and manners of dress bustled everywhere about their mercantile business, shouting in a confused babble of languages. The air was heavy with the odours of spices, exotic food cooking, sewage and bilge water. Tarraco and Emporiae were reduced to the significance of fishing harbours by comparison.

The Axios Brother's warehouse was a two storey structure, the ground floor hidden behind a high brick wall enclosing an enormous yard. As they stopped in front of the double gates, they were swung inwards and a man on foot stepped out. He wore a pale green tunic with a Greek key border in a darker shade and matching suede boots. He smiled over to them and waved a languid hand.

"How lovely to see you again, my dear old things," Cassius Plancus greeted them. "Do come in."

Chapter 21

Cassius looked tanned and healthy, almost his old self but a closer examination showed two deep pain lines running down from each side of his nose to the corners of his lips. His eyes were subtly different, the expression older somehow.

Titus Attius came forward, bowed and saluted.

"It is my pleasure to return your command to you, Prefect Cassius Plancus."

"Not mine anymore, as a matter of fact. I resigned my commission so I am only a lowly civilian. You give the orders here, Camp Prefect but may I suggest we stand the men down so I can brief you?"

The went inside the vast empty space of the warehouse. A table with chairs, bread and wine had been set up inside.

"Immediate business first I think. Prefect Otto, I have requisitioned premises for the overnight accommodation of your cavalry. They belong to an interesting individual who supplies wild beasts for the arena so be prepared for unusual odours. But the buildings are big enough and available so your men will have to make the best of it. Camp Prefect Attius, Prefect Longius, your troops will be split over the marine barracks and upstairs right here. I'll show you where to go shortly and would you do me the honour of dining with me this evening? I have taken over the kitchen of an inn and brought some decent cooks with me so it won't be the usual dockside slop they serve around here."

The animal importer's depot consisted of numbers of heavily gated and barred stalls built around a large open area enclosed by high brick walls with rusting spikes set on top of them. The smell was rank. The men wrinkled their noses but the horses rolled their eyes and capered. They were frightened by the reek of strange beasts and it took over an hour to settle them but even then, they were clearly nervous. The men explored their billet and some of them found the owner's office. It was a large room with pictures of his stock in trade painted on the walls to impress potential customers. Someone ran for Otto and insisted he looked at it. They wanted to know if these creatures were real. Otto spent the next few hours giving guided tours to as many men as could crowd in at one time, stopping in front of each painting and telling them everything he knew, which was not much. The Germans had never seen a lion or a leopard, let alone a crocodile. The elephant astonished them. Otto told them how big elephants were but the men grinned at him at first, sure he was joking. When he insisted that he was telling the truth, their eyes widened in wonder but doubt remained..

At dinner Cassius wanted to hear everything that had happened since he had been forced to return to Rome but the others demanded that he told his story first.

"You know the state I was in when I left camp. The journey to Rome nearly killed me, the ship leaping about in those huge waves, quite dreadful! But I survived and began treatment under the best doctors my family could find. I simply became weaker and weaker. So it was decided I should go to the great centre of medical learning at Alexandria. Mother said the voyage would kill me but my father pointed out I was already more or less dead. By the time I reached Egypt, my hip bones were protruding through my skin and I could count all my ribs. I was treated by one bearded professor and then the next but they could do nothing. I know we are at dinner but I am sure you won't mind me saying I was like a leaking wineskin. However much liquid went in through my mouth, the same amount ran out of my arse. In the end, they gave up and left me to expire quietly on a folding bed in a garden: pretty garden, beautiful pool with lotus flowers and lots of birds. So, there I am, watching the sky through the fronds of a palm tree when another beardy man walks past. But this one was younger, his beard was black and curly and he had long locks hanging down each side of his face. He stopped, came over and looked at me. "Young man, I do believe you're dying." he says. I had to agree. "Correct, sir. I have been poisoned with putrid swine's flesh." I tell him. "Which is inevitable, sooner or later, for men who will insist on eating that unclean animal." He replies, rather abruptly I thought. I said I didn't eat it on purpose and explained how they polluted our water. That seemed to take him aback. He stroked his beard a bit, they all do that in Alexandria, the medical types. Then he said "My name is David Ben Jacob. I am a Jew. Do you want me to try to make you well, Roman?" I told him I was Cassius Plancus and why not? He was as entitled to torment me as any other doctor in the place. He toddled off and I thought that was the end of that but later half a dozen burly Jews turned up with a litter to take me to the house of their master. They laid me under an awning by a fountain in an enclosed yard and that's where I stayed day and night. No more incantations and coloured smoke, no more concoctions made of disgusting parts of animals. His people fed me on watered ewe's milk and nothing else for a couple of days, then a few crumbs soaked in the milk, then a pudding of milk, crumbs and white of egg with honey on it, only small amounts. I was so hungry I begged for more but he was adamant. My bowels stopped flowing. After a few more days, boiled minced chicken breast and half a slice of bread made with the finest flour. Oh that bread! I can taste it now. So we moved on, I was regularly given one new thing to eat. Gradually I began to put on weight. There were massages with oil and then daily exercise until I could stand, walk, even run. By the time I left his care, I was eating normally and couldn't see my bones anymore. One evening David came to my bedside just as I was about to go to sleep and told me I was cured and could leave the next day. I asked him what I owed him and he laughed and said what did I think my life was worth. I named a figure. "Too much" he said. "You'll come to resent your generosity" We agreed on a lower sum. As I left he told me that if

I ever ate pork in any form my malady would recur. He said I should eat a varied diet with fresh fruit and vegetables in moderation everyday and all should be well. Six months after I last saw you all, I took ship to Rome, back from the dead."

"No pork ever? My auxiliaries would think they were in a living hell," Otto remarked.

"I expect the Emperor was pleased to see you," said Boxer.

"Indeed he was. He lectured me for hours on end about how his abstemious habits promoted his own good health. And speaking of Augustus, he will be here to inspect you all one hour before noon the day after tomorrow. Spit and polish gentlemen, you know how he likes his soldiers to shine brighter than the sun. The Master of Protocol wanted to shove his snout in but I told him to buzz off. This is a military matter and the officers concerned know what to do without him flapping about."

The dinner escalated into an impromptu drinking session during which Cassius was informed of every detail of their campaign, illustrated with crude diagrams drawn on the table in wine. They broke up in the early hours. Cassius promised to return the next day and consult on the plans they were going to make to receive Augustus. When the Germans were told they would see their Emperor in person, they said they would acclaim him. It was neither a suggestion nor a request so Otto agreed. However he had a word with Cassius in private and asked him to warn Augustus what to expect.

The entire day was spent in polishing, cleaning and grooming. Cassius approved the dispositions they intended, said that the addition of some refreshments would be appreciated then went back to Rome. The morning of the parade, they were up at dawn re-polishing each item they had attended to yesterday. So it was that the Emperor's carriage entered the square between an avenue of gleaming cavalry. At Otto's signal every man struck his shield with his spear shaft at the same moment. The noise was like the single beat of a giant's drum. It rolled around the port, resounding off the walls. When it died, three hundred men shouted, "Heil!" As the carriage neared the open gates, the ceremonial greeting was repeated twice more. Then the praetorian bugles blew a fanfare and the whole force stamped once. The crash of hundreds of hobnailed boots slamming onto the cobbles added to the storm of sound then fell silent as the first of the three carriages came to a halt and Augustus emerged.

The officers bowed and saluted. The smiling Emperor stepped aside and turned to give a gracious wave of acknowledgement to the men in response to their greeting. Figures climbed down out of the other two carriages in the convoy. They looked shaken. Cassius Plancus had ridden with Augustus who was beaming, the effect on his companions had been exactly what he had anticipated.

He went through the gates and into the warehouse with his party in his wake. There were six of them, two senators, a tribune, a high ranking official of the grain distribution service, a banker and, unusually, a freedman of the imperial private office. Once their eyes had adjusted to the reduced light inside, they saw a neat stack of wooden chests in the centre of the floor and a table set with water and wine flagons, bread, cheese and drinking vessels at the side. There was one chair.

A priest stood beside the chests. He saluted and broke his seal, flinging back the lid of one on the top layer.

"Look at this," Augustus called to his companions. "Gold!" They crowded around not showing anything like the pleasure of their Emperor. "How much is there?"

"Thirty-two chests each containing forty ingots, sir," Titus informed him. "The bullion stolen from your mine, sir."

"All of it?"

"Everything that has been officially reported as missing."

"Found where?"

"Hidden in a cave not far from where Prefect of Engineers Lucius Longius was building your bridge."

"Amazing! Plancus, what do you make of it?"

"It seems odd to steal so much and simply hide it away Perhaps the criminals had a grand design in mind and were accumulating enough treasure to be able to carry it out," Cassius answered.

"Agree. Should be looked into. Find out who or what's behind it."

With the exception of the banker, the proud and powerful men with whom the Emperor had arrived were feeling extremely uncomfortable. Their attempts to hide the fact made it more obvious, the tension almost crackling off them.

Augustus took a sip of watered wine, a corner of bread and a small morsel of cheese to show his appreciation of the hospitality shown him. He sighed.

"Back to work then. Plancus, send this not insubstantial gift from the Gods to the temple of Castor and Pollux under praetorian protection. Then assemble at the barracks, including the Veii contingent. There will be a donative. Camp Prefect Attius, attend an audience at my house this evening. Bring your officers and any of the men who have distinguished themselves and know how to behave. That is all. To our carriages." He stopped and pointed at the freedman. "Not you. Go with my praetorians."

The man staggered and clutched the side of the table to prevent himself falling. He looked at the impassive faces around him knowing that the rest of his life was going to be short and agonizing. They would take him to the Carcer, that jail of horror from which no prisoner came out alive. There he would be tortured and no matter what he revealed, they would not stop until they had ripped his body to rags.

As he stepped into the sunlight, Augustus called Otto over.

"Say something appropriate to these fellows in their own language but don't promise them anything," he ordered, gesturing at the motionless horsemen still in their positions. Otto stood forward and raised his voice to a parade ground bellow.

"Augustus, Emperor of all the Romans thanks you for your service. He will tell his good friend Prince Aldermar how well you have acquitted yourselves."

They responded with one more eardrum bursting "Heil!"

"That went down well. See you this evening."

The carriages rattled away. The gold was loaded onto a cart and marched off with the praetorians. Suddenly the square seemed empty and a sense of anti-climax fell on the remaining officers. Titus would not allow them time to reflect.

"Right, names for the Emperor's bash tonight. Who've we got?"

They left their horses and weapons outside the sacred precincts of Rome where no blades may be carried through the streets and walked with their military escort up the hill to the Emperor's house. It was a warm night so they gathered under awnings in the orchard, lit with flambeaux. Tables were laid out with cold meats, bread, fruit and cheeses. The flagons of excellent wine were greatly outnumbered by ornate jugs full of cold water.

Augustus made a short speech of welcome and directed his guests to the buffets where his household slaves served them with food and drink.

He went from group to group exchanging a few words with each, the perfect, affable host. He was introduced to Boxer's chief mason and carpenter, his second in command and the artillerist who had fired the grapnel. Otto had brought along both his decurions, Sigbold Bearslayer and, against Titus' advice, Lutold Shadow.

Bearslayer? Shadow? What sort of names are these?" Augustus asked.

"They're rather like Mucius Scaevola and Scipio Africanus, sir," Otto replied, citing as examples two heroes of Rome who had been given new names in honour of their exploits.

A slight frown passed over the Emperor's handsome features then he smiled and tapped Otto on the chest with his forefinger.

"Impudence! Spent too much time with Cassius Plancus."

Lutold tugged Otto's sleeve and asked him a question in his own language. All the Germans looked annoyed.

"What did he say?" Augustus asked.

"He wants to know if you've ever seen an elephant, sir," Otto said, reluctantly.

"Does he? Tell him yes."

Otto translated. Lutold posed another question. The Emperor looked enquiringly. Otto translated yet again.

"He wants to know how big it was."

Augustus looked around. There was a balcony jutting out from the house over the entrance to his garden, he pointed at it.

"About that high at the shoulder, maybe a bit more."

Lutold received the information, smiled at the Emperor and spoke again.

"Well, Otto? I'm waiting."

"He says since you have told him it must be true."

"Gratifying, most gratifying."

Titus had been standing alone. He bowed when Augustus approached.

"Titus Attius, former First Spear Centurion of the Second Lucan, lately Camp Prefect. Name not previously known to me. You have my thanks. Assumed command. Succeeded in completing the mission Admirable."

"Only doing my duty sir."

"Military men always say that. False modesty. Now that I know your worth, what can I do for you?"

"I would like the pay due to me and your leave to return to my home, sir. That is all."

"What, no honours, no prestigious posting?"

"May I speak frankly, sir?"

"Yes."

"I was unhappy at how my career with my legion ended. I took this commission hoping to get the bad blood out of me and I have. My soldiering days are done. Time for the likes of Boxer and Otto to take over."

"If only I had that luxury, Titus Attius. No retirement for an Emperor."

Titus did not tell anyone the real reason he wanted to leave the military life behind him. His duel with Adonis Frugi had shaken him. For the first time he had felt his strength failing him and facing defeat in single combat. It was only his greater experience that had brought him out of it unharmed. Frugi and he had fought with swords and vine staffs and it had never occurred to the centurion to be on the alert for any other form of attack. Titus, on the other hand, knew that anything goes, elbows, boots, knees and a solid headbutt, in this particular case. If Frugi had been more of a gutter fighter it was Titus who would have ended in the bottom of the ravine. Time to thank Mars and Fortuna but ask no more of them.

After another half hour Augustus left the party.

"Goodnight and thank you all once more for your loyal service," he said. "Tonight, accommodation in the Praetorian Barracks. Menities my secretary will attend you tomorrow after breakfast. Well done."

It was still relatively early when they entered the Praetorian Barracks. A solid dinner with much more wine was provided in a side-room where they were joined by Cassius Plancus.

"It's a pity you have resigned your commission," Boxer remarked.

Cassius shook his head. "No not really. Look, jolly as it all was, I was hardly a storming success. They almost filleted me like a fat carp on my first campaign and I came back off this last effort like a sack of loosely connected bones."

"You have courage and you're a good soldier, all the same," Titus told him, a rare compliment.

"I greatly appreciate that coming from you, Titus. But I have to accept that, when all's said and done, I'm an unlucky soldier and that is not a career choice I care to pursue. Don't feel sorry for me though, my dear old things. Can you smell it?"

"Smell what?"

"The sweet breeze that is wafting me into the Senate."

Menities arrived promptly the next morning just as they were finishing the last of their breakfast. He had an armed escort and was followed by a slave carrying a satchel. He borrowed an office and invited the officers to join him first. They each received a weighty purse of gold and their further orders.

"I have them in writing for you," Menities told them handing over leather scroll cases. "Would you like me to summarize verbally?" They asked him to please carry on. "Very well, Imperial Prefect Otto Longius, you are to resume your previous duties. Your auxiliary cavalry will accompany you to Luca. The upkeep of the men and their horses will remain at the charge of the treasury until dismissed following a brief period of rest after the journey. With your written orders is a bank draft sufficient to cover their pay. Camp Prefect Titus Attius, I have a draft for your accumulated salary and a travel warrant.

You are to be an honoured guest on board a naval ship leaving for Corsica tomorrow. From there, onward passage to Tarraco has been arranged. Prefect Lucius Longius, your orders are complex and in part personal. You may prefer to read them in private."

The three of them left and the others who had been to the Emperor's informal audience trooped in. They received their smaller purses but there was something extra for Lutold Shadow.

The Civil War had raged for years around the Mediterranean including North Africa where King Juba had allied his forces with their battle elephants to the army opposing Caesar. When he was defeated, bronze commemorative medals were struck, showing Caesar wearing the laurels of victory and a war elephant on the reverse. On the orders of Augustus, one had been found in a storage cupboard and polished to be presented as his personal gift. Lutold's eyes shone as he stared down at his wonderful medal. He gabbled a long thanks in his own language to Menities who kept a vaguely embarrassed smile fixed to his face, nodding his head as if he understood every word.

Titus collected his kit and strolled along the quays looking for his ship, accompanied by Otto and Boxer. The marine guard at the bottom of the gangplank of the first vessel referred him to another moored farther on. It was a sleek liburnian with two banks of oars and a single mast, fast and powerful. Titus presented his papers, the marine saluted and he was ushered aboard after shaking hands with Otto and Boxer on the dockside. They were long handshakes with a great weight of unspoken emotion behind them. Then he turned and marched onto the warship, his back arrow straight, with never a backward glance.

Otto went over to the animal importer's buildings and ordered his men to be ready to ride as soon as possible and make their way over to the warehouse. He rode back on his gelding, giving Djinn an extra day's rest. Boxer was waiting for him inside, the engineers and artillery men were loading up their carts and harnessing the mules. Boxer was grinning widely and almost jumping up and down with excitement in a most un-Roman way.

He pushed a parchment scroll into Otto's hands almost before he could dismount. "Read that," he said.

"To Prefect of Engineers Lucius Taurius Longius, Greetings,

You are to proceed to Luca where you will place your artillery at the disposal of the garrison commander for the added protection of that city. The artillerist you presented to me is to be raised to the rank of optio with immediate effect.

You and the core of your men will remain in Luca forming a permanent cadre of specialist engineers ready to undertake military (and agreed civil) projects as they arise. Funds have been made available for the establishment of living quarters and a depot in or near the city. Again, liaise with the garrison commander, who is being fully informed of all matters.

Aug. Imp.

P.S. You and Otto are of more value to Rome when you serve together. Find a bride my Boxer. I look forward to learning who you have chosen. Wish you really were a boxer. Love the sport. Best thing in the games.

Augustus.

Otto handed the letter back and grabbed Boxer in a bearhug, lifting him off his feet and spinning him around. The engineers whistled at the sight. Good officer that he was, Boxer straightened his uniform and walked briskly over to them to give them the happy news.

When the order of march of the cavalry and transport had been decided, they made their way through the wharfs with their backs to the sea, heading for the Via Aurelia, yet again, and their long journey north.

Titus Attius stood on deck thinking as he watched the coast of Italy dropping below the horizon. The Tyrrhenian sparkled with small sapphire waves dancing on its indigo depths. A few white gulls cried and wheeled overhead in the cloudless sky. He suddenly found that he wanted nothing but to be at home and hold his wife and their child in his arms. The resentment he had felt at the way his service with his legion had ended had evaporated, along with any desire return to the army. Titus Attius exhaled a long breath and smiled. He was content.

As Titus was coming to an acceptance of the fact that a chapter in his life had closed, Otto and Boxer rode towards their futures with hearts full of optimism.

In Rome, a freedman screamed his last in the dungeons of the Carcer. A senator and a high ranking official of the grain distribution service committed suicide by opening their veins with a razor as they lay in their baths. Another senator announced he wished to retire to his estates in the country and take no further part in public life. He donated his villa in Rome to the Emperor hoping it would be sold by auction and the funds raised used to beautify the city. A week later, a tribune was fatally stabbed while walking though the forum. The unknown assailant was never apprehended. It was business as usual for a perfectly innocent banker, if such a person could exist.

"A satisfactory outcome, sir? Menities asked Augustus.

"Very. Send for young Plancus. Time he stood for election to the Senate. There are two recent vacancies I believe, eh?" the Emperor chuckled.

The End

I hope that you have enjoyed reading this book if you did please mention it on social media or leave an Amazon or Goodreads review. I have suggested more of my fictional books which you may like on the following pages.

Thank you for your support.

Malcolm Davies

(You can contact me by e-mail at:-

malcolmdav46@outlook.com

 Best Books by Malcolm Davies on Facebook.

My website is www.malcolm-davies.com.)

The Butterfly Fool Part One

Being an account of the Remarkable Early Life of Mr. Augustus Reynolds of Split Water City, Montana Territory. How he came to leave the Country Of His Birth to travel to the Frontier of the United States of America. His Thrilling Voyages by Steamboat up the great Mississippi and Missouri Rivers. His Dangerous Encounter with a Savage and Fearsome Blackfoot Chief. How he Comported himself in Mortal Combats with Ferocious Wild Beasts and Brigands. And the Many, Remarkable and Diverse Characters he met on his journeys. Also the History of Miss Charlotte Reynolds, Sister of the Above who Heroically accompanied Her Brother on his Adventure. How an English Gentlewoman fared in the Wilderness with neither Cook nor Maid. Her Primitive Domestic Economy. A Romantic Attachment which would have distressed the Many Friends she had left at Home. In Addition, how the Thriving Metropolis of Split Water City rose from the Plains. Its Rude Beginnings and First Development.

The Butterfly Fool Part Two

The Second and Final Volume Depicting the Exploits and Times of Mr. Augustus Reynolds the Celebrated Frontiersman, his Family and Friends. A Theft and Pursuit across the Vastness of the American Prairies. Retribution upon the Felons. Confrontations with Fierce Natives. A Hunt for the Indigenous Bison. A Violent Death followed by Remorse. The Moral Repugnance of Mrs. Reynolds at developments in Split Water City, Metropolis of the Plains. The Arrival of the Mechanical Wonders of our Age in the Remote Wilderness. Celebration of the American Public Holiday known as "The Fourth of July". Wonder at the Resilience of The Inhabitants of The Far Western Territories. Thrill to the Dangers Faced and Overcome by Them with Undaunted Steadfastness

Willy Maddox Went To Texas

Coming off a cattle drive from Split Water City to St. Louis, young Willy Maddox has a bitter quarrel with his cousin Ed which changes the course of his life. Willy is in the wrong of it but for all he cares, Ed can go home on his own; he would rather ride off south with his two new friends, heading for Texas. At twenty years old Willy believes he can handle anything that life throws at him. He has already learned the ranching trade up in Montana, endured the rigours of a long cattle-drive and fended off stock-thieves. What could Texas show him he had not seen before? So, what did Texas show Willy Maddox? Only outlaws, deserts, blizzards blowing up out of nowhere, renegade Comanche and worse but also great opportunity, transforming new technologies and finally, his journey's end. (Willy Maddox first appears in "The Butterfly Fool Part Two", the sequel to "The Butterfly Fool Part One".)

Printed in Great Britain
by Amazon